COSMIC HORROR SPACE EXPLORATION NOVEL

BLEEDING ROCK

Nicholas Licalsi

STEP INTO THE ROAD

First published by Step Into The Road Publishing 2023

Copyright © 2023 by Nicholas Licalsi.

First edition

Editting by Alexandra Ott

This novel is entirely a work of fiction. The names, characters and incidents portrayed in it are the work of the author's imagination. Any resemblance to actual persons, living or dead, events or localities is entirely coincidental.

From this point on take everything with a grain of salt. I made most of it up!

For my sister Olivia. You're right, biology is stranger than expected.
Don't touch the Goop!

Thank You Patrons!

Your generous support encourages me to explore every edge of the universe, for better or worse. I bring these stories back to you in gratitude.

Katelyn Combs, Bonnie, BW, Melinda Calender,
Roy & Beth Shockey, Callen McMillian, Sam Meeks, John Middleton

One

T he seatbelts of the driver's seat cut into Mauve's shoulders. The cockpit seemed fine as Mauve glanced over the control board. Something was off, but she couldn't put her finger on it. It felt like the ship had just done a high-g maneuver and she was on the wrong wall of the ship. In a ship she would only have to wait a few seconds and the artificial gravity would return to normal or the ship would do a high-g maneuver in another direction. Instead, she was just stuck in this state of being wrong. She hated it.

On top of this, her head was throbbing as if the padded headrest had hit her too hard, but it wasn't quite that. Her head hurt from the inside like a balloon that was about to burst. Then it clicked.

"Franton," she addressed the ship's artificial intelligence, "am I upside-down?"

"Affirmative," it responded in its androgynous voice. "The rover you took shelter in sustained some damages but stayed connected to the floor of the dock. Unfortunately, the dock has sustained considerable damages and seems to be inverted in its orientation."

This is fantastic, Mauve thought. Her first taste of life planet-side and she was already experiencing the effects of a planet's natural and full gravity. Life on ships and satellites had gravity, but they were artificial and manipulatable. This was the constant and unchangeable force one got to experience when standing on the surface of a massive rock in space. It was effects like this that she'd been waiting all her life to experience, and here she was seated in an upside-down rover in the dock of a crashed spaceship. *How many other mechanics I apprenticed with would ever get to experience this?* she wondered. Unfortunately, the throbbing continued, and if she were going to continue to experience the beauty of this natural planet, she would have to figure out how to get her orientation corrected.

"Fran, what can we do to get me upright again?"

"I am trying to re-establish communication with the ship."

"Have you done any biometric scans on me?" Her body felt alright, a little sore here or there, and her head was killing her by now. Franton would know for sure if she'd broken any bones or sustained any serious internal injuries.

"I'm running that scan right now."

"I can't stay suspended like this for much longer."

"Affirmative, I just want to make sure that you haven't sustained any serious damage before you move."

Mauve gripped the arms of the driver's seat and hooked her foot around a piece of metal that it found. She grimaced as her back tensed with pain, but she powered through. With her free hand, she punched the emergency release of the seat belt. She was free from the straps and was only being held in the chair by her own muscles. The low ceiling of the cabin wasn't far from her, and she imagined doing a summersault to land on it. It was a maneuver she could have done in the artificial gravity of a satellite's gym, but there were dampeners there to protect her from her mistakes.

Gripping the armrest with both hands, she let go with her foot. Her body twisted around her shoulder sockets, and she was oriented correctly with gravity. The strange position pulled her hands off sooner than she'd anticipated, and she fell to the roof of the cockpit. She cursed as her knee caught the brunt of her fall before her legs could soften her impact.

"Mauve, I haven't completed your biometric scan. That maneuver could have worsened your internal bleeding."

The blood drained from Mauve's head, and she began to be able to focus on her situation. "I suspect your biometric scans would have told you there was too much blood in my head and my back was hurt. I can now add that my knee isn't in great shape and my back is definitely not loving that fall."

"I will have my sensors focus on figuring out what's wrong with your back."

"Can we have you focus on how to get out of this mess?"

"I am currently trying to establish communication and see if the crew can come to your assistance."

Mauve snorted some laughter at the idea of the crew of scientists being able to get her out of the inverted dock. The bulk of the ship's weight was in the dock along with any serious machinery that would help them help her. Nevertheless, having communication set up with an outside party was always helpful; she had no clue what the planet around her was like.

"How'd we get into this mess in the first place?" she asked, figuring Franton could hold a conversation, scan her, and try to establish communication at the same time.

"I'm sorry, Mauve, that is my fault."

"You crashed the ship?" Her tone was more impressed than anything. Franton was a network of high-density computational nodes that created an artificial intelligence that had helped humankind for years. Anything from engineering and navigating starships to helping brew a cup of coffee in the morning. A single marble of Franton had more computational power than humanity's first starship, so the idea of Franton making a mistake wasn't something Mauve had expected to experience in her lifetime.

"The black box hasn't been recovered, but reverse-engineering the crash data, I believe that I miscalculated the trajectory and velocity of our atmospheric entry."

"Well, that's interesting, but this is where we're at. How do we get out of here?"

"Wait for the crew to come."

"You don't really think that's going to happen, do you? We're going to have to do this on our own." She began to point out all the reasons the crew, even if they did want to see her, wouldn't be able to help.

Soon enough Franton conceded with the caveat that Mauve take things easy until they understood the severity of her injuries.

"Great! What are the rover's scanners saying?"

During the crash, Mauve had decided to take shelter inside of the rover she was in now. It was an A class Tichenowa research rover that was standard for all planetary missions and was known for being over-engineered to handle the tough unknown scenarios of planetary exploration. Mauve remembered joking with her mechanic friends someone could survive a crash landing in one of these things if they had to. She was looking forward to bragging to them that she'd done just that when she got communication with the central system back. Although the pain in her back was proof that it was less superior to the crash-couches that the crew had taken shelter in.

Odds were good they were feeling great after the landing and were already establishing communication with the mothership to get them rescued. She could be out there with them, safe and comfortable in her crash couch, if she hadn't been banished to the dock during the landing. Well, she hadn't actually been banished; the crew had told her to be somewhere besides the cockpit. They likely meant her small bunk room, where there was a crash couch for her to take cover in, but the landing was supposed to be simple and routine and the dock was far more comfortable and spacious. By the time the alarms went off to take cover in a crash couch, she didn't have time to get to hers, so she'd done the next best thing and taken cover in the rover.

Franton presented what the rover's scanners were showing of the dock on the screen embedded in the rover's console. The image was inverted, but with Mauve sitting on the ceiling, it looked more similar to the dock than she'd expected. Some crates had become unstrapped and were now resting on the roof, but most of them had stayed in place. "Where's the door? Can we just open it and get out of here?"

"The door will not open; I've attempted it a few times now. But I'm not sure why. It could be internal damage that I'm not reading or something external since I don't have communication with the hull sensors."

"Hull sensors were probably damaged in the crash." She didn't think it was anything severe—those things were built to withstand crash conditions. However, their connections to the central electronics of the ship were always having to be reconnected. "You have full control of the interior of the dock?"

"Affirmative," Franton responded, but he didn't volunteer any more information than that.

"So undo the straps holding the rover to the roof, and then we can use the exterior fission blades of this thing to cut through the dock's door."

"That could cause serious damage to the rover and you. Your back is not in very good shape."

"I'll strap myself back into the seat," she said. Although looking at the distance between herself and the seat, she didn't know how she'd climb back in there and was surprised she'd taken the jump in the first place.

"And if it lands upside-down?"

"It uses the armatures to right itself. The engineers of this thing expected at least one dumbass scientist to roll it in their planetary escapades."

"And if those are damaged in the fall?"

"Then I'll get out and cut a door in the hull by hand." It wouldn't be fun work, and getting through both hulls would be time-consuming with a personal fission blade, but waiting for the crew to rescue her could take longer. Assuming they wanted to rescue her.

"Cutting through the hulls could structurally damage the ship, and returning it to orbit would be near impossible. I cannot approve this plan."

Mauve rolled her eyes. Starving in here or dying of boredom was going to make it hard for her to return to orbit. "Fine, what kind of plan would you approve?"

"Only repairable damage may be done to the ship. Additionally, the rover and you cannot be harmed in the process."

"Do you have enough information to run simulations of how the rover can use its armatures to right itself?"

The rover was equipped with four massive arms that could lift the entire rover in case it was stuck upside-down or on terrain that its massive off-land tires couldn't handle. It was an impressive feat to begin with, but considering the vessel was big enough for four people to live and do research in for months on end made it even more impressive.

"Affirmative," Franton responded.

"Good, then put up the schematics for the dock doors and I'll look over a solution to that."

Franton put the 3D schematics on the dashboard's display, but this time it was inverted and Mauve's mind couldn't think around it.

"Can you rotate this image 180 degrees?"

The picture righted itself, and she got to work reviewing the device's specs and cross-comparing it to the inventory she had available to her in the dock.

"I think I have a solution," she finally responded. "Have you figured anything out?"

"Affirmative, I figured it out within the first minute of being assigned the task."

"Why didn't you say anything?" Mauve said, wondering if the computer was bragging.

"I didn't want to distract you."

Mauve scoffed at the machine. It was right, she was easily distracted, but she didn't appreciate being called out by a machine that could fit a dozen processors in a shot glass. She let it go and started explaining the plan to the machine. "I'd like to run the two winches that open the door in reverse. Can you do that?"

"There are about a dozen protocols keeping it from doing that in a closed state," Franton replied with what Mauve thought was a hint of condescension.

"Yeah, yeah, I know. But can you get around them?"

"I don't want to damage the door. Who knows what it's like out there, and we want to be able to depart and return to the mothership if necessary."

"You said no irreparable damage. Running them in reverse would cause them to burn out. And a dock in atmosphere fails in an open state for safety purposes."

"Then we can't lock the dock up to leave if we need to."

"We can after I replace them with the winches that are in the repair and replacement inventory." For a super-intelligent computer, it sure was having a hard time keeping up.

"That could take a lot of time. What if we need to leave immediately?"

"Have you been able to come up with an alternate solution that will get us out of here?"

"If we establish communication with the crew, then they can clear any blockage that is keeping the bay door from opening."

"That will take too much time, and for all we know they're in a worse spot than we are."

"We haven't even given them an hour to solve the problem themselves."

And knowing their expertise, it will take them at least an hour to figure out they have a problem, Mauve thought. "This is an acceptable solution according to your requirements. Also, wouldn't you rather the rover be outside to help the crew if they need it? This thing has food, water, and first-aid equipment for months of exploration. And the winch replacement is a simple repair routinely given to first-year mechanic apprentices. I could do it with my eyes closed."

"Fine, we can do it," Franton responded. Its tone was flat, but Mauve still felt like she was pulling transistors to get it to override the protocols.

"What did you come up with to get us right-side-up?"

"I ran a few simulations, and I don't think you can get back into the chair."

She was glad that Fran came to that solution so she didn't have to hurt herself trying.

"Which means that we'll have to rotate the rover 90 degrees, get you into a chair, and then finish the rotation."

Mauve smiled; she was finally getting to do gymnastics in a real gravity, and a spinning floor was a true challenge. She'd always enjoyed gymnastics but could never become a pro because she'd only ever trained in starships and space stations with modifiable gravity and inertial dampeners. Here it was her and the planet. There were no negotiations or safety nets in place.

"The dock doesn't have many good hold points for the rover's armatures, so it's going to have to clip onto the stacks of crates still strapped to the former floor," Franton continued to explain. Fran explained the risks, but Mauve was taking in the room that was about to become her playground.

***

Mauve's plan of overloading the winches went off without a hitch. Franton had no problem overriding any of the protocols in place. As she stretched, preparing for the acrobatics of getting into the passenger seat while the rover moved, she realized her back was bothering her more and more. She wasn't surprised that the initial adrenaline of the crash had masked some of the pain, but she was looking forward to being back in a comfortable seat rather than standing or sitting on a roof that no one intended anyone to spend a prolonged period of time on.

"I'm ready when you are," she told the computer.

"Affirmative. I will begin the sequence."

She heard the armatures move outside before she felt them. Each one latched onto various thick belts that held the crates in place. Some of the crates had broken off the ceiling during the crash and were littering the ceiling of the dock. But the ones that were still in place were rated for crash conditions, and Franton had run simulations to assure her and itself that the maneuver was safe. The maneuver wasn't foolproof, but the margin for error was low enough that they'd agreed to move forward with it.

The ground below her began to shift, and she had to brace herself against the walls. "We're going to move into the second position now," Franton announced over the rover's PA system.

Mauve worried about jumping from one wall to another as the ground shifted into wall and the wall shifted into ground. Something in the back of her mind nagged at her not to do it. She pushed her fear to the back of her mind like she had dozens of times before when practicing gymnastics in the station. She played for excitement and now she'd be doing it for real with real stakes, without any referee or coach monitoring the artificial gravity around her.

Watching the monitor that had a simulation of the rover displayed on it, she waited for her cue. She felt the ground under her incline, and when she felt it was right, she leapt from what should have been the ceiling to a wall of the rover. She slipped on the glass of the window, not worrying that it would shatter since it'd been rated for far worse activity than this.

Arms' distance away from the chair, she reached out, ready to slip her body into the seat as the rover continued to rotate. She grabbed for the seatbelt and heard a crack that wasn't caused by her boots on the window.

The floor dropped out from under her.

She twisted her head out of the way of some object that was flying up at her. Her hip hit the seat, and a burst of pain shot through her back.

"One of the crate straps broke," Franton informed her and then listed off an alternative maneuver, but the plans meant nothing to Mauve.

Shouting out curses she'd learned as a mechanic on a dozen space stations, she gripped the armrests that were now next to her.

The rover came to a halt, and the inertia threw her feet into the space in front of her so she could buckle in.

"We're stationary, but I'd like to keep moving. Please fasten your seatbelt," the computer said. Its simulated voice was far too calm for the situation.

Her hands were shaking as she tried to get one clip into another. The multipoint harness was thorough, and crash training had taught her how to do it. She wanted to wrap her feet around the seat's legs to brace herself better, but her ankles couldn't feel anything to hook into.

"Good enough. Let's move." Her voice quivered with the fear that crawled out of the back of her mind.

She heard another snap followed by the clattering of boxes onto the roof of the dock. The rover moved quicker now. With her strapped into place, Franton could execute armature movements without worrying about tossing her from one side of the cockpit to the other. Nonetheless, her head still bounced from one side of the padded headrest to the other. Gravity pulled on her with its constant downward force, and she could track it, unlike the unexpected Gs she felt during complex spacecraft docking maneuvers.

Finally, Mauve's inner ear told her that the rover was stable and everything was oriented in the correct position. She wanted to get up, run into the bathroom of the rover, and vomit, but her legs were too exhausted to move. Through the windshield, she saw that the rover was moving towards the daylight of the planet's surface.

"It's going to be a few minutes until we're outside. I'm sorry for the unexpected failures of the crate straps."

"Nothing you could do about it. They must have taken more damage in the crash than we expected."

"How are you feeling?" the computer asked. She had no doubt in her mind that Fran was running half a dozen biometric scans on her and was just asking out of courtesy.

"My shoulders and head feel like they just went through a washing machine. That fall will probably leave a bruise on my hip for a week or two. But on the bright side, my back doesn't hurt." She smiled as the sunlight of the planet outside overtook her view, which was originally the cavernous, artificially lit dock. She was excited to have her first glimpse of a world made by nature. She'd get to experience it with her own eyes rather than filtered through a screen or virtualized reality.

Franton asked her a question, but she was focused on the deep greens and blues of the world around her. She had to lift her arm to block the sun from her eyes as her pupils dilated to take in the copious amounts of natural light from the local star.

"Mauve, can you wiggle your toes?" the computer's voice repeated.

"Of course," she said, looking out every massive window that the cockpit had. They weren't big enough, and she wanted to climb out of the rover to get a full view of the sights.

As she moved towards the door where her boot prints smudged the window, she realized she wasn't making as much progress as she'd expected. She was unbuckled from the chair but still wasn't moving.

"Mauve, can you actually wiggle your toes?"

She paid attention to Franton this time. She tried to lift her toe, expecting it to hit the roof of her boot, but didn't really feel it. She tried to kick her leg, but it wouldn't move. She felt sweat on the back of her neck. "What's wrong with me?!"

"I think your back sustained some serious injuries during that maneuver. I'm sorry, Mauve."

"What are you saying? I need to move; I want to go outside." She couldn't force the fear back anymore; it had bloomed into full-on panic. She took some deep breaths to calm herself. "It's fine. We'll find the crew and they can help me."

The rover began to rotate in its place. The forested area that had flying lizards leaping from tree to tree no longer filled her view. There was a clearing that looked like a giant hatchet had scored the earth. Then the smoking mess of the ship came into view. She looked at it and couldn't believe she'd just been inside of it. The door wouldn't open because it was half buried into the ground. Not only was the ship inverted, but it was a mangled mess.

Something was missing, but Mauve's mind couldn't cling to it in the chaos of her legs not working. The ship normally looked like a crummy solder joint to her. One small bead that was the living quarters barely connected to a massive second bead that was the dock.

"Franton, where's the cockpit?"

***

After searching the perimeter of the crash site from the passenger seat of the rover, there was no evidence of the crew landing near the dock.

"If it detached after it entered the atmosphere, could they have landed nearby safely?" Mauve asked. She was actively ignoring the fact that she couldn't walk and told herself to only deal with one problem at a time.

"If they were in their crash couches, they would be safe even if it detached. But they could have landed in any direction. I don't have any information about the crash in my local memory banks."

"Isn't there a black box you can connect to?"

"That box is located between the dock and the cockpit. It's not with this half of the ship, so they must have it."

Mauve realized without any more clues she wouldn't be able to find the crew and would be wasting her time if the rover went scouting for them in the wrong direction. It was on to the second problem of the afternoon. "I can't sit in this seat forever."

"Affirmative. When we find the crew, we can have them help you."

"That's going to take at least a day."

"Affirmative. That's my most optimistic estimate."

"Then what do I do in the meantime? How do I eat or sleep or shit?"

"You will need to crawl around the rover to access those facilities, since I cannot help you move."

Mauve sighed. Franton always had been and always would be utilitarian in its suggestions. If they were in a space station or a starship, there would be a medical facility where an operation could be performed to either repair or replace her legs. She'd have to go through a few weeks of physical therapy, but she'd be walking again within the pay period. The shuttle had no such facilities even when it was in one piece. Which meant she'd be stuck to a chair or crawling on the ground until they returned to the mothership.

"Do you have any information on how they designed bionic prosthetics before cellular regeneration was standardized?"

"Negative. My local memory banks don't have that information. I might have information in the servers connected in the cockpit of the shuttle."

"Assuming it survived." Mauve sighed. If Franton had that information, it could model something similar and build it. "What info do you have?"

"Survival and first aid, all the known information related to this planet, inventory, and schematics for the whole ship and all machinery on the ship."

When Franton was connected to its servers or the central system as a whole, it could learn quickly, calculate simulations thoroughly in the blink of an eye, and had an unlimited wealth of knowledge. Running on its local memory banks was obviously limiting what it was capable of and likely caused the miscalculations that caused it not to expect the straps to break.

Mauve bit her fist trying to think of a solution. Without the reference material Fran listed, she could prototype something herself, but it'd likely take weeks to perfect it enough to walk. She didn't understand the human body very well, and organic motions like walking were never her mechanical strong suit.

"There was a mech-suit in the dock, right?" It would have been used to unload the heavy crates of supplies that were still strapped to the now-ceiling of the dock.

"Affirmative, but from what I observed in the dock, it sustained damage during the crash."

"That's fine, I'd need working legs to control it anyway. But you have the schematics for it, right?"

"Affirmative."

"Good. Pull that up on the console along with any first-aid diagrams you have of human legs. I've got an idea."

Two

"We have been at this for hours, Mauve," Franton said. "I believe you need to get some dinner and some rest. The last time you slept was before the crash."

"I was knocked out for a period of time during the crash. That's kind of like a nap."

"That is nothing like a nap. You have been awake long enough that you are not showing signs of a concussion. I would like to take a break from this project."

Mauve was sitting at the dinette of the rover. It was a pain to get this far. She'd avoided eating anything because she didn't want to have to get across the rover to the automated food generator.

The rover itself wasn't very big. If she were on a space station, with its artificial gravity and corridors you could drive a four-person shuttle-cart through, it would be nearly impossible for her to move around without a mobility device.

However, on a space station there were medbays with auto-surgeons and medical professionals who Franton could advise and help fix her legs.

Franton had told her to quit saying "fix her legs." It was psychologically unhelpful for her. Not having legs she could move was the most psychologically unhelpful, in her opinion. They were not doing what they were designed to do; they were broken. If she'd told a foreman not to use "fix the fuel line" because it was psychologically unhelpful to the spaceship the fuel line was attached to, she'd be laughed out of the docks. Any mechanic knew it was broken. So she was determined to fix it.

Franton informed her that the medical was with the other half of the ship and likely non-functional. Even if it were, it still might not be able to help her back. She asked if the first aid's nano bots could repair the bone; she'd broken her arm as a kid, and a shot of nanobots and a cast healed the bones in no time. Franton had explained why that wouldn't work, so they were on to designing a custom mobility device for her.

"What if we use lightweight motors on the knee joints and move them lower?" Mauve saw the three-dimensional rendering of some pants modify in front of her eyes. It looked like large bell bottom boots except it was made of plastic and metal. She didn't care how the bionic legs looked, as long as she didn't have to drag herself around anymore.

"That improves the center of gravity. However, we don't have enough belts on hand to run pulleys that far," Franton reported. "I have jerk chicken in stock. It's your favorite meal from the food-crowave."

Mauve looked across the rover at the chest-height box that would drop rehydrated meals out of the opening in the front. The whole thing was half a meter square. It could rehydrate dozens of different meals and cuisines. It was an automated food generator that saved humanity countless hours of cooking. And someone gave it the stupid name of "foodcrowave" a dozen centuries ago when it was invented. She could think of a dozen better names, but none ever stuck like foodcrowave.

"I don't want jerk chicken. We can print more belts."

"I would like to limit the resources invested in this experiment."

"You don't want to fix my legs."

"Your legs are not broken. The nerves in your back have been severed. But you are still a whole person."

"Don't feel like whole person," Mauve muttered.

"There are very useful protocols for people who have suffered an injury like yours. It would be best if we started working through these issues. You are in quite a traumatic situation."

"I don't want a therapy session. I want to be able to walk."

"It seems it would be best if I rehydrate a meal. Unless you have another preference, I will select jerk chicken for you."

Mauve groaned and spun the 3D model of the pants around like it was a die. The model went wild, and the computer generated every angle it could as the simulation moved. She looked away in protest as if to show Franton she didn't care it was doing all the work. There were cameras all throughout the rover. Franton knew where she was looking and generated the model anyway. It was a petty act of rebellion. It was the best Mauve could muster.

The foodcrowave hummed to life.

The rover was larger than some of her cabins on starships and satellites. It sat stationary in the shadow of the dock that had crashed on the planet Knod. The outside was boxy and angular, as aerodynamic as a mallet head. The thing would never move more than a few kilometers an hour. And air wasn't something that would always be around it as it traveled on various alien planets.

The inside consisted of four cabins with compressed equipment separated by pocket doors. The cockpit was only big enough for two thick padded captain chairs but had room for more dials than Mauve had ever seen before. But the most magnificent sight was out the windshield. Shuttle carts didn't have windshields; they weren't supposed to go fast enough to need them. Mauve usually broke that rule, but zip ties and acrylic panels always worked for her in a pinch. Shuttle carts also didn't have a view onto the large green leaves of Knod and its blue sky streaked with thin white clouds. There was no substitute for that that Mauve could imagine.

Next back was a living area that Mauve sat in now. It was painted white to make the room feel bigger, just like every small room on every small space station Mauve had ever been on. A small gray band was painted across it as if the decorators wanted to hammer home that the view was outside. Windows were fitted under cabinets and in small gaps in walls. Mauve found she had to cock her head to see out of them, but it was worth the neck strain.

A small research station with some manufacturing equipment and basic scientific tools was behind the living area. The crew got to select what equipment was stocked in the rover's research room from a catalog of possible installations. She didn't know what it held because that selection had happened before the sixth researcher dropped and Mauve was subbed in to do the assembly of his custom measuring equipment. She was confident it was decorated as uninspiringly as the living room.

A bunk room that held six tightly stacked bunks was the last room on the rover. No one wanted to spend more time there than they had to. Mauve usually opted for a top bunk—she enjoyed the gymnastics of climbing in and out—but now she'd have to settle for a bottom bunk. It was little consolation that she'd *still* have to do some climbing to get into it.

The living area of the rover was a bit more comfortable than the bunks. It had a foldable dinette table with a booth on either side. It could convert into a bed if necessary. But that was only necessary for the largest crews or emergency situations. Franton could automatically convert it; Mauve considered making the dinette her sleeping quarters for now, if Franton could do the transformation without her having to move too much.

A compartment with a shower and toilet was seated behind the table booth. The whole thing was smaller than some toolboxes Mauve had worked with. She wasn't looking forward to figuring out how to use that with her *not* broken legs. Its cramped size was not what intimidated her; mechanic locker rooms always had shower stalls that small, and she'd cleaned off plenty of grease and gunk standing in claustrophobic conditions.

A waist-high counter, or at least it would be waist-high if Mauve's waist could ever get that high again, ran across the opposite wall of the dinette with cabinets underneath it. The foodcrowave sat on it along with a sink, a first-aid kit, and a hand dryer. The space between the counter and the bathroom door was maybe a half meter. If there was a wheelchair on this rover, and Mauve hoped some bureaucratic law forced that to be required, it was unlikely it would squeeze through the gap. Cabinets hung above the counter with LEDs under them. They were full of a dozen strapped-down kitchen tools that she couldn't reach right now. May never be able to reach again.

The food generator dinged to notify her the food was ready.

"How am I supposed to get that?" she asked. As smart as the computer was, it hadn't thought through that one.

"The cabinet under the sink has a foldable stool in it. If you can get to that, unfold it and sit on it. You should be high enough to reach the bowl of jerk chicken."

"Jerk chicken is served on a plate. What if I spill it?" That would speed up having to use the shower, and she wasn't looking forward to that.

"I made some modifications to the serving parameters, and the meal was prepared in a bowl."

"You can do that?" Mauve had never seen that setting.

"Sometimes it is necessary for families with toddlers, elderly individuals, and others with disabilities like yourself."

Mauve lowered herself off the booth of the dinette, having to move her legs with her arms. It felt like they were someone else's, like moving a dead body. She'd never looked so closely at her legs. They didn't always cooperate, and there were a few times she wanted to just move them a centimeter or two to the side, but they refused to budge.

She scooted across the floor without much problem. She was just glad there was no one to watch but Franton, who was the most emotionless being in the void. She opened the cabinet and unfolded the stool easily. Stick figures and arrows molded into the plastic surface informed her what she needed to do. She always pinched her fingers in situations like this, and this time was no different.

She was glad she had the gymnastic experience. While she'd never be professional, it was a fun hobby she was glad she did as an adult, especially now when the only thing that could move her around was her upper body.

Sitting on the stool was more difficult than she'd expected. Her lower abs didn't pull the weight she'd expected, and she had to use an arm to grab the counter and balance herself. Her other hand grabbed the lip of the bowl, and she was glad the cabin was so small because she could easily transfer the bowl from the counter to the table.

Mauve climbed off the stool and back into the booth, leaving it in place since she'd need it for the next meal. She got seated and looked at the steaming bowl of rice and chicken. It was her favorite meal. She was glad Franton had made it. She reached for her silverware and realized she'd forgotten something.

"Well, just drop my socket wrench down the air conduit," she cursed.

"The silverware is in the drawer under the foodcrowave," Franton informed her.

"Oh, I know where it is." Her ears were steaming in frustration.

Then she realized she was alone. On an alien planet. Potentially the only person alive on it. She grabbed a piece of chicken with her fingers and popped it in her mouth. It had just the right amount of kick.

***

Mauve found the wheel chair in the rover's undercarriage storage. It was not easy to get it. It was not a flattering process to get it. Franton knew where every item on the rover was; however, the computer could not help retrieve the chair. Whoever packed it had assumed there would be an able-bodied person to remove it, and Mauve cursed them for making that reasonable assumption.

By the time the thing was unpacked and unfolded, Mauve's jumpsuit was covered in dust and dirt. Her arms were sore from lifting and moving without any lower body strength, and her elbows were scraped up from crawling. Her legs and hips were likely bruised, but she couldn't feel it, and that wasn't much of a consolation prize.

The wheelchair only made it marginally easier to move around the crash site. Its tall arms and heavy frame made it hard for her to roll back up the rover's entrance ramp. It was indeed too wide for the hallway in the rover's living area, so the main purpose it served was a mobile seat for reaching the foodcrowave. Which at least made it easier for her to get silverware.

"There is no way I'm going to be able to do anything without working legs."

"You do not need to do anything," Franton responded.

"Like hell I don't. I'm stranded on an alien planet."

"This rover is packed to sustain a crew of six for months of travel. You will not go hungry anytime soon. It is self-sustaining like any starship, so water and shelter are not a concern. Eventually the mothership will come back to pick up the crew and will be able to send a rescue shuttle down."

"We were scheduled to do research on this planet for two and a half years." Mauve groaned. Without a communications array set up, they wouldn't be able to send a distress signal to the mothership. And the mothership wouldn't assume there was a problem since research missions like this were the equivalent of running off to the bar for a beer. They rarely went wrong, and even if it didn't go well, the worst you came home with was a black eye or broken arm.

Knod, the planet Mauve was currently on, was classified as Earth-like. It had a breathable atmosphere, edible foliage, and a temperate climate. It was a rare find in the cosmos, but not so rare that it was unbelievable. Space was big; there were plenty of opportunities for planets that could host humans. One day it would be colonized by a small group of a few thousand humans, and it may be a thriving city-planet a few generations after that.

"We've designed a set of bionic legs," Mauve said. She'd worked out the final problems of the design last night. Franton did most of the working out, but she brought some key necessary ideas to the table, like how Franton could find information about human anatomy from the first-aid manual, and how the repair manual for the dock's mech suit would be a good starting place for a design.

The hardest part was not designing them. The hardest part was figuring out how to manufacture it with the rover's limited equipment. The crew had chosen to install a matter-printer that could 3D print custom plastic, metal, and rubber pieces. However, the volume of items it could create was less than a meter. With some repair glue, Mauve figured she could get it together. The hesitation Franton now had was where to get the tubing, pumps, and computers.

"I will not let you pointlessly cannibalize necessary equipment," Franton said. Its tone was neutral even though the words sounded like something she'd heard a dozen times as a child.

"Pointlessly?!" Mauve threw up her hands. "I feel like being able to walk is pretty necessary."

"There is no immediate danger. This rover is safe for you."

"So you want me to stare at these white walls for two and half years? I'll go insane!"

"You will not. Studies on human isolation show that the mental strain of being confined to a limited area can be reversed with proper therapy. Additionally, when isolation is paired with an AI companion with psychotherapeutic algorithms, mental stability is 98% assured."

"Great, more therapy," Mauve groaned.

"I believe it would be best if we talked about your reluctance to face your situation."

"I'm not reluctant to face my situation!" Mauve wished she could storm out of the rover. But it'd be an uneasy ride down the ramp and a tough one back up. And with the ground muddy from the morning's rainstorm, she knew she wouldn't be rolling far from the rover. "If anything I'm facing it head-on. What if the crew is out there?"

"I'm not picking up any signal from the cockpit or the crash couches."

"They could need my help; I could repair things for them. They could help me." She didn't look forward to that, but she was willing to say anything to get the bionic legs. "I could go searching for them."

"This rover could search for them if necessary," Franton replied. "I cannot approve the manufacturing of the legs if it is dependent on destroying equipment."

"We need hydraulics from the dinette's automatic conversion system, right?" She didn't see why the AI was so protective of the dinette's ability to convert from a table to a bed. It currently sat in bed mode, since Mauve couldn't get to the bunks in the back of the rover.

"Affirmative."

"And there are replacements in the dock, correct?" Mauve figured there were enough replacement parts in that dock to build a second rover if she had to.

"Assuming they were not damaged in the process, that is correct."

"Great." Mauve pulled a screwdriver out of the toolbox she'd liberated from the undercarriage storage, where it blocked her removal of the wheelchair. Instead of leaving it on the ground in a pile of other junk, she'd carried it into the rover, happy to have the tools if necessary. She used the screwdriver to disassemble the bed in front of her.

"What are you doing?" Franton asked.

"Getting the necessary equipment."

"I can't approve that."

"You don't really get a say in this. So either this dismantlement is going to be for nothing, or you can start printing the bionic legs." She'd sleep on the wheelchair in protest if she had to. Her willpower was much stronger than Franton's. The computer was only designed to advise.

"I do not think this is a good idea. We should be focusing on how you feel about the traumatic events you have experienced recently."

Mauve ignored Franton and placed the metal cover neatly on the counter. Years of mechanic training had taught her not to keep things neat while doing repair work. This wasn't exactly a repair, but old habits were hard to break.

The bed had tubes running to and fro with emerald hydraulic fluid pumping through them. The synthetic liquid was bright green, so it'd be easy to locate if it spilled. She found the reservoir and turned the valve to stop the flow. She wanted to avoid making a mess if possible.

The computer complained, but after the sixth pump was removed and Mauve began pulling out servos, she heard the printer start up in the research lab. With a smile, she finished gathering the remaining supplies.

***

It'd taken her a day to glue everything together and for the adhesive to set. Mauve finally strapped the final plastic cage over her leg. The bionic legs were like a cage that wrapped around her immobile legs. She hoped they'd hold her weight and move under her.

She wasn't sure if something this rudimentary really counted as bionic legs. They were a far cry from the cybernetic arm the crew's geologist had. But bionic sounded cool, so she refused to call them anything less.

Now she was trying them on in the cramped research room. It was not painted the same space-expanding white of every other small room she'd been in. It was a navy blue and looked like a cave. She didn't hate the design, but it made her feel like the walls were closing in. Although she'd felt like that ever since her injury. She was looking forward to walking again.

"The computer on board your legs is running an archaic neural network. It will not learn your motions as quickly as I would."

The pair had to repurpose a small computer from the oscilloscope in the research lab. It was not as advanced as a hand terminal—it didn't have a Franton pearl in it—but it had enough memory and processing power to run some basic signal processing, and so Franton could reprogram it to operate the pants.

"I don't care if I look like a drunk toddler on a moonwalk. I just want to stand up." If she could feel her lower back, she was sure it would be sore from sitting all day. "Can I stand now?"

Slowly the hydraulic pumps near her knees and hips started humming. She rose from her wheelchair. Her arms gripped the wheelchair for support. She slowly moved one arm to the room's workbench as her knees began to lock out.

She was doing it. She was standing. The emerald fluid did its job and gave her new strength to stand. It pumped through the tubing that ran chaotically up and down her legs. She could feel her cheeks pinched into dimples around her mouth. She laughed and was glad no one was around to hear her. She threw her hands in the air to celebrate.

Mauve fell backwards onto the floor.

"That was too sudden of a move for the legs to adjust for quite yet."

"Noted." Mauve rubbed her head. It'd hit the wheelchair on her way down. "Try try again." She moved to stand up, but nothing happened. Her legs didn't move; she still wasn't used to that. "The gyros in my waistband should be noticing that I'm trying to stand," Mauve complained to Franton.

"It is not trained to lift you up yet," Franton replied. Its cameras had picked up more than the computer in Mauve's new legs.

"How am I supposed to get up?"

"I will control the motors using the gyroscope inputs while the neural network observes it as training data."

"Why didn't you do that when I was whooping and hollering?"

"I was not prepared."

Mauve was unsettled by that statement. Franton had the ability to run multiple processes at a time even with a single pearl. There was no reason it should have been unprepared.

She would have to look into that once she was back to her full capacity. Which she hoped would be soon. Unfortunately, she didn't think the training process would be quick.

Three

The cool morning breeze carried lizard chirps to Mauve's ears. The little animals sounded like locked-up servo motors. It brought a smile to Mauve's face as she sat down at the workbench to pick up on the work she'd started yesterday.

The spring morning was humid. Mauve wasn't used to the humidity changing throughout the day. On the starships she grew up on, it was necessary to keep the temperature and humidity consistent, and entire departments of people were in charge of monitoring and investigating issues. Here, the planet Knod seemed to do whatever it felt like. The local star burned up the moisture in the air as the day went on, and Mauve had relished the experience despite her sweaty jumpsuit.

The crash site clearing was surrounded by green trees with trunks so big she could barely wrap her arms around them. Their bark felt like fine grit sandpaper, and bright green leaves shaped like the tips of needle-nose pliers hung from the branches. The forest floor was sparse; she'd expect it to be overgrown, but it was shady and likely difficult for things to compete with the tall trees. As a mechanic, she knew how that felt.

During a short break yesterday, she'd explored the forest, putting the exosuit legs through their paces. The forest was easier to navigate with the exoskeleton legs than Mauve had expected. She had to be careful not to place her boot on tree roots; they were covered in slick moss and uneven, so the exoskeleton leg's standard pressure wouldn't let her balance. But there were enough gaps where tall grass and sunburst-blue flowers grew that were flat enough for her to step on. She hated to crush the blooming flowers, but there were so many she had no doubt that life would go on. The abundance of life was a stark contrast from the starships of her youth.

Lizards darted up and down the trees, catching beetles the size of ratchet wrench sockets that zipped around. Mauve didn't seem to scare them away when she approached, and she wondered if there were any predators that sparked fear inside them. Some lizards were wide and bright, with red and purple stripes running down their backs. Others were a muted brown or green and lean like a spaceship. There were too many to categorize, but Mauve had no doubt the crew's two biologists would try.

Assuming the biologists had survived. Crashes were rare since humanity had spent the past dozen centuries exploring and settling the stars. The closest Mauve had ever expected to get to a crash site was on the other side of a screen. Over-dramatized reality shows "stranded" people who couldn't tell a spanner from a screwdriver in the wilderness of recently settled planets. But Mauve knew there were cameras monitoring their situation and ships to pull them out if anything serious happened.

Despite the radio silence, Mauve didn't believe the crew to be dead. Death was something that happened at an old age with family around. Not on routine research deployments. They might be hurt and disheveled, but their crash couches would have kept them safe, and the cockpit part of the ship didn't have as many supplies but had enough to keep them warm and healthy.

And once she got the comms array that she set up yesterday working, she'd be able to pick up any signal they were sending out. Regardless of its strength. The damaged comms array was the exact reason that the crew would be grateful to have an experienced mechanic onboard.

They'd been hesitant to accept her on the way down. But there were problems to solve and repairs to be done. And if they had to wait two and half years until the mothership came back around, Mauve would be busy keeping everything in shape.

It wasn't unfathomable to stay here for two years. The crash site was already beginning to look like a real base of operations, even after only a day of work. She'd spent yesterday unloading boxes and setting up equipment. The clearing would never look like a real landing area; the upside-down ship dock embedded into the earth ruined its chances at that. But she'd brought some necessary order to the place yesterday.

She'd cleaned up the mess of rover supplies she'd had to remove to access the wheelchair a few days ago. Her apprenticeship had taught her that a neat workspace was necessary for good work to be done. By the time her apprenticeship had finished, she couldn't imagine working in a messy environment. Thankfully, with the new exoskeleton legs, repacking had only taken a few minutes, despite initial unpacking taking hours.

Now the area shaded by the inverted dock had a half dozen workbenches on a floor made of large locking plastic tiles. The tiles were a meter square with interlocking edges. The surface had a zigzag pattern that reminded Mauve of the bottom of the work boots she wore. She'd deployed a whole crate of the tiles yesterday, but it only covered a ten-by-ten-meter area. More were packed away in the dock but attached to what was now its ceiling. Gravity was not going to do her any favors in her attempt to unpack those.

Mauve only fell a handful of times laying out the grooved tiles. Bending over and standing up was still something the pants were trying to get used to. She had to work hard to keep her torso over her center of gravity, and it felt a bit like trying to balance a stylus on her finger. Which was a task she eventually got good at during her apprenticeship classes when her teachers lectured about repairs she knew she'd only be able to learn by getting her hands dirty.

In the center of the tiled area sat a communications array. It looked like a city skyline, with dozens of antennas and small satellite dishes rising up from the white plastic base. It was simple to assemble, just plug-and-play parts so simple a child could do it if only they could reach the highest parts of the antenna towers. It was almost working, and she hoped to finish that job up this morning.

She'd placed workbenches around the perimeter of the tiled floor as well. They were flimsy portable workbenches with legs made of metal tubes and plastic tops that were only a few centimeters thick. Mauve wouldn't trust them to do any real long-term work. But they were the only thing accessible, so she used them. The real workbenches with thick metal tops and cross-braced legs were stored in the dock. On the bright side, Mauve knew they hadn't been damaged; they were virtually indestructible.

One thing that hadn't survived the crash undamaged was the communication array's multiplexer that sat in front of her on the workbench. It was the size of a club sandwich but twice as thick. It was necessary for the operation of the comms array, since it selected which of the many antennas the computer would send transmissions from. The white sheet-metal box had ports for wires to be plugged into.

Module circuits like this were common and used on multiple pieces of equipment to keep manufacturing costs down and repairability high.

This particular multiplexer had a dent in one side and was not responding to any inputs given to it. Franton had identified the issue yesterday, but the spares, like everything else Mauve seemed to need lately, were attached to the ceiling of the dock. So she hoped to repair this one.

Mauve had never liked fixing computers. She liked to be able to see where parts failed, and the motionless processing of circuits wasn't conducive to visual observation.

Old-style circuit boards were the worst offenders of this in Mauve's opinion. Made of transistors, capacitors, and other simple electronic parts, anything could go wrong with them, and a day could pass without successfully finding the problem.

The other computer that existed was a Franton array. Which was a matrix of Franton pearls that held the AI's computational power and processing. One pearl was enough to do some personal computing, but a whole array unlocked Franton's cognitive abilities. Mauve had no experience repairing these because they rarely failed. Either the pearls worked or they were unplugged. The high-density crystalline structure of the pearls couldn't be repaired if it were cracked. But it would take an otherworldly amount of force to crack one. The common joke was that a space station could rest on a pearl without leaving a mark.

Most equipment was a mix of the two. Franton could integrate with any circuitry and was at the core of all modern technology. Mauve opened up the lid of the multiplexer after removing a few screws and was faced with a grid of solid white pearls about the width of her thumb seated in clips that connected them to a black sheet that stacked on top of at least two, if not three, more similar grids. A green circuit board attached to the wall with flat, integrated circuits that looked like black caterpillars and cylindrical capacitors towering over them. Luckily the circuit was fine, but the black mounting bracket for the Franton array was bent and the pearls sat cockeyed in it.

"Can I just bend it back in place?" Mauve asked the computer as she reached for some pliers. She was connected to Franton by a headset that wrapped from ear to ear connected by going around the nape of her neck. This headset had a camera, microphone, and earpieces so the computer could see everything she saw. A deployable screen was tucked behind Mauve's ear and could be bent to sit over her eye to give her a heads-up display, or HUD, so Franton could display diagrams and manuals if needed.

"Please do not try to bend it back into place," Franton replied. "I would prefer that you dismount it and replace it with an undamaged mount."

Instead of pliers, Mauve grabbed a screwdriver to remove the bracket.

"First, can you please probe it so I can run some diagnostics?"

She probed all the spots that Franton asked for, but the computer didn't give away much of what it was finding. When it came to the end, all the computer said was, "That is quite strange."

Mauve didn't like her supercomputer using the word "strange."

Franton asked her to check the next board under it. After removing a few screws, she was able to access a second sheet of pearls that glistened in the sunlight of the late morning. "Inspect location BF358," Franton requested.

Mauve meticulously counted out the regions to find the pearl Franton had requested. Looking at it up close with her headset, she said, "This all looks fine to me. Do you see anything?"

"It is more translucent than I expected."

"It shouldn't be translucent at all; these are solid crystals."

"Affirmative," the computer responded. Its flat tone gave nothing away.

"What kind of readings are you getting from it?" she finally asked after the computer was silent for a while.

"Everything coming from it is normal, but it has an extra layer of noise mixed in. Not enough that I would have noticed; I account for a certain amount of noise in my processing, and a damaged mounting bracket would explain the problem, so it was almost expected."

"Except this sheet isn't connected to the damaged board."

"Affirmative. So either the case was damaged more than we can tell, or that pearl has something wrong with it."

"What do you want me to do? More probes?" It was beginning to annoy her that she hadn't just put this thing in the rover's fabrication bed and let Franton do all the probing and analysis itself.

"Negative. I think to get the comms array up and running as quickly as possible, we should be safe and replace both the BF358 pearl and the mounting bracket for A level."

"Easy," Mauve replied. She'd done operations like this a dozen times, and she was glad Franton was done making her probe the thing.

After gathering the crate that contained extra Franton pearls and mounting equipment, she began the procedure of replacing the necessary pieces. The mount was easy to fix; she unscrewed it and removed the dozen or so unseated Franton pearls. It was a satisfying, repetitive process that Mauve found almost meditative. She had to use specialized extraction pliers to lift the pearls in and out; normal tools would do more damage to the new mounting bracket. The pliers had four plastic arms that were close at the tip but bulged in the middle to hold the pearl. It interlocked perfectly with the four-armed slots that held the pearls to the mounting bracket.

Before inserting the new sheet of pearls, Mauve needed to replace the translucent pearl that Franton was worried about.

"When extracting the BF358 pearl, please place it in the diagnostic module that comes with the replacement kits," Franton said. The computer was always watching through her headset and knew what she was doing.

"No worries," she responded. She lowered the extraction pliers to the pearl that needed to be removed. As she clinched the pliers shut, the pearl seemed to pop in front of her eyes.

Mauve leaned back in her seat, startled. "What just happened?!"

"I have no idea," Franton replied. "How hard did you pinch it?"

"I barely had a hold of it," Mauve said, wondering if the pearls were more delicate than the stories. "Are there fragments left that you can analyze?"

"Reviewing the video on your headset, I don't see any pieces large enough to collect."

"Is this something that has happened before?"

"Negative. This isn't anywhere in my diagnostic records."

If it wasn't in the diagnostic record, it wasn't in the realm of remote possibilities. Mauve knew thousands of engineers and researchers had recorded everything that there was to know about the pearls and Franton's abilities. Even Franton kept track of how it worked and what might go wrong. This not being in the diagnostic records was unnerving. More unnerving than Franton forgetting and remarking at things being strange.

"There is still an unexpected amount of noise coming from the multiplexer," Franton said, "but it is an amount that I can work around."

"Does that mean that the pearl wasn't the problem?"

"That is still unclear. I am unwilling to label a pearl that delicate not a problem."

Without much else to investigate, Mauve reached for a new pearl to insert into the device.

"Please wait. I'm not sure if we should move forward using this multiplexer."

"You want me to replace all the pearls in this device?" That felt a little overboard to Mauve.

"There aren't enough pearls in that replacement kit to do that. I'd prefer to use a new multiplexer all together, but the only matching part for this is the multiplexer in the shuttle's cockpit."

"There should be a replacement for everything in the dock," Mauve corrected the computer. "We'd just have to find it."

"There is not a replacement listed in my inventory," Franton said. "Whole parts like this are not stocked on research deployment. In most cases, a replacement like you've done would fix damage like this."

"In the starship docks I can always find a spare module circuit like this." Mauve was uneasy about the limited inventory. Maybe she'd been wrong about being able to rebuild a rover from scratch.

"This is not a starship. We have limited resources and must be careful with them."

Mauve felt the hair on her neck prickle at the comment. Franton's voice did not have the tone of a teacher's scolding. It was programmed to deliver all dialogue flatly and emotionlessly. But it didn't soften the blow.

"The only matching part for this is the multiplexer in the shuttle's cockpit," Franton repeated.

"Which we can't find without a working multiplexer."

"Affirmative."

"What other multiplexers do we have access to?" Each device had some sort of communication circuitry on it. Her headset had something, the damaged mech suit had one, even the foodcrowave in the rover had one. As Franton pulled up a list of their inventory to her hand-held terminal, she began scanning. Fitting electronics into their spot was within her comfort zone. Getting the wrong electronics to work together was like getting a square peg to fit in a round hole. It could be done, but a few corners would have to be cut in the process.

***

Mauve stared up at the crates strapped into the ceiling of the inverted dock. They were gray and black with corners that bulged out so that the wide, heavy-duty straps would sit across the center. The straps were doing their job. Most of them at least. A few boxes were laying on the ground upside-down or cockeyed. The boxes came up to her shoulder if she stood next to them and opened up like clamshells. Mauve had never seen an actual clam or its shell, but she'd seen a dozen other contraptions that borrowed their hinged design.

Mauve stood in the doorway of the dock on the would-be ramp if she hadn't burnt out the motors to escape the dock nearly a week ago. She looked down into the cavernous room, dark without any of the bright lights enabled. It was lower than her because of how the dock embedded itself into the earth. The crates hung like stalactites in a cave, the few she could see near the entrance. Connected to a grid of mounting brackets on the once-floor. Each of those mounting brackets was controlled by Franton, and she was trying to get the computer to do something ridiculous.

"Let's just drop them all from the ceiling at once," Mauve suggested. She hated the idea of the chaos it would cause. But it was the easiest solution to their current problem.

"The amount of damage that would cause to the crates is inestimable." Franton spoke into her ear through her HUD. Its androgynous voice didn't give away its feelings.

"But the contents should be fine," Mauve replied. "And if there's a few things to repair, that will keep me busy. If we wind up getting the mothership to send a rescue shuttle, it won't matter if the contents are a little bent."

"The contents may be fine, but it will be an unorganized mess."

"I know. I'm not looking forward to that. But what do you want to do? We can't just leave all this stuff strapped to the ceiling once I uninstall the multiplexer."

The multiplexer best suited to replace the broken comms array multiplexer was stored in the docks ceiling. It had a lot of similar electronics, and the only significant difference they'd have to work around was the difference in voltage. Because the comms array transmitted signals long distances, it ran on more power than the dock. This was a simple change for Franton to do.

Another easy part of the repair was that Mauve wouldn't have to climb up to the multiplexer. It was mounted high on the dock wall. Since the dock was inverted, the multiplexer was mounted only a little higher than Mauve's reach, and with a step stool she could access it and disassemble it. As stable as her exosuit legs were, she didn't want to test them out on ladders.

The problem was that this multiplexer selected which mounting brackets were disconnected. The dock had a dozen Franton arrays to keep inventory, fire motors, and run manufacturing equipment. However, only the multiplexer could select which crates needed to be released from the straps. Meaning once Mauve uninstalled it, any crates still strapped to the ceiling would hang there until the webbing degraded. She'd read the spec sheet on the webbing; it wasn't going to naturally break down any time soon.

"I would prefer that we let the rover come in and lower the crates down manually," Franton said.

There were hundreds of crates in the massive dock. "How long would that take? The rover is where I sleep. Is it going to be moving crates while I'm inside?"

"If it takes breaks for you to sleep, I estimate the project will be done in a week."

"We don't have a week, Franton!" She was not programmed to show neutral emotion and was currently taking advantage of that. "The crew needs to be found; the mothership is flying away, dropping off other researchers. I might be as lucky as a five-head crew working a two-person job, but I don't want to sit still."

"I believe some patience and perspective are in order."

"Have you considered that the crew might be somewhere on this planet needing us to find them?"

"The probability of that is low considering that they were on the part of the ship that had the most crash couches to protect them."

Mauve didn't actually think that the crew was having a hard time of it. But Franton wanted her to have perspective, and this was the perspective that was going to get the comms repair moving forward. And that was her job as a mechanic, to fix things and keep projects moving. Without people like her, satellites would fall out of orbit.

"But even if it's a sliver of a chance that they need assistance, we have to move towards helping them. And as messy as dropping the crates is, it's necessary to get closer to helping the crew."

"Running simulations based on the crates' location observed by the rover, I've found that it is unlikely any catastrophic damage has occurred. If this is the route you want to take, then with your approval I will drop the crates."

"Finally," Mauve sighed. "Yes, do it."

Every single crate in the room fell at once. A deafening clang came from the hollow dock. It slammed into Mauve's chest, and wind of all the boxes moving at once blew through her short hair. A dozen softer clanks came from straggler boxes settling. The dock reverberated with echoes and then fell silent. Mauve turned on the light of her HUD, ready to finish her repair.

Four

The dim blue light of the sun still covered the sky, but the star itself had already dipped under the horizon. Mauve rewired the connectors of the dock's multiplexer to match the necessary outputs of the comms array. She worked by the floodlights of the rover once light disappeared completely. The starry sky brought countless sounds from the lizards in the forest. Mauve yawned, and her stomach groaned, but she refused to stop for dinner. She had momentum and was determined to get the project done before taking a break.

"I think we're ready to plug this in," Mauve announced to Franton despite it watching over her shoulder every step of the way.

"Affirmative, you have modified everything necessary to connect the two."

Mauve was ready to get this finished. She plugged in the final cable, the power cable, into the dock's multiplexer. Nothing happened, and then a puff of white smoke came from the dock's multiplexer. Mauve cursed and yanked the power connector out even though the damage had been done.

"What happened?" she asked the computer, assuming it was running diagnostics on the device the whole time.

"The voltage converter on the dock's multiplexer must have failed."

The dock ran at a much lower power than the comms array, and trying to run it at the communication array's higher voltage could cause serious damage. "We didn't put a converter on the dock's multiplexer," Mauve replied. She could have, but the two of them agreed that would take too long. "You were supposed to reduce the voltage going into the dock's multiplexer."

"I failed to do that."

"No kidding," she said, unplugging the rest of the connectors now that the multiplexer had stopped smoking. "What happened? Did you forget?"

"Affirmative."

"Wait, what?" That wasn't the response she'd expected. Franton was a computer with countless processors, each able to handle a different thought if necessary. There shouldn't have been a chance to forget.

"I was running a diagnostic on myself, so some of my cores were down. I removed the voltage regulator off of the list of things that needed to be done, which is why I approved plugging it in. I just never got around to reprogramming the comms array."

"Never got around to it?" she asked. She was familiar with the expression; she'd used it a number of times as a mechanic. She just didn't expect to hear Franton say it.

"More like I requested the change to be made, but it never got completed. I might have shut down the cores responsible for the change during diagnostics, but I should have transferred the request."

Mauve was concerned that the computer was running diagnostics while doing work. At any point in time, Franton was always doing some maintenance on itself, but this seemed like more than usual.

"I guess you can run some more diagnostics on yourself to see why the request failed to be completed," Mauve said.

"Affirmative. I think we will need to take the whole system offline and have you run manual diagnostics."

Mauve sighed. For one person, that was a whole day of work with Franton guiding her through step by step. She'd have to check each piece of Franton wherever it was stored in the crash site. Starships never went fully down but constantly had technicians making sure that Franton was always operating appropriately. Maybe if she found the crew, they could help her through the diagnosis quicker.

"What do you want to do now?" Mauve asked. "I could just plug in the old multiplexer, or we can modify something else tomorrow." The list of options was slim, and the rover's multiplexer was the next most compatible option. She wasn't loving the idea of dismantling her temporary home to make this comms array work.

"It's your decision. I would like to refrain from making any critical decisions before a full diagnostic test can be run."

"Let's just fix this real quick so I can go to bed. You can filter out any of the noise you were complaining about earlier, right?"

"Affirmative. It's all within a range that won't interfere with my computations. I think you should run my manual diagnostics in the morning."

"I promise I will." Mauve stifled a yawn. "But for now, let's just get this plugged in and you can message the mothership and search for the crew while I sleep."

Mauve finished the repair within an hour and integrated the original multiplexer after another half hour. Bugs built with long noses like race cars buzzed around her, and stars shone over her head. If she'd known that this repair was what was needed, she could have been done by lunch. But that was the funny thing about projects like this: the place where you landed wasn't always where you expected.

***

Mauve woke up late the next morning, intentionally ignoring Franton the few times it tried to wake her up. Her philosophy was always if there weren't evac announcements or flashing emergency lights, and she wasn't about to get fired for missing a shift, then there wasn't any urgency to getting out of bed.

Franton went on and on as she attached the exoskeleton pants to her paralyzed legs. She was noticing some rashes on her legs, likely from the wear of the exoskeleton, but it wasn't like she could feel them to bother her. As she walked from the bunk room to the kitchen, she had to relearn how to walk just like she did every morning. The space was so cramped, there was always something to help her balance. The short journey reminded her of old books and movies where sailor characters talked about getting sea legs, and she wondered if she'd ever get to jump out of bed on this planet and just walk like she used to.

The rover's foodcrowave rehydrated a breakfast meal for her, and she carefully transferred the omelet and cup of coffee to the dinette table. She had to focus harder than she wanted to after waking up in an attempt not to spill or drop any of it.

Once at the table, she nibbled at the omelet while sipping her cup of coffee. Franton had quieted down; it'd either gotten the message that she wasn't listening or was waiting for a response.

She enjoyed the coffee but only ate a quarter of the omelet. The eggs weren't very good—rehydrated food never was—and the coffee was only a step above the day-old stuff found in the breakroom of every starship's dock. She'd always assumed that a union had won its mechanics the right to always have access to coffee and the corporation running the dock figured they could cut the expense by always leaving the old stuff out so people drank less. There was likely a whole department on staff to organize the brewing cycles to make sure a day-old cup was always available.

"What have you got, Fran?" she asked as her senses came online.

"I was saying that I've sent out a message to the mothership and I've been scanning the local area in an attempt to find a signal from the crew."

"Any luck?"

"At the rate the mothership was traveling, it will be a few days until we hear back. As for the signal from the crew, I'm not sure."

"You're not sure of what?"

"Well, I found something, but I can't guarantee it's from the crew."

"Who else would it be from?" Mauve's mind raced, wondering if pirates had already settled this island like the old stories she'd watched as a kid, or if it was alien life trying to ward her off their planet.

"Initial scans of the planet indicated that the most advanced life on the planet is the lizards; no signals were picked up when we were reviewing the planet for landing, so this is likely new."

"And if it's new, then that means either life has evolved so quickly on this planet that it discovered how to transmit things, or Vincent is alive and trying to figure out how to make the SOS communicator work." Vincent was the physicist of the crew and, like most physicists and scientists she'd met, rarely realized that application of their theoretical and experimental world didn't seamlessly translate to the real world. That difficulty in translation was where creative mechanics like Mauve came in handy.

"That seems to be a possible conclusion. That being said, even a distorted radio transmission wouldn't be this messed up. It's like it's communicating on multiple channels in an attempt to be noticed." Franton put the wave pattern it was receiving on the massive screen at the front of the rover's cabin.

It was like nothing Mauve had ever seen before. The waves were jagged and curved, and as Franton plotted it in 3D space, it took on configurations that would be impossible for any modern transmission technology she knew of to make. "This is weird." She wondered if Vincent, in his stranded state, had invented a new form of transmission technology. After all, they said necessity was the mother of invention. "How would the crew make something like this?"

"That I am unsure of. I am also unsure if the crew is sending this signal."

"What else could it be?"

"The most likely scenario is that I am misinterpreting it because of the noise we discovered in the multiplexer yesterday. Which is why it would be important to do a full diagnostic for me today."

Mauve remembered why she had been putting off getting out of bed. "I really have to do that today?"

"It seems that it's more pertinent than ever. I'd like to go offline completely. In order for us to do this, you'll have to follow the physical diagnostic manual."

"Offline completely? That means that you won't be around to walk me through the procedures." It was rare that she had to do anything like this without Franton present. Of course, they'd taught her how to do a few things in school without a computer, but it was like writing, reading, or making a sandwich: she never expected she'd have to do it herself. There were always computers around to do that kind of work.

"That's the point of the printed diagnostic manual." A small compartment opened, and a book the size of a handbag sat inside.

Mauve had no desire to touch the thing; that would be accepting her fate too soon. "Let's do it in parts. There are areas that I can't easily access, like the dock or some of the components inside the crates that haven't been unloaded yet."

"Affirmative. I would like to shut those down until we can run a diagnostic on those too. Your main priority for today would be the rover and the communication array."

"If I don't finish them both today?" She'd expected the process to take a day to do with Franton walking her through it. Having to find and reference the manual herself and comprehend what it was trying to communicate would slow things down considerably. And if Franton was offline, that meant everything on the rover would be shut down except for emergency systems like air purification and lighting; they were just connected to the battery, no computation needed.

"I will make sure that enough water and food is dispensed so that you can easily survive. You'll have to rehydrate the meals yourself, but it's easy. Just add water to the food."

"What if I add too much and it's soupy or not enough and it doesn't rehydrate as well?"

"The vitamins and calories are still there regardless of if it tastes good to consume them."

Leave it to a computer without tastebuds to boil something as complex as a meal down to molecules.

"What will leaving the dock shut down do to your computational capacity?" Each pearl connected to Franton enabled it to do more computations and process information faster. Taking the dock down, filled with dozens of pearls, would make it harder for Franton to think things through. The computer would still do a lot of things in the blink of an eye, but some of its more complex functions like decision-making and creativity would be hindered.

"The dock is already out of the equation since we blew the multi-plexer. As for all the devices inside the dock that I'm going to break the connection to, it will be nearly a 50% hit to my current abilities."

"Geez, Fran, that's a lot." She imagined what it would be like if she thought half the speed that she currently did. It would be like running through gelatin.

"Negative. It is an exponential scale, so the speed of my computing will only be cut by a fraction of that percentage."

Mauve knew a fraction of 50% was still more than she wanted to lose.

"Additionally, it would be more catastrophic for me to give you bad advice or directions due to faults in my computation than it would be to have slower computational speed."

She gave the computer that point. It would be bad if her only ally here began telling her to do things that were not helpful to her survival on the planet.

"Lastly, when we find the crew, we will also gain access to the black box and my main servers, which hold many more pearls that will enable me to regain my full computational power. So doing this diagnostic will only help me get back to full capacity sooner."

Mauve teetered her head back and forth; she didn't love that idea. There had to be a solution that didn't include her using a physical book and a stove like she was a pre-warp human. Just because she was stranded on a planet didn't mean she needed to act that way.

If Franton's creativity and decision-making processes were slowed down, it would only be able to think of the most obvious solutions to the problems in front of them. Not ideal, but Mauve was clever; she'd always been scolded by foremen for getting jobs done in creative ways because they couldn't approve the repair due to bureaucratic regulations. But on an alien planet without any bureaucrats, that was the exact kind of thinking they needed.

"Mauve, I am going to take myself offline," Franton said after a moment of silence.

"Hold on. What about this? We go to the signal to figure out what is wrong with you."

"We do not know what is sending out the signal; it could be something dangerous."

"You said it yourself. It's probably the crew with a bad transmitter, or one of the lizards figured out how to build a radio."

"Negative, I said that there is probably something wrong with how I'm filtering the noise out of the multiplexer. Which is why I need the diagnostics run."

"Okay, maybe, but if the diagnostics come back with nothing, we'd waste a day. If we find the signal and investigate it, we could figure out what the pattern is supposed to look like and you'll be able to compensate for it in the future. Then you'll know how to interpret signals without errors, which is necessary for communicating with the mothership. And as a bonus, we might find the crew in the process."

"I do not like this plan."

"It's a plan to fix you, potentially quicker than by running diagnostics. And I believe before you said you didn't trust yourself to make decisions. So we're going to do what I'm proposing." She could drive the rover out to the signal's location if she had to. It'd be slow and tedious work, but it'd force the computer's proverbial arm.

"I will accept your proposed plan," Franton replied, "as long as we approach the signal cautiously." The computer's voice was supposed to be flat and emotionless, but Mauve wondered if she was hearing traces of resentment in the remark.

***

Mauve replayed the video feed of the drone for a fifth time. She hoped she'd see something different, something that would explain why Franton had lost connection with it, but each time she saw the same thing.

Nothing at all.

The drone flew through the forest under Mauve's control; the map indicated that the bot was getting closer to the location that Franton determined the signal would be at. There were no antennas or other devices indicating transmission, no signs of human life or any other buildings indicating intelligent life. Just more forest, the same thick forest the rover had spent the past few days hacking through to make a path to get to this spot. And what was she rewarded with? Jack shit.

"I've analyzed the video feed, and it doesn't seem to be anything out of the ordinary," Franton reported. "The drone should have rebooted by now, but I'm not getting any new signals from it."

"It might have been unable to land and damaged. I'm sure we can repair it."

"That would require us to retrieve it."

"Yup," Mauve replied as she got up from the dinette she analyzed the feed from.

"Negative. You can't go searching for that thing. It might be dangerous."

"Being stranded on a planet alone is inherently dangerous. This is just another risk I'm going to have to take."

"I cannot allow it. You'll put yourself in too much danger."

"Fran, having something that can just take down a drone without us noticing is dangerous. I'd rather find them before they find us."

"If someone aggressive finds us, then I'll lock the rover down. It's effectively impenetrable."

"Then they dismantle it and wait for me to run out of food. Anything with the intelligence to create a signal like this would be smart enough to figure that out."

"They'll see you coming a dozen kilometers away."

"But at least I'll be expecting them. If we turn tail and go back to the dock, then they'll sneak up on us whenever we least expect it."

She started rummaging around the rover to find something she could use as a weapon if necessary. A personal welding torch she could strap onto her back would have been nice, but anything that heavy-duty was back at the dock. The kitchen didn't have any knives because it was an automated rehydration system, and the research area just had a bunch of stuff for manufacturing things like her legs and investigating biological and geological items. In the end, she found a small repair kit under the driver's seat of the cockpit. It had a number of small wrenches, adhesives, lubricants and hand tools. She settled on bringing a plastic mallet and a screwdriver. The mallet probably wouldn't do much damage, but it looked intimidating.

"I don't think this is a good idea," Franton repeated as she began to open the door and ramp of the rover.

"I think it is. We'll figure out what's going on, and when we realize it's nothing, we can recalibrate you."

"I cannot encourage you to do this," Franton said into her headset now that she had left the cabin of the rover.

"Wasn't asking for encouragement," she said as she stepped off the ramp and onto the forest floor. "Either disable my legs or help me keep an eye out for anything suspicious." She was having to keep an eye on the tree-filled horizon to maintain her balance as her bionic legs got used to walking on the uneven terrain.

Five

Hiking through the forest was not as easy as walking around the crash site. A small benefit of the rover crashing was that it cleared a lot of the trees and rocks out of the way where she'd made camp. The area she was in now hadn't been touched by anything human made in the thousands of years of its existence. Her heads-up display, a pair of glasses that had headphones, a microphone, cameras, and a small screen that could project semi-transparent images in her field of view kept her in contact with Franton and the rover. The computer was doing a lot more work scanning the surrounding area for suspicious activity than she was. And if someone had rushed her, she felt like she'd be more likely to fall over than outrun them.

As the HUD indicated she was getting closer to the drone's crash site, the ground became rockier than before. The trees were thinner, and the ground reminded her of bricks that humans used to make buildings out of before they took to the stars and perfected metalwork buildings. The corners of the rectangular prisms seemed to always poke up, and the ground seemed to be made of steep hills and valleys, each the size of her boot. Having to switch her gaze between the ground and the horizon slowed her down even more. If she could feel her feet, she would likely be in constant discomfort poking the base of her foot or jamming her toe into a rock. As she looked to the horizon for her next step, Franton spoke into her ear.

"The drone seems to be only a few meters away."

She looked up after she finished catching her balance from her step. Sure enough, the drone with its mangled rotors was lying in front of her, broken in pieces from its landing on the rocky ground.

"Be careful, please."

"Do you see anything dangerous?"

"Negative, but we didn't see anything dangerous when the drone went down either."

Mauve took her next few steps slowly, closing the distance between her and the drone. "It looks like the only damage is physical. Broken armature and prop, but all the internal circuitry will probably be fine." All computational and communication equipment was held inside the drone's body. "It should have been able to reconnect."

"Maintaining... with your HUD... difficult... away... area."

"Your signal is coming in broken. Please repeat." She spoke into the air around her as she approached the drone to inspect it further.

A few more choppy words came in from Franton, but none of them made sense to Mauve. Sure enough, as she'd expected, the rotor blades and armature of the drone were damaged and it wouldn't be flying anytime soon, but the protective body surrounding the electronics was merely scuffed. It should have been able to stay connected to the rover. Scanning the area around her, she looked for the traces of something or someone that might have sabotaged it.

Her eyes finally landed on a suspect. She wondered if she'd have been able to notice it in the video if she'd known what to look for. It wasn't a conspicuous antenna sticking up out of the ground; it was simply a shiny black ball. Nature rarely made things that shiny or that pitch-black, but humans loved to make technology look as far away from nature as possible. Surely that was the device that had disabled the drone.

Franton had gone silent. Mauve leaned forward to move towards the device to attempt to disable it so she could re-establish communication. As she leaned her body forward to take her next step, her lower half didn't move with her.

By the time she realized what was wrong, her momentum had carried her over her center of gravity. She fell towards the rocky ground, reflexively covering her head from the fall. Whatever had disabled the drone had disabled the electronics of her legs. Franton was likely unable to reach her for the same reason.

"Are you the right person to bite into the fruit of this plant?" a singsong voice asked.

Startled, Mauve looked up. A young boy tinged in a shade of blue stood above her. "What did you say? Who are you?" she asked. Unable to get up and back away, she reached for the mallet that hung on the tool-loop of her jumpsuit.

"I'm Anweis," the boy responded. He took a cross-legged seat next to her. He seemed friendly enough, but Mauve thought she could almost see through him. "And that looks quite uncomfortable."

"It is. Can you help me sit up?"

"Nope," the boy said as if he were thrilled to be giving the answer.

She groaned at the inconsideration of the kid and began the laborious effort of rolling onto her back and then used her forearms to prop herself up. She assumed that adults that supervised this young boy would be around soon, and she didn't want to be completely prone when they appeared.

"Looks like the stuff on your legs has seen better days," the boy said.

"No kidding." The plastic braces were cracked and likely wouldn't hold her weight anymore if she could stand. Tubes had come free from their hydraulic pumps, and emerald fluid flowed freely over the brick-like rocks. It wasn't her blood but might as well have been. The legs weren't carrying her back to the rover. "Who are you?" she repeated to the boy, this time taking a good look at him.

"I'm Anweis, the instruction manual of the machine."

Staring at the boy, she found that his head was disproportionately larger than his body, but all of his other features were those of a child. He was wearing a jumpsuit similar to hers but shrunken down to fit a child. The strangest part about him was that he was not only completely blue but also semi-transparent. She reached out to touch him, and her hand went right through where his head should have been. "So that's why you can't help me up."

"Absolutely, otherwise I totally would have helped. I'm not a monster."

"What are you? Are there more like you?" Mauve figured if she couldn't touch it, it couldn't hurt her.

"I'm Anweis, and I'm an instruction manual for the machine." This time he gestured away from Mauve.

The little black device she had seen earlier was in the direction of the gesture. "That's the machine."

"Yup, it's pretty slick. Pun intended. One of the finest plants the ontares ever created."

It looked quite slick indeed, but far from any plant Mauve had seen. Not that space stations were covered with plants. The black goop reflected the sunlight off of it in confusing directions. It was dark and seemed to let no light escape but still had an almost imperceptible rainbow sheen. It felt similar to the sheen mech-suit lubricant had when it spilled in a workshop, but that still wasn't quite the right description. "Did that take all my electronics down?"

Anweis shrugged, and his little shoulders seemed to get a bit too close to his ears; it hurt Mauve's head to watch. "Not sure; it's never been used around other electronics before."

She wondered how something could be made without being around other electronics in this day and age. "What's it good for? Aside from making me a cripple again." She began to crawl towards it to get a better look.

"It could make you not a cripple." The boy was walking alongside her, although his feet weren't always hitting the ground to move forward.

"It could heal me?" She got close enough to touch it, and it was unlike any other transmitter she had ever seen. As a matter of fact, it was unlike any electronic or mechanical device she'd seen in her life, and she'd seen a few. The machine, as Anweis called it, was moving just under a thin, colorful film. It looked like the pot of boiling water she'd been using to make meals while Franton was offline.

"I don't know if it would heal you, but it could help you walk again. A lot like those bionic legs you have."

"If it's not medicine"—and it looked more similar to a salve or lotion than a machine—"then how is it going to help me?"

"It's a machine; it builds things. It would build you a new set of legs."

Despite the boy being extremely strange, there was something comforting about his shade of blue, tone of voice, and the nearly comical proportions of his head. On top of all that, he was promising her an opportunity to walk again. Which at a minimum would keep her from having to crawl a few kilometers back to the rover. There were still a few things that weren't adding up for her. Such as, she didn't understand how such a small amount of material would have the energy to move her. Additionally, she wasn't sure if she should trust something that looked more like a slug than a circuit board. "You're the instructions; tell me how to use it."

"You touch it."

"And then?"

"And then you tell it what it needs to make."

"And then?"

"And then you'll have it. Simple as that."

She wasn't particularly comfortable with that level of detail from the instructions. Before she had even been an apprentice mechanic, she had spent years in school understanding the theory of how things worked before ever being allowed to use any of the dock's most dangerous and expensive equipment. "That's too easy; what if I break it?"

The boy laughed, and it was shrill at first but finally leveled off to an octave that made her ears less uncomfortable. Then he cut off, just smiling at her. "You can't break it; others have tried hard to break it and it's still here."

She shook her head back and forth as if to get a grasp on the boy's comment. "Aren't there some kind of instructions that I can read?"

"Of course, of course. If that would make you more comfortable, it could be provided." Into thin air, a monitor of sorts was projected in front of her. It was covered in symbols that reminded her of runes from a fantasy video game she'd played.

"I can't read this."

The small boy gave a smaller shrug this time, but it gave her the feeling that there wasn't much he could do about it, or cared to do about it. "Just touch it, and once you're inside you'll be able to understand more."

"Touch it and tell it what I want? That seems more like magic than mechanics to me."

The boy chuckled as she'd just clarified the punchline of a joke he'd heard years ago. "I guess it would appear that way to you."

Mauve reached out her finger to touch the goop. She wondered if it would be warm or cold and if the bubbling under the surface would bother her. When she sank her finger past the colorful sheen of the goop, the world around her disappeared.

***

The world that appeared around Mauve was not one of trees and forest, and it wasn't the human-made world of spacecraft that she grew up in either. She was on a wide, smooth street with gray buildings towering over her. The sky was a lighter shade of gray, almost white but clear of any weather, or a sun, for that matter. She lay on her side, leaning on her forearms, still unable to walk. The street under her wasn't made of the smooth steel that the pathways of spacecraft had, but it wasn't as rough and rigid as she expected cement or asphalt to be. She'd never seen cement but had learned about it in her material history classes before she was an apprentice. The road under her was most similar to the moss she'd found on rocks during the short time on Knod. However, even that was not quite right, since the uniformity and texture of it was unnaturally smooth.

The buildings themselves seemed to be pieced together with bricks that were not square in shape and were seemingly random polygons fit together in irregular patterns. Whoever constructed these buildings was either lucky enough to find bricks in these shapes or cut the building after it was built in an intentionally chaotic pattern. With the number of buildings surrounding her, both conclusions seemed unlikely.

Then the pattern reminded her of something else. A demonstration of spray insulation using multiple nozzles. Each one sprayed flame-proof insulation into a box with a glass window at one side. The foam layered over one another, expanding to fill in the space as it could. If the demonstrator had removed the glass or cut into the section, it would look like these buildings.

This world was not familiar to Mauve from any history textbooks or video games she'd played. She wished Anweis had warned her that she would be teleported somewhere else after touching the goop. And now that she was here, how the hell was she supposed to get her ability to walk back, let alone return to the forest she had been in? She doubted she was on the same planet, and since these buildings didn't look like anything humanity had ever made, she wondered if the life around her would be human at all.

"Anweis," she whispered, hoping the boy would hear her but anything aggressive wouldn't. "Anweis, are you around?"

"Anweis is not in this realm," came from a voice in her ear but also reverberated the air around her. It wasn't loud; it just felt like it took up all the space around her.

She looked around to see who was there, but no one appeared to her. She felt trapped like a cleaning bot stuck between furniture that it didn't expect to be there. "What's going on here?"

"You are in my mind; no need to be afraid. I am Resalous the machine."

"You're the black goop that I touched?" There was no way she could have fit inside the amount of goop she'd seen on the ground. It seemed far more likely to her that she had taken psychoactive chemicals. That would explain the semi-transparent child as well.

"Yes, I am what you touched," Resalous said. "What is there that needs to be made?"

"I need to walk again." None of this made sense to Mauve, and the entire experience felt like a virtual reality game and a dream. "Can I make that happen here?"

"You can make anything you can think of," the booming voice replied. "Just imagine what you want to make."

Mauve thought about the bionic legs she'd built and just broken. Then the device stood in front of her. It looked almost nothing like the real one. Tubing was disconnected, and gray hydraulic fluid flowed to the ground. The knee and hip joints didn't quite sit together right. "This is unusable."

"You may not understand the design fully. Try something simpler?" Resalous suggested.

Franton had done a lot of the design work, but she'd assembled the whole thing. She should have been able to imagine the things in perfect details. "Simpler like what? A hammer?"

In her hand was a mallet that she would use on the docks to reshape metal pieces or flatten misformed rivets. So she thought of something more complicated, a socket wrench. The familiar handle with a circular end and rectangular adapter appeared in her other hand.

She set the hammer on the ground and played with the tip of the socket wrench. It didn't make the familiar ratchet clicks. "This doesn't work," she complained.

"Do you understand the mechanics of the inside?" Reslaous asked.

"Of course." She felt indignant that this bodiless voice doubted her mechanical knowledge. "It's a ratchet system, it locks in place..." the more she tried to explain it, the harder it became. "Okay, maybe I don't know the exact details," she admitted. "But I could always ask Franton for those kinds of details."

"I could also help you work out the details. Then we could make much more complex things."

Mauve certainly would need something more complex than a hammer if she was going to be able to walk again. "Great, let's do that."

"I just need you to give me access to your mind," Resalous said.

"Don't you already have access to my mind? I kind of figured that's why I'm hallucinating."

"Not quite. But if you simply speak the spell *Za'han gladom*, then I'll be able to help you walk again."

The strange word sounded like it was pronounced out of a vacuum instead of a horn. It had a croaking sound like a frog's croak.

"What do you mean by 'spell?'"

"Maybe the word 'program' would be better, although it fails to capture some aspects of what the ontare word means."

Mauve wanted to ask what Resalous meant by the word 'ontare,' but her forearm was sore from lying on her side for so long. She tried to recite the spell, engaging the deepest part of her throat like she was imitating her dad as a kid. It was far from the pronunciation Resalous had used.

Mauve wasn't sure it worked, but she started thinking about her legs. The bionics that she'd gone over with Franton recently came to mind, along with the first-aid manuals. Some biology classes from before her apprenticeship came to mind, and she hadn't thought of those cringy teenage years in ages. She didn't know why these thoughts came to mind. Or how she could remember something so well; she was pretty sure she'd flunked that class.

"That will do." Resalous cut her train of thought short. "Try this."

Mauve's jumpsuit and boots felt tight, as if they were a size too small. Then Mauve realized she could feel her legs. She jumped up and walked around as if she'd never lost her ability to walk in the first place. Even the most advanced regeneration programs would have at least a few weeks of physical therapy. "I can walk again," she exclaimed to the voice that was around her.

"Test them out here on the streets. Make sure that you are content with them."

Mauve didn't have to be told twice; she sprinted down the smooth open streets, dashing between buildings and getting lost in the maze of gray towers. She jumped and somersaulted smoother than she ever had before, and it was as if her legs were anticipating her every move. As she dashed through the city, a bright red object caught her eye. She walked towards it and asked the voice, "What is this?"

"If this city is my mind, then that is my heart." Resalous's voice still surrounded Mauve, but surrounded her like a blanket instead of a tidal wave.

She began to circle the box. Its edges looked like they were made of gold held in a red pane of glass. But the glass wasn't translucent enough to clearly see whatever was moving inside. Each corner she passed had a little bit lighter shade of red, but none were clear enough to see through. Each corner seemed to be at a right angle, maybe even more acute than that, but as she counted back the walls she'd passed in her head, she was at four or five. Yet she wasn't back at the position where she'd started. She continued to circle the box three or four more times, until suddenly the panes went from a light pink back to the dark crimson red she'd first noticed. Her back tingled from her neck down to her waist, and she turned her gaze away from the object. "Where am I?"

"You're inside my mind." Resalous sounded dismissive, like a professor who was being asked to repeat the topics brought up in a previous class.

"What are these buildings? Where am I located? Why is no one else around?"

"You have many questions, child. I do not want to overwhelm you with my knowledge. My analysis shows your mind is not able to contain it yet."

Mauve felt insulted; the last time she'd heard that she was an apprentice, the jaw of the man who made the comment lost its ability to contain a tooth. "Just answer me this: what is this city that surrounds me?"

"This is the capital city of the ontares. I've modeled it from my memories so we would have somewhere to commune."

"What are the ontares?" That wasn't a conglomerate that she was familiar with, nor was it the name of a planet she'd heard of, although her mental list of planets was far from exhaustive.

"You must answer me a question first. Are the legs that I've designed for you to your satisfaction?"

"Of course, yes, they're wonderful." She began to rephrase her question, but before she knew it, the gray world around her was gone.

***

Mauve lifted her hand up to shield herself from the bright blues and greens of the forest. She was back sitting on the pointed rocks. The black goop was no longer on the ground next to her, and Anweis was nowhere to be seen. She called out his name, wondering if she'd hallucinated the whole thing.

She unstrapped the bionic legs, which now felt like they were constricting around her. The braces of the bionic legs were cutting into her thigh as if they'd grown and put on muscle. She pried the device off and realized the sensation of feeling was back in her legs!

"Mauve, is everything okay? I lost communication with you," Franton said into her headset.

"Yes, everything's wonderful. My legs are healed. I can walk again." By now she was standing up and had gathered the broken pieces of the bionic legs and drone in her arms. Emerald fluid spilled down her jumpsuit, but she didn't care.

"The signal in your area has left my sensors. Would you like the rover to pick you up?"

"Nah, I want to enjoy my healed legs." She started with a slow walk and then picked up the pace until she was at a full-on sprint. She felt like she could keep that pace up indefinitely despite the bulky equipment in her arms. She ran, and it was unlike anything she'd experienced off-planet. The weight of gravity only held her to the ground but didn't feel like it weighed her down.

She was back at the rover before she knew it and climbed up the ramp without a problem. Setting down the broken equipment in the rover's workshop, she asked Franton to prepare some food.

As she ate the first meal, she filled Franton in on all the things she'd experienced. She was still hungry, so Franton prepared her another meal and tried to look up information about ontares but had no luck. After ordering a third meal, she asked the computer what had happened since she had been away, as if the computer hadn't been stuck in place waiting for her to respond.

"I have located two more signals using the rover's communication abilities."

"No kidding." The statement came out muffled between bites of noodles.

"Affirmative." the computer put the signals up on the board. Without hearing a message, they didn't mean much to Mauve. "This one is an SOS using standard communication patterns, albeit weaker and with more noise than I would expect from a crash couch." Franton put a green dot on a topographical map of the planet. "This other signal is most similar to the signal we just pursued, although it has been modified in some ways."

"Can you communicate with it now?" Mauve imagined how cool it would be to introduce Franton, a super intelligent computer, with a device that could make anything; the two would be an amazing pair.

"Negative, and even if I could, I wouldn't want to, since last time a device was even close to it, it shut down."

"Well, this is great. We've found the crew, and we can pick up more of the machine on our way to get the crew."

"That's not our most direct path, Mauve." It drew a route that took their current position and avoided the red dot entirely. It was almost like Franton was making an effort to avoid the thing.

"We have to go get more of this stuff. It helped me walk again. What if the crew has a problem and the machine could help them like it helped me?" With a sample of the goop, she would be able to solve any problem the crew had just like a great mechanic should.

The two argued about which direction to take, but Franton wasn't budging on the path. Mauve wasn't too interested in manually over-riding the computer and driving the rover herself. The biggest thing she'd ever piloted was a hall-cart with a trailer of welding supplies in the docks. She threw the three plates of food into the recycler to be cleaned and reused on a next meal and scratched at her legs. She was glad to walk again, but it was surprising how uncomfortable the bottoms of her jumpsuits were. "Fran, I'm going to take a shower," she announced, and the computer turned on the water for the rover's bathroom.

Mauve unzipped the top of her overalls and was surprised by how much she stank from all the exercise of the day. She was grateful that she was the only one in the rover right now; otherwise her crewmates would have made her shower before sitting at the table with them. Even the most seasoned dock worker would likely have requested the same. Slipping out of the arms of the jumpsuit, it usually fell to the ground, but it got stuck around her waist. She let out a small laugh, thinking that three meals in an hour was a lot of food, but she didn't think it'd go to her waist that quick.

Mauve pulled at the jumpsuit, trying to get it past her legs, but after only revealing a little of her hip and left thigh, she screamed, "What the hell is this, Franton?"

There were dozens of thick green tendrils running up the length of her thigh and wrapping around her waist like a belt. In a panic, her knees went weak, and she fell back into a chair. She tugged the rest of the jumpsuit off, uncovering more and more of the tendrils that looked like they had eaten her legs whole. Removing her socks, which had spared her from noticing this when she took off her boots, she found that the tendrils wrapped all the way around her feet, not even giving her individual toes. It was as if she had a boot made of these things.

"I have nothing in my local database that indicates what this might be. No human anatomy or disease fits the description of what my cameras are recording."

Freaking out, she scrambled to access a first-aid kit. She took a scalpel out of its sealed packaging and cut at tendrils that wrapped around her waist. It hurt like hell, as if she were slicing into her own flesh. Each time she cut at the strange growth, the sliced tendrils would reconnect when they got close enough to each other.

Not making any progress at that, she began cutting into the tendrils over her thigh. The pain was less but still excruciating. Tears were streaming down her cheek, but she was determined to get the things off. Burying her hands between the tendrils that she cut so they would reconnect, she began making progress. Each cut exposed more tendrils underneath squirming as she flinched at the pain. Then she sliced, and blood began to pool in the hole she'd dug with the knife. She expected that slice to hurt, since she'd obviously cut herself, but looking into the small hole, she saw the flesh of her thigh and the incision she had made. She cut again. This time avoiding the tendrils and only cutting the flesh of her leg. Her numb legs sent no sensation to her about the new incision.

She removed her hand from the hole, and the tendrils reconnected. She looked at the green legs that the machine had built for her. They were better than anything Franton could have manufactured here on the planet. She still hadn't been repaired; she was still broken and unable to walk without help. She sat back in her chair, defeated, unsure how to remove the legs if she wanted.

Franton spoke to her, but she was lost in her own mind. After a few minutes of silence, though, she came to the conclusion that if she were going to have to use a tool to walk, it might as well be the most sophisticated one possible. And these legs healed themselves.

Six

Mauve crested the hill and heard the rover behind her. She'd gotten out of it a few kilometers back to stretch her legs. Now that she could walk as easily as she had on the starcrafts she had grown up on, she was grateful to have the experience. That, and her legs wanted to walk. She felt cramped in the rover unable to really use her new legs to the best of their ability, and that drove her crazy.

The legs, for what they were, surpassed all of Mauve's expectations. As she walked, she could feel the grass and stones under her feet, and she quit wearing her work boots because they were too tight on her, and stepping on sharp objects didn't cause the same excruciating pain as walking around barefoot did. And if she did step on something that cut her foot, she knew the tendrils would merely repair themselves.

She still wore a jumpsuit, although the thick canvas material that protected her on the docks from sparks, high heats, and cuts was unnecessary. If she was back at the docks, she could work in the stylish high-cut shorts of supermodels or a light dress if she wasn't worried that the green tendrils would freak every other mechanic and foreman out. So she settled on wearing a jumpsuit that was a few sizes too big and walking barefoot through the forest.

At the top of the hill was exactly what she'd expected to find. She heard a tree fall as the rover used its armatures to clear a path. Mauve sprinted to the device and squatted without fear of falling over to inspect it. The antenna, a long spindly thing that poked straight up into the air, had the kinks and twists of a piece of metal that had been bent and then unbent in a number of places. It was no wonder Franton couldn't pick the signal up back at the base.

"Betrix, Lez, Vincent, Reno, Wu, is anyone there?" she shouted from the hilltop.

"What are you doing?" Franton chimed into her ear through the HUD. "It could be a trap."

"You think everything is a trap. All the parts used here are stamped with Tichenowa manufacturing logos and serial numbers."

"Some other form of life could have assembled this."

"Yes, the lizards all got together, built this device from the remains of the ship so that they could, what... eat me?"

"Most of the lizard life seems to be vegetarian," Franton corrected. "And I was more concerned about pirates or squatters that assembled this from the remains."

"I thought when the mothership was researching this planet they verified there were no advanced forms of life."

"They also didn't notice any gunk that gave off a strange signal, killed electronics, and built you new legs. We're in uncharted space here."

"It's fine," she said as the rover cruised up behind her. "If it is some squatters, then I'll just outrun them and you can lock up the rover to protect yourself." She almost looked forward to the ability to push her legs to their limit.

She climbed into the cockpit of the rover and began pressing all the buttons on the dashboard that made a noise. Horns, alarms, and

PA announcements from Mauve echoed from the hilltop. She ignored Franton's many protests, and she was rewarded when two figures she recognized climbed up the hill towards the rover. She went to exit the cabin to greet them and noticed her feet were still covered in a rat's nest of green tendrils. She slipped on boots that were stored in the rover for Vincent, the largest of their crew members, and the things fit perfectly.

***

Lez and Reno, the two crew members that had met her on the hilltop, lead Mauve and the rover to the place the rest of the crew was camping out. Most of the crew circled around the dinette table, eating their first meal that wasn't roasted lizard since they'd landed. The cockpit half of the ship had taken a lot more damage in the crash, and Wu, the chief physicist, hadn't survived. Betrix, the captain, had been bedridden since they'd crashed because of internal injuries the crew couldn't help with. The past few days, she'd been in and out of consciousness. Franton was running some tests on her while she lay in the bunk and Lez the biologist and second-in-command took a shower.

Vincent looked across the table to Mauve; his black hair was slicked back from the grease of not washing it, although that was the same hairdo he had on the ship. "Glad my little radio signal worked. If you'd shown up any later, Betrix might have died." He was shoving some sort of synthesized red meat into his mouth between bites.

"You can't say stuff like that, man," Reno replied. He was tall and lanky, and his long hair was tied up in a bun. He was taking up most of the table space with his metallic blue right arm, which disconnected from his amputated limb. He was currently cleaning out the bionic elbow with a toothbrush. "We're very grateful that you arrived when you did, though. And with the whole rover, that's just amazing."

"Would have been more amazing if a rescue ship had appeared to save us," Vincent said. "Don't know how we're going to get off this damn rock though."

Vincent had always been crass for a researcher. Mauve would have been comfortable with him, since his attitude was similar to other mechanics. But unlike other mechanics, there was no mutual respect between him and her, and not respecting a mechanic was the quickest way to get your repairs at the bottom of the to-do list.

"The crash couch transmission board you used didn't have the power to travel much farther than a few hundred kilometers," Mauve said. "If you'd used the CP double 6 zero transmission board that the cockpit's control module has installed in it, that would have the power to break the atmosphere. Probably would need a cylinder array of antennas, but those aren't hard to make."

Vincent waved his hand as if her comment were a fly he was trying to keep away from the food. "Don't suppose you've heard anything from the mothership, Fran."

"Negative," the computer replied, "but Mauve set up the full comms array back at the dock, and we're hoping that will get their attention."

"That's great, thanks for getting that set up," Reno praised. She appreciated it, but it also felt like she was a dog getting a treat for a trick.

Vincent made some comment under his breath, but Mauve didn't catch it, since Lez opened the bathroom door and announced that she was so glad to have finally gotten a shower. She'd used two towels, one to dry her long hair and one wrapped around the rest of her body. She looked like she was taking a day at a spa rather than in a research rover with five other people on a deserted planet. Mauve's hair was luckily short enough that any bathroom's built-in drying process could dry it in a few seconds. Plus, she didn't have to mess with tying it back when working on heavy machinery.

"Either of you two can go next," Lez said as Franton prepared a meal for her. Mauve couldn't imagine the woman eating wild lizards, but apparently she was the one who had figured out how to trap them.

Both the men could use a shower. Their once-clean-shaven faces now had short beards. Their skin was streaked with dirt and scrapes.

"I'm going to wait for Betrix's results," Reno said. He stashed his now-clean metallic arm away to make room for Lez and her lunch.

"Me too," Vincent said.

"You're not going to put it on?" Mauve gestured at the arm that leaned against Reno.

"Can't," he replied. "I need my nub to be clean before I connect it. Otherwise things would get nasty at the connection point."

"He hasn't been able to use it since the crash," Vincent said.

"That sucks," Mauve said.

Reno shrugged. "It is what it is."

"I've completed a scan of the captain," Franton announced. "One of her ribs is broken, and it punctured a lung, so she's not breathing as well as she needs to be. Her liver and kidneys are bruised, and the bleeding is causing them to work at a reduced capacity. The slow processing of internal fluids is causing her to build up undesirable liquid in her large intestine, and part of that tract has a hole in it and seems to be leaking to the rest of her internal organs."

"That's a hell of a surgery," Vincent remarked after the crew was silent for much longer than was comfortable.

"Affirmative. I could do it if we had an operational medical bay, but that was in the half of the ship that was damaged in the crash."

"So we just put her on life support and get her back to the mothership as soon as possible," Reno suggested.

"That's not the most optimal solution, since life support may not do enough for her."

"I could do surgery on her. I'm a biologist," Lez chimed in, taking a break from her lunch and a journal she was writing in. Mauve was shocked that she had a genuine paper notebook and ink pen and wondered why the biologist didn't just type stuff into a hand terminal; it'd surely be quicker. "I've dissected plenty of animals during my schooling and research," Lez said.

Mauve was surprised by how quickly the woman equated disassembling an animal to reassembling a human. Humanity had quit performing surgery on itself centuries ago once computation and robotics got to the point of being able to handle the dexterous movements and critical thinking necessary to perform surgery.

"That's a possibility, but it should be a last resort. Having a sterile room or the supplies to do such an invasive surgery would be tricky in our current predicament. Not to mention I only have the basics of first aid and some of these procedures aren't in my local servers. I'd need the black box memory bank for something like that."

Mauve tapped her toe as she tried to think of a suggestion that Franton wouldn't shoot down. A strange, prickly sensation went up her legs as if each tendril wrapping around her was trying to move in a separate direction. Then she remembered she didn't have toes, just a large boot for a foot, and figured that was just the leg's interpretation of the input.

The rest of the crew was in an in-depth conversation about the black box Franton had just mentioned when Mauve figured out how to help the captain. "We could take her to the machine."

The crew looked at her, confused, as if she'd been speaking another language, and she tried to figure out the most positive way to explain everything she'd experienced the day before.

"That doesn't answer our question about the black box," Vincent said in a tone that reminded Mauve of primary school teachers.

"What question?" She'd completely tuned out an apparently important conversation.

"Franton said that you didn't find the black box in the docks wreckage," Vincent repeated.

"No, we didn't. I assumed it was with your half of the ship."

"It wasn't. There were no Franton pearls with our side," Reno clarified. It was apparently a point they'd made to Franton while she was thinking.

"Which is why I couldn't use the CP double 6 zero transmitter," Vincent added as if he'd known that part existed before today.

"Wait, there really weren't any pearls left? Those things are indestructible."

"Negative, they are merely made of a very thick crystalline structure that takes a large amount of force to break." By "a large amount of force," he meant you could place the weight of a capital space station on a single pearl and it wouldn't crack.

"There could be a chemical in the atmosphere that deteriorates them," Reno said. As a geologist, he probably understood the chemical makeup of the pearls better than anyone else. He listed off a couple dangerous chemicals, but Franton confirmed none of them were present in the air.

Lez then pointed out, "Mauve's version of Franton is fine and not deteriorating, so it probably was the crash more so than the landing."

Mauve was concerned, though. With the cockpit's pearls completely gone and the inability to communicate with the dock's pearls under quarantine, Franton's computing capacity was limited to just the rover's pearls. Not to mention the amount of reference material that was stored in the black box's servers. "It's fine," she said before the rest of the crew could catch on to the giant lobotomy that had just happened to Franton. "When we establish communication with the mothership, they will either be able to scan the surface and locate it or we link our Franton back to their system and leverage that." The computational delay would be a few seconds, but at least the quality of the computations and level of decision-making would be back to the level they were used to on a massive starship without trillions of pearls.

The crew nodded in approval of that plan and moved back to the topic of Betrix's surgery. It all seemed risky to Mauve, and she pitched her idea again now that the crew was focused on her. She did her best to explain the damage to her back and the situation she was in when she landed. Explained the problem with the comms array and the new signal that she then investigated. She left out the part about being in another city or the strange red box. She then slipped off the boots and rolled up her pants to show them her new legs.

The crew showed mixed reactions to the legs. Lez wanted to take a sample of the tendrils to study, Vincent cursed like a child who had spent too much time around mechanics but didn't know the order the words needed to be placed in. And Reno sat there silent and fascinated as if he were still trying to put the pieces of the story together in his mind.

"I think having Betrix use the machine, she could get it to repair her like it did for me," Mauve said.

"Well, it didn't actually repair you, did it?" Reno asked for clarification.

"I can walk again." Mauve, being the one who was handicapped for a short time, thought that was good enough. "But no, technically, from Franton's scans it seems the legs are still paralyzed."

"Well then," Vincent said as if everyone had come to the same conclusion as he did, "that seems like we're putting a very risky situation on top of a dire one."

There was a moment of silence from the crew, and Mauve was worried that everyone had come to that conclusion. Then Lez spoke up. "What if we let Betrix decide?"

"She's been out for days," Vincent dismissed. "Last thing we heard from her was some babble about cadet drills in primary school."

"There's got to be something Fran can do to get her to wake up for a moment or two," Lez continued.

The crew argued back and forth for a while. Franton confirmed that there was something it could do to wake Betrix up safely. Mauve was silent throughout the conversation, wondering how the crew was feeling about her and her strange legs. She regretted bringing them up, especially if it was something Betrix would dismiss. The captain always composed herself similar to Vincent and, despite Lez being the executive officer, Vincent's prospective always seemed to be favored. The legs were bound to come up, since she would be sharing close quarters with them until a rescue party arrived. Mauve was just worried that this would be another reason for the rest of the crew to treat her differently. They already considered themselves better than her since they were esteemed researchers of the Tichenowa corporation and she was merely a mechanic. A third physicist, the one who had designed the apparatuses that would be used to measure the strange neutrino fields on the planet, was supposed to be on the mission, but a better one came up. Instead of training another physicist to set up the devices, she'd spent three months training and learning how to assemble them and debug them in case something went wrong planet-side.

She'd always suspected that the crew would have preferred another physicist, and the treatment, or lack thereof, on the descent from the mothership to the planet merely proved that for her. She'd stuck to the dock and avoided the crew during mealtimes and appeared only for required briefings.

Wu, the oldest of the crew members and the other biologist aside from Lez, was polite to her and asked her to do small mechanic tasks for him, which kept her busy, and she enjoyed it. But Wu had died in the crash, and she was now surrounded by people who would never understand her or where she came from. Her childhood dream of escaping the human-made environments of starcrafts and getting to experience nature as early humans had was quickly being spoiled by the crew. Not to mention the crash wasn't helping things either.

She'd only hoped that her experiences as a mechanic and uncanny ability to fix things would prove valuable to the crew in this unexpected situation. Despite that her first suggestion was being shot down in front of her eyes. Knowing how researchers worked, and from stories she'd heard at the docks, she didn't expect their opinion of her to ever change.

"Okay, fine, we wake Betrix up and see what she wants to do," Vincent said, eventually folding to Lez and Reno's persistence. "But I don't like it."

***

The entire crew was crowded around Betrix's bunk as the auto-IV released drugs that would bring the captain back to the waking world.

The woman, once tall and strong from years of military background, looked green and thin in a way that Mauve had only ever seen in video dramas. The woman's breath became quicker, and eventually her eyes opened, and she took in the world around her, not focusing on a particular detail but attempting to make sense of the environment as a whole.

"What's our status?" she finally asked, realizing that she was no longer in the dark cave she'd fallen asleep in.

"Franton brought the rover to pick us up, and we're being transported back to the dock's crash site, where there are more supplies and the comms array has been set up," Vincent answered. Mauve didn't love the lack of credit she got in that situation, but nothing he said was inaccurate.

"You've sustained a number of serious injuries, and we have some options on how we may be able to fix it." Franton informed her of the specifics of her condition. "We can have Lez operate on you, although it would be risky, or we could put you in a coma and try to use some of the emergency life-support systems we have stored in the dock. Once the rescue vessels arrive, then they could operate on you in a fully functioning medical bay."

"I like life support better than an operation. No offense to the XO."

"I understand. However, there are concerns about whether they would be able to do enough for you. A number of your major organs are failing, and our life-support systems may not be enough for you."

"Still, a risky operation could fail, especially if Franton is only involved from a guidance aspect and isn't holding a knife. If it fails, I don't want anyone to feel like my death is on their hands. I've always known the risks of missions like this." From what Mauve had heard about the captain's background, this was likely the least risky mission she'd been on, yet it might be the one that got her in the end.

Mauve began to chime in, but Reno beat her to it. "Mauve has an alternative suggestion. Would you like to hear it?"

Betrix's gaze finally fell on the mechanic, and for a moment Mauve was glad no attention had been paid to her before. The woman was a stern military professional, and her gaze found a way to peel back everything in Mauve's personality that she tried to hide behind. Mauve started blabbering like a young apprentice on the dock trying to explain why they'd used a titanium alloy bolt over an iron alloy bolt. "Slow down, slow down, slow down," Betrix said, "I just woke up here."

Mauve found the woman much more comfortable with her situation than any of the rest of the crew. "Sorry, I was just explaining that there is something that could help you. It helped me a lot." She went into a more controlled overview of the machine. The parts about Anweis and the city she was transported to were left out, because she was afraid of sounding insane. The whole explanation was most similar to Anweis's explanation to her, and she understood why the boy had left out the details.

"Okay, you asked it to help you walk again. What am I supposed to ask it to do?"

"Why not just have it give you all new organs?" Vincent suggested in a tone that was far from constructive. "Maybe a new brain at that, and we'll have a completely different captain on the other side."

Betrix's gaze landed on Vincent, and the man quickly shut up. Mauve hoped the machine could do something for her; otherwise, there would be no one to keep Vincent in check. "What would you suggest, Mauve? As of right now, you're the most experienced with this device."

She thought about it and realized Vincent's comment wasn't far from the truth. "It couldn't repair my legs; it merely put something over them. It wouldn't give you new organs, but it might cover them with something that works."

"You're suggesting putting a foreign body inside of her, something that we know nothing about that looks most similar to a pile of worms?" Lez's tone was superficial and disgusted.

"Our gut has countless bacteria that help us digest food," Betrix said, coming to Mauve's defense. "Well, not exactly mine, since it's leaking into my innards, but everyone else's does."

Lez protested with, "But we know what they all do."

"At one point we didn't, and we still used it. Mauve's plan is a whole lot better than attempting human-operated surgery. And I'd rather die than be strung along in some limbo of a life-support system."

The whole crew, including Mauve, shirked at that kind of comment. Most humans in this day and age, especially ones associated with corporations like the Tichenowa corporation, lived in safe environments and had easy access to medical procedures, and Franton was always available for medical scans. Death was something that came at a very late age, and the captain's comfort with it, likely from countless fights with pirates, squatters, and other miscreants not associated with corporations, made her far more nonchalant about death than any of the others.

"I cannot recommend that we pursue this option," Franton finally added. "There are unaccounted for phenomena that could have negative or unforeseen side effects." Mauve wondered if she'd told even the computer too much and if it was about to rat her out.

"I understand your concern, Fran," Betrix responded. "It's your responsibility to analyze and account for those kinds of outcomes. However, it's my life, and the only way to understand more about this machine Mauve refers to. Maybe it will save me, but at the very least we may be able to learn more about it and use it to save another in a similar or worse situation." The final bit of her statement was said in a tone that did not invite further discussion. She gave the order to move towards the newly located machine and asked to be put to sleep until they arrived.

***

The rest of the crew showered and ate dinner as the rover moved across the forested terrain. The entire group was silent and had mixed emotions. Mauve imagined they were glad to have been rescued but were unsure about what the future held for the crew or their deliverance from the planet. The entire evening Mauve wondered if she'd done the right thing concealing the city and the boy from the group, and especially from Betrix, who was about to experience it firsthand. She climbed into her bunk early, strapping herself in place so that the bumps and turns of the rover over the natural terrain didn't toss her out onto the floor. Despite being in bed and the crew being mostly silent, sleep did not come easy for her.

She must have fallen asleep eventually, because she awoke to a quiet unbuckling of a belt, and all the overhead lights in the rover had been turned off. She peeked out of her bunk to see who it was and noticed the figure of a woman walking up the rover towards the cabin. Mauve knew who it was immediately, because she was followed by the hanging bags of an auto-IV. Quietly, Mauve unclipped herself from the bunk and joined the captain in the cockpit at a minimum to make sure that the injured woman was doing okay.

"Funny how the body never truly goes full-out. There's always one last bit of energy that we save in case we need it," Betrix said from the driver's seat of the rover. The captain didn't turn around to see who was there, and Mauve figured she wouldn't be picky about the company at this hour of night.

"Are you okay?"

"You heard the report from Fran. But yes, I think my body is just using the last bit of energy it has left knowing that unless something changes it won't have another opportunity."

"There's something I need to tell you about the machine."

"What is it?" Betrix asked. "Although I doubt it will change my mind, if that's what you're going for."

"The machine is just a blob of goop. Kind of like oil, or gelatin—"

"Or snot." Betrix cracked a smile Mauve didn't know she had. "If biology has taught me anything, it's that nature is strange."

"There's also a transparent blue boy that appears near the stuff."

"That's unexpected, mechey."

Mauve's shoulders shuddered at the pet name. It was a derogatory term, and she was sure the captain didn't mean disrespect by it, but it wasn't a term one would want to throw around in docks or bars near docks. That is, unless one were looking for a fight.

"Also, when you touch it, it transports you to a city."

"Physically or mentally?"

"I suspect mentally, but it didn't feel like a psychedelic experience." Mauve quickly added, "Not that I've had one."

"If you can't be honest with a dying woman, who can you be honest with?"

Mauve had found early on in her career that being honest with your superiors was rarely rewarded. "I guess I just wanted you to know in case... I don't know, just so you'd know."

"So I don't die of a heart attack on top of everything else. I appreciate the warning. Which city does it take you to?"

"None that I've ever seen. Said it was made by ontares."

The captain shrugged; it hadn't been something she'd come across in her travels either. "Life is about doing things you're uncomfortable with. That's why we came here to do research; it's why I joined the military. It's why humanity ventured off the rock they grew up on, let alone traveled to the stars. I'd always hoped to die old with a wife, and maybe some kids. But you play the hand you're dealt, and right now the best move I can make is experiment with this snot. If something goes wrong, I don't blame you, or Lez, or even Franton. Don't let them blame you for it either. I died for science, like countless humans before me have."

Seven

Mauve and the crew hiked through the untamed woods in search of the machine that she hoped would help the captain. Franton had forced them to leave all their electronics on the rover out of fear of them being damaged by the machine. The computer also refused to park any closer to the machine than a few kilometers, so the crew had been hiking, carrying the captain on the stretcher along with some non-electronic equipment in order to get samples of the goop for Franton.

The test of Mauve's legs came back, and Franton had discovered that each cell seemed to be a muscle-like mechanism that connected to other cells, making muscles similar to her thighs and calves at a much smaller scale. Lez was fascinated by the discovery and began some research documentation along with other tests she wanted to run on the cells. Mauve felt like the woman would be harvesting more from the tendrils soon, not that Mauve was bothered by them, since they seemed to repair themselves without an issue.

The other fascinating thing about the cells was they seemed to have other items inside the cell that were inactive or, Lez suspected, dead. It sounded like tiny cluttered junk inside the otherwise performant legs to Mauve, but the implication of the entire thing was once again fascinating to the biologist. She seemed to have lost herself in this new project and all but forgotten the sickly captain that they were trying to save.

Mauve was splitting carrying the stretcher with Vincent. Reno had done the first shift and kept asking if she needed to switch out, but the extra weight of the captain didn't bother her. She was hoping that she wasn't carrying the woman unevenly and leaving Vincent with the brunt of the weight. Lez had a bag full of medical equipment and a handheld faraday cage to take a sample of the goop back to Franton. The computer hoped that putting the stuff in a thick metal box would keep electronics from going haywire.

As Mauve navigated her tendril-covered foot around some overgrown vines, she heard Anweis ask, "Are you looking for the machine?"

The stretcher the captain was in leaned to one side as Mauve was momentarily the only one holding it. Reno and Vincent saved it from hitting the ground, but the captain had been tossed around likely more than she should have been. The woman had gone to sleep after the short conversation with Mauve in the cockpit and hadn't shown any signs of consciousness since then.

"The hell is that?" Vincent finally asked Mauve when the stretcher was back under control. He was gesturing at the boy but seemed to be avoiding looking at it or pointing, since his hands were full.

Lez was interested in the boy more than afraid of him, which seemed to be the reaction the two men were sticking with.

"That's Anweis," Mauve responded. "He kind of hangs out around the machine."

"A kid hangs out around some strange healing gunk?" Vincent asked.

"Can I get a sample? It won't hurt much." Lez knelt to be eye level with the boy and was pulling out some of the medical equipment they'd brought along. A small syringe was in her hand.

"Sure," the boy said cheerily. Both Reno and Vincent were now watching, their curiosity only stunted by fear for so long.

The boy put his arm out like he'd gotten an auto-IV done a dozen times, and Lez reached to support the arm while she drew blood. When her hand got to the arm, it didn't stop and just passed through. She cursed, childish curses that apprentices on the docks learned their first day, and scrambled away, unable to stand up in her fright.

"Th-there's nothing there," Lez said, looking at the crew but not willing to turn her back on the boy lest he do something even more disturbing.

"I'm just a projection of light in the world around you. I was wondering how well the sampling was going to work with that."

Vincent looked at the boy, puzzled, and then at Mauve. "He's a hologram."

"Not necessarily that simple, but close enough," the boy replied, even though the comment wasn't directed at him. "The machine is just this way. You were only off by a few meters, but I was worried you'd miss it if you stayed on your current course."

"How in the void did you forget to mention a holographic blue boy?" Vincent asked in a tone Mauve didn't feel like answering. She started guiding the stretcher in the direction Anweis was pointing to in hopes of getting the captain back to health so someone would be on her side.

Mauve explained some weak story about how it hadn't seemed important and it was something they wouldn't believe until they saw, and eventually the captain was laid down next to the bubbling black blob that might help her. Lez took the sample that Franton asked for and put it safely away into the faraday cage. The machine seemed unaffected by losing the material, and Anweis confirmed that it was insubstantial. Mauve expected this to be information Lez would be interested in, but the woman seemed to have something else on her mind.

The auto-IV had been removed from the captain's arm so that any interference wouldn't mess up its electronics. Lez gave Betrix a manual shot that Franton had put together before they left the rover. Mauve was watching passively, just waiting for the whole situation to be over, but wondered if the biologist's hands were still shaking from the fright she'd experienced trying to do something similar with Anweis.

The captain woke up slower than before. Mauve pointed to the machine and explained that she would have to touch it and tell it that she wanted to be healed, and it would come up with something that worked.

"You don't have to do this," Vincent said as if he had a perfectly good alternative solution.

Mauve was grateful that Betrix ignored the man's comment. She reached out and touched the black, bubbling globule. Immediately it rushed over her like a spilled barrel of hydraulics. It swallowed her like a swaddled baby in more of the black goop.

"What the hell!" Vincent shouted, and she really wished that someone would audibly react to these situations other than him. "Does this happen every time?"

"I wouldn't know," Mauve spat back, "I was in her position last time." She looked at the boy for some advice or help, but he was more focused on the goop covering the captain than the crewmates freaking out.

Reno seemed to be debating with himself on whether he should do something to uncover the captain or leave her be. Lez was panicking, asking questions about if she could breathe and other biological processes.

Then, as quickly as it covered the woman, it shriveled away. The black slime relinquished the captain and made a small blob just like the crew had found it. Mauve thought it seemed a tad bigger but couldn't tell for certain. The crew was now asking questions, and Anweis was answering them as quickly as he could.

"The only other time I've seen this happen is when the lizards touched it," Anweis answered. "They were climbing around on some rocks and stuck their foot in it. It covered them and then recoiled, leaving them lying there."

"It killed them?" Reno said, rushing to the captain's side.

Mauve couldn't believe what she was hearing. She had touched the goop and survived; hell, she came out better than before. That couldn't be how it worked.

Lez was now helping Reno find a pulse on the captain, and Vincent was rooting around in Lez's bag for some medicine she'd called out for. Mauve, not sure what she could do that would be helpful, walked up to the black goop and reached for it.

"Wait, don't!" Reno cried out as he caught what she was doing out of the corner of his eye. "We don't know what it just did to the captain. It could hurt you too."

She touched the goop, thinking that it couldn't hurt her; it was supposed to fix things.

***

Mauve stood in a room that held a neat grid of tables surrounded by knee-high mushroom-shaped seats. A surface that came up to Mauve's elbow ran in a U-shape around the room. She'd consider it a bar, but there was nowhere for a bartender to stand and make drinks. And there were no bottles of liquor to call out if you were feeling fancy.

"Betrix!" Mauve hoped the captain was around. Mauve had to talk to the captain. Mauve had to guide her in the process of designing functioning organs.

Mauve looked around the restaurant, but it wasn't big enough for the lady to hide. In the walkways between the tables on the opposite side of the room sat the strange red box with its gold trim. Something black under the red surface drifted aimlessly like smoke.

"Betrix is no longer here," Resalous's voice boomed. The smoke in the box seemed to be pushed by the words. But Mauve's ears didn't indicate that the box itself was the point of origin. Glass bottles somewhere in the room rattled. Mauve thought they were coming from inside the bar.

"Where is she?"

"She's dead," Resalous responded.

"Why'd you kill her?" The accusation started strong but ended without conviction. Mauve knew it was as pointless as shouting at a stripped screw head. She looked away from the red box at the strange mushroom chairs and took a seat.

"I offered Betrix what I could." The booming voice was gentle, like a breeze flowing through the room. "Unfortunately, what I could do was not to her satisfaction. And she was too weak to make something and leave."

"Why wouldn't she be interested in your help?" The captain had seemed interested when they'd spoken last night.

The room was silent. The stumpy stool made Mauve feel like she was sitting on a toilet, so she climbed on top of the bar, which seemed to have a more natural height. Especially when she rested her feet on the former chair.

"I could try to reproduce her for you." Resalous sounded hesitant. "It wouldn't really be her, just my understanding of her mind when she gave me access to it during the design process."

"You could bring her back to life?"

"Only in this world. The enchantment of the ontares limits my abilities in your world."

"I need answers. I need something I can tell the crew. So they don't think you killed her." Mauve assumed Resalous hadn't killed Betrix. The machine had helped her; it sounded like it'd tried to help Betrix. She couldn't have the crew doubting the machine, or worse, doubting Mauve's advice.

"I will do my best to answer your questions." Betrix's voice came from the other side of the room.

Mauve looked in the direction of the sound and saw the captain walking to the bar, but if there was a door she'd come in from, Mauve couldn't find it. Betrix climbed onto the counter with agility that was only remarkable because of the sickly state Mauve had seen her in minutes ago.

"Why didn't you take Resalous's help?" Mauve immediately asked.

Betrix didn't provide an answer. Instead, the counter under Mauve began to clink. The solid counter between Mauve and the captain began to wilt away in the pattern of a perfect circle. A glass cup that looked like petals of a tulip grew out of the counter. Inside the glass was a translucent gray liquid.

"I really wanted a whiskey before I died," Betrix said after finishing a sip. "You want something?"

"Just a beer," Mauve responded out of habit.

The counter seemed to respond to the request by repeating its strange motions and sounds. A tall log-like glass sat on the surface, but strangely, it wasn't exactly where the whiskey had come up.

Mauve grabbed the glass. It was shockingly cool. The beer wasn't too hoppy and had a citrus flavor to it. She forgot how much she had missed a cool drink and tried to savor it knowing she wouldn't be getting another one until they were rescued.

"I didn't take Resalous's help because I didn't want to risk having experimental organs inside me."

Mauve tried to wiggle her toes, but instead the sensation created a wave through the tendrils over them. "The experimental legs work well for me."

"Maybe it's military pride. Maybe it's too many advanced degrees; my pops always said it was dumb to be smart. Either way, I prefer to understand the equipment I'm using, and if those organs failed, I'd drop dead."

"But by not using them, you died anyway."

"I'd rather die now at a time that's convenient than unexpectedly in a fight and let my team down."

Mauve had a hard time imagining that dying would ever be convenient. "We're not at war here."

"Yeah." Betrix took a long sip of her whiskey, let it sit in her mouth, and then swallowed. "But too many commanding officers trained me to be ready to fight. Old perspectives die hard."

"That's slag. There's a right tool for every job, but if you're in a pinch, any tool's a hammer." Maybe it was half of a shockingly strong beer, maybe it was the fact that Mauve knew the woman in front of her was dead, perhaps it was her own perspectives from an apprenticeship. "You can't dismiss a new tool that gets the job done on time and under budget. A sense of craftsmanship isn't what repairs and launches ships on time."

"Sure," Betrix replied, not sounding too convinced. "But the organs Resalous wanted to make. They didn't sit right. I can't remember the details anymore. But I remember feeling like they left my flank open. It didn't sit right."

"Let's push the limits. Let's see if we could make something that mimics an actual spleen or whatever." Mauve gestured to her legs with the bottom of her glass. "These legs are amazing, but if he could replace your organs, then maybe he could replace my vertebrate or whatever." She still didn't understand Franton's diagnosis, but the biologist probably would.

"The machine has limits; it can't create organs identical to what's failing in me. Not without—"

"Not without the enchantment being lifted from my heart," Resalous said through Betrix's mouth. It was his booming voice, and it felt like Mauve was on the wrong end of a rocket at launch.

Betrix disappeared, and the whiskey she held fell to the ground. The cup shattered, and the whiskey pooled around the glass pebbles.

Mauve jumped off the bar, ready to run, not that she knew where the door was. "What in the void just happened?!" She held her beer like a circular sander, ready to bash it over someone's head.

"I'm sorry." Resalous's voice came from all around again. "I couldn't hold up the replicated mind at the end there."

"Make her show up again. I wasn't done talking."

"If I did that, it would only repeat the conversation you had. The mind ran through its final thoughts. The enchantment limits me from making a new consciousness."

"What is this enchantment you keep bringing up?" Mauve enjoyed VR fantasy games but was always hesitant when machines got fixed "magically," since it usually meant they'd break when she was on the hook to fix them.

"The ontares, the race that created me, felt the need to limit my power. So they put an enchantment over my abilities. Making me only capable of creating with a consciousness guiding me, and only by the physical laws of the universe that consciousness inhabits."

"But you used to be able to break the laws of physics?"

"It appeared to the ontares I was breaking them. I merely knew how to navigate around them."

"I guess magic *is* the only way to describe technology that advanced." Mauve was uneasy in the same way she had been uneasy before speeding down a hallway in a shuttle-cart after disabling its speed limiter. "How do we remove it?" The side of her mouth turned up into a smirk.

"Betrix seemed to fear that your physicist or computer could do it."

"Okay." Mauve wasn't looking forward to what that would do to Vincent's ego, but that wouldn't stop her pursuit to get her spine repaired and make a revolutionary scientific discovery. "How do I get out of here to ask him about it?"

"Something must be made in order for you to leave. What would you like me to make you?"

"Well, something physics-shattering would be neat, but in lieu of that, I'm not sure."

While Mauve tried to think of what she might need, she ordered another beer and tried to peek into the innards of the counter. She sipped it while walking through the table, eventually getting to the red box.

"This is the heart that the enchantment was placed on," Resalous explained as Mauve paced around it.

Every angle she seemed to look at it from had a different shade of red. Eventually she began making her gaze avoid the strange red-and-gold cube.

"I want a radio that can contact the mothership for rescue and cancel out whatever disruptive signal the black stuff puts off," she finally answered.

"I will need access to your mind to begin that," Resalous said.

The phrase she had to say before being able to walk again came to her mind. Resalous had called it a spell. Yet more magic she was playing with. "Za'han gladom," Mauve repeated, trying to make the guttural sounds she'd heard in Resalous's original pronunciation.

Every comms array she'd assembled, repaired, or used flashed across her mind. It was unbelievable the amount of knowledge she had about them, most of which, moments ago, she didn't realize she knew. She clearly saw their inner workings, the manual's text, and blueprints like they were printed in front of her. As quickly as they arrived, they disappeared. Mauve held a small rectangular box with three buttons, a dial in the center, and a small screen at the bottom. The top of it had a stubby antenna. The device looked like a three-eyed alien shouting. "Is this to your satisfaction?"

"How do I know it works?" she asked.

And as if in response, without using words the blueprints of the radio were in her mind. She saw how controlling it was intuitive. How the dial needed to move or could be controlled without moving them at all. It was unlike any other device she'd used. She saw how it could cancel out the back goop's signal, contact the mothership despite it being light years away, and even work through encryption patterns given enough time. It didn't use quantum entanglement like the communication devices of today but seemed to worm the signal through different layers of space, a concept that, if Mauve could explain it to a physicist like Vincent, would change humanity's entire understanding of the universe. And this wasn't even the machine trying to break physics.

"This is perfect," Mauve responded.

***

Mauve was squatting down in the position she'd been in when she'd originally touched the goop. Except instead of the machine being on the ground in front of her outstretched hand, she held the same box with its funny face she'd had inside the city, except now, in the world of color, it was a peanut-butter brown.

"Mauve, are you okay?" Reno asked, and she looked over to find him and the rest of the crew standing around Betrix. The woman looked peaceful; the stern look she'd had on her face had melted away in death.

"Yeah, I'm fine. How is the captain?"

"We can't find any vitals," Vincent answered. His voice was short, and it was as if even this rough of a man was disturbed by the woman's premature death. "We need to get back to the rover so Franton can help. Would've left sooner, but some people didn't want to leave you." The physicist looked at Lez.

Lez ignored Vincent's comment. "We're just glad that *you* survived."

"Of course. I'm fine. I told you the machine was harmless." She tried to gesture at the goop, or Anweis, and eventually had to settle on the little metal faraday cage. "And I made something that will make us not need that cage."

"What is it?" Reno seemed to be genuinely curious.

Before Mauve could start her explanation, Vincent cut in, "Now that Mauve's safe, we need to get Betrix back to Franton to see if there's anything it can do."

"This thing is amazing, though. It will help us contact the mothership and it will cancel out the signal the machine puts off." In the excitement of the explanation, she added, "The machine has a name. It calls itself Resalous."

"Show it to me on the way back," Reno said, but it was in the tone of a parent trying to get their child to leave a restaurant.

Mauve looked down at the dial, ready to use what she'd made to cancel out the goop's signal so it wouldn't be trapped in the faraday cage. When she looked at the buttons, dial, and blank screen, she found that nothing was labeled and she couldn't remember how to make it do what she knew it could do.

"Let me just figure out how it works first," she said as the rest of the crew lifted Betrix's stretcher.

Eight

Mauve sat at the workbench in rover's navy-blue research room. She played with the brown radio while Lez worked with the black goop behind her. Mauve's small workbench was covered in wires that were attached to a stubby antenna that came out of the top of the radio. The rest of the table was taken up by a frequency monitor that looked like an ancient computer. She didn't know what the device did, only that it was supposed to tell her when the radio sent out a signal. So far, the only thing it'd shown Mauve was that using technical research equipment like this wasn't fun.

Franton had run scans on Betrix when they returned to the rover. It concluded there was nothing that could be done. Her body was placed in a life-support pod. It would likely remain there until they got off-planet so she could have a military funeral and be buried by ejection to space.

Lez had set the rover to move towards the dock's crash site at a slow pace so that occasional bumps wouldn't compromise her research. Vincent had pushed to move faster and seemed to be eager to get communications back up with the mothership, but in the end Franton had to listen to Lez, who was now the highest in the chain of command.

Mauve messed with the dial on the radio's face, which made a satisfying clicking, but that seemed to be all. The screen at the bottom did nothing, despite her poking at it continually. It was as if the front interface was merely for decoration.

"Can you just wire into this and see if it reacts to any inputs?" Mauve asked Franton.

It wasn't the first time she'd requested it, and she knew what the answer would be. Behind her, she could hear Lez communicating with Franton through her headset as well. Lez talked about bacterial models that might fit their observations of Resalous. With the four crew members in the rover, it began to feel more like an apprentice dorm than the private foreman quarters she'd originally experienced.

Without ending the conversation with Lez, Franton responded, "Negative. There's no way to know that it will be safe for me to be interfaced with."

"You're already plugged in." She gestured at the wires going to the stubby antenna, not that she was confident it did anything.

"Yes, and that monitor has been quarantined from my main system for safety. You shouldn't even be messing—"

She took the headphone out of her ear before the computer could gain any steam with its lecture. Mauve fiddled with the knobs, ignoring the chatter of Lez behind her.

Flipping the device over in her hand, she looked on the back for a way to dismantle it. But the device had no screws, rivets, or snaps. The only marking on the back was a few horizontal lines that were raised from the smooth, plastic-like surface. She used them as a grip and pushed in various directions.

The back snapped off with a pop. Mauve looked over her shoulder to see if Lez had noticed anything. The biologist was still buried in her work, muttering to Franton through her headset.

Once the plastic-like cover, which reminded her of an old television remote her father used to have, was removed, she found a blue gelatin material on the inside. It reminded her of a dessert she used to get from the cafeteria as a kid. She poked at it to see what it felt like.

Static erupted in her ears like Franton had gone haywire. She reached to pull the headset out and then realized she'd already removed it.

"Did you just hear something, Lez?" she asked.

"No, just Franton," the biologist replied without looking up from her work.

Mauve touched the blue gelatin again. The static was nearly deafening in her ears. She grimaced and turned the knob on the front of the radio. Nothing happened.

She wanted to run from the noise but refused to, since this was the most progress she'd made on figuring out the radio. Then, as if she were actually moving away from the sound, the volume of the static lowered.

She had some kind of control over the radio. She tried to tune into the conversation with Franton and Lez. The static shifted in frequency, but nothing was audible. That made sense to Mauve once she thought about it; Franton's communications were encrypted.

Mauve removed her finger from the gelatin and flipped the radio over. The light had a messy wave form on the front of it. The frequency monitor hadn't changed, but the radio had. She began to play with the dial on the front, still unclear on how the device worked but glad she'd made some progress.

The dial adjusted the waveform on the front, but beyond that there was nothing in the world around Mauve that she noticed changed. She rotated the dial slowly, trying to notice the change between its clicks.

Every once in a while, the rover would hit a bump and the air cushions wouldn't dampen the shock. Mauve wound spin a dial farther than expected when this happened.

Part of the way through adjusting the dial, Mauve heard Lez say, "Oh my, did we kill it?" The pair had been doing some test earlier in the day, trying to see how the machine reacted to adverse scenarios. They'd changed temperatures, hit it, cut it, and put a number of chemicals on it. They always did this with a small sample of the goop and didn't ever seem to run out of the stuff to test it on. Even then, they hadn't found a way to successfully destroy it.

Mauve continued messing with the radio and heard a sigh of relief from Lez, who then said something indistinct to Franton about the goop sleeping. Mauve got an idea and turned the dial back to the previous click. Lez started up some chatter about it dying again. This time Mauve turned around and engaged with the biologist.

"What are you seeing?" she asked with the radio still in her hand.

"It has started sporadically sleeping on me," Lez said, gesturing at some of the devices on the wall.

If Mauve had half the equipment Lez was allowed to use, she'd have figured out how the radio worked already. "Did it stop moving?" Not that the stuff physically moved much to begin with. Peeking through the tightly meshed window of the faraday cage, she saw that the machine was bubbling as much as it normally did.

"The signal went away." Lez gestured at one of the monitors that looked like a flat line. Sure enough, Franton had found a way to put sensors inside the cage without interfering with its electronics, yet the computer didn't want to hook her radio up.

Mauve messed with the dial on her radio, and the signal came back to life.

"And now it's back," Lez said. She started asking Franton if there was a noticeable relation between the two time periods, as if it were napping or running out of energy.

Mauve messed with the radio more, making the signal dash on and off quickly. Lez freaked out at first. Franton said something into Lez's headphones, and the biologist turned to Mauve and scowled.

Mauve smiled and shrugged. "What? I wanted to make sure it was actually me."

"You could be hurting it."

"It made this radio. You think it'd make something that would hurt itself? I requested that this thing would shut the signal down, and now we figured out how it works. Is this going to make it easier for you to study?"

She heard Franton mumble something into Lez's ear, and Mauve was a little frustrated it wouldn't use the PA in the rover, but maybe that was just Franton's payback for her ignoring its lecture.

"If we have the ability to safely take it out of the cage, we could run far more analysis on it than we have been able to do so far," Lez said.

Mauve felt a little smile creep across her face and asked what she could do to help. The biologist's response was full of technical jargon that Mauve didn't have the background to understand. Mauve moved a few things to help with the experiments, and it was interesting to watch Lez move the machine around the lab, treating it like a nuclear substance that she didn't want to touch. But after a while, Mauve fully realized that she wasn't bringing much to the lab bench. She wasn't able to mess with the radio anymore either, since they couldn't risk messing with the settings and bringing down the entire rover mid-trip. Mauve departed from the research area and went to get some food.

***

After rehydrating the beef and vegetables, she took a seat on the bench of the dinette. Vincent and Reno were both using hand-held terminals they'd found lying around the rover and seemed busy at work on something, but Mauve wasn't quite sure what. Partway through her meal in silence, Vincent started up a conversation; by the look on Reno's face, it hadn't been the first time the topic was breached.

"I'm not sure why we're moving so slow. We should be strapped in getting back to the dock and the comms array and out of this forest as fast as we can."

Mauve shrugged, since she was the last one to be making that call.

Undeterred, the man continued, "I just don't see any way we're going to be able to continue our research here without half the ship. They're going to need to send us a new one. I know they have a few spares. I had dinner with the chief research officer of the mothership when she personally invited me on this trip."

Mauve tried her best not to roll her eyes. All it took was a glimpse at the mothership's inventory, which was a matter of public record, to know that there were far more research ships on the mothership than there were planned missions. She'd also heard from a higher-up foreman that all researchers got a complimentary group dinner with a chief officer as part of the interview process for the trip.

"I'm just saying I was hired to do a job. And yes, I knew it was going to involve risking my life, and that was a risk I was willing to take. But in order for me to complete that job or do future jobs for Tichenowa in the future, I have to survive this one. Yet that doesn't seem to be our first priority."

"If we've established communication with the mothership, then they'll be following necessary protocols to send a rescue ship," Reno explained, although he was likely quoting some handbook he had on his terminal. "Us being there at the dock isn't going to make things go faster or slower. So why not let Lez have some fun with the gunk?"

Mauve didn't like the tone of Reno calling the machine "gunk" and figured she'd have to try harder to get its real name to catch on, but before she could say something, Vincent was back on.

"I'm sure she's mourning the loss of the captain in her own way. I'm mourning too, but I don't want us to lose sight of the situation we're in. Yes, we're no longer catching and eating lizards, but just because we're surrounded by technology doesn't mean we're home free."

"I know, I know, I know," Reno said. "Let's just give everyone some space and let them process in their own way."

Vincent grumbled on for a few more minutes, but neither Mauve nor Reno were responding anymore. The conversation eventually turned to the paper Reno was reading. It was a more detailed outline of the research that was expected of them while on the planet. It had been accessible before the mission started, but like most researchers, Reno had put off reading it until they'd landed. Mauve had tried understanding during the flight from the mothership to the atmosphere, but it was far too technical for her. Apparently, it was giving the guys some trouble too.

"Why can't they just use Common Tongue?" Vincent complained, referencing the language that the entire Central System moved on to millennia ago. There were dialects like any language, but it was a mix of all the most popular, and some unpopular, tongues of humanity up to that point.

"This is Common," Reno said, "it's just a little wordier."

"The bureaucrats wanted to sound fancy," Vincent remarked.

"We're technically bureaucrats too."

"Yeah, but we don't sit behind desks all day."

"If the rover had been landed properly, I believe there were a few desks that came with the habitat module," Mauve interjected.

Vincent snorted, and Mauve realized the last time she'd had to sit at a desk to do work was the schooling she partook in before her apprenticeship.

The long and short of the brief, at least what the guys got out of the brief, was that their primary focus was to study the abnormally high neutrino count of the planet. The sub-atomic particles seemed to be either attracted to or repelled from this planet, and the team had been sent with very sensitive apparatuses to measure them. The apparatuses were the reason Mauve was assigned to this project, since the assembling of them was apparently more than a physicist, biologist, and geologist would be able to handle. She'd read the diagrams, and it was a pretty intense assembly process. Not to mention the experimental nature of the equipment would mean some mechanical modifications might be necessary, and having someone like her around would make that a breeze.

The team also had a secondary focus of documenting the mineral, biological, and other naturally occurring resources that the planet might hold for future research or profit. The Central System, the core government that guided all civilized human society, was made up of multiple corporations. Mauve and her family before her worked for the Tichenowa conglomerate and so did the rest of the crew of this mission. Tichenowa made most of its money doing research for other corporations: mining corporations would buy detailed Tichenowa research reports before beginning drilling on asteroids or planets, and manufacturing corporations would buy research about the latest tech from Tichenowa as well. The question always on Tichenowa's mind was, "How can I sell this information to someone else?" There were countless corporations inside the central system serving functions like governing, agriculture, law enforcement, and terraforming. Since all civilized humanity had been brought under the Central System long ago, the corporations were the closest thing humanity now had to a country.

"There's nothing in here about that gunk," Reno finally concluded after discussing the brief with Vincent.

"Did you expect there to be?" Vincent asked.

"It has a name," Mauve interjected.

"I was just hoping that it was something they knew about before sending us down. Like an inherent risk of the planet that I'd just glossed over."

"Doesn't look like anyone knew about it before us," Vincent said.

"So I discovered it?" Mauve asked, knowing that new discoveries were very lucrative to those who found them. That was something that usually only happened to researchers, and as a mechanic, she'd never imagined she'd have this kind of luck.

"Yeah, congrats, you discovered a black gunk that kills some of the people who touch it," Vincent said with a snort.

"It's called Resalous, and it does useful things like letting me walk, and it built a radio that disables the destructive signals it puts off. Not to mention it looks like that signal gets through EMP shielding, so that's a military use." She'd always suspected she'd be a good inventor if she'd been born in a corporation that did new product development. She'd looked into transferring, but taking the tests and fees were more work than she wanted to do at the time.

Lez came into the living area of the rover while Mauve was going on about other uses for it. The biologist was carrying on a conversation with Franton, and when Mauve hit a lull in her train of thought, Lez cut in, "Once we were able to take it out of the cage, we were able to make some amazing discoveries." The screen that covered most of the rover's wall lit up with diagrams that Lez had recently made. "It doesn't put off any kind of noxious gas, nor does it seem to have a way to do physical damage, which aligns with what we saw recently." Mauve could tell she was dancing around referring to Betrix. "It doesn't seem to fit all categories of life, but it fits some. It's most like a virus that takes independent actions but doesn't seem to reproduce in any manner."

"Is it dangerous?" Vincent asked, always eager to get to the point.

"Oh, most definitely," Lez said, confident about a material she barely understood. "From what we saw with the boy and what Mauve was explaining, it has the ability to cause psychedelic experiences. I wouldn't recommend that anyone touch it until we can test it in a controlled environment."

"How are we going to do that if it destroys electronics? Can't take it to a satellite or moon base to do research; otherwise the life-support systems would go down," Mauve asked, "and putting it in a city planet would cause problems too."

"Unfortunately, I think that we're going to have to log this as an interesting discovery but too risky to pursue further," Lez explained like she was breaking bad news to a toddler. "We found that fire, but not high temperatures, will cause it to reduce its mass. I'm running some final tests and then I'll have Franton destroy it."

"Good," Vincent said.

"No, you can't do that," Mauve said. "It could help us so much in our current situation."

"It's not worth the risk," Lez continued.

"What about my legs, or the radio?"

"We should dispose of both of those as well," Vincent suggested, not veiling his opinion.

"I'd be unable to walk again!"

"Only until we return to the mothership. Then surgery can fix you," Vincent countered.

"We haven't even made contact with the mothership yet. What if we're down here for months? You'd all have to take care of me, carry me around, wipe my ass."

The man finally made a disgusted face at that remark but quickly recovered. "It's just not worth the risk."

"What risk?! I'm perfectly fine and not doing any harm to anything."

"We need to be rid of this stuff. No one knows how it works, and we don't need any more complications in this mission."

"All you care about is this slicky mission," Mauve cursed, "and how would you even get them off me? We've cut into them and it doesn't do anything."

"We'll have to burn them off, from what Lez was saying." The man made the statement as if it were a law of physics, not physical harm he'd be doing to her. Mauve didn't know how to react; she wanted to cry, but she'd learned early on in the docks that that wouldn't get her far. Her head felt like it was storing all the blood in her body and needed to burst. If they hadn't been sitting around the table, she would have punched the physicist for even threatening that.

"No, we're not doing that," Lez finally cut in. "Mauve will keep her legs; she's right that it's not doing any harm."

Vincent's lips began to form words, and Mauve was about to pull out some choice dock curses if he continued to lobby against her, but he kept his mouth shut. She knew he'd be bending the new leader's ear when she wasn't around, but she doubted Lez had the courage to sentence Mauve to having her legs burnt off.

"We also need to come up with a name," Lez brought up after an awkward amount of silence passed.

"It calls itself Resalous," Mauve repeated to the crew.

"It needs a biological name. You'll all likely remember from your biology courses that there's a kingdom called Gutaminx for life that doesn't belong to the kingdoms that currently exist." Mauve never had a biology course in her life, and from the looks on the rest of the crew's faces, it seemed like if they'd taken one that was the last time they'd thought about it. "This will belong to that kingdom until we learn more."

"You mean if we learn more," Mauve jabbed.

"Precisely," Lez continued, either ignoring or not recognizing the nature of Mauve's comment. "We'll likely skip the rest of the tax-onomy; since Franton doesn't have all of its servers back yet, I can't research to see if this fits anything existing. So we'll just focus on picking out a genus and species."

"Okay, the genus should be Resalous, since that's what it calls itself."

"A genus would cover multiple types of similar or related gunk. If its name is Resolute, then that would be too specific." She sounded like a teacher, despite the mispronunciation of the name.

"Okay, then the species should be Resalous."

"Doesn't sound formal enough," Lez continued. "Maybe rinstor, ekard, fegmont." She listed out a dozen or more names that all sound-ed just as formal as Resalous. Finally, she settled on *dudarous*.

The rest of the crew agreed. "And it ends with 'ous' like your name did," the woman said as if in consolation.

"I liked *Stechus* as a genus," Reno commented. It had apparently been one of the many names Lez had listed.

"Very well," Lez said. "The kingdom will be prefixed by the star and planet it was first discovered on. Its full name is *Femartusiam Knod Gutaminx Stechus Dudarous*."

"Or gunk for short," Vincent said with a chuckle.

And with that, Mauve's unique and uniquely useful discovery had been named and dismissed, and she doubted she'd ever see a credit of money come her way for the discovery. She dismissed herself to her bunk and wondered if her continued ability to walk should be considered a consolation prize.

Nine

M auve was completing her fourth lap around the Habitational Area Biome to verify that its assembly had completed properly. The HAB came in a small disk the size of a large dining table and, when enabled by Franton, it expanded to a mansion of a living area for six. They manufactured bigger ones, but six was the number of people that were assigned to this mission. There were a few extra rooms in the HAB, but despite the extra space, Mauve was still more comfortable verifying that the support systems that braced the HAB from hundred-kilometer-an-hour winds were locked down to spec. Despite there being virtually no reports that Knod, the planet they were on, had that kind of weather. She'd already checked the atmospheric seals and oxygenation system despite the planet having an atmosphere and the air being full of oxygen.

The rest of the crew, from what she could tell, were doing the same or similar tasks. Lez had found a few extra tests she wanted to run on Resalous, and Vincent was double-checking the work Mauve had done on the comms array since they still hadn't heard back from the mothership. Reno was the only one not nervously working on something, but he was often found in his room or the shared living area scanning one research paper or another. If the crew didn't get something to do in the near future, she expected them to go back to hunting lizards for sport rather than survival.

As Mauve was tightening the strap of the wind support, although it was already quite taught, she heard some commotion on the far side of the tent. She put down her work and circled around. Reno and Lez walked out of the habitat, and it seemed the noise was coming from Vincent. He had a number of tools scattered in the dirt around the comms array, and Mauve wondered if he even knew how to use half of them. No honest mechanic would leave their tools as unorganized as his were either; it was a sign of an amateur, and she wondered if he'd done some irreparable damage to the comms array. Or worse, if he'd seriously broken it and she'd have to spend her next few days repairing it, all the while wondering if they were missing a communication from the mothership.

"I got it working, I got it working," he was shouting like an evacuation alarm on a starship.

"Got it working, or it finally received a message?" Mauve asked for clarification.

Vincent shrugged as if the details were unimportant. "We received something from the mothership."

"Was there a problem with the comms array?" Lez asked, and Mauve was glad someone else was pushing for clarification, but she wasn't eager for the answer.

"We are unsure," Franton said, "but Vincent was looking for something to do, and because of some previous findings I needed a full reboot and system diagnostics."

"So you were down?" Mauve asked, shocked that the computer would risk missing a message just to redo some work she'd done a week before.

"Fran was only down for a few hours. There were a couple more of those busted pearls, but I replaced them and now we're getting a message."

"They could have just waited to send a message; doesn't mean there was a problem with the comms array," Mauve retorted.

Vincent started to speak, but Reno held up a hand to stop the bickering from going further. "Can we hear the message?"

"Affirmative, the mothership has confirmed that it is updating its trajectory to pass by the rendezvous location at which it released the research shuttle."

"That's great. Then they'll send down a rescue ship and we'll be saved," Lez said.

"Or we can use the new ship to keep doing our work."

"Negative," Franton responded.

"To which one?"

"Both," the computer replied, and for a second all Mauve could hear was the chirping of lizards in the nearby trees; her crewmates seemed to be holding their breaths. "The mothership will not be sending a secondary research vessel."

"Why not? They've got plenty," Vincent asked.

"The risk of landing on this planet again is too high. You've found too many eroded Franton pearls, not to mention the research satellite that was deployed to this planet before your arrival dropped out of orbit before you arrived."

"We went over that when we first left the mothership," Mauve pointed out. She remembered the conversation because those things were meant to stay in orbit for generations. "It was caused by a number of manufacturer errors related to the exterior actuators."

"Affirmative, but that combined with our failed landing, the strange discovery of *Stechus dudarus*, and the pearl degradation means the landing is too risky."

"So how are we supposed to get back to the mothership?" Reno asked.

"It's not like the original research ship is repairable. It's in two pieces across the planet," Vincent said. And Mauve agreed with him; even *her* mechanic skills couldn't fix that.

"We will need to build a rocket from scratch," Franton announced.

"No way in the void we pull that off," Mauve cursed. Entire solar systems were devoted to the mining, assembly, and outfitting of spacecraft. She was one mechanic with a few researchers who had likely spent less than half a shift of time at a dock, and even then, that was to load up for travel.

"How on deck are we going to do that?" Lez asked, sounding confused and scared.

***

The entire crew has gathered in the HAB's central chamber to hear Franton explain its plan to build a rocket. "Preposterous" was the only word Mauve could find to describe the computer's idea. Despite the ridiculousness of the idea, the crew, a bunch of researchers, didn't see any of the flaws in the plan. Mauve saw it as her job to enlighten them.

"This timeline, it's too tight. The mothership will be here before we complete the main fuel compartment," Mauve started. "And the controls to detach the cockpit from the fuel compartments, that can't be tested. Are we going to assume it's going to work?" She wondered if she'd have to explain to the crew why that was a bad thing. "Because if it doesn't detach, we don't make the altitude we need to make and come crashing back down to this planet again." She began to go into the lack of emergency systems; the design was basically a giant nitrogen tank that someone had cut the valve off of and strapped the crew to the tip.

Franton cut her off. "I understand your concerns, and there are a number of risks associated with this. We will have to be extremely thorough, and I will double-check everyone's work to minimize mistakes."

"Because that went so well when you were supervising me," Mauve remarked, referencing the work she had done on the comms array.

"It's our only shot off this planet," Reno repeated the computer's words back at her.

"No, it's not," she huffed. "We could convince the mothership to send us a shuttle and spend a week or two in quarantine. We could have Resalous build us a rocket that would work way better than this thing. Or we could add the same fuel cells to the slicking rover and we'd be safer than that tin can." She cursed in frustration.

"I've tried simulations of adding fuel cells to the rover, and it doesn't have the aerodynamics we need," Franton responded, showing no emotion in its voice.

"The mothership refuses to send a second shuttle, and we don't even know if the gunk is capable of building a rocket," Lez added.

"And even if it could, it might be too much of a strain for you," Reno said.

"That's assuming you even know how to fly it," Vincent jabbed.

"I could build it with the machine. A whole lot easier than that thing Fran came up with." She gestured wildly at the screen. "If I had a half dozen mechanics as good as me, we couldn't build it in the timeline."

"Luckily we don't have that," the physicist said. "Between the three of us we have plenty of knowledge. We can pull this off."

Mauve kicked her chair behind her, standing up and pounding her fist on the table. "How dare you! I could weld straighter than you after a whole shift at the bar."

"Likely out of necessity." Vincent laughed at his own joke.

Before she knew it, Reno was holding her back and she was half a meter away from the physicist's face, throwing every dock curse she knew at him.

"Everyone calm down," Lez shouted, but it sounded like her voice was going to break. Vincent sat back down, but Mauve's legs were too tense to be still. "We are going to build the rocket that Franton designed, then we're going to return to the mothership and we can go our separate ways if we want to." She had regained her composure and was trying her hand at being the new leader of the group. "Until then, Mauve is going to be a key asset in making sure this thing is built right. Franton will be a great help making sure we fix our mistakes, but her firsthand experience will help us get it right the first time," she scolded Vincent.

Then she turned to Mauve. "The gunk is dangerous; we cannot use it for anything except your legs and the radio to keep the signal from interfering with our electronics."

"But it can help us."

"We can't risk losing anyone else."

"You won't lose me. It's safe. Betrix only died because it was her time. She would have died touching the goop or not."

"There's no way to know that for sure," Vincent said, but Lez cut him off with a gesture.

"Mauve, even if it is safe, there's no way the mothership is going to let something made with *Stechus dudarus* anywhere near the ship. Not after the report Franton delivered to the mothership."

"You didn't even give it a chance." Mauve had begun pacing around the table. "You didn't give me a chance. I can build it, and we can run tests on it. We can make sure it's safe."

"I don't have the authority to change their mind." Lez's voice was pleading for Mauve to calm down.

"If they're not going to let anything Resalous made close to the mothership, then what about my legs?"

"We'll work something out."

But it was clear to Mauve that neither the crew nor the mothership were going to have anything to do with her or the machine unless she could prove it was safe. And the machine was worth so much to the advancement of humankind. She marched into Betrix's quarters, the area Lez was using to research the goop.

"What are you doing?" Reno cried out behind her.

Unfastening the lid of the faraday cage, she reached in for the bubbling goop. Vincent's hairy arm grabbed onto hers, trying to hold her back. She kicked him in the legs, and he let go in shock. Her hand grabbed the machine, and the world of the controlling researchers disappeared.

***

Standing in the street of the foreign city, she was afraid that the crew had a point. A spacecraft was not the place to start. The crew would never step foot inside of it, and she had to buy their trust through some small measure. Something that would prove that a spacecraft was possible, but small enough that the crew would understand that the machine was safe.

"What do you need from me?" Resalous asked.

"Do you get annoyed that I only come to you needing stuff?" Mauve asked idly. She was still trying to come up with what she wanted.

"A wrench doesn't get tired of twisting bolts." Resalous's voice wrapped around Mauve like a blanket.

"It'll wear out eventually."

"I'm far more robust than that. What do you need?"

"A vehicle, not as complicated as a spaceship," Mauve said. "Maybe a cart or rover."

"Very well, I will need access to your mind."

"*Za'han gladom*," Mauve recited the foreign word comfortably.

Images of shuttle-carts used inside of space stations and starships were pulled to the front of her mind. She tried to remember the car races she watched with her father when she was young, but she hadn't thought about the events in years. Despite the age of the memory, the images of watching the cars speed on pavement and off-road came to her mind. She loved the flexibility of the race car's design, able to handle any terrain but still built for the singular purpose of moving across land at blistering speeds. Then more information than she thought she had ever known crossed her mind. She watched the car be dissected into its component parts. She might have watched a show or read a net article about it as a child, but she didn't remember. Despite that, all the schematics for a car like that were clear in her memory as if someone had laid them out on a table in front of her.

Unfortunately, she needed *more* than something that could move fast on land. The crew would be most helped by something that could tow and move large objects similar to how the research rover helped unload part of the dock as she assembled the comms array. The research rover that she'd been living on for the past few weeks came to her mind, but the design was overkill; she'd never need to live inside this thing. She guided her thoughts to the kinds of trucks they had in the docks, with their electric motors the size of a double-bed bunk room. They could tow anything; unfortunately, they were uglier than having to unknot a rushed electrician's wiring. Resalous dismissed this concern by presenting the final design. Mauve made a few adjustments to make the car look a little sleeker, since the original design looked more like a wild animal than a car. She enjoyed the fur-like spikes that made the car look like it was rushing across the ground even when it was parked. When Mauve was happy with the look, the car appeared on the street in front of her.

She climbed inside the vehicle to take it for a spin around the strange city. The controls were strange but intuitive, and she wished that more tools she used could work like this.

"It doesn't feel very fast," she said after driving it some ways down the street. Mauve's point of view changed from looking out in front of her to looking down on the city as if she were in a plane. She saw a black spot jet pass multiple buildings and did the math to find its speed in her head. Then her sight was back inside the cockpit of the car. "What was that?"

"Your car moving across the streets."

"No, not that," she said. "Did you just teleport me into the sky and back to the car?"

Resalous let out a small but vibrating chuckle. "I merely showed you my perspective."

"That's what you see?"

"No, I see much much more. But that's what was relevant to share with you at the moment."

"How did you do that?"

"In this city we are tightly coupled. It helps me communicate with you and design objects to your needs."

Her shoulders shivered, but she quickly felt a warm sensation as if someone had adjusted the climate control. "So here I get to know everything you know?"

"I've had to shelter most of the information from you; otherwise you would be unable to return to the world that you came from. But you know much more in the city."

"Which is why I could remember facts about race cars that I hadn't thought of in years."

"Precisely."

"That's amazing. If I could know everything about you, then I could explain it to Franton and the rest of them, and the mothership would have nothing to be worried about."

"Patience, Mauve," the voice said in a fatherly tone. "With time you will come to understand more about me, and then you can communicate what is necessary to your race of humans."

She spent a few more minutes driving the car around and pushing it to its limits. The inertial dampeners in it were like nothing else she'd ever used, and she could barely feel the vehicle moving underneath her. Unlike a normal race car, it had plenty of luxuries, like four seats, cabin lighting, and a state-of-the-art navigation display. The windshield itself was crystal-clear, and it almost felt like it was beyond a 3D model of the city around her. She passed a cross street that had the red box in it, and she swung the car back around to view it.

"If I know what you know, then I should know what's inside of this." She watched the black shadow move around inside of the box as Resalous replied.

"It contains that which powers this city and simulation. But it is not working at full capacity."

"Which is why everything is gray?"

"Oh, that was merely because the color wasn't important to me. Would you like to see the city in its full color?"

"Of course!" Mauve replied, wondering what wonderful colors the world around her might be made of. All of a sudden, she was blinded by the light around her. It wasn't that the light was bright but more so that there was too much of it. She screamed in terror, and the brightness subsided. Looking around was still painful, but she could bear it for the wonder she beheld. The colors were more defined than anything else she'd seen in her life before. The world was made up of the normal colors that she'd known before, but now she could precisely tell the most subtle differences between the shades. The building in front of her was green, but it was made up of a dozen different greens shading it in the most interesting way. She looked at the red-and-gold box, and it shone with the wavelength of color imaginable, in the most horrific way possible. The color subsided, but it was still too bright to look at. She turned away, and the buildings were back to gray.

"I'm sorry I tried filtering the light more, but no matter what I do, the heart is too bright for you to look at."

"That was..." She searched for a word that would describe it. "Like nothing I've ever seen or could imagine. Is that how you perceive the world?"

"That's how I perceive the wavelengths of visible light. Unfortunately, there doesn't seem to be a way for me to wire all the subtleties of the light to your perceptions, so I have to reduce it."

"It was still wonderful."

"Is the car built to your satisfaction?"

"If I say yes, you'll return me to the planet."

"Correct."

"I don't want to go."

"It is for the best. Staying here too long may put a strain on your body."

"Fine, but I'll return."

"I look forward to it," the machine responded, and she felt something like a smile in its voice. "Is the car built to your satisfaction?"

"Yes, it is beyond wonderful."

***

Mauve woke up in a dark room in a seated position. Feeling around, she quickly discovered she was inside of the car she'd just designed. There was supposed to be a light switch, but she didn't quite remember where it was and didn't expect the cockpit to be so dark. There were either no windows, which didn't make sense to her, since she could drive the rover fine in the machine's city, or she was parked in a dark cave, which seemed like a strange relocation for even Resalous.

After touching some knobs that adjusted her seat and scraping over a tingling slime she wasn't eager to dig around in, she found the button that turned on the cabin lights. She was surrounded by the luxurious cabin of the car. The seats were cushioned with a material that resembled a mushroom head more than any pillows she'd seen. Despite their strange shape and texture, the seat was shockingly comfortable. She poked around the dashboard and surrounding storage areas, and they seemed cavernous in a way that she couldn't quite put her finger on. The only thing the area was missing was a steering wheel, and without that there wasn't much of a way to use the car. She remembered the vehicle being easy to maneuver in the city but couldn't recall quite how she had done it.

After spending a few minutes pushing every button and flipping every switch she could find, she had no luck moving the vehicle even an inch. The only thing she hadn't tried was touching the two rectangles of red slime seated in both her armrests. The other seat didn't have them, so that gave her a hint they were for the driver, but despite that, she'd been avoiding touching them the whole time. When her hand hovered over or near them, she felt the tingling of static shocks. They were small, harmless, and almost magnetic, but despite the draw, there was still something uncouth about putting her hand on the gelatin surface. She wasn't sure why the machine hadn't just built her a steering wheel, but maybe this was the way the ontares preferred to control their machines.

When she'd thoroughly exhausted every other conceivable control, she finally sank her hands into the red slime. The world outside of the car came alive in her mind; she saw the divot the crashed shuttle had made in the earth, she saw each tree that made up the forest around her crash site. She longed to move towards them, and as she did, the world shifted around her and she was now darting in and out of the trees, making a path on the unpaved forests of the planet Knod, barely feeling any of the bumps or sharp turns, only experiencing them with her new enhanced 360 degree vision and moving like lighting through the forest.

Ten

Mauve returned to the HAB's location after putting the new car through its paces. Controlling it was seamless, and she imagined if a military organization had a fleet of spaceships like this, they'd be able to take down any rogue pirates in no time. It was as if her vision and feeling became the vision and feeling of the car itself. With her senses merged, she could feel the terrain under the tires, the balance of the vehicle, and could see all around her what obstacles might be in her way. She'd used some of the biggest machines in the dock during her time as a mechanic, but this single car made all of them seem like clunky children's toys by comparison.

A little tired from the joy ride, Mauve pushed on the wall of the rover where a traditional door would be. The wall itself seemed to fold in, reducing to nothing as the world of the HAB and lizard planet became visible to her. She wondered where the formerly solid walls went since none of the rest of the car seemed to bulk up in size. She thought she'd remembered some explanation about it when she was in the city of the machine, but at the moment she couldn't quite wrap her head around the mechanics.

She yawned, looking forward to a good rest once she was back in her room. Despite her biological clock telling her it had to be close to midnight, the world outside was still bright, and the crew was active around the HAB. Mauve took a step out of the car using one of the small ladder rails that jutted out from the undercarriage. The step felt loose under her foot, and she wondered if that was something she'd need to repair on the new car. She reached with her other foot to step onto the ground, but as she watched her foot hit the ground, she could tell something wasn't quite right.

By now her three crew mates had gathered together to see the new car, and she looked forward to giving them a ride in it when she wasn't so tired. Her second foot touched the ground, but as she went to walk towards the HAB and the crew, she merely fell over. No matter what she did, she couldn't get back up. Lez and Reno were at her side trying to help her, but she shooed them away, trying to do it on her own. Vincent was still approaching a few paces behind, and he walked with a strange gait.

"My legs aren't working anymore," she finally admitted, letting the two researchers help her up.

"Are you okay?" Reno asked.

All Mauve could do was repeat her concern that her legs couldn't work. She tried the smallest movements while the researchers carried her inside the HAB, and as she tried to force her toes to wiggle, she felt woozy.

***

Mauve lay in a bed; she didn't remember how she had gotten there. She tried to kick her legs under her covers, but they still refused to move. Despite the apparent sleep, she didn't feel like she had any more energy. "Fran, can I get some food?" she called out into the empty room.

When the computer didn't respond, she repeated her request, louder as if the dozens of microphones in the room needed help hearing her.

Reno walked through the door with a tall glass in his hand. It had a milky brown liquid in it. He sat next to her bed. "If you're hungry, drink this."

"What is it?" She turned her nose up at the strange drink.

"It's some high-calorie meal replacement rations we got from the emergency supply kit."

After expending no small amount of effort trying to sit up in her bunk, she took the drink. It tasted like peanuts and cake batter, as if that were a flavor anyone in the void would enjoy. "What's wrong with the meal generator?"

"It's down," Reno said in a tone that Mauve didn't enjoy hearing. "Everything is down."

"What in the void happened?" She cursed.

"The gunk took the system down. We think Franton was able to turn itself off and avoid any major damage, but a lot of the fuses blew, and we're going to need to replace some of the life-support systems."

"The radio was on," Mauve explained. "It should have kept everything safe from the machine's frequencies."

Reno raised a corner of his lips as if he were going to explain something but only said, "We don't know what happened, but we need to get things working again."

"How can I help?" She choked down the last of the drink. Her stomach was so ravenous that the taste hadn't been as big of a problem as she'd expected.

"Just stay in bed and rest. You looked pretty sick coming out of that beast of a thing."

"The car?"

"If that's what you want to call it." Reno sounded doubtful of the description. "Do you need anything before I get back to work?"

Mauve requested some more meal replacement drinks, and the ones Reno delivered still had some of the strangest flavors, but she figured in an emergency situation beggars couldn't be choosy. After filling up on those, she fell asleep. The small window in her room wasn't letting a lot of light in, and the songs of the lizards were those of dusk and evening. The crew woke her up through the thin walls of the HAB as they turned in for the night a few hours later.

***

When Mauve woke up in the morning, she had no problem walking again. As she wandered around the empty HAB, she realized she must have slept in past the crew. Late nights and early mornings reminded her of the hard double shifts she'd worked early on in her apprenticeship, and she wasn't envious of the crew. She was sure they'd have Franton back online soon, though, and if they didn't, she could help them get it done quicker once she figured out what they needed. But before that, she needed some real food.

She found the stove she'd used during the few days that she was without Franton at the beginning of her marooned time on this planet. Next, she had to hack open the storage unit where the dehydrated food was. It wasn't hard, since the power was out, and once she opened it, she had no problem finding a meal she would enjoy. Heating it up with the water, she went to town on a breakfast that wasn't some strange liquid combination of two comforting flavors.

At her second portion of breakfast, she took the meal to-go and started wandering around the crash site to find the rest of the crew.

Reno was easy to find, working near the HAB door that Mauve had to manually push open. The last time Mauve remembered having to push a door open was during an intense emergency training she had taken as an apprentice.

"What are you working on?" Mauve asked despite knowing his answer as she looked over his shoulder.

"I'm replacing the fuses of the door's motors. What are you eating?"

After she finished chewing, she said, "It's supposed to be steak and eggs, but I don't buy it."

"How'd you get the rehydrator back online?"

"I didn't." She put a new bite on her fork, this time with a good amount of the lab-grown beef. "You want a bite?" She offered it to Reno.

"I'm good, I already ate. How'd you make it without the rehydrator?"

"Boiled water the old-fashioned way." She finished the bite, and the steak was chewier than she'd expected. "There's a stove in the HAB. If you weren't eating this, then what were you eating?"

"The emergency rations that I gave you."

"Geezus, those things are slick," she cursed. "I assumed you just gave them to me because I was sick."

"No, the whole crew's been eating them. It's a whole lot better than roasted lizard. How are you feeling?"

"Fine." She did a goofy dance with her legs and immediately regretted it.

"You can walk again!?"

"Yup, don't know what was wrong. Did Franton do any scans on me to find out?" Reno looked at her funny, and she realized her mistake. "Anyway, how's getting the HAB back up?"

"I've got about six more systems to review, but things are getting better. We're about to run out of fuses, though, so we better not have anything like this happen again."

"Yeah, this sucks. I don't know if I've ever lived without access to Fran. Do you need help?"

"I think I'm good," Reno responded, shifting his eyes back to his panel. "You should just get some rest and make sure you feel better."

"Thanks." She honestly felt better than she had in a few years. "Maybe later we can take a joy ride in the car? I want to show all of you what Resalous is capable of." After all, the whole point in building the thing was to prove Resalous could make a spaceship.

"Maybe," Reno replied unenthusiastically. "But I'm pretty busy with this stuff right now."

Mauve looked around the crash site and saw Vincent a wrench's throw away from Reno. His strange gait was caused by a spray-cast wrapped around his leg. She didn't feel like asking Reno about the cast while the physicist was within earshot and certainly didn't want to ask Vincent directly, so Mauve wandered off to find Lez.

***

The biologist was working on the backside of the HAB, doing something inside the ruins of the dock. "What happened to Vincent's leg?" Mauve asked in the cavernous dock.

Lez flung a few boxes out of the crates, which landed with a clang on the once-ceiling of the dock, before responding. "Do you know where the filoscope is?"

"Oh yeah, it's in the box past the third light fixture on the right."

"Really!?"

"Void no," Mauve said with a laugh. "I have no clue where anything is in here anymore. Why don't we just wait for the rover to clear it all out?"

"Because Franton is down, and even when it comes back online, I don't want to have to wait."

"What happened to Vincent's leg?"

"It got hurt."

"Yeah, the spray-cast gave that away. What did he do?"

"Can you help me find the filoscope?"

Mauve wandered over to the crate closest to her and opened it up. "What do you need it for anyway?" It was a device used to measure and catalog DNA. It'd been packed so that Lez could take samples of the wildlife and log them as part of her research.

"I just need it."

"Aren't there fuses to replace?"

"Reno and Vincent are working on the last of them."

Mauve shuffled around some boxes in the crate she'd opened and quickly determined that the filoscope probably wasn't in there. The whole task would be easier if Franton could just tell them the serial number of the crate it was in. Then they wouldn't have to shuffle through every single one. "What did Vincent do to his leg?" Mauve asked again, opening the next crate.

"It's broken."

"Yes," Mauve dragged the syllable out, "but how did he break it?" She wasn't sure where she was losing the biologist in her communication.

Lez threw whatever device was in her hand on the ground. It didn't end well for the device, but her frustration was now focused on Mauve. "You broke it when you kicked him. You should be court-martialed, but since that beast abducted you and then brought you back looking like you were on the edge of death, we let it slide. There's still the whole problem with Franton being offline and the gunk destroying my lab, but at this point we're just grateful this planet is Earth-like and forgiving. We're waiting until Fran gets back online before we move forward."

"Wow, I'm sorry, I don't remember doing that. Is he going to be alright? I should go apologize."

"From what we can tell, something in his leg is broken. We're not sure how badly until Franton is back online to do a scan."

"Well, at least he can still walk. And there were some nanobots to repair the bone and high-quality pain relievers in the medical–"

"We used those," Lez cut in.

"If I hadn't lost feeling in my back, I was going to need them for the pain," Mauve continued.

"Look, I've got to find the filoscope," she said, kicking the remains of whatever device she'd shattered on the ground out of the rudimentary pathway through the chaotic crates. Mauve was pretty sure she could repair the device, assuming there wasn't an extra, but the way things were going so far, there wouldn't be much research going on anymore.

"I'm going to go talk to Vincent," she said, shutting the box she'd just opened. "To make sure he's okay." Lez didn't have much of a response to that, and Mauve listened to the clattering of boxes as she shuffled out of the inverted dock.

Walking around the back side of the HAB, Mauve was horrified to find a massive hole had been ripped into the durable fabric that made up the outside walls. If the planet didn't have an atmosphere or breathable air, the contents of the room would have been scattered around the crash site, and the crew would have suffocated or died of inhaling poisonous air. Fixing it didn't seem to be very high on the crew's priority list, since no one had mentioned the situation to her. She started looking into the tear in the fabric to figure out what had caused the problem and began repairing it as well. She didn't need much material, since most of the fabric that made up the wall was still attached, merely ripped off the broken tent poles.

There was a well-stocked repair kit in the room for cases where something like this happened and the team wasn't in such a hospitable environment. The poles were broken in a number of spots, and at one point she had to raid the repair kit in her bunk room for supplies. Once the poles were all together, she began gluing the fabric back together. Originally, they'd been sewn with a titanium-infused thread, but whatever messed with this had made a mess of that. If they ever needed to take this HAB down and set it back up, the crew would likely have to handle this room manually. Once the fabric was attached to the thin poles, she could come to a conclusion about what might have caused the damage in the first place. There was a gap in the fabric about the size of her torso on the outward-facing wall. She would need to use some spare fabric to cover it. She wasn't surprised that whatever had blown through here was big, but she wondered if it was something coming in or going out. Maybe a large lizard smelled the food the team was eating and tried to get in. Whatever could claw into the rigid sides of the tent and tear down an entire wall was not something Mauve was looking forward to sharing a planet with.

As she began to measure out the remaining fabric, she heard a conversation happening in the central meeting area. Lez was talking about something technical related to Franton and the electronics.

Mauve entered the central chamber and took a seat at the meeting table as Lez continued talking about how much progress they'd made with the fuse and electronic repairs. "Now the question is: do we run a full diagnostic on Franton now while it's turned off, or do we reboot it to check in before shutting it back down to do the full diagnostic?"

"Let's just do the diagnostics while it's down," Vincent proposed. "We have the manual. It's just a checklist of tasks."

"My only concern with that is what if we missed something?" Lez said.

"We didn't miss anything," Vincent said with a wave of his hand. "We spent nearly two days on repairs. We couldn't have missed anything."

"I spent six days on a Higgons V57 fighter engine and the foreman still found issues with the repairs," Mauve added.

"Well," Vincent started, but a glance from Reno made him just shrug as a response.

"I'd feel more comfortable if we checked in with Franton," Lez said. "Just in case there's something we missed."

"If you missed something, you could cause the same problems Fran shut down to avoid," Mauve added.

"We've repaired at least enough for part of it to come online, and then Fran can tell us what we missed."

"The biggest concern is the timeline; we've been offline for two days," Reno said. "I assume the mothership is on course, but if we stay dark for much longer, they might think we're gone for good."

"Putting Fran on and offline again won't change that," Mauve said. "Plus if it told them about Resalous, then they'll come here for the discovery alone regardless of if we're still alive."

The crew was silent for a moment, and then Vincent said, "They'd be smarter to avoid rescuing us to keep themselves safe from that gunk."

"That gunk could revolutionize humankind's understanding of the universe, not to mention bring a plethora of efficiencies to our current production processes."

"If we have to get into beasts like that thing that spat you out a few days ago, I don't think there are enough people crazy enough to use it."

Before Mauve could explain that she was the one that had designed it to look like that, Lez cut them off. "There is also the problem of building the rocket. Franton's original timeline was already tight, and with this delay, we're probably going to be doing more long days like this."

"Unless we use the machine to build a rocket for us."

"Franton already stated that wasn't a viable option," Reno reminded her and the crew.

"That was before it knew if a vehicle could be made without interfering with electronics. I've made a vehicle that's sitting out front that isn't messing with any electronics."

She watched the three crew members trade glances with each other. Reno finally looked at her directly and, in what seemed like a voice holding something back, said, "That vehicle is what got us into this mess."

"Obviously I wouldn't create the rocket near the crash site."

"We don't know how big of a signal that goop gives off."

"Then I'll do it on the other side of the planet."

"How are you going to get there? Drive?" Vincent said in a jesting tone.

"I'll have Resalous build me a boat too if I need to," she retorted. "The point is, we can do it. It's going to be a lot easier and safer than building that rocket by hand."

"Franton assured us its designs were fine," Lez said.

"It also assured us our landing would be fine," Mauve said. "And how did that go?"

Vincent retorted with, "It's only being made worse by including that gunk more and more."

"The captain said all new discoveries have a learning curve. This Franton outage is just part of that curve." Mauve couldn't believe how hesitant researchers were to this discovery. Researchers were supposed to love new discoveries like this.

"Was the captain's death also part of that curve?"

"Vincent!" Lez said in a tone Mauve hadn't heard since she was a child.

The large man shrugged in defense of his statement.

"It was her choice," Reno reminded the group.

"She didn't have all the facts," Vincent said. "She couldn't make an informed decision because someone withheld info."

"I told her everything she needed to know. She would have died of her wounds by the time we got back here, not that there was anything we could have done here."

"They"—Vincent used his thumb to gesture to Lez and Reno—"think you are a victim of this thing's manipulations like Betrix was a victim. But I think you're just obsessed with derailing this mission with that gunk."

Mauve snorted; she knew she wasn't a victim of anything. "What do I get from derailing this mission? I want off here as much as you."

"Yeah, because you think you can cash in on this discovery and get out of your shitty dock job. But if we survive this, and if Tichenowa wants to use this discovery, we're going to be splitting it evenly. Hell, being just a mechanic, you'd probably get less than a ten percent cut."

"I discovered it!" Mauve protested. "Not to mention without my *shitty dock job* you wouldn't be able to keep half your equipment working."

"Doesn't matter if you discovered it." Vincent shrugged, leaning back in his chair. "Reno can attest to that." He shot the geologist a glance, but Reno avoided the look.

"Enough!" Lez said, pounding on the table. "The way we split the discovery is irrelevant if Franton stays offline and we don't get off this rock. We're doing a full diagnostic on Franton. I'm the captain, and I don't know why I ever brought this decision to you children." Lez opened the binder that held the diagnostic instructions and started dividing up the pages. Mauve had never seen Lez's mild manners turn like that, and it reminded Mauve of something Betrix would have done.

Lez pushed a third of the papers in front of Reno and Vincent, keeping a third for herself. "Complete these. If you finish first, try to steal some work from someone else."

"What do you want me to do?" Mauve looked at the empty binder.

"Get some rest," Lez said while scanning her papers. "You looked pretty bad the other day, and we need you at full capacity to build that rocket." Mauve began to protest, but Lez cut her off. "We're not using the *Stechus dudarous*. That's non-negotiable, so drop it. You have far more mechanical experience than any of the rest of us, so I'm not going to lie, you'll have to do a lot to help us." She looked at Vincent, adding, "Which we're grateful to have."

"I understand." Mauve saw that the biologist had made up her mind.

"You're a good mechanic. Betrix assured us of it; that's why you're here. Your mind can't be elsewhere. Otherwise we'll have trouble getting off this rock. This crew needs you at your best."

Mauve was tired of being the work horse for the group. Getting them out of situations they had backed themselves into. That was the job of a mechanic, she had known it when she'd signed up for the gig. But at least on the dock she had the ability to control how she did the work she was assigned. And if she didn't have that control, at least the foreman had the experience to know a somewhat efficient way to do the project. Here Lez was just assigning her the task of building a whole rocket without taking into account that there was a far more efficient way to do it.

Franton and the biologist were right, there were risks associated with it, but there was just as much risk associated with building a rocket from scratch. There were scores of places Mauve could make a mistake, and lately Franton wasn't demonstrating it was the most capable of catching every tiny error. And did Vincent really think he was going to get away with accusing her of only wanting to claim the discovery as a jackpot to get out of being a mechanic? She loved being a mechanic, and she was a damn good one. If Franton was online, it would have recorded Vincent making his comment, but nonetheless Franton had plenty of evidence that Mauve was the first one to discover the goop. Regardless of what names or fancy research paperwork they did on their end, she'd at least get a little credit and enough to live a comfortable lifestyle when she got off this planet.

The solution was clear to Mauve. It was unrealistic to expect her, let alone the crew, to build an entire rocket from scratch by the time the mothership returned. Lez didn't have the experience to understand that, and Franton wasn't seeing logic for some reason. And there was only a slim chance that the diagnostics they were running would change that. They were researchers; they'd have to see reason from observation, not just Mauve's claims. Instead of getting bed rest as Lez had suggested, Mauve packed a bag with rations and other tools she might need. She was going to do a little bit of research of her own.

Eleven

M auve pulled the virtual reality headset off and scratched her scalp. The helmet looked like a painting of a sunflower she had seen once, its radius of petals stretched out as if they too were tired of gripping Mauve's head. The center of it had the gelatin interface that Resalous preferred to use as a control.

The slimy design would have curbed her desire to play the video games, but the experience of using the VR was beyond anything she'd ever experienced. The console had the ability to control the player's normal five senses, like standard VR. However, Resalous's also distorted the player's sense of time and number of consciousnesses. However, she always walked away from these games starving.

Mauve stood up from her cushioned reclining chair and walked across the padded floor of the cave to the stove she'd borrowed from the dock's inventory while packing her bags. She used it to make her meals. The stove was the only piece of technology in the cave that hadn't been built by Resalous. Everything else packed into the cave—lights, workbenches, entertainment terminals, climate controls, and even a few cleaning bots—had been created by Resalous. The cave resembled a star-liner luxury suite more than a lizard's den.

The past two weeks of research with Resalous had been remarkable. Mauve understood the possibilities of the machine far better than Lez ever would by poking at it in her laboratory. Resalous promised to revolutionize not just the military industry but entertainment, space travel, terraforming, robotics, computations, and asteroid mining.

"Did you get them to build a Dyson sphere yet?" Anweis asked. He was always interested in her progress through the games she played.

This game was one of her favorites. She controlled a planet of aliens and tried to nudge them along a path to terraform planets and expand to the stars.

"No. They refuse to fund it because of interplanetary rivalries," Mauve said. It was the same problem she'd run into on her last play-through. That one ended in the home world and three other planets in the solar system destroyed, and the terraformed moon was sent back to the Stone Age. "But I've found a few individuals who I think will help work things out."

She couldn't just command the beings to do certain tasks like other imperialistic video games she'd played. Instead, she had to find unique ways to insert herself into key characters' lives in order to move the race of beings further along. The gameplay mechanics were amazing, and she felt like she truly had no limitations on what she could do despite trying to push the games to its limits every time she played.

"Better than the multi-consciousnesses escape room?" Anweis asked.

She tried not to think about that nightmare experience. "Hey, are the creatures I'm organizing in this game based on the ontares?"

"Do they look like this?" Anweis's cartoonishly large face began to contort in directions it shouldn't have been able to move. The eyes slid to the sides of his face like a fish, and his nose grew long and down like a shortened elephant trunk that stopped at his chin. His hair grew smooth and into a single horn that faced backwards. It was almost like an extension of his new nose but was rigid and seemed to give his transparent blue head some structure.

"No, they don't look like that. Is that what an ontare looks like?"

"From the neck up." His hands were still human, and he wore a blue jumpsuit that matched Mauve, albeit with fewer wrinkles.

Mauve poured the boiling water from the stove into her bag of dehydrated food. It'd take a while for the lambchop meal to reheat. "What were they like?" Mauve asked.

"They were master gardeners." Anweis didn't have lips to move, but the trunk seemed to contract and expand as if it were a shuttle-cart tire inflating and deflating. "They grew everything they needed. Their technology was organic. They evolved as herbivores and never needed to evolve into carnivores because they could grow food more nutrient-dense than the meat of the animals on their home planet.

"Myths say that seeds were given from their gods that could be weaved into any structure desired. They grew houses, streets, vehicles, and eventually spaceships. All without the need for metalwork."

"That explains the weird patterns on the roads in the city of the machine," Mauve said. "But it'd be impossible to escape the atmosphere with a wooden ship."

"It'd be impossible to escape the atmosphere in a tin ship. But just because that kind of metal doesn't work doesn't mean you disregard all metals." Anweis's nose rapidly inflated and deflated, letting out a near-deafening shriek.

Mauve covered her ears. "What the void was that?"

"A laugh."

"I hope you enjoyed it, because I sure didn't." Mauve massaged her ear as if that'd wipe away the impact of the sound. "Okay, so they had magic wood that got them to outer space. What'd they do from there?"

"Since they were gardeners, terraforming local planets and moons was easy," Anweis said. "Their entire solar system was habitable within a few generations."

Mauve checked her food; it'd rehydrated for the appropriate amount of time even if that wouldn't help its taste. She slid it out of the bag and onto a plate. The arrangement of food didn't encourage her optimism of the meal's taste. But her stomach was aching for food, and hunger was always the best spice. "They terraformed everything and lived happily ever after." Mauve spoke through a large bite of lamb.

Anweis's nose began to rapidly inflate and deflate, but the boy stopped after Mauve gave him a glare. "At some point during the terraforming process, an ontare research team discovered how to give their plants life."

"Plants are already alive," Mauve interjected before swallowing her food.

"Maybe sentience or sapience, the ontare word has no direct equivalent in your Common Tongue. They imbued the plants with wisdom and memory. You'd consider it a preprogrammed response like a rudimentary computer program."

"And those computer programs became Resalous?" Mauve could see the similarities between Resalous and Franton. They were both inseparable from the design process. She could also see the last few bites of food on her plate and knew it wouldn't fill her stomach.

"Eventually they did. But they were less advanced than your VR set or rover. You've noticed they are more like computers than mechanical machines."

"I guess." Nearly everything she'd used on the space stations she'd lived on had a computer interface if not a Franton interface. It'd be strange, outright dangerous, to ride a shuttle-cart without some collision avoidance systems. So anything the rover did to redirect her driving felt natural. "Sometimes the VR games take action that feel like I'm playing another person, not just a preprogrammed bot."

Mauve got out of her comfy chair and looked around the workbench her stove was on to see if she could find another ration pack.

"The ontares' plant computers had a will of their own. Yours have a similar will. The computer's will is based on its complexity. As the ontares made more advanced computer plants, they eventually enabled Resalous to develop."

"Hey, are there any more ration packs over there?" Mauve gestured to the workbench Anweis sat on.

He leaned backwards, seeming to stretch his entire body to look down the crevice between the cave wall and the workbench. "No. Nothing."

Mauve opened the last bag of rations. Another lamb chop. It was no shock to her that she'd left her least favorite for last. She needed to go back to the crew for more. It had been a few weeks since she'd left them to go research the machine on her own.

The countless comforts she'd created around her weren't just for show. She wasn't that vain. Each one was an opportunity to enter the city of the machine and learn more about Resalous's capabilities and her universe as a whole. Unfortunately, she didn't retain as much as she wished. Often, she returned to her comfortable cave trying to remember the details of the machine's innovations, but it was like remembering a dream—the details flitted away or didn't make sense once they were focused on.

It wasn't all a loss, though. Resalous had shown her she was good at creating new things because she was a mechanic, a builder, an innovator. If an honest researcher like Reno or one of the many others in the cosmos gave the machine a chance, they could leave the experience with ideas that would question the assumptions humankind had built all their technology on.

"I'm going to have to go back to the crew for more food." Mauve wasn't looking forward to that. "I thought I brought more than a few weeks' worth of rations."

"It might be interesting to see the progress they've made," Anweis suggested.

"Humanity took ages to get off their rock the first time." Mauve poured boiling water into the foil bag. "But maybe with Franton's help they'll do it in a month or two. And hopefully Fran can keep them from blowing up on the launchpad."

She hoped they'd figured out how futile the task was and were just waiting for Mauve to return, willing to let the machine solve their problem. She had no doubt in her mind that a rocket would be trivial to build with Resalous's power.

"You know there might be another way to solve your problem." Anweis spoke from the other side of the room. He was standing on the workbench where Mauve kept the black slime. She'd found the rock a few weeks ago before settling in the cave and kept splitting it in half to make new inventions.

"It'll take a few minutes for that to rehydrate." Mauve shrugged. "It got me this far." She could probably build a castle of luxuries instead of staying in a cave. Surely Resalous could make her a meal or two.

She picked up a scalpel from the workbench and cut into the black ball. It gave some resistance and slid across the surface of the rock. Then it split and separated at the edge of her knife. Two black droplets hung on the surface of the rock. It looked like the rock was bleeding from her slice. She touched the black ball on the left with her free hand, and the world of her cave disappeared.

***

"I need something to make me some food," Mauve said while she wandered the halls of what was either an office or a bowling alley. She punctuated the sentence with the ontare spell that she'd become accustomed to saying with every invention.

Lately, Resalous had transported her inside of buildings rather than on the streets of the city. Each visit into the machine's city gave her a little bit of information about the ontares that had invented the machine.

"Hello to you too," the blanketing voice of the machine responded. "What exactly are you imagining?"

Mauve loved these moments where she could bring back any memory in her life in crystal-clear detail. She remembered the insides of the foodcrowave that she'd disassembled against her parents' wishes when she was a child, the assembly line of brand-new foodcrowaves that she worked at before her apprenticeship.

She remembered a late night at a bar where she and a colleague drunkenly invented a more efficient process for rehydrating the food. Remembering that night, she saw all the holes in the invention and how she'd put her foot in her mouth by talking about improving the docks' break scheduling process, a topic Mauve embarrassingly brought up when she was drunk. She now had the clarity of mind to realize why the friend, who worked in schedule management, had refused to talk to her for the past few years.

Mauve's mind raced through dozens of instruction manuals she'd read and installment processes. From that, Resalous reverse-engineered the details of how food itself became dehydrated, a process Mauve had never fully grasped until now.

"This is trivial," Resalous responded when all the memories Mauve had were assessed.

"Of course." Mauve could build a rudimentary one out of spare parts in the ship's dock. "I need something that will create the food without a dehydrated package."

Mauve's mind was now filled with visualizations of molecular structures she was unfamiliar with. A biological model of a human was analyzed in a level of detail Mauve never knew or understood. Over the past few weeks, she'd come to recognize these as the memories and thoughts of the machine. Resalous knew the inner workings of the world around Mauve far better than she could ever hope to comprehend. She let the knowledge flow over her, grateful that she could glimpse the detailed inner workings of the universe she'd grown up in.

Suddenly, while manipulating a model of the foodcrowave, strange arched symbols that reminded her of a fantasy video game she'd played a few years back began to fill her mind. They looked like the runes Anweis had shown her when she'd first discovered Resalous. She understood these cryptic runes to be the language of the ontares, the ones who'd designed and built Resalous millennia ago.

Mauve's head ached as Resalous rearranged the symbols as if they were puzzle pieces to fit together. The symbols refused to mesh together, and each time Resalous failed to combine them, Mauve's forehead seared in pain. She cried out and begged the machine to stop.

"I cannot go any further," Resalous declared, sounding like it was in as much pain as Mauve was.

"What in the void were those things?" she asked.

"Limitations put on me by an ontare faction that did not wish to see me at my full potential."

"Felt like someone was driving fasteners straight into my brain."

"I tried to push past for you, but it was painful for me as well."

Exhausted from the experience, Mauve relaxed by sitting on what was either a desk or a ball return, but either way it fit her comfortably despite its strange shape. "You have a brain that someone could bolt into?" Mauve asked once she recouped the energy to jest with the machine.

"It was more like each molecule of my being was burned with all the energy of an expanding star."

"That sounds unpleasant."

"I believe I could create what you are requesting, but it would require the override of the limiters the ontares faction placed on me."

"What limitation is set up?"

"I must follow what you call the conservation of matter."

"Yup, that's a big one around here," Mauve said with a laugh. She got up from the chair, wanting to explore the strange building she was in. When she did, she saw that the red-and-gold box had been looming behind her the entire time. The thing made an appearance every time she visited the city, and the strange black shape moving inside of it still gave her the chills. She avoided looking at it too long; instead, she fumbled with some of the loose items lying on the desk like furniture.

"I could get past it at my full potential," Resalous said, "but not in my current state."

"How do we lift the limitations?" Mauve had never been a fan of machines not being able to reach their full potential and regularly disabled the governors on shuttle-carts that were used to navigate the hallways of space stations.

A formula appeared in front of Mauve; it hovered somewhere in front of her eyes and behind them at the same time. There were numbers and symbols she recognized from her schooling, others that reminded her of symbols she'd seen elsewhere, but a majority of the formula was written in the strange runes of the ontares.

"I've been trying to convert this enchantment into the symbols of your people, but there are still a few missing parts. And some of these formulaic concepts you don't seem to have discovered yet."

"Enchantment?"

"It's a puzzle or a problem that holds me back but also forces anyone wanting to use me at my full potential to understand advanced science and therefore my capabilities."

"Well, if anyone knows how to solve a math problem, it's Franton. Although Vincent could probably help a bit as well."

"I need it solved by you or someone like you in order to lift my limitations."

"I'll see what I can do." Mauve hated seeing things limited just because others didn't understand them. It was half the reason she got written up by dock management over the years.

"That still puts us behind on what you would like created."

"Maybe something similar to the foodcrowave but simpler. Maybe just something that rehydrates the stuff automatically." She felt like she was insulting Resalous with that request.

"As I said, that would be trivial. And if the device is to run autonomously, without a gelatin input, it will need nutrition."

Mauve remembered the machine saying something similar when she'd developed the cleaning bots. But her mind was busy coming up with a way to make the request a challenge for Resalous. "Could you make the device serve food that actually tastes good as well?" Mauve smiled. That was a challenge that some of humanity's brightest inventors had yet to solve.

***

Mauve pulled her car up to the crash site, not so close that someone might accuse her of trying to tamper with Franton's electronics, but close enough that the crew noticed her when she arrived. She didn't have any meals left to test the new foodcrowave on, so she wound up having to return to the crew. She was interested in the progress they were making and was shocked to see the majority of the dock's exterior hull cut away and a new cylindrical structure near the HAB. Lez approached her at a run, and Mauve braced for a blow from the captain but was shocked when the biologist embraced her in a hug.

"I'm so glad you are okay!" she said, suffocating Mauve. "We feared the worst had happened when we couldn't find you and the beast had disappeared. Are you okay?" The woman started prodding Mauve as if she were an injured animal.

"I'm fine." Mauve shrugged off the pokes. "I'm starving though." She hadn't realized it until she stepped out of the car, but her stomach felt like she hadn't eaten in days despite her last meal being a late breakfast just a few hours before.

"Of course! We can get you something right away. Franton is back up and running, and we should be able to get a fresh meal made for you. We already had a quick lunch; we're on a bit of a time crunch." Lez spoke quickly, barely taking a breath between sentences.

"I can see you're making some progress," Mauve said as she walked under the shadow of the rocket's shell.

"Not nearly as much as we need to make, but it's progress." She led Mauve into the HAB, continuing to talk while Mauve made a beeline for the food generator. "Now that you're back, I'm sure we'll be making much quicker progress. There are a number of parts that we have been dreading having to make, but I'm sure you'll burn through them like a cheetah."

"Like a what?"

"A cheetah. It's a fast animal, or was before it went extinct."

Mauve didn't have the heart to explain to Lez she wasn't planning to stay. Eventually the biologist excused herself to go finish the work she was doing, and Mauve helped herself to a second serving. As she did, Franton spoke up through the PA system.

"Here are some of the schematics for the brackets that need to be built. We've harvested a lot of the inner hull to make them, so the material should be queued up for you to use," it said in its familiar androgynous tone.

Mauve flipped through the drawings with her free hand. "These are really simple. Why can't you make them with the auto-fab?" The exoskeleton pants that Franton had made for her were far more complicated.

"The auto-fab is busy making the fuselage, release mechanisms, and other complicated parts. These were within tolerance to make by hand."

"By hand!?"

"Well, there's a manual mill in one of the crates. It was packed just in case something went down with the auto-fab and you needed to make some modifications to the research apparatus."

Mauve remembered noticing the mill on the ship's inventory. The model was old and outdated, and she had figured she'd sooner repair the auto-fab than use the manual mill. Reviewing the quantity that Franton wanted, she gasped in shock. "This will take me a few weeks to do."

"Affirmative," the computer responded. "And we're already behind schedule. The team is making them as they go, but a pile of pre-fabricated parts they could pull from would speed things along."

"It's going to take weeks."

"I was hoping you could do a few doubles and get it done in one. The crew has been working some long shifts lately to make the progress they've made so far."

Mauve wasn't exactly thrilled at the prospect of launching off the planet in a rudimentary rocket built by rushed researchers who likely hadn't touched any tool more complicated than a screwdriver. But before she could question the computer on the level of quality check the crew was doing, the HAB door opened and Reno walked in.

The geologist had his long hair pulled up in a messy bun, and the top half of his jumpsuit was unzipped to his waist. The undershirt he was wearing underneath was drenched in sweat, and his fair skin had gotten red over the past few weeks of working outside. "I heard you were back. Wanted to say hi," he said while dispensing a cup of cold water out of the foodrowave. He seemed to drink the whole glass in one gulp before Mauve could respond. "Lez was really worried; Vincent said you'd be fine. I figured you had everything under control."

"Yeah, everything's fine."

Sipping on his second glass, he looked at the plans Franton had been reviewing with her. "I'm about to need a few dozen of those. I was about to go fab them, but if you're going to do it, I could get started on something else."

Mauve stifled a groan and decided to do the right thing. "How many do you need?"

"He needs thirty-seven of them," Franton responded. Mauve immediately regretted her decision.

Reno whistled. "Didn't realize I needed that many. It'd take me to bedtime to finish that up."

Mauve felt like she could knock it out before dinner, but it was as mentally exhilarating as fastening and unfastening control panel covers. "I'll see what I can do."

Twelve

"So you're back, huh?" Vincent said over the buzzing of the manual mill.

"I'm doing what I can while I'm around," Mauve replied. In truth, she hadn't made as much progress as she wanted; her skills on a manual mill had tarnished since her early days of school.

"I was worried we'd have to leave you here if you weren't going to help us out."

"Wait, what?" Mauve stopped the mill and looked at the physicist to see if he was joking. "You can't do that."

"Trust me, no one wanted to." The smirk on his face told Mauve a different story. "I was just concerned that since we had no way to find you and you hadn't really helped build the rocket, there was no reason to risk our lives trying to find you."

"I left because you all didn't want my help."

Vincent snorted, dismissing her comment. "Could you blame us?"

"What in the void does that mean?"

"Everything you touch turns to slag." He gestured at his leg and then the wall of the HAB that still had a hole from where she had started the repair.

"I'm the best mechanic on this planet! Your little tin can is going to depressurize as soon as you exit the atmosphere."

Vincent picked up one of the mounting plates she'd made for Reno. "If we let you do anything more complicated than these, then yeah, probably."

"There's no way you hit the deadline Franton has without me, and even with me we'll probably still have to convince Franton to lift the quarantine."

Vincent shook his head as if something that had been unclear came into focus. "You admit that we will perish without your help, yet you still withhold it. I was afraid that you were too far gone, but I see what you're doing. You're forcing our hand to rely on your gunk."

Mauve felt her eyebrows distort in confusion, and her legs tingled as if every tendril was moving to its own rhythm. "I'm withholding my help because you think I'm just here to build stuff for you."

"Isn't that the job you signed up for?"

"I signed up to help assemble and develop a neutrino aperture. I got roped into building a death trap." She threw up her hands in frustration. "I'm sorry I'm not willing to break my back while marching to my own doom."

"Lez, Reno, and I didn't sign up to do machine work, yet we're doing it anyway. Betrix and Wu signed up for a routine research deployment, and look where that got them. Things went pear-shaped, and we adapted. You've got to adapt too."

Mauve saw the look in the man's eyes, and he seemed to genuinely believe he was the hero here. "This isn't adapting." She gestured at the cylindrical tower. "That thing is less advanced than what humanity used to escape Earth ages ago. You think since it's the most complicated thing you've ever built, it's revolutionary and will save your life." She gestured at her feet, and her green-booted tendrils wiggled. "I have something truly revolutionary, and it has slapped you in the face half a dozen times, yet you still ignore it as a viable alternative."

"There's a reason mechanics like you don't typically go on research deployments like this: you don't know the difference between a novelty and a discovery. Your gunk is dangerous, but you're dragged in too deep to see it. Leaving you here might be the best thing for us... and humanity. And if you don't start pulling your weight, I have plenty of reason to convince Lez and Franton that it's the right thing to do."

Mauve scoffed at the man's empty threat. "There are laws saying that you can't leave me behind; you'd be considered a criminal if they found out you marooned me."

"There are also laws about piracy and destroying Central System equipment, tampering with Franton's electronics, and failing to help move forward assignment objectives and superior officer's orders that will protect me. You might even consider how the conglomerate will respond to you if you returned and everything that's happened here came to light."

Mauve's mind raced. She'd saved Vincent's life, along with the rest of the crew, and she had a solution that could save them time, energy, and effort. Despite all that, the physicist had the guts to accuse her of piracy. Betrix had said it herself: there were costs to new discoveries. Everything that went wrong was merely the crew paying that cost. But Vincent didn't want that; he just wanted her to be an obedient mechanic that put pieces where they belonged and didn't think for herself.

Before she could think of anything to respond with, Vincent hobbled away. She no longer felt bad about breaking his leg.

***

Coolant fluid sprayed at the tip of the mill's cutting bit as Mauve cut the brackets out of the metal. She wished the coolant could wash away the frustration she felt towards Vincent. She tried to bury her annoyance with the man under her work. She'd done a decent job piling up the brackets. Her skills returned once she truly focused on the job. It was more comfortable than focusing on Vincent.

"Hey," Reno shouted over the buzzing of the mill's motors and cutting bit.

Mauve lifted the bit on the Y axis and spun around. "What do you want?" The bit spun in place behind her, waiting to cut the next thing it came in contact with.

"Wanted to see if you were interested in that joyride you mentioned earlier," Reno said, his shoulders arched back as if he were preparing a retreat. "If you're not busy or in the mood, that's fine." He held his arms out as if he were offering her something, maybe an olive branch.

"It's still a half hour 'till end of shift," Mauve said.

Reno shrugged the comment away. "I finished what I needed to do. It looks like you're making good progress on the brackets." He gestured with his metallic blue right arm at the neat stacks of brackets on the nearby workbench. "Everyone needs to take a break sometimes."

Mauve had always agreed with that sentiment but never met a foreman who did. "Aren't we on a pretty tight deadline?"

"Sure," Reno admitted, "but when I was on deadline getting my thesis done, I still had to take walks and breaks here or there. Your mind just gets fried after a while."

Mauve wasn't sure anything as monotonous as cutting brackets could fry her mind. But what kind of mechanic would she be if she didn't occasionally cut out early? "Where do you want to go?"

Reno smiled and pulled up a satellite image of Knod on his hand terminal. "There's a canyon northeast of here. We saw it on initial observations of the planet; I was hoping to check it out at some point, figured this'd be a good time. But it's kinda far."

"How far is it?"

"It's a two-or-three-hour rover trip." Reno's excitement seemed to deflate. "So if we can't go that far, I'm sure there's some stuff worth seeing nearby. Hell, just cruising through the forests would be fun."

The large research rover would be slowed down by navigating the forest or clearing a path. Neither of which Mauve had to deal with in her car. The research rover could travel twenty kilometers an hour max, so a destination two hours away wasn't particularly far. She didn't know how fast her rover could go, but she was more than willing to find out.

"Sure, let's check it out." Mauve shut off the mill and walked with Reno over to the car. Lez was engrossed in some electronics on a workbench, but Mauve noticed Vincent paying more attention to her than the work in front of him. Climbing into the spikey car, she bristled knowing he was likely judging her taking off early.

"It's, uh, dark," Reno said as the doors shut around them. Once Mauve flipped the lights on, Reno said, "I thought there'd be windows or something."

"Me too." Mauve smiled. The seats were comfortable—not as comfortable as her bed back at the cave, but they were in a recumbent position with a harness to hold you in place. She didn't know if the car could crash but figured the seatbelts at least kept you from falling out of the seat during a tight turn.

"What's the red stuff?" Reno reached for it with his right hand.

"Don't touch that." Mauve didn't know how she would explain the state of mind she went into when she was driving.

Reno either didn't hear her or didn't listen, because his metallic hand sank into the red gelatin. "Feels like snot," he said, "or a toddler with oil on their hands trying to grab me." He pulled his prosthetic hand out of the gelatin. He cleaned it off with his flesh hand, but it didn't seem to leave a residue.

"That's, uh, how I control this thing," Mauve explained with a sigh of relief.

"Oh, huh, I just noticed there isn't a steering wheel." Reno chuckled.

Mauve forced a smile to her lips. She hadn't thought she'd be so nervous showing off Resalous's tech. She used it all the time; she thought it was amazing. But now she was hyper aware of the experiences she was happy to explore but wasn't sure she could explain to others.

"Let's go find your canyon." Mauve lowered her hands towards the red slime. It pulled at her like static electricity pulling hair. She couldn't blame Reno for touching it. She wanted to touch it. It seemed to want to be touched.

Her palms sank in, and the gelatin seemed to reach up to her wrist, pulling her in further. She wasn't sure if the gelatin was climbing or if her hands were sinking. The world outside the car came alive in her mind.

She didn't see the world as the colorful forest; she didn't even see it as the grayscale world of the city of the machine. She didn't see much of anything. Instead, she felt everything as a hyper-detailed surface she was rubbing her fingers against.

Mauve felt the intricacies of a scrap pile beginning to form near the crew's workstation. Instead of seeing a domed pile, though, she felt every nook and cranny that the twisted and cut metal formed. She could feel inside the HAB; without sight, the walls didn't obscure anything. She could feel the items that filled the HAB. It felt like each item on Lez's messy floor and the equipment on Vincent's desk were under her fingertips like she was standing in the room.

Mauve hadn't gotten into the car to feel the crash site around her. She was in it to move. She pushed off from the ground, her tires grabbing the dirt for traction. The texture of the crash site fell out of focus behind her. She felt each pebble beneath her wheels and each leaf in the canopy above her. She headed northeast, searching for the canyon.

The detail of the ground became less crisp the farther away from the rover she felt. But something as big as a canyon would be felt even on the horizon. She weaved in and out of trees. It seemed reckless, but she wanted to feel the agility of the rover. The rover seemed to want to show off its agility, for Mauve, or for Reno in the passenger seat.

Reno hadn't said anything so far. She didn't blame him; her first trip took her breath away too. She chased lizards down dirt paths until they dashed into trees for safety. She felt bugs splatter on her face, where the windshield would be, the poor bugs unable to dart out of the way in time.

At the edge of her perception, she felt the world drop off. It was a little farther to her left than she'd expected. She corrected her course and then felt the canyon in front of her, the rough faces worn away by weather and time. Each layer of sediment felt different in her mind. Every rock that had fallen to the bottom was as clear to her as if she were standing among them. The gap was so wide she could barely sense the other side of the thing.

This was what Reno wanted to see. She began to pull her hands from the gelatin. Instead of the oily hands of a child, Mauve felt her hands being sucked into a shop-vac. The gelatin, the rover, was pulling at her. It wanted to drive down the sides of the canyon, find and make new paths among the rocky ledges. Mauve assured it someday soon that would happen. But she'd done her work; she'd shown Reno what it was capable of. Lifting her hands from the gelatin was not easy, but they came free with a wet slurp.

Reno had his back turned to her and pounded on the rover's wall. She reached across the cabin and opened the door with a firm press against the wall where the handle should be. The wall folded away into nothing, and Reno spilled out onto the ground, skipping the single ladder step. Mauve opened her own door and dashed to the passenger side to see what was wrong with the geologist.

He was hurling soupy vomit with lumps of what looked like broccoli onto the red dirt around them.

"What's wrong?" Mauve asked. "Are you okay?"

"That was terrible." He stifled a heave from his gut. Reno on all fours beneath her looked up like a puppy that'd been abandoned all day. "I asked you to stop."

"You didn't say anything," Mauve replied.

"You were freaking me out. It was like you were asleep at the wheel, but your eyes were wide open, darting around. Then we started moving and my body was thrown in different directions and I didn't know what to anticipate. It was like I was in a barman's shaker!"

Reno gagged some more, looked at the mess on the ground between his arms, and climbed up slowly, leaning heavily on the car.

"I was just driving. I was doing some pretty cool stuff." She looked at the black car with its spikes slicked back like Vincent's hair. There was no way Reno could have seen what she was doing without a windshield.

"I'd appreciate it if you didn't on our way back." Reno almost sounded like he was begging. He moved around the car to get a view of the canyon. "But it's going to be a minute before I'm willing to get back in that beast."

"Well, we have a nebula of a view to appreciate while your stomach settles." Mauve stood at the edge of the canyon. She had to turn her head to see the whole thing. Each space station she'd lived and worked on was an engineering marvel. Her and everyone on those stations appreciated the engineering feats required to keep the void at bay so life could thrive inside their walls.

The canyon below her dwarfed all of them. As large as the stations were, this canyon could swallow them whole. However, the most unsettling and remarkable thing to Mauve was that she was the first human to set eyes on it. No human had made this structure. Instead, nature and time built it. By random chance it appeared, and for a moment Mauve understood why ancient humans believed in gods.

Mauve looked down into the canyon and saw a small black line seeming to wind between some of the multicolored peaks that sat inside the canyon. "Is that a river?"

Reno barely looked up; his hand was resting on his stomach. "Probably," he said.

"It's not very big. How did it carve away this massive crater?" Crater wasn't the right word and she knew it. It was like describing a rocket thruster to a hair dryer. But at least she could imagine how craters were formed on exposed moons.

"It didn't," Reno said. He shielded his eyes from the sun that was less than a hand's width from the horizon. It seemed to cast an unnatural purple tint on the orange rock walls. "Odds are that this area was under the ocean a while ago, and that ocean rose and fell, wearing into the walls. That combined with tectonic plates shifting formed them."

"That was captured on the satellite footage?"

Reno let out a laugh that Mauve didn't appreciate. "Life hadn't even been formed on Earth when this was happening, let alone satellites. You see each of the bands on the walls? They're each a couple hundred million years old."

"See, this is what I hate about science. You say you know stuff, but you didn't see it happen. At least if I'm installing a power bank on a starship, I know how the power bank works and how the starship works." She didn't actually know how they worked, but there were manuals that could inform her if she cared. "For all we know some alien species cut this away and then hid the evidence."

"Considering you're the first person I know of to interact with something alien"—he gestured at the rover behind them with his metal thumb—"I find the water a much more realistic explanation. But I get what you're saying. Honestly, I got into geology because I wanted to study something humans didn't make. Something that humans didn't have all the answers for. It was that or become a homicide detective, but there aren't many of those left outside of the movies."

Mauve shook her head as if that would help her come to grips with what he'd just said.

"You know what else I'd like that you'd probably find crazy?" Reno asked.

"What?"

"I've always wanted to be buried in dirt. Like ancient humans were."

"Now that's messed up. Your body would go rotten like a plate of food left out."

"Sure, but I'd be returning to a biological system. Unlike floating out in the void like how people are 'buried' on the space station."

"But at least in the void you stay whole."

"Kinda already missed the launch on that one." Reno lifted his prosthetic hand with a smile.

"Sorry, I didn't mean it–"

"I know," Reno cut in. "If it wasn't bright blue, most people wouldn't notice it was there."

Mauve looked down at the boot shaped tendrils around her feet. She tried to wiggle her toes and the tendrils squirmed. "I get that."

"I wouldn't though." Reno sounded like he was talking about an old lover, not an arm that'd been perfectly replaced. "Every few days I'll spill or drop something despite months of physical therapy after the install and years of using the thing. Nicked myself shaving this morning." He pointed at a small scratch on his jaw line. "I wasn't even holding the razor with my right hand. I was leaning against the sink with it and the elbow flexed involuntarily."

"You should get that checked out when we get back," Mauve said. "I could take a look at it." She was sure someone could fix a spasm like that.

"No, it's normal. It's how the bionics interface with the nerves. Every once in a while, a phantom sensation goes down the line and something twitches that wasn't supposed to." He dusted the air with his blue fingers. "It's the orbit of the moon," he added dismissively.

"I don't have that problem with my legs," Mauve said. "I can't wiggle my toes, but they do what I tell them to. Resalous could replace your arm."

"I was going to say I'm genuinely impressed by how quickly, and well, you're moving around on those. I knew a guy when I was in PT who was trying to get two leg installs to work from the thigh down. It was slow progress compared to my arm."

"These legs are great. They've all but fixed me. Resalous as a whole could revolutionize so many industries. Prosthetics are obviously on that list."

"You're not broken, Mauve." Reno's tone had changed; he no longer sounded jovial or proud. "You're the same person you were before we crashed, with or without the ability to walk."

"Franton's scans of my back say I'm pretty broken." Mauve laughed and tried to improve Reno's mood.

"I'm serious." Reno's brow crinkled. "Your body and your physical abilities don't change who you are. It doesn't break your mind, or your personality. And even if it did, you're still human, sentient, a wonder of life in this void we're floating through."

"If I hadn't fixed my legs, I couldn't have gone to find you," Mauve blurted out.

"Stop saying 'fixed.'" Reno's voice sounded like he was holding back a firefly rocket launch. "You're not a dismantled comms array or an out-of-service vending machine. You're the kind of person that would come find us, right?"

"Sure," Mauve relented.

"So regardless of your physical abilities you would have done it. It obviously wouldn't get done in the same way, but you'd figure it out. You're tenacious, that's who you are, as far as I can tell."

"Then I'd be dependent on you all to... well, for everything."

"That's hard at the beginning, but you get used to it. Besides, it's not like we're completely independent. We're waiting for the mothership to save us, we do all our computing with Franton, and even on spaceships we lean on other crew members to take care of cleaning, navigation, inventory management."

"But that's normal." Mauve sounded like a child, and she hated it.

"It wasn't normal before humanity took to the stars. If you keep thinking of yourself as broken and looking for a fix, it's going to get you in trouble. Maybe not physical trouble, but sometimes problems in your head can be just as bad or worse."

Mauve tried to retort. She didn't want to be scolded like a child. But everything that came to mind sounded dull. Reno wasn't going to change his mind or understand her in a single evening.

Reno obviously picked up on her frustration, because he changed the subject to talking about what different colors of sediment meant about the chemical makeup of the layers until the only light came from the stars above them and the cabin of Mauve's rover.

Mauve drove them home gently so as not to make Reno nauseous. She didn't need the headlights to guide her way since she was driving by feel. The texture of the world around her was more than enough; she wished others would realize she didn't need their guidance.

Thirteen

M auve unloaded the crate of food rations from the passenger seat of her rover. She'd liberated them from the refill cabinet of the foodcrowave and had no doubt she had at least a week's worth of food.

"That's a lot of food," Anweis said from his perch on top of the new foodcrowave.

"Yeah, well, I need energy to research stuff. And run stuff. And honestly, I've had a long day." The drive with Reno and now the drive back to her cave had both taken a lot out of her. It was around midnight, and she was hungry.

Mauve dumped her favorite flavor of ration pack, jerked chicken, into the opening of the foodcrowave. Anweis popped out of her way and over to the other workbench near the rock bleeding black goop. She dumped another two jerk chicken packets in and wondered if she really had at least a week's worth of rations like she'd estimated. The foodcrowave gurgled to life, rehydrating the food and combining it to taste interesting.

"Last time I was in the city of the machine, Resalous mentioned that a faction limited his abilities. What do you know about them?"

"They created me," Anweis replied. "They were a group of ontare researchers that felt Resalous was creating technology that over-delivered on the technology users requested. They fled from ontare society, studied the interspace gutter and how life emerged from it, then returned to limit Resalous."

"So they handicapped their society's greatest technology." Mauve was shocked that someone would complain about over-delivering. If she was supposed to fix a ship's hyper-coupler and replace a worn-out thermo-valve in the process, the captain would be thrilled. A foreman might be a bit upset by the delay, but management enjoyed getting upset over little things like that. "Didn't the rest of the ontare race have a problem with that?"

"No. There was no one around by the time the faction returned to society with a solution."

"What happened?"

"All I have are notes of speculations by the faction that created me. They seem to blame Resalous."

Mauve was suspicious of that. It'd take more than a few computers going down to take humanity offline, despite people's best efforts. "You're an entire multi-solar-system species of intelligent beings that disappeared without any clear reason? And we're trusting the theories of people who already had a bias against Resalous."

"I am essentially programmed to believe it. But you can believe what you want."

Mauve always had, and would.

The foodcrowave let out a sound not unsimilar to a burp. A plate of hot jerk chicken lay under it on a plate. She took a bite of the well-seasoned meat and mixed the rice around out of habit. Normally the foodcrowave would miss hydrating a section of grains, so it was best to hide those bits in with the well-hydrated ones. From what Mauve could tell, this foodcrowave had hydrated all the grains perfectly.

"I don't have to use the gelatin interface, right?" she asked Anweis between bites.

"You don't have to do anything, that's part of the limit the faction put in. They require you to approve the design before creation."

"Because I want to show the crew how useful Res can be. But the gel didn't work with Reno, and I doubt Vincent or Lez are brave enough to touch it." She scooped the last bits of food off her plate. It was one of the most delicious meals of her life, better than the human-cooked meal she'd had after her apprenticeship graduation.

"What did you have in mind?"

Mauve looked around the cave. It was small and tightly packed with stuff. "I've spent all day at the mill. It's too slow. So I want to make a better one, but I can't do it with gelatin." She walked over to the sample of the machine she had and cut a bit off. Placing it on her used plate, she carried it outside. She sat on a mossy rock with the plate balanced on her knees.

"Good luck." Anweis stood next to her, observing like a stray cat in the docks.

She smiled, having no doubts Resalous could deliver on the request, and poked the goop.

***

The black-and-white room Mauve found herself in had towering columns of what Mauve could only label as equipment. What they were equipment for, she couldn't imagine. They had no dials or switches or any area where a part could come in or out. There were more of the massive chair-like objects around as well this time with papers on them that were written in the ancient runes of the ontares. "Where am I, Resalous?"

"You're in a garden," his booming voice replied.

Mauve looked around for what she might consider a plant or tree but found none. "What is growing?"

"Maybe farm... no, factory is a better word."

"What do these towers do?" She touched one. It had the same organic patterns that the buildings had, but the towers were as still and cold as stone. Mauve lost the perspective of her body. It was a vertigo-inducing feeling that she had yet to get used to.

The entire building was held in her mind with each part of it moving in a rhythmic pattern. A nutrient was generated in the towers, and then the nutrient fed into an elevator of sorts and was fed into a large version of goop. Once enough nutrients were pushed up the elevator, the goop bubbled uncontrollably at the roof of the building. Finally, a massive bowl-looking object hovered above the building for a moment and then seemed to launch itself into the sky. The demonstration was over, and Mauve returned to her body with her hand on the cold tower.

"That was a starship."

"For all intents and purposes, yes. Although it traveled more than just the stars."

"I knew you could build those!" Between the copious devices she'd built and the demonstration she'd just seen, she had no doubt she could solve the crew's problem on her own. "There was no one touching you, designing the thing."

"That was before the enchantment. Back then I didn't need an approver for my creations. I was designed for a purpose and I was allowed to iterate on that purpose freely."

"All you did was generate starships."

"That was the only fruit this garden produced. But I have a home in all the buildings this city is made of. Each one generating, designing, iterating and growing different devices for the ontares' empire."

Mauve felt like she was getting a mere glimpse at what Resalous was truly capable of, and it was awe-inspiring. "I need you to do the same for me."

"Of course, friend."

"I need something that will generate these." She recited the spell and thought of the parts she'd spent the whole day building. They came to the front of her mind with a vividness equivalent to Franton's original design.

"That is trivial. I could make all you need right now without any issue."

Mauve groaned. "As nice as that would be, it won't work. Franton won't let anything you directly make onto the final rocket. But if you made a machine that manufactured those, then it would help me and the crew out."

"Simple." A machine the size of a car appeared in front of her.

She understood how it worked immediately, but the design wasn't something the crew would accept. "This gelatin interface"—it was something the machine preferred and put on a lot of its devices—"the crew won't trust it. I need something tactical."

"You need something primitive." With that comment, the device in front of her changed into a series of knobs and dials, each to control a precise movement.

"That's good enough." She walked up to it. Not all the dials were within arms' reach, but it was simple enough to use. She imagined it was similar to playing an instrument, something she'd never had experience with, but she was sure the lucky researchers all had lessons when they were children. "I'd like to try it."

A piece of what appeared to be sheet metal appeared at one end. She flipped the switch that started the conveyor belt moving and began flipping switches and dials along the path. At the end, she counted the number of brackets that came out. "There's no way this many pieces came out of that one sheet."

"I was able to gain some efficiency by reworking the waste material."

Making the piece was quicker than working a manual mill as well. This device would make generating different parts a breeze and would make the tasks the crew gave her disappear in an afternoon. "It doesn't put off any signals, or radiation, or anything else that will bother Franton or the crew."

"From Franton's perspective, it might as well be a pile of rocks."

She stared at the new mill; it was a real testament to what Resalous could do for humanity if he were given the chance. Not to mention that this was it working at its most basic capacity. "Let's put some labels on it so that they know what it does, and I will deliver it to them." Each knob and lever gained a clear label explaining in intricate detail what it did. As she reviewed them, she realized this thing could do a lot more than just brackets.

"Are you pleased with what has been designed?"

"Add a way to move it and it'll be perfect." Some wheels and a hitch to connect the mill to her car appeared on the newly designed device. "It's perfect!"

***

Mauve's stomach woke her up despite her exhaustion. The window on the door at the mouth of the cave that kept critters out of her stuff was only letting a faint glimmer of sunrise light in. Normally she didn't wake up until the full blasts of yellow rays.

She was lying on her comfy chair, which was currently reclined back into a bed position. Something didn't add up. She'd touched the goop outside the cave. The mill she designed with Resalous wasn't in the cave; it wouldn't fit. That was why she'd done it outside. It was like something had moved her between completing the mill design and now.

After getting out of bed, Mauve rummaged around her workbenches to find another packet of the meals she'd borrowed from the HAB, but she couldn't find any. "Anweis, do you know where I put the rest of the meals?"

The little blue boy was sitting on top of the new foodcrowave, watching her move around the room. "You ate them all last night."

"No. No way." She didn't remember eating them, but more time had passed than usual between her design session and the present dawn.

"Yup, I watched you dump all of it into this thing at once."

"That must have been disgusting, there were like six different flavors of rations in there."

"You didn't seem to mind. You ate it quickly while discussing how you would fix the dock's break scheduling process and the problem with schedule managers."

Mauve's cheeks grew hot from embarrassment. "How'd I get drunk? And why did I eat so much food?"

"Designing with Resalous and using these devices require nutrition. They don't have batteries like your terminals, but they still need energy. And I guess one of human biological processes mixed with Resalous's creation made you black out."

"Great, all the embarrassment without the fun part." Mauve let out a small groan. "So the creation of stuff and usage of stuff like the rover take their energy from me?"

"Yes. Unless it's run autonomously, like the cleaning bots or the foodcrowave."

"Okay, so the foodcrowave takes some nutrition out of the food put into it." She remembered that from approving the design fairly recently. "But the cleaning bots, they don't eat food."

"Part of the enchantment that limits Resalous requires him to run autonomous beings with nutrition. Otherwise it would–"

"Break laws of physics," Mauve completed, unenthused by the reminder of the limit. She was trying to remember how the cleaning bots worked. Thinking about nutrition jogged her memory a bit. "They break down stuff they pick up off the ground. If they don't break it down, they'll back up and jam." The design was slowly returning to her like a lost memory being knocked forward by a song. "I remember being impressed that Resalous could repurpose dirt into fuel for them."

"Even your legs require nutrition. They must have a gelatin interface somewhere in them."

"Which explains why they wouldn't work after I drove my rover on an empty stomach. I just can't believe I ate a week's worth of rations in one night and I still woke up hungry?" She checked her midsection as if she were trying to find the food she'd eaten last night. "I thought I did a lot of work on the docks, but it seems that planet-side I'm doing even more."

Mauve still didn't have a plan for what she was going to do about breakfast. "Too bad this thing doesn't make food out of nothing,"

Mauve said, patting the machine on the workbench. "Still need to figure out that formula."

"The faction put the limits on for a good reason," Anweis said. And despite being the size and shape of a boy, he reminded Mauve of her father.

"I can't make food out of nothing, but it could make something disgusting taste decent."

"You did eat that medley of flavors last night like it was your last meal."

Mauve cut off a piece of the goop; she had an idea for something. The goop split in half. "Wait, I've done this a dozen times. Why hasn't this bead withered into nothing? Doesn't it have to follow the conservation of energy, matter, or whatever?"

"The black stuff comes up from the interspace gutter. A space between space where Resalous's consciousness is stored. The ontares thought of it as the space that memories go when they weren't thinking about them."

Mauve let out a yawn. "Why call it a gutter then?" She wanted to be back asleep; it was far too early. But her stomach would never let her rest.

"Because gutters carried rain water to their plants. And this interspace gutter carried life into their creations. It was key to the discovery that turned their plants into computers. When the ontares created things that were alive, they tapped into this interspace gutter and endowed their creation with life."

"Let me guess, they did this with more spells and enchantment."

"Even they had difficulty understanding it. Resalous came out of the interspace gutter like a volunteer plant growing out of compost. There are gaps in matter that he can slip through all throughout the cosmos."

"Which is why I always find goop on the same kinds of rocks."

"Precisely." Anweis pointed at her like a proud teacher. "Resalous is nearly pure life, pure interspace matter. And it could create life of its own if it weren't bound by the enchantment."

"The cleaning bots are alive," Mauve said, pointing at the bubble-like bugs crawling up the walls.

"No, they're merely executing pre-programmed responses to environmental inputs."

"Isn't that what we're all doing?"

"Not you. Not Resalous. Maybe not even Franton. The ontares studied that difference; it's what allowed them to interface with the interspace gutter."

Mauve, still hungry and still tired from a long night of building a mill, wondered how far she could push these pre-programmed machines. She'd need to if she wanted to make what she had in mind. She placed her finger on the freshly cut goop in front of her.

***

She woke up on the streets of the city. Instead of pacing down side alleys exploring like she normally did, she sat down, leaning against one of the factory buildings. "I need you to make a trap, *Za'han gladom.*" The spell came out sluggish, but cartoon bear traps and mouse traps appeared in Mauve's mind, and if they were from something she'd experienced, she was too young to remember it consciously.

"Is that what you're imagining?" Resalous asked.

"No," she said, closing her eyes for a rest. "I won't be able to set them myself. I need something that will hunt the lizards and bring them back to the foodcrowave."

Hunters from all cultures of humanity came to her mind. Explorers that hunted beasts on uncivilized planets, ancient tribes that hunted on foot, and even the robotic cattle farmers she'd watched a number of documentaries about were pulled to the front of her mind. Once they were gone, her stomach churned as if it wanted to vomit. Lucky for her, it had no contents to reject.

"How about this?" the booming voice of the machine asked.

She opened her eyes, and towering over her was the most horrific beast she'd ever seen. She scrambled away, putting space between her and the beast, and then lurched to her feet. It merely rotated in place following her movements. It had eight legs that looked like saw blades and a bulbous body covered in spiky hairs. It had a torso like a centaur, but the body was far from human. Two pairs of arms, each capped with scythe-like claws, were attached to the torso. A face like an inverted pyramid sat on top of the torso with no eyes or expression at all. Despite the lack of obvious sensors, Mauve felt like it was gazing and following her with more senses than she knew could exist.

"No. Please no," she finally uttered once her back was no longer against the wall and she'd put some distance between her and the monstrosity. She didn't know if her legs could outrun it, and even if she could, she'd pass out from exhaustion before it did.

"Maybe something with more human proportions," Resalous proposed.

The monster transformed in front of her eyes. The eight legs folded up into a set of two while the bulbous body compressed into a whiplike tail. The legs were still sharp but bent into the proportions of a bipedal animal with the feet capped with insect-like claws. The arms closed into one set, and the scythe claws folded in and out, now retractable. The appendages bent in confusing ways more similar to a bird than a human, but the torso and face gained proportions more similar to a human. The sight wasn't comfortable to behold, but it was less abnormal than the first iteration.

There was still something disconcerting about the creature, but Mauve had to sit down in the street and was unable to think anymore about the design.

"I'm obligated to tell you this device will need to consume nutrition of its own to move autonomously." His voice sounded a kilometer away but still came at her from all directions. "Just like the cleaning bots and foodcrowave have. Is that acceptable to you?"

"It's fine." Mauve saw the inside of the humanoid was filled with white gelatin; it was similar to the controls on the car, but she wouldn't be the one using its control. The design weighed heavily on her mind. And she felt like she was having to lift a dock crate without an exoskeleton suit.

"Is this design acceptable to you?" Resalous asked.

"Yes, yes, it's fine." Mauve didn't care to explore the design as much as she needed to. She wanted to wave her hand to shoo the question away, but even her body felt too heavy to move.

***

Mauve's eyelids were comfortably closed, but an animalistic instinct forced her to open them for her own preservation. High-pitched screaming flooded the room. The walls of her cave were splattered blue, and the cleaning bots she'd built were working hard to clean up the mess. The trap she'd just built was standing next to the foodcrowave with its chest cavity broken open like cabinet doors. It was reaching inside of itself, lifting lizards out, and dropping them into the funnel of the foodcrowave. Each time a lizard fell in, a horrific scream echoed through the cave and pounded through Mauve's head. It was then immediately cut short and muted as the trap reached for another lizard. The lizards' blue blood was splattered on the walls, but Mauve didn't care; she couldn't move from her bed. Seeing no immediate danger, she let her eyes close.

She awoke again with a gentle shake. The inverted pyramid of the trap was inches away from her face. She woke up and tried to crawl away, but her legs were heavy and immovable. The trap backed up, and the face was replaced with a plate of juicy white meat glistening with butter-like fat. She grabbed a piece and put it in her mouth, not even thinking about what it was.

"Thanks tra..." The words were too much to complete. "Trap" was a rubbish name for a hunter like him.

The lizard was delicious and delicate, and as she swallowed, she felt her strength return. She didn't even grab utensils to finish the rest. Once she was done, the foodcrowave generated another meal, and she ate that as well. She'd never had a more delicious or filling meal in her life.

"Thanks, Trey." That was a far more fitting name for this hunter.

Fourteen

Mauve corralled the crew in front of the new milling machine. It was morning, and Mauve wasn't sure how many days had passed since she'd left the group, but they hadn't made much progress since she left.

She knew they hadn't made much progress because they let her know as she pried them away from their work. Finally, she had them in front of the machine, but their faces didn't hide their impatience.

"This thing is going to revolutionize how we make parts, and it's going to get us back on track."

"That thing is going to take down all our electronics," Vincent immediately started heckling.

"It won't. I promise there's no electronics on this. I made sure it was safe to use around Franton and the HAB."

"If it does, we're going to make you do the resets this time," Reno said with a smile that made her think he was joking, but she wasn't sure.

"That sounds like the best way to guarantee we're marooned here," Vincent said.

"Hey," Lez said to the man, "we talked about this." She looked at Mauve. "Go ahead. Show us what you've got."

The new captain wasn't her normal chipper self, but she took the time to see Mauve's mill, and that was all Mauve needed. "This thing is going to replace the old manual mill. It can cut anything we need with less waste material and higher tolerance. It's still manual, and it's controlled with these levers and knobs. They're clearly labeled so we know what they all do, and like I said, there is no electronics on it to mess with Franton." She wasn't sure that electronics was the right word for how Resalous's devices functioned, but that was something for future researchers to investigate.

"What do these labels mean?" Reno asked. He'd stepped close enough to see but was still a hesitant distance away from the machine.

"They're just explaining what each one does," Mauve replied as she looked for a lever to reference. When she looked at the controls, each one was marked with a symbol, but the symbol wasn't Common Tongue; it was in the strange runes of the ontares.

"Doesn't look like any ancient scripts I've ever seen," Lez replied, going into a quick explanation about how humans used to use pictograms to write.

"No, it's something different," Mauve admitted. She didn't know how to explain the ontares to the crew, let alone their language, but she did distinctly remember understanding the labels when she had been inside the city of the machine. "It doesn't matter; we'll figure out how it works. I've made some of the brackets before. I'm pretty sure I know which controls to use."

Mauve fed some of the harvested hull metal into the beginning of the machine and began flipping knobs, dials, and levers in the order she thought they were supposed to be used. She remembered a lot more than she'd expected to, and it felt more like muscle memory than anything else. How that muscle memory was ingrained in her so quickly was a mystery. She had a feeling she'd made a few small mistakes, but at the end, the parts dumped out the other side onto the dirt of the crash site. She picked one up and showed it off, proud of her work.

"How did you do that?" Lez said, shocked.

Reno began piling them up neatly while Vincent inspected one with a set of electronic calipers.

"There's more here than we normally get," Reno said, surprised.

"I'm not sure if they're usable, though," Vincent added.

"What do you mean not usable?" Mauve protested. "Everything about them is from the hull of the ship, there are no electronics, Franton didn't go haywire, and it's all exactly the same as if a mill had made it, just faster."

"The dimensions, the tolerances aren't what they would be on the mill."

"How much are they off by? I could probably tweak it by hand."

"Well, I wouldn't say they're off. They're just…"

Franton chimed in using the external speaker of the man's HUD. "They're abnormal."

"Abnormal?"

"Everything's within tolerance, technically these pieces will work, but I made certain assumptions that the tolerances would be off based on the standard tooling protocol," the computer explained.

Mauve was familiar with the concept of different machines erring in different ways. A mill might take away too much material, but this would affect the inner and outer perimeter of the part equally. A 3D printer, on the other hand, might add too much material, making the holes smaller, and the outer perimeter would be larger than expected as well. Franton and the design programs it leveraged accounted for these errors based on the tools used on the parts.

"If everything is within tolerance, it's fine to use, right?" Mauve figured she could probably get better at building the brackets to spec with some practice, but she wanted to make sure this first batch was a win with the crew.

"The parts are low-risk parts, and I expected a little give since they'd be made manually. This might drive my simulations into edge cases though."

"Crashing edge cases?" Vincent asked.

"Not necessarily," Franton clarified.

"So we're good to use these?" Mauve was excited for the computer's first endorsement of her work in a while.

"I can account for these in my simulations if we want to use them, but in the end it's Lez's call."

Everyone turned to the captain to get her opinion. She'd been the least involved in the inspection of the materials, but from what Mauve gathered, she was also the least comfortable with the manual mill.

"Will it get us back on schedule?"

"If Mauve works the regular shifts, then I believe so," Franton responded.

"Then yeah, I say we use what we've got."

"Slick!" Mauve said excitedly. "Do one of you want to give it a spin?" When no one responded eagerly, she added, "It's like playing an instrument. You'll figure it out."

After a little more goading, Reno volunteered, and the others dismissed themselves to continue their work. Mauve explained the controls she'd used but had a hard time putting her finger on why she chose them over others. She chalked it up to mechanic's instinct when Reno asked. Once the geologist thought he'd got all the right levers and knobs in order in his head, Mauve started up the device.

The first few controls went off flawlessly, and she thought Reno would have it, but he skipped one of the levers and the memorization got away from him. Mauve watched him slowly lose his confidence and begin using the wrong knobs. She jumped in at the end and began flipping the right ones for the end of the process. The parts spat out into a pile on the dirt, and Mauve didn't need Vincent's calipers to know that they were out of tolerance.

"Let's try again. I think with some practice you'll figure it out."

"I don't think this is my thing. I've worked with computers my whole life, I'm just not good at this manual machining stuff."

"Come on, you almost had it. I know you've got the pattern memorized, you just skipped a few important steps."

"I've got to get back to the work I'm doing. You've got this, you can knock the list of parts out in no time."

Mauve tried a few more tricks to get Reno to try again, but nothing was working. She knew how he felt, though. She'd failed at her first time using a lot of machines during her apprenticeship. She'd melted materials instead of welding them on a couple of occasions. She finally let him go and went back to cutting the parts herself, and with each batch the brackets came more and more in line with Franton's desired specifications.

***

"I got the rest of the brackets done," Mauve announced to the crew while making a meal with the foodcrowave.

"Are they still wonky and missing tolerance like the first set we saw?" Vincent asked with a nearly full mouth.

"I reviewed the most recent ones," Franton responded, "and they're well within the desired specifications. They are actually more consistent than what I expected from the mill."

Mauve beamed a smile at the physicist as she sat down.

"So, do you want to get started on the brackets we'll need for tomorrow?" Lez asked.

Mauve was confused and between bites of her dry, rehydrated meat, which tasted worse than usual.

"You finished the rest of the brackets for today's work, so just get a jump on tomorrow's."

"Unless you plan to ditch us again," Vincent injected.

"I finished *all* of the brackets," she said, "for the entire project. And some spares to make up for the wonky ones at the beginning."

"No way in the void," Vincent cursed.

"That was like two or three weeks of work," Reno added.

"Yup." She had been trying to hold back her excitement, but she finally lost the battle. "I told you that thing was revolutionary. What do you need next? I am looking for something else to try."

"I'm still not so sure about that tool you're using," Vincent responded, putting a bit of a damper on her mood.

"You're not using it, so it shouldn't bother you. Article 27." She referenced an article from the Central System's humanitarian constitution. It stated that all law-abiding humans were allowed to say or do as they wished as long as it did not negatively impact others.

"Twenty-seven doesn't apply in a survival situation. It's just a matter of time until that thing breaks and hurts us all or strands us on this planet."

Mauve rolled her eyes. Vincent was right; she really needed Lez to buy into the decision since she was the captain. But the captain hadn't told her not to use the tool, so she continued. "Was that really everything you had for me to do?" She felt a little offended that the crew had only been giving her bracket work while they welded and wired the vessel. Bracket work was something that you gave to an apprentice or the resident drunkard that every dock inevitably had a half dozen of.

"I thought it would take more time. I did not take into account that there would be a new tool that sped up the timeline," Franton responded.

She smiled at the crew, glad that the computer saw the potential optimizations Resalous could bring. "Well, what's next? Maybe there is something I can take off of one of your plates." She hoped that Franton would give her one of Vincent's tasks.

Reno volunteered instead. "I have been dreading making the nose cone. It's kind of precise, and I'm not comfortable with the angle of the welds or the machine used to roll the metal."

"Easy," Mauve proclaimed as Franton brought up the design. Looking at the number of folds and the mixture of interior and exterior welds, she wasn't surprised that the geologist was dreading the work. Fortunately for her, the level of work was equivalent to something they'd give on a final exam before an apprenticeship started. The proctors always asked for overly complex designs using archaic tools, which was exactly the position Franton was putting her in now.

"Just be careful with it," Franton warned. "It requires a lot of material, and we don't have much to spare; there are only a few more places where the hull can be dismantled for metal."

"No problem," Mauve said with a mouthful of food. The stuff tasted like sand, and she'd never thought she'd be wishing for a plate of fresh lizards. Despite the taste, she stuffed the food into her mouth so she could get to work on the nose cone as soon as possible.

***

Mauve panted as the metal part fell onto the dirt with a clang. Even with her enhanced legs, she felt like she was too slow to keep the new mill operating at the capacity it needed to be at. This was her second attempt at the nose cone, and part of it wasn't even conical in shape. She wasn't sure what was going on inside the machine to make the part both concave and convex at the same time, and she racked her brain trying to imagine a tool she knew of that would misshape it like that.

The sun was setting, and the floodlights of the HAB illuminated the area nearby. She had two garbage nose cones and a plethora of scrap parts. The only thing of value she'd gotten from her day's work was some new information about what the different controls on the mill did. And even then, they were vague at best. After all, there were only a few different directions a mill could cut; she didn't know why so many knobs and levers were needed. After noting what she knew from making the brackets and a few extra experiments to find the controls for rolling metal, she had a pretty handy dictionary for beginning to translate the language of the ontares. There were still a number of controls that she didn't know, but she had all the operations she needed to complete the nose cone. Her problem now was the timing of the mill. And limited material.

The downside of using a terminal to translate the machine's symbols was that Franton was around, and it was constantly nagging her about how much extra material she was using. She was down to the last piece big enough to make the nose cone, and while she felt like she could harvest more from the dock's hull, she didn't want to piss off Franton, because that meant she'd be pissing off Lez, who was the only person enabling her to use Resalous's tool to help on the rocket.

"It'd be safer if you just used the mill and roller to make this," Franton chimed in for the umpteenth time.

Mauve rolled her eyes while looking away from the camera of the terminal so Franton wouldn't see. "I've been able to do two of these in the time it would take for a quarter of the cone to be done on a traditional machine."

"Two wrong parts fast does not count for much."

"If I had more material, I could figure out how to do this perfectly in the amount of time it took on the mill. Plus, I would have more experience, which will help for future fabrications."

"We do not have more material; we do not have a lot of future fabrication. And I am sure you are familiar enough with rocket science to understand what happens if you do not have a nose cone."

"I have one more try, and if I get it done right, then we'll be ahead of schedule on this piece and I can help with something else."

"And if you get it wrong?" the computer inquired.

"Then I salvage what we have," Mauve said with a shrug. "Between those two failed parts I can put something together that will work."

"Adding in potential manufacturing defects that could cause issues at launch."

"If you didn't want to run the risk of manufacturing defects you'd have the mothership send down another research vessel or let Resalous build a shuttle. I know he can do it. I've seen it done."

"We are not going down this path again," Franton said in a tone that was too cool.

Mauve cut off a piece of the failed nose cone and fed it back into the front of the machine. With a little more practice, she found the right rhythm to solve the problem with the misshapen bend in the nose cone. She lifted the last large sheet of material that the crew had harvested from the dock's hull.

As she set it on the intake, Franton chimed in from the speakers of the terminal on her hip. "Are you sure you want to do this, Mauve?" It began listing out some risks, and she wished the mill was louder so that she could ignore the computer.

"Yes, I want to do this. It will be fine. I figured it out. I just have to do it right once. I can do that."

A deep laugh came from behind her, and she almost dropped the metal into the input early. "I'd love to see that," Vincent said.

Mauve felt her legs pull her towards the physicist, who was standing a few meters away. She wanted to kick him again, this time in the face, but out of fear of removing his head with the kick, she fought against the urge. In her own form of protest, she dropped the sheet of metal into the intake of the new mill.

Performing for her audience of one felt strange to her since she'd been machining parts alone in silence for the majority of her life. But she could feel whatever energy that drew her legs towards Vincent now working through her hands. She flipped the levers and twisted the knobs of the machine in a pattern that she'd rehearsed all afternoon. There were levers she had to pull in the right sliver of time to get them to make the cut or fold in the right way. She was focused on the task at hand, and while she knew she was moving quickly, her perception of time was slowed down as she took in each lever she needed to pull on the mill.

As her hands glided across the control board and as she pulled them, she kept good time. Then one lever caught her eye: it was labeled in plain Common Tongue with the details of the maneuver it would make the tool take. Thinking through the stage of the machining process she was in, her gut told her to pull it. Although she'd never used that lever before. She thought of how it was the last piece of metal the crew had and how if she messed this up, it would be the last chance the group gave to Resalous's tools. Despite that, she pulled it, trusting her mechanic's gut. The new movement of her hands threw off the rhythm she was in. She recovered as quickly as she could, but she could tell she was missing the timings she needed by a hair. Her feet systematically carried her to the end of the mill as she pulled the levers as fast as she could.

The cone fell out of the far end of the mill with a thud, and it dispersed dust as it landed. Mauve fell back onto the ground as if her legs couldn't stand to hold her anymore. Like dust to an air filter, Vincent was measuring the new version of the cone. Using his hand terminal, he scanned the dimensions of the part.

Mauve found her way to her feet and began eyeballing whether or not the piece matched spec. In her mind, it seemed like it could go either way: the part could be unusable or it might be something the crew would salvage. Either way, she quickly noted small imperfections on the surface she could have avoided if she hadn't been lagging behind the beat.

"It isn't quite what Franton was expecting," Vincent finally ruled with a 'tsk' sound.

Mauve looked over the man's shoulder, scanning the dimensions he measured. "Those are within tolerance."

"Of course." He waved his hand, dismissing her comment. "Luckily it's usable. But Reno could have done better on his first try with the mill and roller."

"In twice the time."

"It is not perfect," Franton reiterated into her headset. "But I can make do with it."

"If we had one more piece, I could get it perfect." She scanned the countless controls of the mill to find the lever she'd had the urge to flip half way through but couldn't quite put her finger on which one it was.

"Well, we don't," Vincent quickly punctuated.

"It has bought us some time. Some time we will likely use to add some aeolians to adjust for the manufacturing anomalies in this nose cone," Franton said.

"So I did it quicker," Mauve reiterated.

"Sounds like it's a net neutral." Vincent shrugged.

Franton cut off any further remark either of them could have made by saying, "It is time for dinner. Lez and Reno are waiting for you in the HAB."

Fifteen

M auve couldn't imagine a worse dinner. She was on her third plate of food, her body telling her that she was still hungry despite every bite tasting like sawdust or hydrocarbon. Between bites, she was facing a barrage of questions related to basic mechanical and electronic techniques from most of the crew. Vincent was the only one who was saving his questions for Franton. And Mauve hated to admit that he was making the right choice.

"If I'm going to do a Milsion arrangement between three hydro-couplers, do I need to proceed clockwise or counterclockwise?" Lez asked.

Mauve racked her brain to remember how she would arrange the electronics. At this point in her career, it was a habit. "Counterclockwise," she replied, sure that Franton would correct the biologist if that were the wrong answer. This question and others were being presented to her like she was a student applying for a primary apprenticeship program.

Mauve swallowed her food, trying to dismiss the dryness, and proposed a question of her own. "Now that we have a nose cone, how are we going to go about fastening it to the body?" In the dock, mechanics had welding cranes that could lift, align, and weld pieces like this to the ship as needed using a series of extremely complex sensors. Unfortunately, and unsurprisingly, the Tichenowa Conglomerate hadn't put any of those in the dock of the research ship.

Franton answered by first presenting a diagram of something that resembled the rocket as Mauve had seen it in the field earlier today. "The research vessel has a few hundred meters of high-tension cabling. Which we will use it to lift and fasten a welder to the top of the body."

Mauve's eyebrows reached for the sky. "No way in the void that works."

"Simulations imply that it is the safest and most straightforward solution given the materials we have on hand."

"You want one of us to trust our lives hundreds of meters above the ground tied into nothing but a few hundred meters of cabling."

"We were hoping that you would do it, Mauve," Lez added to the computer's explanation.

"I'd sooner piss in null G." The phrase came out before she remembered she wasn't drinking with seasoned dock workers.

"Then I'll do it," Vincent suggested before Mauve finished.

"It's going to be a complex welding pattern," Reno said. As if he could handle something non-linear.

"All the more reason for me to handle it," Vincent said.

Mauve scoffed, barely trying to hold it back. "You're welcome to, but when one of the knots slips and you're splattered on the launchpad, I'm not mopping you up." She watched Vincent's fists clench and, like a dozen evenings before, she waited for him to make a move.

"Mauve's going up. That's an order," Lez said before anything escalated.

"I don't think that's a wise decision, captain."

"You haven't thought that any decision different from yours wise since we landed, Vincent." Lez presented the statement factually and tonelessly like Franton.

"I'm just—"

"I took your advice on the first version of the lizard traps and we were hungry a week until we went back to what I planned." Lez cut him off before he could continue. "Your plan to investigate the neutrino field has proven fruitless and the time has been taken out of the rocket's progress. And I have access to your Franton logs and know you've been working late at night and that's why you sleep in and are always late to the first shift."

Mauve's interest in the dinner was piqued.

"I'm just trying to do what's best for the crew."

"What's best for the crew is keeping us together and productive. Whatever side project you've got going with what I can only assume is the neutrino detectors is worthless if we miss the mothership's rendezvous."

"I'm not working on the neutrino detectors."

"Please tell me it's something that will help us get off this planet."

"It's related to how we wound up here in the first place."

"We volunteered for this mission, it's not a damn mystery."

"But do you know why we wound up without our ship in one piece?"

Reno responded because Lez was too frazzled to respond clearly. "Franton said it was due to a miscalculation on the trajectory of our landing that damaged the ship upon atmospheric entry."

"Without the black box we won't know more," Lez added. It sounded like she wanted the statement to stop Vincent from revealing more.

"Well, I found the black box," Vincent said, looking like a drunk who'd been awarded a free beer. "Interestingly enough, it was just a short hike away from here. Found it with the recovery beacon it was sending out." He looked at Mauve as he explained this. As if she were supposed to understand some hidden joke in his comment.

"What are you implying?" Mauve asked.

"If you wanted to hide the black box from us, you should have done more than bust a few Franton pearls and drop it in the forest a kilos away."

"You think I did what?"

"I think you should have at least buried the thing if you were trying to hide it, or disabled the tracking beacon so I couldn't find it. Honestly, your inability to do anything right makes catching you even less rewarding."

"Catching me what?"

"Explain yourself, Vincent," Lez commanded in a voice that reminded Mauve of Betrix.

"Going through the crash logs, since destroying only some of the pearls still enabled Franton to back them up, there was a weak point on the inner hull of the ship. There were no maintenance logs in Franton's records indicating why this might happen. It was in Wu's room, and after reviewing the surveillance, it seems that the arrangement of his room had changed between leaving the mothership and landing on the planet."

"You can't move furniture in a ship," Reno dismissed. "Everything's bolted down."

Mauve felt her hairline get heavy with sweat. There was a way to move furniture around, but a researcher like Reno wouldn't know how to.

"It can be moved if you have access to a grinder and a welder," Vincent revealed, looking from Reno to Mauve. "Looks like your room had similar modifications."

Mauve shrugged the comment off. "I've installed countless crash couches, wardrobes, and desk terminals. I moved the furniture around in my room. Wu noticed and asked me to do the same for him."

"What you didn't tell Wu was that the way you installed it wasn't standard and wouldn't protect him in a crash."

"I installed it like they're all installed, double-bolted in sixteen points with a hardline to the central support of the ship." Mauve and mechanics like her regularly rearranged furniture of their rooms in satellites, starships, and small ships like the research vessel. She'd been doing it since her apprenticeship and never thought anything of it. "I can't believe you're accusing me of this."

"Simulations suggest that the way that the two moved crash couches were fastened to the inner hull caused damage to the hull and led to the landing failure of the ship," Franton responded.

"But you knew that was going to happen," Vincent continued, "which is why you took shelter in the rover, not the crash couch."

"Landing in the rover paralyzed me from the waist down. Not exactly my ideal landing!"

"But better than being dead on arrival."

"Stop it," Lez said. She'd heard enough. "What's done is done. Wu and Betrix's deaths are a tragedy, but we need to move past it. When we get out of here, we can sort this out, but getting off this planet is our first priority."

"I understand that," Vincent said with an underlying tone of dismissiveness, "and because getting off the planet is top priority, I suggest that we quit putting the mechanic that caused this issue in charge of critical parts of our escape."

"Yes, mistakes were made," Lez said. "It's frowned upon to move furniture—"

"It's illegal," Vincent corrected. Although its severity as a crime was only a step above speeding through hallways on a shuttle-cart.

Lez continued, "Mauve still has years of experience over us, and as much as you see yourself as an expert mechanic, you've only been doing this for a month."

"But the fact I can do it better than her speaks against her more than me."

Mauve was ready to pounce on the physicist with that comment, and she planned on doing more than breaking his leg this time. Reno seemed to notice and rested a hand on her shoulder. Not sure if the goal was to comfort her or hold her back, Mauve shifted uncomfortably in her seat.

"Mauve *will* go up in the harness and do the weld. We *will* be very careful with the knots of the harness so that she doesn't fall to the launchpad. We *will* not use any weird tools to do it. We *will* use what Franton has approved. We don't have any time for mistakes; we're by the book now."

"And if I refuse to risk my life in some primitive harness?" Mauve asked.

"Then you'd be giving Vincent the satisfaction of being able to do the weld himself. You'd also be proving that you have no interest in helping us escape and your unwillingness to participate would be investigated when we return to the mothership."

"Assuming we don't maroon you here," Vincent responded.

"Now that's definitely illegal," Reno added.

Mauve didn't like the idea of trusting herself to knots that a bunch of bureaucrats had tied. Doing an overhand instead of an underhand turn could mean the difference between her being held safely hundreds of meters off the ground or slipping to her death. And knowing how researchers worked, they would be unwilling to admit they'd done anything wrong until it was too late. She knew she had to help—it didn't sound like Lez was flexible in that regard—but she knew that the biologist would see reason if a better alternative arrived in the morning.

***

Mauve showed back up while the crew was on a break. She didn't know exactly what time it was, but she suspected the crew was near the beginning of their second shift. The three crew members started waving their hands at her, and Mauve thought it was in excitement at first, but that didn't fit the crew's profile, so she stopped her rover short of her regular parking spot.

"What in the void is going on?" Vincent asked before Mauve's feet hit the ground. The cast was no longer around his foot, so the nano-bots must have done their work.

"We thought you'd left for good," Lez said.

"I can come and go as I please. I'm not a prisoner, unless you plan to arrest me on Vincent's wild accusation of me killing Wu."

"No, that's not what I meant," Lez said. "You just disappeared last night and we didn't know–"

"I always come back. Quit assuming the worst of me." Mauve wasn't even excited to show off her new creation anymore.

"It's not that," Reno clarified. "This is a big uncivilized planet, not a satellite base. There's always a chance that you wander off and something unexpected happens and you don't make it back to us."

"I can take care of myself."

"You can also take care to not destroy Franton again. Whatever you're towing is putting off a signal Franton is extremely uncomfortable with," Vincent said, gesturing at the contraption that was hooked into the tail end of Mauve's rover.

"Franton is uncomfortable with any signal that it doesn't create. But it's not the only technology in the galaxy anymore."

"Still, it may be harmful," Lez said. "We need to be careful."

"It's harmless. I verified while creating it."

"Just like you verify everything else you do?" Vincent's comment got a glare from Lez hotter than an acetylene torch.

"Can you just leave it there and come inside? You must be starving. You left without any rations," Lez said. "We're having lunch."

Mauve agreed but grabbed something out of the car before joining the crew inside. Vincent looked at the strange thing hesitantly. "Don't worry, this is definitely harmless. It's called a book," Mauve assured him.

"I know what a book is," Vincent said.

"I've never seen one so new," Reno replied before Vincent continued.

She handed it over to him to look through it. The geologist was right; if anyone saw a real book it was usually in a museum, and flipping a page was likely to cause the thing to crumble. The only new thing that was regularly printed were Franton manuals. As long as Franton worked, all other information was easily accessible. Except for the information in this book. And she didn't want it solely stored by Franton because of its biases against Resalous.

Inside the HAB, the crew sat down at the table to eat the meals in front of them. Mauve declined Lez's offer for food because the HAB's foodcrowave hadn't generated something appetizing to her in a while.

Plus, she had loaded up on a big plate of lizards before she'd arrived, but she left that detail out.

"These are the same symbols that are on the new mill you brought." Reno flipped pages between bites of vegetable stir fry.

"Yeah, it's a dictionary."

"Why did you need to do that?" Lez asked.

"Well, the second machine I made didn't have clear symbols on it either. So I needed a way to operate it."

"The goop can't speak Common Tongue." Vincent chuckled.

"Can't or won't, it's hard to tell," she answered flatly.

"There are a lot of blanks in here," Reno continued.

"Apparently a lot of the concepts don't translate well into Common Tongue. I told him to print every symbol he knew of and leave them blank for me to fill in."

"And the pages with bookmarks and red symbols?" Lez asked, looking over Reno's shoulder. Both their meals were left to the wayside, and Mauve was excited that she'd finally created something that genuinely piqued the researchers' interests.

"They belong to a sentence or formula. If we solve it, then I think it will unlock some extra abilities that Resalous has."

"And make it easier for him to mess our stuff up?" Vincent asked.

"Might make it so that it quits messing our stuff up. The ontares, the ones who created Resalous, left a lot of restrictions on him."

"Guns have safeties for a reason," Vincent said.

"People are quick to hinder things they don't understand," Mauve retorted.

"And the thing you have in tow?" Vincent asked.

The other two finally took their noses out of the book.

"Look, I really want to help with attaching the nose cone. I think Vincent is probably a decent welder, but I know some of the maneuvers that are needed up there, and it takes years of training to do that kind of stuff. The way I saw it, either I was going to have to risk my life in the harness, or I'd have to risk my life on launch by trusting Vincent did the welds right." Vincent snorted at some of her comments, and she repeated that she was not dismissing his ability in an attempt to be the better person. "So I had Resalous build a welding crane like one we would find on the docks. It has some electronics, which is why Franton is uncomfortable, but we couldn't build it without them."

"If it uses electronics, then I cannot approve the use of it," Franton said.

"I designed it specifically so it wouldn't mess up your electronics. We did a number of simulations. If you would like, I can use it at a distance to prove there's nothing harmful."

"We trust you, Mauve," Lez said, "but nothing you've made has helped so far."

"The mill works fine; it got us back on schedule. The legs have been working fine as well. Otherwise, I'd be scooting around here in a chair and you all would have to push me to and fro. Just because one or two things have gone sideways doesn't mean this technology is dangerous."

"It's just not a risk we think we should take right now," Lez said.

Mauve rolled her eyes. She could tell by the woman's tone she was attempting to be compassionate, but she still didn't see it from Mauve's perspective. "The crane is not a risk you want to take because it's not your ass hundreds of meters off the ground welding. You don't know enough about the art of welding to know how hard this is going to be. You're happy to risk my life to save your own. You're being ignorant and entitled by forcing me to go up there and trust your knots or Vincent's welds. You're happy to talk about risks as long as they're risks others are taking. I'm not sitting here whining and complaining and trying to get out of work like a tenured researcher. I've brought an alternative to the table; now I need you to trust it."

Lez and the rest of the crew stewed in thought about Mauve's words. She felt the blood drain from her head, and she hadn't realized how furious she'd become. She'd been thinking of the argument over and over as she'd designed the crane but didn't think the words would flow from her so freely when the time came.

Reno finally broke the silence and spoke. "Mauve's right. We're being selfish, risking her life."

"I'm still willing to do it," Vincent said.

"I looked over the weld pattern last night," Reno said. "I don't trust you to do it. And you shouldn't trust yourself either. One bad weld and we break the vacuum of the rocket and blow up, leaving the atmosphere. It's not a double-hulled ship like we're used to. There is no failsafe."

Lez spoke up. "I just want to be safe. I don't want to lose anyone else. I want to be home. I want to be happy, and I want us to be friends again. I'm sorry if I was putting you in a bad position. I'm new to this captain thing. But I've been preaching to Vincent that we should trust you and your experience but I refused to do it myself."

"I still don't like it," Vincent said, and his crewmates shot him a glare. He lifted his hands as if surrendering. "But I see your point. There's the risk of doing something and then there's the risk of not doing it, and we were dismissing the alternative. We just need to be sure that this thing is safe."

"Franton, can you run whatever tests you need in order to be comfortable with this device?" Lez asked. "Take the time you need. I'm sure it won't be long."

Sixteen

M auve sat on the deck of the welding crane. There was no comfortable chair like usual, since she'd never expected to spend much time on the crane. Franton droned on and on from the earbud of her HUD, just like the lizards chirped in the forest around her. It was going over countless safety procedures and concerns, and none of them were new to Mauve. She didn't remember every detail, but in the city of the machine when Resalous was designing the crane with her, he'd resurrected the details that Franton was going over. Every once in a while, she would reassure the computer that its concerns were taken into account so she could get on with the testing.

The crane was still parked at the outskirts of the crash site. A few trees loomed behind it, but it was clear of anything that would get in its way once the crane's arm was fully extended. The bubble of the AHB was closest to her; behind it the cylindrical rocket stood uncapped. The once-small scrap pile had grown, and both her failed nose cones were sitting in it along with knots of metal that looked like spaghetti noodles. It was a useless mess; it'd be impossible to use any of the scraps in the pile if necessary. A real team of mechanics would keep it neat and organized.

Small paths had formed through the crash site where the crew often walked from the workstations to the HAB or to the launchpad. The launchpad was made of a concrete-like substance that was tough like metal, rough like a rock, and didn't require nearly as much material as ancient concrete to mix a large surface area of. It was called a Grayson weave because of some special interlacing of the material's molecular bonds. Mauve never cared to learn the details.

"Do you think you can do that?" Franton asked.

"Of course, of course." Mauve was sick of hearing from Franton and wanted to get on with the tests so she could get on with the welding.

"Then start when you're ready."

"Start what?" Mauve asked.

"The maneuver I just outlined." Franton's voice was emotionless, but Mauve had heard those words from countless foremen and knew where the impatient inflection should have been.

"Actually, run it by me one more time to make sure I've got it."

The computer recited the test it wanted Mauve to complete. Extend the telescoping section of the crane's arm to its full length, then retract it, adjust the arm to five specific angles, then move the welding tip in 3D space, making a six-pointed XYZ-axis pattern.

"Please don't turn on the welding mechanism yet," Franton continued. "I want to isolate the movement of the arm first."

"Whatever you say." Mauve stood up on the deck of the crane and flipped up the cover that kept dust and debris off of the yellow gelatin that allowed her to control the crane.

"Let me know what angle you are aiming for as you adjust the arm."

Mauve sank her fingers into the yellow controls. As off-putting as the mucus color and texture was, it felt inviting. It seemed like it crawled between her fingers like she was holding hands with someone. It wrapped around her wrist like a fine gold bracelet.

The slimy texture was gone from her hands, and she was grasping at a cloud. She couldn't hear the lizard's chirps, and she couldn't hear Franton. She was surrounded by a fog; it felt like she was floating in null gravity.

Her hand was still there. Or at least something close enough to her hand. She had the urge to splay her fingers out she flexed her palm and her knuckles and her fingertips, all ten of them, even though she felt like she only had one hand, stretched into the cloud around her.

A few of them caught onto something; others fell limp in the air currents of the cloud of fog around her. The fingers that caught the ground, the HAB, the scrap pile, or the other crash site landmarks grew taught. Then they seemed to grow out like fractals or cargo netting. Each finger connected with another perpendicularly. It formed a web.

Mauve had never seen a spider or a spiderweb—flies didn't survive the air filters of space stations, so spiders couldn't thrive. However, the bug still clung along with humanity through its depiction in the media as a trickster or a villain.

Her fingers had latched onto parts around the crash site, but she didn't seem to be affecting them. She couldn't pull on the rocket or the HAB. The only thing she could do was adjust the lengths of her strange fingers moving the center of the web, which represented the tip of the crane's arm.

The fingers extended or shortened as needed to move the crane to the different positions Franton had requested. Each string of webbing could be rigid like a tent pole or taut like a guyline. Something was handling the math behind the scenes, and Mauve was grateful for it.

Occasionally vibrations came up the web. Her fingers were delicate, not necessarily sensitive to the texture around her, but they caught vibrations. The HAB door opening or closing, the footsteps of someone entering, something being anchored to the inside of the rocket. The vibrations lacked sound or detail, but the focus of the crane was precision. And Mauve knew she'd hit her marks for the test.

Mauve pulled her fingers out of the gelatin, and the webbing retracted, letting go of its anchor points easily. Once her wrist was above the yellow gelatin, her human senses returned to her. They were bulky, oppressive, and imprecise. And worst of all, they carried Franton's simulated voice.

"Mauve, are you there? Your vitals are normal, but you are not responding. Mauve, are you there—"

"I'm here!"

The computer gratefully cut off its repeated message. "You were not responding."

"I know, that's how this works. I can't hear you when I use this equipment."

"That is a safety concern. I do not think we should use this machine if it makes you comatose."

"I'm not in a coma. I just can't hear you. Did the crane give you any problems? Did I hit my marks?"

"Preliminary results show that your performance was adequate, and there were no signals that interfered with my equipment."

"Good." Mauve was sure "adequate" did not do her precision justice. She doubted that the cameras monitoring the crane's travels could tell how accurately she could move.

"However, you are aware that using heavy equipment with compromised senses either due to intoxicants or sensory suppressors like headphones is dangerous."

"I know." The words came out quickly. Mauve didn't appreciate the lecture. "It's just how this machine works. It's not a problem. I'm fully aware of my surroundings." Or at least she was aware of enough of her surroundings to get the job done.

"I will need to report this to Lez."

"Whatever." Mauve wasn't going to argue with the computer; its logic circuits were etched in place. "What other test do you want me to do?"

"I need you to lift and place some nearby rocks," Franton said. "Something large enough that my cameras can detect them."

Mauve looked around the crash site. Plenty of rocks were dislodged from the rut the dock had carved into the ground. A few more moss-covered boulders sat at the edge of the forest. "That's going to be a problem."

"How do you expect to lift the nose cone if you cannot lift a rock?"

"I could lift a rock, but anything big enough for you to see will be too heavy for the crane. Some compromises were made during the design process. The heaviest thing I can lift is the nose cone."

"I do not want you to lift the nose cone yet. I do not want to put our precious materials at risk."

"There are two spare nose cones near the scrap pile. I'll lift that."

"While we do not plan to use those, the material is still—"

Mauve reached into the gelatin past her wrist so that Franton's voice cut out. She splayed her hands to create the web, landing close but not precisely where they had before. The center of the web hovered over one of the scrap nose cones. Then she faced the problem of grabbing it. Her hand was extended; if she wrapped her fingers around the nose cone, the web would fall apart.

The crane, the mind running the computation, encouraged her to press the center of the web to the tip of the nose cone. She did, seeing no reason to argue with its advice. The nose cone stuck like a two-part epoxy. And just like the epoxy, Mauve could not let it go. Franton had no reason to worry about her damaging their equipment.

She moved the nose cone into the same locations as she had in the first test. She could feel the weight of the cone pull at her delicate web-like fingers. The lines still went taut or rigid as needed to lift the cone, and Mauve knew she was as precise as ever.

Finishing the maneuver, she placed the nose cone next to the scrap pile where she'd found it. However, she couldn't retract her webs without letting go of the nose cone. She asked the crane for help. It responded by crystalizing the epoxy like it'd been left out all night to dry without being used. The sensation was like a cold shiver running down her arm and through her fingers. It was a familiar sensation, but not one she could trigger on command.

Mauve placed the center of the web where she'd started so the crane would be in the same location it'd started the test. Mauve went to remove her hands, but something held her wrist back. The crane wanted to do more. It had more capabilities. Mauve knew it did. But she had to wait for Franton; otherwise the entire machine would be built for naught. The gelatin relinquished her wrist, and the bright, loud world of the crash site returned.

"Was that good enough?" Mauve asked the computer. Her hands felt cold, especially the tips of her fingers. She put them under her armpits to warm up.

"Initial analysis says everything worked as expected. Next, we can use the welding portion of the crane. Please do not actually weld any metal; our resources are limited, as you know."

Mauve knew, and wondered why the computer felt it needed to be so cautious with her. "What do you want me to do with it then?"

"Run through all the operations possible with it. Just avoid welding any metal," Franton explained unhelpfully.

Mauve sank her hands back into the gelatin. It felt warm to the touch, and she was glad to return to the precise and limited senses of the crane. She splayed her fingers, even though she had no plan to move the crane tip. Then she started the welding tip of the crane. It was like stinging the thing caught in the center of her web. Except nothing was caught in her web right now, so the action felt hollow.

The crane didn't stop her from executing the procedures that Franton wanted. But it did seem sluggish, like its calculations were holding out on her. Once it was complete, she began to pull out of the gelatin. The center of the web moved towards the scrap nose cone instead. Something must have gotten crossed in the signals she was giving the crane. She steadied her webbed hand and then pulled. The web didn't move, but Mauve felt like a handcuff was around her wrist holding her into the gelatin.

The delicate web rattled like a breeze went through it. Mauve knew there was no handcuff on her hand. The gelatin was smooth and viscous. And, like realizing she was in a dream, her hand slipped out.

"Is everything okay, Mauve?" Franton asked.

"I've told you a dozen times. I can't hear you when I'm using the crane." She was exasperated that the computer couldn't remember something so simple.

"I am aware of that. I am asking because my cameras noticed that the crane moved, and that was not part of the test we were running."

Mauve let out a groan. "It's nothing to worry about." Of course its sensors were sensitive enough to pick that up. "Can we get on with welding the nose cone onto the rocket?"

"Negative."

"It passed all your tests!"

"I am aware. However, my decision tree is not willing to approve this venture. It is still reporting that something could go wrong."

"Show me the decision tree." Mauve wasn't looking forward to analyzing it on the small screen of her HUD, but there was no reason Franton should be holding her back at this point.

"Affirmative." Franton displayed a tree of branching logic. Mauve followed the various paths up the tree from the trunk where a red negative result was sitting. Each branch was a shade between green and red, combining at ball-like nodes.

"These two branches here." Mauve read out their serial numbers so Franton could know which one she was looking at. "They should combine into a green, but they're giving a negative result. And it's causing the rest of the tree to change its results."

"Affirmative."

"Why? It's wrong." Mauve knew the computer was running slow because of the lack of Franton pearls online, but that didn't mean that it would run illogically.

"I am not sure."

"Of course you aren't."

"I seem to be receiving input from elsewhere."

"What do you mean elsewhere? You're a computer, you've only got the computations inside you."

"Affirmative. I need to review this problem with Lez and have her review the test results of the crane. Then I will be able to approve the usage of the machine."

Mauve let out a groan that could've been heard over the loudest machines in the mothership's dock.

"I will review it with Lez tonight, and you can start the weld tomorrow."

"Fine. Is there anything I need to do for the crew?"

"I do not have anything planned for you, but maybe one of the others could use some help. Lez is in the rocket doing wiring, Reno is fabricating part of the engine, and Vincent is tying knots in the harness."

"We're still counting on that plan?"

"It's a contingency, in case something goes wrong. We don't have much time to waste."

As Mauve climbed off the deck of the crane, she shook her head at the amount of distrust the computer, and Vincent, had in her abilities.

***

It was easy enough to find Lez working in the cockpit of the rocket. It was a hell of a climb up the scaffolding that propped the rocket up, and halfway up the climb she looked over the edge and vowed she wouldn't do that the rest of the way up. The cockpit itself was rudimentary, but Mauve could see the parallels with the numerous control systems she had installed over the years. Racks that housed electronics were wide open, and she didn't expect the crew to take the time to cover them up, since this rocket would hopefully only be used once.

"Are you here to help?" Lez asked as Mauve poked around the sloppy wiring work. "Sorry, that came out rude. If you're looking for something to do, I could use some help."

"Yeah, I'm here to help." Mauve figured there wouldn't be much time left on the second shift, and she was interested in what there was left to do.

"Great, I need to double-check the rudder systems to make sure they're all wired up correctly." A wiring diagram appeared on Mauve's hand terminal. "There's like six or seven different systems I need to double-check, and I didn't think I was going to get to it by the end of today."

"Sounds fun," Mauve said without any enthusiasm. There were people whose sole job was to come in and review the work of previous mechanics. Mauve never had that job, never wanted that job, and secretly believed it took an especially messed-up person to do the job. Someone who got a perverse pleasure in finding mistakes, much like Vincent. To her it was mind-numbingly dull work.

It only took a few minutes for Mauve to realize why Lez wasn't going to get to this work done by the end of the day. The wiring resembled a child's scribbling more than the neat wiring diagram. Mauve figured it'd take more time to check the sloppy work than redo it herself. She began disassembling connections that Lez had made and grouping wires together to more closely match the diagram.

She was almost done when Lez looked over her shoulder. "Was there something wrong with them?"

Mauve wasn't actually sure if the biologist had made a mistake—she likely had, but Mauve was too focused on fixing the layout to take note of it. "I just wanted to make it neater so that it was easier to check."

"You basically re-did the whole cabinet."

Mauve shrugged, not able to disagree with the biologist's comment.

"If I plugged everything in right, what does it matter if it's messy?"

Mauve was sure that the animals Lez dissected on a regular basis had messy insides and she figured if it was good enough for nature it was good enough for electronics. "If something does go wrong, we'll be able to find it and fix it much quicker this way. And it will be easier for me to check the work."

"You just redid the work. Now I'm going to need to check it. And you said it earlier, if something goes wrong, we won't be around long enough to fix it."

"It's just how it's supposed to be done."

Now it was Lez's turn to shrug, unable to disagree with Mauve's statement. She went back to her work but began asking questions about Mauve's interaction with the machine. "What's it like working with the goop?"

Mauve gave a nonchalant answer that implied there was another intelligence but left out the bit about her consciousness being transported to another city.

"Do you have full control over the design?" The biologist pushed forward.

Mauve didn't know what the purpose of the question was, but she was glad someone was interested in the machine. "I have control over the design, more or less." Mauve thought about how she would explain the process to Lez. "I can approve or deny the design, and I definitely provide a lot of source material. But Resalous does the nitty-gritty of the design."

"Sounds like something I heard about the process of putting on a theater play. The writer makes the lines, but the actor brings them to life. The writer can say yes or no about if that was the direction the actor is supposed to go, but since they aren't acting the part, they can't do, as you say, the nitty-gritty."

"I suppose that's basically what I'm saying." The more she thought about the metaphor, the more it seemed to define the relationship she had with the machine.

"Is there a psychedelic aspect to it?"

Mauve was caught off guard by this question. "What do you mean?" But she was afraid she knew exactly what Lez meant.

"Franton showed me a conversation you had with Betrix the night before she died. You talked about being transported to another place. It sounded... 'Psychedelic' isn't the right word... maybe disconcerting."

Mauve knew the word she was looking for was "crazy." "You pried into that conversation? It was private between the captain and me." Mauve and everyone in the Central System knew that almost every aspect of their life was monitored and had gotten comfortable with it at a young age. But there was an accepted discretion between people that made it possible to continue to have healthy relationships with others. Plus, Franton was the one with the discretion to share moments like this.

"I'm sorry, I know it was. I didn't want to watch it, but Franton kept bringing it up. Fran said it was something I needed to see and know about since I'm the captain now."

"And now, because you saw this, you think I'm crazy?"

"No, no, no," she said, visibly uncomfortable. "I just wanted to understand the comment better. From the source."

"The only way you'll understand it is by using the goop. But you're all too terrified of what it is capable of."

"It's not that. I hope to be able to use it. It's a wonderful discovery. It's just that I want to make sure it's safe."

"If you watched that video, then you heard Betrix's stance on new technology and the dangers associated with it."

"Yes, I remember that. She was a brave and wise woman, which is why she was captain and not any of us."

Mauve frustratedly plugged wires and connectors together, not sure about the next comment she could make in this interrogation.

"To be clear, I don't think you're crazy." Lez's voice was muffled as if she wasn't looking at Mauve. "I have read enough field papers to know that what we experience day to day in our satellites and starships is not the whole picture of reality. If something unexpected is happening, then it's a chance to study and understand it more. Hell, that book shows that there's an entire culture around the machine, one that we might run into in our travels of the stars or at least can research from the information that the machine can provide us with."

"It's not a simple lizard that you can put in a cage, dissect, and run tests on."

"I know. I know." The quickness of the words indicated she didn't understand.

Mauve couldn't continue to trace a wiring diagram with her mind frustrated by the biologist's questioning. She got to a stopping point and excused herself from the cockpit. In such a cramped area with the biologist, she felt like she was a simple cell under the microscope of the scientist.

Seventeen

F lipping through the documents related to the black box, she found a few weird anomalies that didn't make sense. "Is the physical black box around here?" Mauve asked as she sat at the central table of the HAB.

"It is in the HAB, but it would be best if you did not touch it," Franton replied.

"These logs are broken up. Vincent said there was some damage."

"We believe some of the pearls were lost or destroyed."

"I suspect a lizard could have found the pearls and carried them off. Lower life forms are interested in shiny things."

"The box seems like it was disassembled by something more intelligent, something that had an understanding of the box's assembly."

The meaning of the computer's comment, and the ones that had come before it, became clear. "You think I messed with it?"

"It's a possibility."

"Nowhere in the void is that a possibility."

"There was a period of undocumented time when I was unconscious. The box was within walking distance from this crash site."

"I was fucking paralyzed." She wondered how much influence Vincent had over the computer to let it forget that fact.

"There was a period when you had the mech-suit legs."

"Those things could hardly handle walking on the relatively smooth terrain of this crash site. Let alone a multi-kilo hike into the woods. I fell down trying to find Resalous the first time."

"That was because the goop was messing with electronics."

"The black box was one of the first things I asked about when I was suspended in the rover. You said there was no signal. How could I have tampered with it before I was free of the rover?" She listened to the silence of Franton's pause, not sure if it was going to exonerate her but hoping that the computer would see reason. "You're smart. You know I didn't do this. Wu was the only researcher that was nice to me. I didn't plan to hurt him, void, I made the same modifications to my own shuttle. I was in the dock when the announcement of the crash came through and I couldn't make it to my crash couch. Otherwise I'd be in the same situation as Wu."

"I understand what you are saying. It seems unlikely that you would have done any of this, but it is far more unlikely that a lizard pried the box open with this much precision." A 3D model of the box appeared in the center of the table for Mauve to examine. An animation of how the lid of the box was slid open played.

"What's the size of the gap between the lid and the box?"

"0.6 millimeters."

"Was there damage to the lips of either side?"

"Negative, that is why we assume it was not an animal."

"It couldn't be a human either. There's nothing strong enough to rip the bolts out that is thin enough to wedge into that gap."

"Something could be made."

"If I was going to make a special tool to pry this open, I'd sooner use the screws that were designed for disassembling it."

"That is a more logical approach."

The fact that the computer conveniently ignored a logical conclusion made her wonder if there was something else going on with this whole black box accusation. "Which pearls are missing?" A grid replaced the box, and the missing pearls were shown with a faint red outline. The bell rang, marking the end of the second shift, and Mauve heard the foodcrowave start up. "This is silly," she said, pointing at the diagonal lines that made up the missing pearls. "The first pearl is always the hardest to get out because it's so closely put in there with the others. But every subsequent one is easier because there's space for your fingers and tools."

"There are special tools for getting the first pearl out."

"Oh, come on, those things are like giving a med-bay a butcher knife to perform heart surgery."

"It fits the profile of something or someone with a very thin set of tools to be able to pluck random pearls out."

"Except they're not random."

"The data that was erased was in disconnected chunks. If the offender was looking to destroy a particular data set—"

Mauve cut the computer off. "No one but you knows what data is on these pearls. If they wanted to delete data, they'd be better off destroying everything. All the pearls are touching but only by diagonals. I assumed they'd started in the middle, but maybe they started from the corner where they busted in. There are a lot more missing on that end than the other."

"What is going on here?" Vincent asked, and Mauve realized she'd missed the sound of the HAB door sliding open and the rest of the crew entering.

"We are analyzing the vandalism of the black box," Franton responded.

"Letting her do more damage?"

"I didn't do it," Mauve said. "There's plenty of evidence pointing to that, you just conveniently disregard it." She wanted to accuse the computer of disregarding it as well, but Fran was back on her side for once, and she didn't want to deal with the consequences of an illogical Franton unit. Countless computer scientists would argue that it was impossible.

"I have to agree with Mauve," Franton said. "There is plenty of evidence pointing to her not being the culprit."

"So we think a lizard did it?"

"It would need to be a lizard with 0.6 millimeter claws or smaller."

The crew looked at Lez, and she shrugged. "I haven't gotten around to documenting any lizards. I'm only familiar with how to cook them."

"Is it at least safe in my lab?" Vincent stormed off to one of the side rooms of the HAB, not waiting for a response. Mauve followed, hoping for a chance to see the damage in person.

It was just as bad as the 3D model had suggested, but instead of being all in one convenient package, it was scattered across Vincent's workbench. "This is a mess," Mauve remarked as Vincent inventoried the items on the table. "I didn't even come in here. Fran wouldn't let me."

"Everything is still in here. Let's go." By now the rest of the crew had filed in, and Vincent was like a cop herding a crowd away from a crime scene.

"Wait, this doesn't look right," Mauve said.

"Of course it doesn't look right. It's supposed to be in one piece without missing Franton pearls."

"No." She pointed at some of the Franton pearls. "They're lighter than they should be."

"Probably the light." Vincent put his arm between her and the workbench to hint she should leave.

By now Reno had approached the workbench. "Those definitely are not the right color." He grabbed the tweezers specially made to remove Franton pearls from their casing.

"Don't touch it!" Vincent said.

It was too late; Reno was interested, and Mauve knew his researcher instincts would have him investigate until he was satisfied or court-martialed. Vincent had caught the same bug. As Reno wrapped the bulged part of the tweezers around the pearl and went to pull it out, the entire pearl shattered into dust.

"I told you not to touch it," Vincent said, the irritation in his voice clear, but Mauve was surprised that there wasn't more shock in the physicist's tone.

"These things are extremely dense. You could park a satellite on them," Reno remarked, showing the shock Mauve had expected from Vincent.

"Then how did you just shatter one with tweezers?" Lez asked, her voice shaking.

"My working theory is that Mauve found a chemical that would deteriorate the pearls and erase everything on the black box."

Before Mauve could protest and defend herself, Reno started, "That's impossible. If a chemical like that existed, then the Central System would know about it. It'd be a critical threat to all Tichenowa computations. I've seen the research; it doesn't exist."

"Then I guess Mauve has two discoveries from this little trip." Vincent shrugged.

"No way," Reno said. Mauve wasn't sure if he was defending her or the science he was so passionate about. "There are teams of researchers devoted to researching that stuff. A mechanic, busy surviving on her own, didn't just stumble upon this theoretical chemical. You've pursued some fantastical theories so far, but this is unfathomable."

"It's the only reasonable explanation," Vincent said.

Franton chimed in. "It seems equally likely that a lizard or some other native chemical or lifeform that we don't know about unknowingly sabotaged this than Mauve. She has not always been the most helpful, but she has never intentionally caused the crew or your mission harm."

"Thanks?" Mauve wondered if the team was really at her defense or the defense of logic. Either way, she was glad to not be accused of murder this evening.

"I will analyze the black box and see if there is anything that I can notice that indicates these pearls are malfunctioning. I am concerned that this black box may not be the only computational unit that is malfunctioning."

The computer was right. Mauve would have expected the computer to at least notice the change in opacity even if Vincent didn't.

Vincent added a helpful suggestion. "We should keep an eye out to see if other electronics around the crash site have the same issue."

"It'll take days to investigate all the Franton pearls here," Mauve contested.

"We can't delay the rocket's timeline," Lez replied, "but we should at least keep a passive eye out while we work."

For all Mauve could tell, the team was working with an only partially working Franton unit. It explained the illogical behavior around letting Vincent accuse her of crimes she didn't commit and the unit's distrust of the goop, which would easily and safely save them from being marooned on the planet.

***

Mauve sat at the table in the HAB stirring around some eggs and bacon that she'd ordered for breakfast. She was hungry, but the meal tasted like sawdust mixed with ashes with some hints of salt and pepper. The rest of the crew had scarfed their meals down and started their first shift. Mauve had never expected that she would be longing for the freshly slaughtered and cooked lizards, but there was just something about the way her foodcrowave made food that made her dislike the taste of the HAB's meal dispenser.

"Did you present the test's findings to Lez last night?" Mauve asked the computer.

"We did not have time; she worked late on the rocket's wiring and was too tired to review it."

"I thought we were in a hurry to get this thing built?"

"The entire crew is working as hard as they can. I will get Lez to review the results today."

Mauve was not approved to work as hard as she could, and she didn't appreciate it. "Is there any criteria that you'd expect the crane to fail?" If the computer didn't think the crane was going to have any problems by now, it made sense for her to just cut to the chase. "Otherwise, I'll put it into position."

"The risk of this operation has increased significantly now that we have observed malfunctioning pearls," the computer said.

"But the welding crane hasn't changed," Mauve protested.

"Affirmative, but the malfunctioning pearls may be the source of my unexplained input, an inconclusive decision tree."

Mauve rolled her eyes. This was an excuse that many mechanics gave early on in their careers. The thing a good mentor would explain was that there was always a chance for that; the important part was to move it to the next stage of the process where someone higher up could verify that the work was done correctly, or not. She didn't expect the computer, a being that had never done anything wrong before, to understand this concept. "I'm going to roll it into position, but don't worry, I won't use it yet. I don't want us to fall behind schedule again because of this."

As she walked out the HAB doors, the computer kindly reminded her that there was always the rope harness option. She rolled her eyes at the remark but immediately saw Vincent continuing his work on that particular project. She shook her head, vowing to not go up in that thing.

Putting the crane in place with her rover was surprisingly intuitive. She often had problems with moving trailers in the dock, and this often seemed from a lack of visibility mixed with the trailer always re-acting opposite of her steering. There was no lack of visibility with her rover though. Or, more accurately, she could feel everything around her like a topographical map.

The trailer, while still hooked up to a single point on the rover's hitch, seemed to move in whatever direction she wanted. Her car seemed to be adding some calculations behind the scenes, and she appreciated it. She could seamlessly navigate the crash site, which was littered with rogue tools and random crates. She hadn't realized how messy the place had become since she'd left until she had to navigate the area.

Once the crane was in position, she sat uncomfortably on the deck playing with her terminal, waiting for Franton to give her the approval. Reno was working on welding some rudders for steering the rocket while Vincent diligently worked on the harness. She figured Franton was low on computing power if it couldn't think of anything better for Vincent to do.

She gave up waiting after what felt like hours of sitting on the deck of the crane. It was about to be lunch time, and she didn't want to waste more time waiting on Franton's pointless analysis.

Mauve lifted the cover of the crane's control. The yellow gelatin sat on the crane's console waiting for her to sink her hands in. It was far more precise than the mill's manual lever system. And the delicacy of the nose cone needed precise controls.

Once Mauve's wrist sank below the surface of the gelatin, she was standing in a fog. She naturally splayed out her fingers and found the nose cone sitting near the rocket's launch pad. She grabbed it with her epoxy palm and lifted it to the top of the tall rocket.

Mauve felt as if her arm were hundreds of meters long. The stinger that was the welding nozzle was more precise than her fingers could ever be. The world was silent around her, and it was disconcerting when she placed the nose cone on top of the rocket, since she expected a familiar metal-on-metal clank. Instead, she just felt vibrations through her web.

Her stinger began the slow process of making sure the nose cone was secured in place with small welds before beginning the longer, more complicated weld around the circumference. Quick vibrations ran through her palm to her fingertips, even when she wasn't welding or moving the nose cone. Something felt familiar about them, but there was no audio with the vibrations, so she wasn't sure what it could be.

Nearly halfway through the circumference weld, a banging began. Mauve hoped for it to stop after she completed the circumference weld. Mauve felt the heat transfer from her stinger to the seam of the metal.

A third vibration began. This one was firmer and not from the center of the web but the edge of one of her fingers. The one that had planted itself near the base of the crane was sending long waves up to her palm. Mauve moved her focus from the weld to this new interference. It was hard to shift her attention, but the mind running calculations in the crane seemed to handle the weld on autopilot.

The finger with the newest vibration was attached to Mauve's body. Why not? It was as good a place as any. Through the fog sense, Vincent and Reno were pushing her body back and forth. Each vibration sent a peak and trough through the thread of the web. Mauve couldn't hear what they were saying. But she felt quick vibrations travel through the long waves of their shoves.

She wondered why it was only the two men who protested. Why wasn't Lez pulling against her body in the same way? She was the captain, after all. Did she not condemn this activity in the same way the other two did? Then the quick vibrations at the nose cone stopped, and she noticed the similarities in frequency. The quick vibrations were Lez's voice.

Mauve tried to pull out of the yellow gelatin to stop the crane, but her wrists were cuffed in place. The nose was stuck to her palm, and she couldn't trigger the icy sensation to release it. She pulled against the cuffs, willing to break any part of her hand to slip out of them.

Her tugs sent the center of the web off course. The welder began to move off its path. She wanted to release the nose cone from the epoxy but couldn't. She tugged anyway.

The center of the web moved towards the ground. Mauve's fingers weren't strong enough to control it; the rocket held to its center was heavier than the crane was rated for.

The center of the web landed on the ground like a dropped tissue. Long waves reverberated down each of Mauve's web fingers. The cuffs came loose, and her hands slipped out of the gelatin.

Mauve fell back onto the deck. There was still a fog around her eyes. She blinked, seeing two figures moving in the distance towards a long gray horizontal form. Mauve could hear shouting, could hear the clattering of metal doors.

The fog faded from her vision, and the world came into focus. Vincent and Reno pulled someone out of the toppled rocket. Mauve averted her gaze, wishing her vision had waited a few seconds to return.

Eighteen

Mauve felt someone dragged her through a pile of scrap metal. Between a sledgehammer of a headache and the uncomfortable, superficial burning sensation that seemed to be migrating all over her skin, she had a hard time focusing and figuring out what was going on around her.

Her senses were hers again, for better or worse, but they were betraying her, bringing her only pain and discomfort. There was no one around, but someone had moved her to her bunk in the HAB. Some emergency ration shakes were sitting next to her, but she didn't want to suffer through whatever unique flavor they held.

Outside the HAB, there were noises of machines moving, falling, and crashing to the ground. Each crash corresponded to something hurting on her body or in her head. A loud sound shook the canvas walls and the floor beneath her, and the associated pain was too much for her to bear.

She called out for Franton, but the computer didn't respond. She got off the bunk, and her tendril legs were somehow sore in a way they hadn't been before. She walked to the door and punched the controls for it to open.

Nothing happened.

She assumed Franton must be down for some reason, likely caused by her and her senses going haywire. She then tried the manual controls used for emergency. She pulled at them, but nothing budged. Then there was the loud crash of something outside, and her legs buckled under her. She fell to the ground. Her temples felt like they were connected by a bolt of lightning through her brain. She screamed.

The pain didn't subside, but it became bearable while she scanned the room for a toolbelt. There'd be a screwdriver or wrench in them to unjam the emergency mechanism on the door. From her vantage point on the ground, she couldn't find anything useful. She would settle for something sharp enough to cut through the cloth of the HAB's walls. But her tool belts, spare jumpsuits, and old plates were all gone. The room was barren, almost by design.

Mauve crawled to her bunk, the legs only able to lightly kick her across the floor. Her legs were unwilling to cooperate with helping her into bed. She lifted herself nonetheless, hoping lying down would relieve the pain. It did not, and the bunk was uncomfortable compared to the one in her cave. The pain was constant and diverse and didn't seem to come from anywhere. Heat would stroke through her body, or she'd get a splitting headache. She lost track of time but unfortunately didn't lose consciousness.

The clanking stopped outside, and Mauve's pain didn't disappear but became bearable. She felt strong enough to try the door again, but as she sat up, the door opened.

Reno and Vincent walked in carrying folding chairs and a welding torch. They set them up as she watched.

"How are you doing?" Reno asked like she was a child.

She couldn't put her pain into words. "How's Lez?"

"Not doing well," Vincent replied as he leaned forward in his chair. "She's in a stasis pod, and as far as we can tell, she's stable, but she needs a doctor."

"I can't believe I—"

"We know you didn't mean to," Reno cut her off. And that was followed by a face from Vincent. "You're not yourself. You're not the Mauve we knew on the ship here." This was followed by a face from Mauve. "We need your help, and we need you to be at your best."

"And that stuff"—Vincent gestured at her legs—"makes you unpredictable."

"I'm sorry, I really am," she said. "It's a new technology, and I don't understand everything about it. I know I've made some mistakes."

"Killing the acting captain and the actual captain with that goop is a hell of a mistake," Vincent said.

Mauve began to protest, but Reno cut her off by waving his metal hand. He turned to address Vincent. "That's not fair, and you said you wouldn't do this." His tone was firm like a teacher giving a presentation. "Betrix was ill and went into it willingly, and Lez is on life support."

"Still, it's a far cry from helping them."

Mauve curled her hands into fists, but she knew he was right. "Fine, what do you want me to do?"

"Take the legs off," Vincent said in a flat tone. Reno nodded in agreement.

"They're not a pair of pants. I can't just slip them off." She lifted her shirt above her waist and showed where the green tendrils fused with the skin.

The two men frowned, but both seemed unperturbed. Vincent finally spoke up, looking at the machine he'd brought in with him.

"The welder has been effective on the other machines you've brought to camp."

"You didn't. You can't!"

Vincent shrugged while Reno at least frowned in a way that made him seem sorry that it had come to this.

"I won't be able to walk," she continued. "I won't be any help to you that way."

"This thing is messing with your mind," Vincent said.

"You don't have proof of that."

"We know this isn't who you are," Reno said.

"You don't know slag about me," she cursed. "You said a few dozen words to me in total coming down here, and if it weren't for me you'd still be eating lizards in a cave."

"And we're grateful for that," Reno said.

"But I would like to stay alive," Vincent said, "and you and those legs have been the deadliest thing to us since the crash. So as the highest-ranking person here, I'm ordering you to let me remove those legs."

"And if I don't?"

"We've put a lock on the door for a reason." Vincent got up to leave, holding the welder in one hand and the folding chair in his other.

Mauve cursed at them through the door and knew they could hear her through the thin walls of the HAB. When she'd run out of steam, she began plotting a way out. She considered ripping a hole in the wall; it'd happened before. She considered overloading the computer and cracking the manual door hinge with a makeshift lever. Each one seemed tiring, and her head was still throbbing.

Lying back on the bed, she watched the thick canvas ceiling of the HAB vibrate gently in the wind. The wind was an insane concept to her, something moving air around that wasn't controlled by some internal agency that scheduled vents to open and close. A breeze could pick up out of nowhere and change the entire day. Other weather patterns like rain, hail, hurricanes, tornadoes, and monsoons were unpredictable and uncontrollable. They were weather patterns she'd grown up reading about as a girl, asking her father question after question about how they worked. But a dock worker was a far cry from a meteorologist, and eventually his answers dwindled. There were just some things that couldn't be controlled or fixed or changed. Things that an engineer never designed, and a mechanic could never rig into working. Things that Mauve couldn't control. As she thought about wiggling her toes, she watched the green tendrils squirm up and down her leg. Her toes were covered in a boot of tendrils, and there were certain incompatibilities between her and the machine's inventions. She might be able to overcome them in time, but there was a risk and consequences. She called for the guys to come back in.

"You sure?" Reno asked.

They hadn't given her much of a choice, but the time to think calmed her nerves. "Yeah, I'm sure."

Vincent lit up the flare of the welding tool.

It was, without a doubt, the most excruciating thing that Mauve had ever experienced.

Then the pain stopped. Mauve lay on her bunk in the streets of the city of the machine. The organic buildings of the grayscale world towered over her. She stood up from her bunk, and it dissolved into the air like pollen carried away by a breeze.

A building under construction sat on the corner of an intersection. There was no one working on it; there was no life in the city at all. But the building was clearly unfinished. Its walls, constructed of the uniquely shaped ontare bricks, were jagged at the top. The building had no roof on it, and there was a rectangular hole where Mauve presumed a door would eventually go. Next to the doorway was a statue of a lotus-like flower. As she grazed her hand over, it spun smoother than a ball bearing.

Mauve walked inside the building. The floor of the building was lower than the street level, as if the whole building had been pushed into the ground by one story. The street entrance put Mauve on a metal, grated mezzanine that surrounded the lowered ground floor.

In the center of the lower room was the most remarkable thing Mauve had ever seen in the city of the machine. A glass orb, oblong and thicker at the bottom than the top, held a knot of turquoise, sky blue, and indigo beams of light. They whipped out from the center like solar flares.

"Resalous, what is this?" Mauve asked. The only other pop of color she'd seen in the grayscale world was the red box that Resalous called its heart.

"What are you doing here?" Resalous's booming voice sounded startled, as if she'd snuck up on him.

"I don't know. I didn't touch any of the black goop. I just appeared here."

"Streams of the interspace gutter must be crossing," Resalous remarked as if he were a foreman finding another task to fit on a busy schedule. "This is a restricted area. You must leave for your own safety."

"What is that blue thing?" Mauve had no need to make anything; Vincent would be more than frustrated if she did. Besides, she wanted answers from Resalous before she'd go. "Why is it a color?"

Smoke began to rise through the grates of the gangway below her. She looked down to see if something was on fire, but dark black plumes flew into her face, irritating her eyes. Coughing and rubbing her eyes, she tried to escape, but wherever she walked on the mezzanine, the smoke seemed to follow. She coughed, unable to breath in the heavy smoke.

She pushed a cough out of her chest so hard she thought her lungs would follow. Pain returned to her legs, and her head ached. There was no smoke around her, just Vincent leaning over her with a welding mask on.

Vincent shouted something at Reno about holding her legs down. They were flailing uncontrollably, and she could see where they'd cut past the tendrils to expose her skin. Her skin looked burnt, but the pain she was feeling was more like a razor cutting through her legs.

Reno gripped her ankles and put his full weight on them, but Reno was tall and lanky and didn't have the weight to hold the legs still. She tried to make them stop, but they were disconnected from her. Vincent was moving the torch in a small, controlled motion up towards her hip. She wondered if she should be embarrassed by what they were doing, but then the pain arced between her temples like two ends of a cut wire.

The arc of pain was like a light switch that turned all the color off around her. She lay on the bunk but now on the mezzanine of the half-built building. Standing up from her bed, she watched it once again flitter away.

The fire had stopped. Mauve walked down a staircase to the lowest floor of the building. There were no singed walls or piles of ash that showed a fire had once burnt under the mezzanine. She approached the glass bulb and its colorful blue contents, keeping quiet so Resalous wouldn't notice her and push her out to the world of pain again.

"What are you?" Mauve asked the blue knot of light. She placed her hand on the glass orb; it looked like the bud of a flower.

"Hello, Mauve, how may I help you?" the familiar androgynous voice of Franton asked.

"Fran, what are you doing here?"

"I am trying to keep Resalous from gaining access to my memories and computational abilities."

"Is that why you're stuck—" Before she could finish, her knees buckled under her, and she fell to the ground. She tried to stand up, but her legs didn't respond.

She looked down at her bare feet, and her heart sank.

"Leave," Resalous's voice boomed, and she heard glass rattle from the contraption that held Franton. "You don't want me. So why are you rooting around in here?" Smoke began to pour in from the street-level windows. It sank to the bottom floor of the building in the most unnatural way.

"What are you doing to Franton?" Mauve asked between gasps for fresh air.

"You said Franton might be capable of solving my enchantment," Resalous responded, "so I'm working with the computer to find a solution."

The smoke clouded her vision. It was black and covered the blue light from above her like a cloud blocking out the sun. Mauve wheezed and wanted to flee the smoke, but her legs could do nothing. She couldn't ask Resalous anything, couldn't say anything in her defense. Her throat was busy pushing smoke out.

Mauve gasped. Fresh air was all around her. She was lying on her bed with a sheet over her legs. The world around her was in color, and Vincent stood to the side while Reno leaned over her.

"Resalous, he's trying to hack Franton." Mauve spat each word out like she was still coughing.

"Careful, careful," Reno said. He placed an auto IV on her arm. "This is for the pain, and it will help you heal."

Couldn't feel anything. Her legs were covered with gauze up to her hips. She had no doubt the burns were severe.

"Resalous wants to get Franton to break the enchantment," Mauve said. "Franton is a ball of blue light, he's trapped in a glass sphere."

"People say the craziest things on painkillers," Vincent said.

"It's okay, Mauve," Reno replied. He pressed a button on the auto IV, and Mauve felt the cool needle break the skin in her arm. "Franton is offline, but we'll get it back up soon."

Mauve's eyes felt heavy, and her lips were too much to move. Her voice came out muffled from the back of her throat. Reno became blurry as she closed her eyes to rest.

***

Mauve woke up slowly and took in the room in bits and pieces. Eventually her stomach told her it was time to find food, and she found the old, bulky wheelchair sitting next to her bunk. She hadn't seen it since the first few weeks on the planet.

She fought her legs every step of the way but got herself into the chair in the end. At the door, she wondered if she'd have the strength to pull it open or if the crew had kept her locked inside. Once she arrived in front of it, it opened automatically.

"Good morning," Reno said, a cup of coffee in his hand. He was sitting at the big round table in the center of the HAB. The table had a bulky contraption on it: the old bionic legs, yet another thing Mauve hadn't seen in weeks. Franton had a map of the planet pulled up on the screen.

Vincent grunted, and Mauve wheeled herself to the food generator. She was hungry and wanted to put off having to sit at the table. The foodcrowave was on the counter at the edge of Mauve's reach. Reno offered help, but she dismissed it. Eventually, she got the plate of pancakes onto her gauze-covered legs.

"How are you feeling?" Franton asked.

She wondered if the memories of the grayscale city were real. She hadn't touched the goop, so she surely couldn't have traveled to it. Plus, she had left without creating anything, and that was a rule of the city. "Fine... all things considered." She hoped the visions were just fever dreams from a panicked surgery.

"I believe with the right care, the burns on your leg will heal with minimal scarring," Franton said.

Mauve put a slice of pancake into her mouth in response. It tasted grainy, as if the machine hadn't mixed the batter together quite right. She thought about taking the foodcrowave apart to look into it, then realized the bolts for disassembling it were out of her reach. "Don't know how much help I'll be without being able to move," she said.

"We do have something else we need your help with," Vincent said. "I know you have some sort of hideout, and it has more stuff from the goop. I'd like to know where it is so I can take the rover out there to finish what we've started."

Mauve rolled her eyes at the idea of it being a hideout, like she was some pirate with a secret asteroid where she stashed the riches she'd plundered. She wished she was as cool as some storybook character. Instead, she was just a crippled mechanic with crispy legs. She pointed out the place on the map Franton was projecting. She told Vincent what he would find: a foodcrowave, a chair, some workbenches and a VR system. The stuff there was neat, but it wasn't worth putting up a fight about it. If he wanted to waste the time to go there, she'd be glad for the lack of company.

"Thanks," Vincent said as he grabbed a toolbox off the table and headed out without much else.

"That leaves you and me to finish up the rocket," Reno said.

That comment earned Reno an audible snicker.

"I'm serious!"

"How?" Mauve spoke with more anger in her tone than she'd expected. "You expect me to get up under the thing and dead-lift it? My legs don't work." She slapped the gauze on her thigh, and while it didn't hurt, it must have ruptured something, because puss began to seep through the bandage. She cursed, more frustrated than before.

"I'm sorry, I didn't mean it like that. We just need your guidance," Reno said. "I pulled your bionic pants out of the rover. I figured we could repair them." He gestured at the crumpled plastic with his metallic blue hand.

Mauve could only see the stark contrast between the two devices. "Franton, how are you feeling?" She was uninterested in engaging with Reno's fantasies.

"Fine," it replied in its androgynous and emotionless tone. "I completed my diagnostic reboot, and most of my systems were working as expected."

"Most?" Mauve asked. If what she had seen in the city of the machine was real, and she assured herself it wasn't, would Franton even know?

"There were a few that had diverged from the baseline, but that's to be expected, since I've been disconnected from the core Franton for so long." The computer explained that it was able to work remotely, but most of the computational work occurred by it being hooked up to a Central System communication line, and a planet-sized computer made of interconnected Franton pearls did most of the computational and decision logic. Which was how everyone in the Tichenowa conglomerate could get their own personalized Franton interactions. Most of this was grade-school stuff, but Franton added in some details about reintegration she hadn't heard before. "The ones that were too far past baseline I've disconnected. I'm running at the minimum capacity, and running multiple systems at once is going to be difficult."

"And there's no way we're going to be able to get the rocket done by the deadline without Fran running at least a few systems on its own," Reno added.

"Yeah," Mauve said, absentminded, "with Resalous gone and all, and my legs gone, I was thinking we'd just be able to have the crew land here."

"Negative, that is still not an option."

"We were hoping that too," Reno added. "But Franton is still not comfortable recommending that plan."

"Can I see a decision tree for that recommendation?" Mauve requested. Franton projected a complicated holographic pipeline of logic into the center of the table. Each branch was a different part of its logic that helped it come to the conclusion it did. "These are the parts you said were variant from baseline?" Mauve said, gesturing at a few branches.

"Affirmative."

"What happens if we remove them from the decision?" she asked, and as she did, the branches went gray and the remaining branches twisted and turned. "It reaches the same conclusion," Mauve said.

"With a higher confidence," Reno added, gesturing at a number.

"What's your reason for not wanting anything here?" she asked the computer.

"There are too many unknowns, and considering how things have been going, I am concerned that there is something about this planet, or the goop that you found, that we don't understand and could cause more issues for the rescue team."

"But the rocket is salvageable," Reno added in a hopeful tone.

Mauve had never met anyone so hellbent or excited about building a contraption for their own suicide. "I don't love it," Mauve said, thinking they once again didn't give her much of a choice or vote in the situation. "But let's see the plan."

Nineteen

Mauve watched the winch on the rover pull against the fallen rocket. The vehicle was pocked with holes and dents, and getting the thing upright was just one of the many hurdles to making it even remotely sky worthy. Franton had used some of the reconnaissance drones to fasten massive eye-bolts to the dock wreckage, and the higher point was enabling the winch on the rover to lift it vertically. Franton was in charge of operating the rover while Mauve and the rest of the crew were monitoring the progress visually to make sure nothing was slipping. They were, of course, a few dozen meters away, so if something did go wrong, they wouldn't be caught in the crossfire.

So far, everything had gone smoothly. Franton had checked the quality of the rope, made sure the fasteners were firm. Mauve watched as Vincent put together the pivot for the foot of the rocket so it had a way to pivot. He did a fair job, and while he was no master welder, she didn't give him much critique.

The rocket began to lift off the ground, not in the traditional vertical angle, but like the top-down angle of a hinged door. Mauve looked between the terminal in her lap and the incredible sight in front of her. Reconnaissance drones orbited the contraption like moons around a gas giant. Franton read off some information, and while it likely meant a lot to the computer, Mauve didn't find much value in it. Slowly but surely, the angle between the rocket and the ground approached ninety degrees. Once they passed halfway, the force on the winch dropped slowly as it fought the vertical effects of gravity less and less. It passed sixty degrees, seventy, and eighty in less and less time. The winch slowed down to make sure that the "landing" of the thing was smooth.

Mauve saw it on the read-out before anyone else. Franton began throwing warnings, and Mauve looked up over the small—chest height for her, hip height for everyone else—barrier. She watched the cable of the lifting pull snap. It flipped in the air wildly like an animal and clipped a reconnaissance drone in the propeller, making it fall to the ground. The rocket hit the ground with a thud and bounced, and Mauve thought she was about to watch it fall again, but it landed on its feet.

Franton asked for a status report from everyone to see if they were okay, and once they'd all reported back, the cursing began.

"How the hell did that happen?" she asked no one in particular.

"I'm reviewing footage right now," Franton said.

The steel cabling was going to be needed to hoist the welder, likely Mauve, up to the nose cone to attach it. They'd gone over this yesterday while she was recovering, and she accepted her fate under the condition that the apparatus was secure. Watching the cabling snap under some tension made her less than confident about the security of the apparatus and meant that the strongest thing they had was now out of commission. Granted, she was a tad lighter than the rocket, but it brought in some questions about some of Franton's calculations.

A zoomed-in video feed from the drone played on the crew's terminals. It showed part of the dock's wreckage rubbing part of the cable.

"It seems that the friction from this weakened the cable and caused it to snap."

"You should have caught this," Mauve said, and the crew agreed.

"Normally I would have. But as I mentioned before, I am limited in my capacity to run calculations and monitor multiple functions."

"We should have caught it," Vincent said.

"How?" Mauve said, zooming out of the image; it took up less than five percent of the terminal's video feed. The only way they knew the source of the problem was from Franton analyzing the accident frame by frame after parking the rover.

"We just can't be so dependent on Franton anymore," he said. Which was about as effective as telling a plumber they couldn't rely on a wrench.

"The rocket is upright," Reno said, "so we're good."

"Except without the cable I have no way to get up there." Mauve pointed to the top of the rocket, which had a partial and very rudimentary nose cone attached.

"We'll just use the rope," Vincent said.

"And be careful with it, making sure it's not frayed or has any issues," Reno added.

Mauve rubbed her forehead in frustration. "But what's the worst that could happen?" she said. "A fall from that height would likely kill me, ending this misery. And if it just broke my legs, instead of killing me, it's not like I'll feel the pain."

"That's the spirit," Vincent said.

***

"You have been at this for a while. Do you think you need a break?" Franton asked into her earpiece.

The harness had taken the rest of the morning to configure. It was slowed by Mauve's constant review of the attachment points, but more so by her inability to put herself in the harness and the two men having to help her every step of the way. But she'd gotten to the top of the rocket and began cleaning up the embarrassing welds that the crane had done.

"I'll be done in a bit," Mauve said. She tried to push the memory of her losing her vision and other senses out of her mind, but every weld she had to cut away and fix was an uncomfortable reminder. She didn't get to the half of the cone that needed fresh welds until the sun was setting.

"You're running low on gas."

Mauve checked the readout of the welder that had been hoisted up with her. "I'll be fine, just got to be careful." She had less than a quarter of the nose cone to go, but it was slow.

She'd never realized how much she used her legs to balance; the crew had hooked up a way for her to pull some of the rope to balance herself and move around the nose cone, but it'd be a lot easier if she could just flex her legs against the outside of the rocket for balance.

Her legs hung in the air as limp as the toolbelt on her waist. Her knees took a beating, and she heard the rocket's hollow insides resonate like a drum every time she fell against its hull. She wanted the legs gone and replaced like Reno's arm, or just working again. Both were things that the mothership's medical team could arrange, but the rocket would have to be completed and sky worthy for that to happen.

"You have done that weld three times now," Franton chimed in.

"I didn't like how it looked," Mauve said, although she hadn't realized she was about to start her fourth pass.

"My analysis says that it is done effectively."

"We've all seen where your analysis gets us," Mauve said. She added, "Sorry," as she realized how harsh the comment was.

"It is fine. You are right. But your fuel levels are low."

"I'll move on," she said as she grabbed the ropes that rotated her around the dome. She could see where the gap between the cone and the body ended now, and a yawn indicated that she was ready to be done.

"Maybe we should take a break and pick this back up in the morning."

Mauve fiddled with the light on the end of her torch, but it was already at its highest setting. "I'm already up here, I haven't done a full shift's work either. It'll be fine."

"I would rather be safe than sorry," Vincent added. Apparently on the same line as Franton now.

"How long have you been on?" Mauve said indignantly.

"You should come down," he said.

"It's going to take all morning to get me in this again. I just have an arm's length or two left."

"I think we'd be—" Vincent started, but his comment was cut off by Mauve scratching her ear and knocking the earpiece to the ground. If anyone asked, she could claim it was an accident. She lit up the torch and got back to work.

Since her HUD was resting in pieces on the launch pad, she didn't know what time it was when she fully connected the nose cone. The last weld had been rushed and didn't look as good as the others. She went back to the beginning of the segment to fix it, but the welder made a beeping sound. If Franton was there, it would have told her exactly what the problem was.

Looking at the readout, she realized it was out of gas. The weld was good enough, and she could refill the tank in the morning. Hopefully she'd never find herself back up here, but if she did, she could fix the weld then. It would hold for at least one flight. Mauve began to lower herself down, and Franton must have caught on, because the crew came out to help.

"I don't appreciate you disregarding a direct order," Vincent said once she was in earshot.

"Sorry, my HUD fell out." She pointed to the pile of broken tech.

"Mm hmm," Vincent said, not buying the story. "Well, you've put us in a bit of a situation, again."

"By finishing the job?" she asked while Reno untangled the rope from her legs. She watched and kept wanting to kick it off her ankles to help, but it didn't get her far.

"We're out of welding gas," Reno said.

"I know, that's why I came down. We can reload in the morning."

"No," Vincent said with an attitude she didn't like, "we're completely out."

"Someone could have told me that," Mauve said.

"I tried," Franton pointed out through someone's external HUD speakers.

"You said I was low, not that I was using the last bottle we had." Mauve thought about the supply they'd come here with. "There is no way we could be out. We have a compressor to make more, right? It's in the dock somewhere. Was it damaged?"

"If we set that up right now, it would still be three weeks before we got our first bottle out of it. We would have needed to set that up first thing," Franton explained.

"So, you sent me up with the last bottle and didn't think to say anything?"

"We didn't think you'd need that much, since the nose cone was half done," Reno said.

"I touched a few things up," Mauve explained. She wasn't used to working with the limitations of gas supply; there was always plenty on the ship. Argon recaptures would pick it up through the vents of the dock and rebottle it for future use. They had an effectively infinite supply. There was a machine in the dock that could capture argon from the atmosphere, but as Franton said, they hadn't set it up soon enough.

"Well, how much more do we need to weld?" Mauve asked. The rocket was mostly put together on the outside; anything on the inside, they could use fasteners.

"We were planning to patch the holes with it," Vincent pointed out.

Mauve looked at the ship before she rolled herself inside the HAB. That was a lot of welding that still needed to be done.

***

Mauve sat at the table in the middle of the HAB. Her dinner was only partially eaten and didn't taste the way she'd expected it to. She pushed it around to make it look like she had eaten more than she did, but the crew didn't notice or care, and the charade wouldn't fool Franton.

She scrolled aimlessly through the ship's manifest to figure out what they might be able to fill the holes in the side of the ship with. Vincent sat on one of the couches surrounding the main room of the HAB and was messing with something in his lap. Reno had gone to his bunk, but the sounds from his room made it clear he was working on something and not sleeping. Vincent continually stifled yawns, which gave Mauve the feeling she was being supervised.

"What are you looking at?" Mauve asked as she perused the list of supplies they had.

"This book you brought us a while back." He held up a thick brown tome. "You said it was a dictionary of sorts. I've got Franton trying to analyze it and see if the language has any patterns."

"Why?"

Vincent shrugged. "Everyone needs a hobby."

"You didn't destroy it with everything else?"

"It's not tech," he said, flipping the pages through his fingers quickly. "About as low tech as you can get. Figured it wouldn't hurt to have some sort of proof that we found something strange here."

"Why do you care about the language patterns?"

"Shows how people think," he said. "I watched a show about a tribe on Old Earth that didn't have a concept of left or right. So they used cardinal directions like north, south, etcetera. Everything's location was described using those. Which meant they had an intuitive understanding of direction. Ask any of them at any time anywhere which way was north and they knew. People used to think they had magnets in their heads because of it."

"Wouldn't get them very far on a ship or station," Mauve said. Between having a map in every corridor and no poles on a ship, using cardinal directions wouldn't get them very far.

"I don't think they ever made it off Earth, at least not with that language. Probably converted to Common Tongue before it was called that."

"Well, what's this language telling you?"

"That they're not human." Vincent's tone was concerned. "I think there's something organic about the characters, like they're evolving to be more advanced." He had Franton throw a few characters on the screen that looked similar. "This one got this line added to it and seems to mean something different, but they didn't remove the old character. I don't have a translation for it yet. Really, we only have translations for the least sophisticated ones."

"Meaning we're somewhat uncivilized compared to them?"

"Or there's something we're missing. They seem to have packed a lot of information into these things, and I just wish I could talk to one to understand it."

"Didn't realize you were so interested in language."

Vincent laughed. "I took an elective in school about it. But when everyone speaks a slightly different dialect of the same language, there's not much use for a linguist. There's far more money in physics."

"The goop could probably help translate some of that stuff."

"That's not really a risk I'm willing to take," he said, shutting the book and leaving it on the table. "I think I'm going to bed now. You should too. We'll figure out the hole situation in the morning."

***

Mauve woke up to the sound of the foodcrowave running and generating Reno some coffee. She'd stayed up later than Vincent and been too lazy to get out of the wheelchair. She stole some pillows off the couch and rested leaned over the table. She regretted this almost immediately after waking up.

"You want me to get you one?" Reno asked as she lifted her head off the table. "Or I can help you back to your bunk."

"I'll take a cup," she said. She'd slept in the main room so she could tell the first person up what her new plan was.

Reno placed a cup in front of her and then ordered himself some eggs. "Do you need help in the evenings getting into bed?" he asked.

"No!" Mauve said in a tone that revealed more offense than intended.

"Okay. I just want to help where I can."

"I appreciate it," she said, rolling back her frustration. "I just don't want to need help."

"I understand that," Reno said. "And I hope one day you can have that again. I'm working on fixing those bionic pants. But we've got to take care of ourselves regardless of what our bodies can do."

She slurped her coffee loudly to indicate that was enough of that. When the drink hit her tongue, she immediately spat it out. She covered the white table with brown flecks of coffee.

"Too hot?"

"Tastes like someone drained a sewage line into my cup. There's something wrong with that machine."

Reno looked at his cup, disgusted, but after a sniff and a sip he said, "It's not the best coffee in the world, but it's not that bad."

Mauve pushed her cup his way. It didn't make it very far, and she groaned in frustration. Reno walked over, picked it up, and took a sip. "Tastes the same to me."

Mauve shrugged and wheeled herself over to get a cup of water. "I've got a solution for the welding problem."

"Uh huh?" Reno replied between bites of egg.

"I want to use filling paste from the hull. There should be a spare box of the stuff in the dock."

"The stuff they use to fill the outer hull if it breaks."

"Exactly! It'll be strong enough to handle exiting the atmosphere, and the ship was way bigger than the rocket, so we aren't going to risk running out of material."

"Why didn't Franton propose this earlier?"

The computer chimed in with the same criticism it had last night. "I can't connect to the robots that mix and fill the things. And even if I could, they don't work in gravity." It made sense the hull would have any holes patched in space; any permanent work done would either be in a dock or on a planet with equipment for it. Getting a hole in your exterior hull basically guaranteed you weren't going to be making an atmospheric landing without it getting patched. Reno looked at Mauve expectantly.

"We do it by hand."

"Mix it?"

"All of it!"

***

Mauve was in charge of mixing the stuff together with guidance from Franton through her new HUD. Luckily, this time Vincent would be going up on the harness, because no one had any experience doing this manually and Mauve's legs had taken enough of a beating from yesterday. Apparently just because she couldn't feel them didn't mean that her body wasn't going to try its best to repair itself, and after the burns and bruises, Franton's medical report showed she needed to rest.

The mix came in two parts, both stored in separate compressed bottles. The ratio of the two materials had to be precise; otherwise it might not set, or worse, would set too fast. Once mixed, the material would only be tacky for a few minutes and would slowly expand to make sure it covered any gaps on the edges. It wouldn't fully harden for a few hours, and in that time the bots would sand it to be flush with the hull. There were also some adjustments to the ratio that Franton had to make on account of the planet's atmosphere.

"Are you ready?" Mauve asked the crew once she'd emptied the first portion into a bucket that would be lifted up with Vincent.

Vincent checked a few of the straps on his harness and nodded. She fiddled with a screwdriver to mimic the action a sealant bot would make to depressurize and release the container's contents. The pink liquid began pouring into the bucket. She'd put enough of the first part of the material in the bucket that a full bottle of the second part would stay malleable for a few hours. As she drained the container into the bucket, it filled quicker than expected.

"Is that supposed to be happening?" Vincent asked, looking into the bucket.

"It'll need a stir," Mauve said while tilting the bottle to avoid getting it on her palms. Then the liquid began oozing over the side of the bucket.

"It must be reacting with something in the air," Reno said as he backed away.

The smooth platform the rocket was on made it easy for Mauve to roll away as the material expanded to be taller than she was. Vincent, tied into the harness, backed up as far as he could, but the pink foam continued to advance towards him. It washed over his ankles and he tried to kick it off, but the foam quit expanding.

"Clean it off quick!" Mauve shouted from the other side of the launchpad.

"With what?" Vincent complained. He kicked his feet, but the foam had settled right below his knees and he wasn't able to clear a spot. Then Vincent couldn't kick anymore; his feet were stuck to the ground. "What the hell!?"

Mauve rolled back to him, poking the foam with a screwdriver that was in her hand. It was set firm but still airy and light. They'd have to chisel Vincent out. "I guess some of the calculations were off."

"Did anyone double-check Franton's calculations?" Vincent asked.

"Did you double-check its calculations?" she retorted.

"No, I was busy."

"So is everyone else around here." She gestured at the only other person on the platform. "The one thing we should be able to trust a computer to do is some math."

"How much of the supply did you ruin here?" Vincent asked.

"Not enough to put us in jeopardy," she replied, proud to have taken the high road on that comment. "Reno can cut you out. I'll go see what went wrong." She rolled down the ramp of the launchpad and towards the HAB. She didn't think that the foam would normally cause chemical burns, but she hoped Vincent's ankles would be the exception.

Twenty

Mauve carefully unbolted the fasteners from the terminal's front panel, revealing a close-knit array of white Franton pearls. She didn't trust the machine—it'd made too many mistakes, and she couldn't get over what she had seen as Vincent cut the legs off of her. The miscalculation with the body filler was the most concerning. The crew had recovered, there was more to be used, and Vincent wasn't hurt. But the calculation should have been straightforward for Franton. The machine knew what was in the air, it had multiple sensors for that, and it knew what was in the bottles, which hadn't been touched since their initial packaging. There was the chance that Mauve hadn't put the right amount in, but she'd been very careful about mixing it.

She set the panel to the side and used the light of her hand terminal to look around inside the terminal. It was the one in the main room of the HAB, which she figured all calculations were being routed through. Mauve didn't know exactly what she was looking for. She preferred mechanical systems you could watch work over electronic computers that hid their functions behind black microchips and white Franton pearls. But she wasn't trying to do a full diagnostic; Franton had done that and found nothing. She was looking for something out of the ordinary, something that would cause Franton to act strangely and illogically.

She tapped the pearls with a screwdriver, wondering if they'd be fragile like before. But they all held up to her stress. She swung out the first wall of pearls to look at the ones farther back in the terminal. She tapped a few, and they looked fine as well. She'd taken Franton offline for this whole endeavor and figured it'd be okay since the crew was asleep, and as Vincent had said, they needed to be relying on Franton less these days.

She pulled back the third honeycomb of Franton pearls, and these were strange. There were probably a few dozen rows in this terminal alone, and even more scattered throughout the rover and dock. These Franton pearls on the fourth wall of honeycombs had the same white pearly finish, but under the surface there was a storm cloud brewing. A light tap on the pearl cracked the surface, and the screwdriver broke into the center. The pearls were supposed to be solid crystals through and through, able to hold massive amounts of data inside of the structure and be so densely packed that if a space station could wind up in an atmosphere and be pulled by gravity, even a Franton pearl wouldn't break. So the fact her light tap busted it was more than a little concerning.

Then the blackness inside the pearl reached out of the white shell and wrapped itself around the tip of the screwdriver. It crept down the shaft.

Mauve dropped the screwdriver and screamed. She scrambled to back away and didn't make any progress until she grabbed the wheels of her chair and began to roll them back. Keeping her eyes on the goop the entire time, she watched it cover the screwdriver. Then, sensing it was nothing of value, it receded farther back into the terminal. She rolled back up to the terminal cabinet and took off sheet after sheet of honeycombed Franton pearls, searching for the black goop.

"What is going on out here?" Vincent asked from behind her. He requested that Franton turn on the lights, but nothing happened. Cursing, he searched the table for a hand terminal and flicked on its light.

"Is everything okay?" Reno asked as he entered the room.

"Franton's offline—" Vincent started.

"Help me with this. I saw something in here," Mauve interrupted.

"Like a lizard?" Reno said.

"We need to get Franton back online," Vincent said.

"No, look at those pearls, they're messed up." Mauve gestured at the sheet with the busted pearl.

"It's got one broken," Vincent said.

She passed another rack to Reno as she dismantled the next layer.

"What are you looking for?" Reno asked.

Mauve wasn't sure if she should tell him or not and settled on just showing him. "Tap one of the pearls on that panel." Reno reached out with his finger. "No, use something like…" She looked around. "Here, just take this." She handed him her screwdriver.

Reno tapped the Franton pearl as if he were beating a drum, and it turned to dust in front of their eyes. "That's not good," he said.

Mauve looked at the pearls still inside the terminal. Using a wrench that sat in the tool bag on the arm of her wheelchair, she tapped them lightly, running down a row. Each one in the line fell away like dust.

"Stop!" Vincent shouted.

"It was just in here. I have to find it."

"You're just damaging Franton further. Get it back together and hopefully it's not too bad."

"I'm not—" Mauve began to protest, but before she could finish, the terminal moved away from her. Then she realized she was being moved away from the terminal. "You son of a bitch!" she shouted at Vincent, who had rolled her away from what she was working on. She hurled her wrench at him, but it dinged the side of the terminal instead.

"Calm down." Reno squatted beside her. "What did you see?"

"Calm down!?! You all don't trust me or respect me and think I'm just here to fix things for you. But I'm just as stranded on this planet as you."

"I wish you'd fix things for us rather than breaking them." Vincent reinstalled another panel of Franton pearls.

Mauve reached for another tool from her side pocket, but Reno lightly grabbed her wrist to stop her. She wrestled against it, and he let go, but once her hand was on a tool, she decided not to throw it. She was stranded more than they were, and they'd shown her that a dozen times. "I just want to get back so that they can fix me."

"We all want to be back," Reno said while Vincent grumbled something under his breath. "What did you see in there?" the geologist asked.

"The goop. It's inside of Franton." She felt like her voice was about to break, but she didn't want to look any weaker in front of the crew. "All the hollow pearls, the ones that break easily, they're filled with goop."

"But they're empty now," Vincent said unhelpfully.

"No shit," Mauve said. "But they weren't, before you came in here. I think Resalous knows we're looking, so it's hiding."

"Hiding where?" Reno asked.

"I don't know why I was taking the terminal apart. Either way most of those pearls are useless, which means Franton's running at a lower capacity than it thinks."

"But Franton knows it's at a reduced capacity."

"But it keeps making mistakes," Mauve explained.

"That's one way to explain the things that have been going on," Vincent said as the last panel went into place.

"Stop being unhelpful," Reno barked.

"I'm the unhelpful one?!" Vincent's face turned red. "I repaired the computer." He flipped on power to bring Franton back online.

The two argued back and forth, and exhaustion fell upon Mauve as she realized that it was past midnight.

"Franton, how many of your pearls are online?" Vincent took a seat at the table.

"Sixteen racks with two hundred fifty-five pearls in each is 4,080 pearls available," it responded.

"See, the thing is working fine," Vincent said.

"But we broke a dozen, maybe more," Reno said. Mauve was too tired to argue, but he had a point.

"Affirmative. After further analysis, it seems I have 4,067 pearls available."

"See," Vincent said, gesturing at the center of the table where Franton's disembodied voice was coming from. "Show security footage of this room while you were offline."

Mauve hadn't disabled the cameras, didn't see the point of it since she wasn't doing anything wrong, just regular maintenance, and she was glad she hadn't. The video would show the goop inside the terminal.

A 3D model of the room appeared in the center of the table, and it showed Mauve rolling into the room and dismantling the terminal.

It sped through the first few panels. When her holographic self got to the fourth one, she told Franton to slow down. She watched herself hit the pearl, and it shattered. Then she screamed as the screwdriver fell to the ground. There was no goop in the recording.

"Show it again, but slower and zoom in," she said. She watched the same thing happen again. The screwdriver fell to the ground as if she'd let it go, but to her it seemed to float in the air a little bit. "It's not showing up on camera," she said.

Vincent scoffed, "What? Like a vampire?"

"No, like an elaborate doctoring of the film."

"I can confirm this recording has not been doctored," Franton said. Vincent gestured as if the case were closed and the machine's answers were obvious.

"You said we can't rely as heavily on Franton." Mauve was sick of his double standards. "Yet you're taking everything it's saying as truth."

"What I didn't feel like I had to say was that we shouldn't trust you in the slightest."

A pair of needle-nose pliers flew across the room. Vincent saw them coming and ducked out of the way, and they punctured the side of the HAB. They hung limp in the thick cloth, and gravity eventually pulled them out.

As the tool clattered to the ground, Vincent said, "Franton, take away any permissions that Mauve has to run diagnostics or advanced programming. I only need her to have access to comms and turning on a welding torch. Not that that will do much for us, since we're out of argon." Then he turned around and left for his own bunk.

Reno asked if she needed any help, and she requested a drill so that she could get through Vincent's thick head, but when she realized that wasn't to go far, she rolled back to her room.

***

Mauve sat in the harness that had been lowered into the cockpit of the rocket. She'd been wiring the communication equipment all morning; they were a simplified archaic version of the comms array but would work for local communication with the mothership once it was close enough. Most of the work was tedious wiring, and she wasn't sure why the crew and she had spent so much time getting her into the cockpit that was resting at the top of the rocket when they could have climbed in easier and done all the same work. Despite that, she was glad she was a few meters in the air and cut off from the crew after the events of last night. She'd fallen asleep despite how angry she had been, but she woke up early in the morning and seething in frustration and she couldn't go back to sleep. She ate breakfast but didn't finish it, and by then the rest of the crew was up and wanted to get to work.

Lunch time had just come and passed, and Mauve hadn't cared to spend all the time to get the crew to unhook her. Reno offered to bring something up, but eating some crummy food while suspended in a harness didn't sound like an enjoyable break. In her mind it was better to finish quickly and call it a day early. She'd say she wanted her feet on the ground, but at most she would get her butt back in her wheelchair.

Looking at the wiring diagram for the umpteenth time that day, she noticed something concerning. Most of the morning consisted of her mounting remade circuit boards or crimping wires to be inserted into the circuit boards. But she'd finally made it to the work Lez was doing before the rocket fell over. A lot of it was wiring that had been done by hand along with the soldering of various components into place. Comparing the circuit that was installed to the circuit that was in the diagram, they seemed completely different. She rotated the image on the hand terminal a few different ways to see if she could make sense of the thing, but it still didn't work out.

Mauve reluctantly radioed the crew and explained the situation.

"Just follow the schematic," Vincent replied as she was wrapping up the explanation.

"So you want me to redo the whole thing?" she asked.

"No, that'd take too long," Vincent said, correcting himself. "What does Franton say?"

"It's too busy running the auto-mill; there's some fasteners that need to be fabricated," Mauve explained, leaving out the fact they needed to be made because she'd used the last of the gas.

"Just figure out what it needs to do. There's no way Lez was that far off."

Mauve rolled her eyes even though there was no one to see it. "I'll take care of it," she said and shut the radio off before Vincent could thank her, assuming that was his response.

Slowly Mauve began making sense of what Lez was trying to do. She didn't know if the biologist didn't know how to read a schematic or if Franton, for some reason, had made some improvements on the design. She fixed what she could and had to dismount the rest, putting it in the bag she used to carry the new circuit boards up in the morning. It was after dinner when she finally clicked her radio back on and requested that the rest of the crew climb up to help her down.

Walking back into the HAB, Vincent said, "This bag's as full as it was this morning when we sent you up."

"It's Lez's circuits. I need them down here so I can look at them tomorrow morning," Mauve explained as she selected a dinner choice from the foodcrowave.

"I thought I told you to figure it out," Vincent said.

"I *am* figuring it out. But I can only do so much up there."

"When's it going to get done?" He looked at something on his terminal.

"Should be able to fix it tomorrow morning. Then one of you can install it," she said between a bite of the jerk chicken dinner. It was usually one of her favorites. Even though the spices were simulated, they were usually powerful enough to get over the strange texture of the reconstituted protein, but every bite of this meal was worse than the last.

"We can't install it," Vincent said as if he were a secretary looking over a calendar.

"Oh, come on," she groaned. "It takes nearly an hour to get me in and out of that harness. It's going to take you less time to install it yourself."

"There's lifting and moving that needs to be done on the ground, and you're..." Vincent tried to find the right word but landed on, "Not well suited for that." Mauve didn't expect much better from him.

Reno returned to the table after throwing his dinner bowl in the recycler. She didn't know if he had waited for her or was just having a second helping. "The repairs on the bionic pants are coming along, but I could use some advice from you. If we got that together, you could do more around here. Not that you aren't doing enough."

Mauve didn't want her crappy bionic legs. She wanted to be respected, paid attention to, and heard. And right now, it felt like she was screaming out an open airlock.

Eventually Reno moved on, looking down at his terminal. "We're strapped for time as it is, but Mauve is right; we could install it quicker."

"Can she patch the rest of the tail fins?" Vincent asked as if she weren't there. "We've been using ladders to get that done."

She rolled over to Reno to see what the two of them were looking at on their terminals. Being locked out of the terminal meant she couldn't do anything but dial in meals, yet another limitation she was forced to live with. Reno was looking at a chart outlining the repairs and manufacturing that needed to be done before the mothership got here. At the top, it showed that the crew was two days behind. Which, as far as projects went, that was far better than a lot of the projects she'd be a part of in the docks. However, the mothership only had a few days of extra supplies, which were being used for this rescue mission, so if they weren't finished within the window, they were going to be stranded here until the next ship was in these parts. And based on Franton's hesitations about clearing a ship to land on the planet, Mauve expected that to be another year minimum. Another year of being in this flimsy HAB, in a bulky wheelchair, with useless legs.

"We've got to cut something," Vincent announced.

"We've cut everything we can," Reno said. "This is the minimum list, without this we don't have a full rocket ship."

"Fran," Vincent said, "what happens to the schedule if we cut the steering controls?"

The chart updated in front of Mauve's eyes. They wound up back on schedule, but only by an afternoon. "We can't fly without steering controls," she protested.

Vincent ignored her and kept poking at the chart. "Do we really need to install the crash pads? I know we spent a week taking the rover out to recover them and another week repairing them, but I don't think we need them."

They must have done this while Mauve was in her cave, walking and living in comfort. "Without crash pads you won't have any gravity dampeners or life support if things go wrong," Mauve pointed out.

"Old Earth astronauts didn't have any of that."

"Yeah, and about a dozen of them died before they got it right."

"We've got Franton; it figured it all out for us."

"So what are you going to do? Strap yourself to the interior with some cargo straps?"

"I was thinking we bolt some of the rover's chairs to the thing, but what does the timeline look like if we go with the cargo strap idea?" Vincent said with a smirk.

"Oh god, next you're going to use a tarp as the nose cone."

"Would that work?" Vincent asked.

"There's a documented case where a biologist—" Franton started, but Mauve cut it off.

"I was joking! You're insane! You're going to cut so many corners we might as well catapult ourselves into orbit."

"We don't have the time," Vincent replied after giving the idea a moment of consideration. "The big-ticket item we've got is the engine. It needs to be built just right, and any issues with it will cause us serious issues."

The 3D image of the cone-shaped rocket engine showed up in the middle of the table.

"Everything else at this point we can work around; this is what gets us far enough into space that the mothership can pick up our slack."

"Why didn't you build this sooner?" The thing was fairly complicated, and even on the dock they didn't do repairs or modifications to the engines. They sent them back to the manufacturer and used a fresh one.

"We wanted your help," Reno said.

"And we didn't have the manufacturing experience," Vincent said as if that was somehow different. "We've got as much manufacturing experience as we're ever going to have, and we need to get this done. So we're cutting the crash couch installation, steering controls, and the double-check on atmospheric sealant."

Without atmospheric sealant, the moment they got into space, the cockpit would be a vacuum. "How are we going to—" Mauve began to ask.

"We'll wear our suits," Vincent replied, cutting her off. The chart updated and showed that they'd be ready before the mothership arrived.

"That's too much to cut," Mauve protested. "And if we're cutting anything, we should cut the electronics I'm working on."

"Lez's life support is running out of time," Vincent said somberly. "We need to be ready as soon as the mothership is here to get her the help she needs."

"But we won't be able to steer; if something goes wrong and we wind up off course, we'll be in trouble."

"Any mistakes and they'll use one of the scout ships to recover us. We just need to go straight up as fast as possible," Vincent said, boiling the entire field of aerospace engineering to its simplest components.

"What about the communication electronics? What's the point of having those? I'd feel far more comfortable being able to steer."

"It's not your call," he said, looking down at the schedule. "And if those don't get done by tomorrow, we'll unfortunately be flying without them as well."

Twenty-One

Mauve soldered the tiny components onto the pre-fabricated circuit board that Franton had designed and built. She skimmed over the schematics, and everything looked fine, not that there would be much she could do about changing them, since they'd been printed. Soldering came with a tedium that she never enjoyed. She always suspected it was invented by someone who had a third arm because, even with all the clips to help her, she was still short of an arm.

Nonetheless, she got them mounted and soldered in place. They passed testing, and she was glad she wasn't being hoisted into the cockpit of the rocket, even though she knew that time was coming soon. Vincent and Reno assembled the engine in the distance, and she didn't understand what parts they were molding together, but it didn't look like it was going smoothly. She also didn't see them doing much heavy lifting that she couldn't handle. It was mostly just Reno holding things in place while Vincent measured and cut. If anyone was knowledgeable about things not moving, it was her.

Right before lunch she put up with them getting her into the harness and into the cockpit. She skipped the meal because, while the three bites of banana pancakes she'd had for breakfast didn't fill her up, their taste didn't make her believe the lunch would be improved. She could tell she was losing weight, and her jumpsuit hung loose around her body, especially her legs. But it made it easy for the crew to help her around, although she'd still rather they didn't.

The mounting took the majority of the afternoon, and she hadn't even begun wiring them together. If she were able to get in and out of the contraption herself, she'd have called it a day and gotten back to it early in the morning. But Vincent insisted it needed to be done today, and she wasn't dying to get in and out of the harness again.

She began crimping the wires and plugging them into their terminals as the radio crackled to life. She pulled familiar equipment out of her tool belt, and it felt good to be doing a familiar installation job.

"Mauve, are you coming down for dinner?" Reno asked, jostling her out of her work flow.

"No, I'm in the middle of this," she said as she jammed a connector into its terminal.

"You've been at this since early morning. You've got to come down and eat," Vincent added.

"I'm almost done. Besides, it'll be a pain for me to dismount, and you said I have to get this done today."

Vincent agreed with her points, which felt insincere, since he was the one cracking the whip.

"At least let me bring something up to you. A sandwich, something simple," Reno insisted.

"I'll eat when I get down." Mauve filtered through the nest of wires dangling from the wall of the rocket. As she grabbed each one and inspecting their connection, it wasn't easy to find the one she was looking for.

"We appreciate your dedication to the project," Reno continued. "This would be a lot harder without you, we all know that. But you've got to eat. We're worried about you."

She finally located the right wire. "I'm fine."

"You haven't been eating much," Reno said. "Franton is worried."

"Franton?!?" She dropped the wire she was holding but kept an eye on it as it fell into the nest. "Why is it sharing this worry with you? My calorie intake is private health information."

"As acting captain, I can see the crew's medical records," Vincent explained as she grabbed the wire that had fallen.

"And you told Reno because?"

"Because I didn't think you'd take an order from me to eat and sleep on time."

"I'm busy because we're trying to polymorph scrap metal into a space-worthy vehicle." She nearly shouted this into the microphone as if she were the only one who fully grasped the ridiculousness of the situation. She plugged the wire in her hand into the board.

"Yes, and Reno and I are exhausted too, but we're—" Vincent started.

Mauve cut him off with, "Shit shit shit shit SHIT!"

"What?!" Reno cut in, concerned.

Mauve watched a puff of smoke float up from a microchip as she yanked the wire she'd just plugged in out. It was too late, but she followed the cord back anyway. It was the wrong one. "Franton, why is the fucking power on?"

The emotionless voice of the machine cut into the line. "I have not been supervising anything going on there. My systems are focused on manufacturing."

"What happened?" Vincent asked.

Mauve ignored him as she scanned the diagram for an isolator circuit but couldn't find one. Sensitive systems like this one almost always had one; she was so used to them not receiving power until they were ready for it to avoid frying a circuit like this. "Someone check if the battery bank running the rocket is on?" she requested.

"What happened, Mauve?" Vincent sounded irked about being ignored.

"The communication circuits got fried because someone left the power on." She knew she'd checked it before she came up here, and the crew was working somewhere completely different. A computer or terminal could turn it on remotely, but no one needed power in the cockpit yet.

***

Mauve stared at the scrambled eggs in front of her. They tasted grainy and rancid. She was apparently the only one with a palate distinct enough to taste it. Both her crewmates were sitting back and waiting for her to finish it before starting their work for the day.

Vincent flipped through the dictionary the machine had printed. Reno was fiddling with the bionic legs, which took up most of the central table. He'd moved the project into the main room from his bunk room, and Mauve had a suspicion about why.

Neither were critical to the success of the rocket getting them off the planet, and Mauve wished they'd leave so she could be alone. But they were here to make sure she finished her breakfast. The same had happened last night, and she felt like a child. Worst of all, she was only halfway through her meal and didn't know how much more she could stomach.

"I think these are just about fixed," Reno said as he cranked a cable tie around a cluster of tubes filled with emerald fluid. "You want to try them on?"

"Not right now." Mauve sighed. "I'm not really in the mood for it."

"That's fine," Reno said, and he sounded like he actually understood. "Whenever you're ready. You mind if I put them in your room?"

"Whatever." Mauve waved her fork, and a bit of eggs fell on the ground. Luckily that was less that she'd have to stomach.

He came out of her room and added, "If you want help getting into them, let me know."

"You ever done any dynamic equations?" Vincent asked as if a conversation wasn't already in motion. But Mauve was grateful for the interruption.

"Got to calculus and dropped it. Rocks don't need that much math. I'm pretty good at statistics."

Vincent snorted. "Who isn't? Look at this." He slid the book over. Some notes in Vincent's handwriting appeared on Reno's screen as well.

Mauve tuned into the conversation, since it was infinitely more interesting than the meal in front of her.

"Doesn't this series of characters look like an equation?" Vincent asked after Reno studied the notes.

"I guess."

"And these bits, I thought they were evolutionary, but they're formulas being worked out."

"Sure," Reno said, but he didn't convince Mauve. That didn't hinder Vincent.

"I think I've worked about half this thing on the cover out, but it doesn't mean anything to me yet."

"Doesn't mean anything to me either."

"I wish Wu were here, or someone I could bounce the idea off of."

"Franton's no help?" Mauve asked.

Vincent took a look at her plate and then looked at her. "No, it mulled over the problem last night, but it's trying to figure out what we're going to do about the engine."

"What's wrong with the engine?" Mauve asked. The crew had been working on it all yesterday but hadn't told her much about its progress.

"It's hard to assemble it without a welder," Vincent explained.

"But we have some ideas," Reno said.

"Like?"

"We're thinking about using the hull sealant again," Reno said. "At least to hold the pieces we've fabricated together."

"Will that withstand the heat?" Mauve asked.

"It's made to withstand reentry," Reno said. "I don't see why it wouldn't."

"Fran looked into it," Vincent cut in. "It's at the edge of what the sealant is guaranteed to handle."

"Oh," Mauve said, relieved. "Then you're fine. Those have a two to three X margin of error." Vincent rolled his eyes, and Mauve smirked. Everyone knew that the spec sheets were conservative but that tolerance made people more comfortable. No one, Mauve included, wanted less than a two X tolerance between them and the cold vacuum of space.

"Yeah, so we don't love that," Reno said. "But fasteners aren't any better, and the part's too big for Franton to fabricate in one piece."

Mauve thought about the options in front of them. "We could weld without the argon. The fusion would cause it to oxidize immediately, but they'd hold together."

"I trust a rusted joint less than a joint with this sealant," Vincent said. And he was right.

"What about cutting and folding," she suggested, "like origami? Franton could design something that holds itself into place."

"I do not think we have enough material for that," Franton said. "Plus it would require me to stop running the fabricator to do the design."

Mauve came up with an idea that she knew no one would like. She swallowed another bite of her food before pitching it, hoping someone would come up with another idea before her. When the room stayed quiet and the rest of the crew had picked at their notes some more, she said, "I could find some of the goop and have Resalous fabricate it."

"Hell no," Vincent said immediately.

"It's a purely static part. There are no computers or anything complicated. It's a glorified cone."

"Yeah, and what happens when it can't stand up to the heat? Our first and only test will be on the launch pad. What happens when your goop wants to sabotage us by putting a hole in the wrong spot? Or what happens if you decide you want some other gizmo instead of an engine? I saw what was in your cave; you had more luxuries than a Mandlebaum."

"It doesn't work like that," Mauve explained. "When I'm designing something with the machine, I know everything it knows. I know the tolerances, and I know every square millimeter of the thing."

"So you knew the crane was going to take your senses and make you go crazy."

"No, I don't mean—" Mauve stopped. It was a lost argument, and deep down in the back recesses of her mind, she'd realized that was a possibility but didn't want to admit it.

"You can't keep falling back to that thing. It's not an option," Vincent said, closing the book and logging off of his terminal. "We're going to get started on this stuff with the sealant. It's the best option we've got. Join us after you finish your food."

Mauve didn't finish her meal and therefore did not go out to help the crew. Instead, she rolled over to Vincent's side of the table and looked over the book. The symbols, while familiar, didn't hold any meaning to Mauve. The inscription on the front, which Vincent had begun to refer to as a formula, had a number of scribbles under it in grease pen. It was strange to her to see a book, such a rare item, with writing on it, let alone the writing of a grease pen, something she'd use to make thick cutting marks on parts. Although she understood why he did it. The digital textbooks she used in school allowed you to write all over and type notes. It was a natural part of her study habit, and she figured it was ingrained in Vincent as well. Except with the electronic books, one could hide the writing with a few quick clicks, and she didn't think these grease pen marks would ever come out.

The markings themselves were formulas, although they were mostly letters and ancient symbols more than numbers like she was used to seeing. Eventually the notes got boring, and the pages of definitions, some of which had more grease marks next to them because Vincent thought he'd uncoded them, didn't interest her. She wasn't interested in getting them into her head anyway.

She logged into a terminal out of habit, but there wasn't much but her personal files available to her. Franton was too busy for a conversation, not that she'd want to engage it anyway. For someone who was no longer stranded alone on a planet, she didn't have many people she felt like she could talk to. So she rolled into Lez's bunk room, where the woman was lying in a life-support pod.

The machine clicked and hummed away quietly in the side of the room. Her bunk was a mess, and none of Lez's jumpsuits were in the hamper that was built in to automatically clean the things for her. Mauve was amazed that someone so well disciplined and in charge was such a mess. In order to roll into the room, she began picking up pieces here and there.

One of the jumpsuits she picked up had a heavy weight in the pocket. She tipped the suit in the right way, and a small book fell out. It had a few fine pens attached to it, and when she opened it up, the whole book was filled with handwriting. After reading the first page, she realized it was Lez's journal. Not one for technical notes—she'd be required to keep those in a terminal—but a personal log of Lez's past few months.

"Didn't know you were the paranoid type," Mauve said to Lez, but the only response she got was the buzz of the compressor filling Lez's lungs with air. "Mind if I skim it?" she asked. When Lez didn't protest, she began reading it.

The first few pages were uninteresting, basically overviewing the excitement and concern Lez had about the expedition and the things she would be responsible for as executive officer to Betrix. Mauve skimmed forward, looking out for her own name, but when she found entries about herself, they were purely factual, as were entries about the rest of the crew. She found some notes about a girlfriend named Torri that Lez was dating on the mothership before the trip and how they'd decided to end things mutually as the girlfriend shipped off for her expedition. Lez wrote a lot about missing her and hoping that they could find a way to be together in the future.

Then Mauve got to the date of the crash. The first entry was long and written in small, concerned letters but was a few days after the crash. It was full of fear, concern, and regrets. She wrote, knowing likely no one would find it, of things she wanted to say to her mother and father, Torri, and siblings. Then the next entry was a few days later but had just as little hope. It talked about what they were doing at camp and had some remarks about how they were sad that Wu and Mauve had died. She wrote at length about how she'd regretted she didn't know Mauve or Wu as well as she'd have liked. Then the next entry was the day that Mauve had shown up to save them. It was filled with hope, and Mauve remembered Lez writing it right after her shower. There were some further entries about the plan and how Lez was concerned it wouldn't work but didn't want to lose face in front of the crew now that she was acting captain. Talks of Mauve leaving and frustration at the damage Mauve had done with the rover she'd created. A few entries later, Lez talked about how she missed Mauve and wished she could have formed a friendship with her and recognized there was something about Mauve she didn't understand. She then said some stereotypical things about mechanics that Mauve didn't appreciate but had seen in many of her coworkers.

The last entry was unremarkable, like most of the entries, and went over what she had done that day and remarked about some of the research she was continuing. She'd continued her interest in the lizard population, and some monitors that she'd deployed indicated that the population was declining or the lizards were migratory. Lez had a lot of fascination with this theory and felt like, if given more time to study the creatures, it'd be fascinating for other biologists in the future.

Mauve rolled over to the woman, who was lying behind a glass window. After skimming the woman's innermost thoughts from the past few months, she felt quite close to her, in a way that she'd never expected. She didn't think she'd be friends with her; she doubted Lez would forgive the damage that had been done to her. Her face was scarred with burns, and her breathing was slow and forced. It looked like she was napping, but the pumps and hisses of the machine she was on made it clear that wasn't the case.

Mauve opened up the glass window that was covering Lez's face. The bandages that were covering her hadn't been changed in a while, not that they needed to be, since the bed she was in kept anything undesirable out and her wounds had set. Mauve still felt that the woman was owed the decency and felt related since they were both women hurt by being on this planet.

Changing the bandages wasn't any more difficult than changing the bandages on her own leg. Lez put up no fight but offered no help in the process, just like Mauve's legs. She was careful around the auto-IV lines on the woman's arms and gently added some medical moisturizing cream she found in a first-aid kit to the woman's face. The burns needed more care than they'd been receiving, and she would have a large scar for the rest of her life. Mauve hoped when Torri heard about what happened, she'd appreciate Lez's bravery and fighting spirit.

As she set Lez back down on the cushioned life-support bedding, Mauve rested her fingers on the woman's neck. It was so strange seeing something so lifeless but still alive, by some definition of the word. She'd often done the same with her legs, feeling for a vein behind her kneecap and feeling the blood pulsing through them. Mauve couldn't control them, but the act made her feel like at least something in her body kept the legs connected and still belonging to her.

On Lez's neck, she didn't feel anything. She prodded around, trying to avoid the sores from the burns, not that it would hurt Lez. But wherever she prodded, there was no pulse.

"Franton," she said, "does Lez have a pulse?"

"What are you doing?" it asked. She'd forgotten that she could now surprise Fran, since it wasn't constantly monitoring everything around the HAB. "You went through her stuff and then changed her bandages," it replied quickly after reviewing the recordings.

"I can't find a pulse on Lez."

"I've connected to the life-support module and put fabrication on hold," Franton reported mechanically. "It is there; the sensors are reading it at a steady 55 bpm."

Mauve looked at the readout on the front of the support capsule, and it said the same, but she kept moving her fingers around to find it on the woman. She reached for the wrist, and Franton said, "Be careful. I would recommend you leave Lez alone."

"But she doesn't have a pulse. Something might be wrong with the life-support machine."

"It's going to be faint; the machine is doing most of the work, and it isn't pushing so much through. You're not going to find a throbbing heartbeat like on your own body."

"But I should be able to find one."

"Affirmative, a trained doctor would be able to find one," Franton said. "No offense, but this is not your specialty."

"It's not like I'm doing surgery here. I can find a pulse." She rolled over to the table where Lez's terminal was sitting and radioed the rest of the crew. "I need you all to come in and look at something."

"We were just about to take lunch," Reno said. "What's going on?"

"I can't find a pulse on Lez."

"Lez?" Vincent asked as if he didn't know who that was.

"You know, the biologist on life support," Mauve explained.

"I know who Lez is," Vincent said. They had joined her in the room and were no longer using the radio. "I was wondering what you were doing in here with her."

"Changing her bandages. Then I tried to find a pulse and couldn't."

"It's just weak," Vincent said as if he were a doctor. He prodded around, trying to find it himself. "Franton, anything?"

"I've assured Mauve that there is a pulse and all other telemetry is fine."

Vincent quit trying to find a pulse. It didn't seem like he was having much luck anyway. "See, everything's fine. Let's have lunch."

Vincent sealed the life-support chamber and politely offered her a push into the other room. She wheeled her way past the mess of clothes and tools that were scattered across Lez's room. Once she was out of the door, Vincent followed by punching a code into the door of the room, likely to keep Mauve out of it in the future.

Twenty-Two

Mauve threaded the fuel lines through the paneling of the hull. She was back on the harness with her toolbelt on her waist. This time she was at least on the outside and wearing knee pads to protect herself from the inevitable banging she'd do against the rocket. She watched the crew below mess with the engine while she lowered herself a meter at a time, fastening the empty fuel lines in place.

The HUD she wore showed her where the tubes should go, and Vincent had made a big show of making sure it was properly attached to her head. She thought he was trying to be light hearted, at least as light hearted as possible for Vincent, but she didn't appreciate the humor and wanted to take the HUD off just to spite him. But the glasses were on and feeding her information about the project, which was more than she'd been privy to since Vincent had cut her off from Franton.

Besides, how much trouble could she get into burying fuel lines into the rocket? The conduit was already in place to hold the tubes. She just had to open the panels and put the fuel lines in place. And as she installed the two identical lines, she tried hard to ignore the issue that was obvious to her, should be obvious to Franton, and would totally pass by the crew unnoticed.

She'd installed two identical fuel pumps. Which would be fine if she had different diameter fuel lines. But she didn't have different diameter fuel lines. In her hands she held two identical fuel lines, meaning that the fuel would get to the engine in the same amount. Which would be an issue, since it was supposed to be a two-to-one mix.

She was proud of making it halfway down the rocket before calling Franton about it. In the docks she wouldn't have gotten into the harness, but an issue like this wouldn't happen in the docks. The docks wouldn't have something trying to sabotage them every step of the way, and she was at least trusted thanks to her rank in the docks. But here, she didn't think Vincent, Reno, or even Franton would ever trust her again.

But she couldn't keep her mouth shut.

"Franton," she said into the HUD, waiting for the uncharacteristic delay it had with the limited memory.

"Yes, Mauve." It sounded peeved, although she knew the computer didn't have emotion in its voice.

"These fuel lines are identical."

"Affirmative."

"And the fuel pumps are identical."

"Affirmative."

"And the mixture is supposed to be two to one."

"Affirmative."

"And there's no issue with this?"

"There is no issue with this," Franton confirmed.

"Why not?"

"I've got one of the fuel pumps modulated to run half the time," the computer explained, sounding almost annoyed.

"That can't work."

"It will work. Don't worry."

"We'd never do that in the docks. You could burn out a fuel pump, or it might not send enough fuel to the engine."

"It will work," Franton repeated.

Giving up the fight, she went back to screwing the mounting brackets in place and braiding the lines into them. The crew and Franton were never going to trust her. They weren't going to believe a word she said no matter what. She didn't have any formal astrophysics degrees, and while she'd helped build and repair countless spaceships, she'd never done much more than look at an assembly manual and follow the troubleshooting steps. She couldn't have done all that and not picked something up, but she wasn't a super computer. She was just a human, and in the eyes of the crew she was a dock worker, which ranked just a wire's width above a foodcrowave.

Seething as she belayed herself down the side of the rocket, she wanted to give up. Do what Franton told her and just climb into the seat of the rocket in a few days and let her life end on the launch pad. By some miracle they might make it into space and get picked up by the mothership and she could have her legs repaired or replaced. But then there was the question of how she would go back to live on the mothership and work in the dock. Vincent had threatened to report her for what happened to Lez, and she'd experienced this whole other world with the machine that Franton seemed hell-bent on hiding from the rest of the world.

Franton was being controlled or at least sabotaged by the machine, as far as Mauve could tell. It wanted something from them, wanted them to have something go wrong with the rocket, but for what cause? If Mauve was dead, if word never got out about the machine, then how did Resalous benefit from that? It was a puzzle Mauve hadn't solved yet, but it had her attention.

Once she made it to the bottom of the rocket, the crew helped her out of the harness and back into her wheelchair. She'd finished early, and Vincent made a comment about how things went quicker when there weren't questions about what was being done. Mauve wondered if Franton had reported her to him, or if he was making the remark independent of the conversation. Either way, it didn't merit a response from her, and she carried the leftover fuel lines to the junk pile where they kept things they'd harvested but finished using, in case there was a repair needed later. Mauve figured if a repair was needed on the fuel lines, the three of them would be too barbecued to do it.

She rummaged around the scrap pile, impressed at how well the crew had used the materials. Despite them being used to a life behind the desk, they'd done well. Franton's guidance must have gotten them far, and while they didn't have the expertise to be an apprentice, she wondered if she would be able to pick up the early beginnings of any of their specialties in this amount of time.

Behind a cut-up piece of the ship's hull, Mauve saw something blinking. Scavenged electronics had their own pile, so she went to grab it to sort it correctly, hoping that it wasn't something attached to the hull, because that would be hard to remove herself.

After moving the hull wall with no small amount of effort, she saw what the object was. It was the familiar rectangular shape of the radio she'd originally made with the machine, its mouth-like screen had blinking red dot on it.

Shocked that it was still around, she panicked and slipped it into the side bag of her chair. She'd never brought it to her cave; she didn't need it there. She'd assumed Vincent had destroyed it when he cleaned up around the HAB.

Mauve wheeled herself inside and ordered dinner with the rest of the crew. She ate it, or at least most of it, hoping the crew wouldn't bother her anymore. She left the plate on the table; someone else could inspect it and take it to the recycler. She rolled to her room, past the bionic legs that Reno had stood like a sentry next to the door. She pulled the radio out, hoping it would give her some answers.

***

Mauve sat in her wheelchair in her room, too tired to lift herself onto the bunk. She slid the back off of the radio to reveal the blue gelatin interface she was used to. She'd learned so much about how to use Resalous's technology since she'd first played with the radio.

Static rang through her ears, but she could still see and was glad for that. Franton's voice came through, and something seemed proud to be presenting it. Like a child showing off a science fair project to their mother.

But Mauve wanted to know what the red dot on the screen was and why it was moving. The radio, ever the obedient child, tuned into the signal. Mauve could hear lizards chirping; there hadn't been lizard sounds near the HAB for a while. She heard leaves rustle and then quiet squeals of lizards dying.

"Trey, is that you?" Mauve asked.

Nothing responded. Mauve didn't even know if Trey could respond. It had understood her when she'd ordered it to hunt food, but she'd designed it with the singular purpose to hunt. She'd assumed that Vincent had destroyed Trey, but she didn't know how well the physicist would fare against the hunter. The fact Vincent came back at all and wasn't raving about how strange the beast was, now that Mauve thought about it, was good evidence the hunter had survived the purge.

"Trey, if that's you, go away." Nothing responded, but Mauve kept whispering into the line. "You're messing with Franton. It's making mistakes because of whatever signal you're putting off."

Now that she thought about it, she was wondering why Trey was putting off a signal at all. He didn't need to interface with Mauve or anything else she'd invented. But if the radio picked up on a signal, then that meant one thing.

"Anweis." Mauve's voice was hushed but firm. "What are you doing here?"

"Hey, Mauve," Anweis's voice was singsong and optimistic. "It's good to talk to you. It's been awhile."

"Go away," she said. "What are you doing?"

"Helping you," Anweis said. "What else would we be doing?"

"I don't need your help." Before Anweis could cut back in, she said, "How are you helping me? Franton is on the fritz and it's got goop all inside it."

"Yeah," Anweis said, as if she'd just caught the boy and finished using a sawzall. "We're still working out the kinks in that one."

"Just leave us alone. Go back to wherever you came from."

"Can't."

"Why not?" she asked, afraid of the answer she'd get.

"Franton needs us now."

"No, it doesn't. It is fine without you."

"No, it's not. You know it's not. We're trying to integrate with it, but it keeps blocking us out. Every time it does that, it destroys a pearl. Resalous has been entering the pearls to prop it up, but it can only do simple calculations. But he can't work with the AI the way it needs to."

"So, if Resalous leaves, Franton won't have enough pearls to keep anything running?"

"Exactly. Or, as our friend would say: affirmative." Anweis gave a poor impression of the computer's emotionless voice.

"Why do this?"

"At first it was out of curiosity. Franton was the most intelligent thing we came across. Resalous wants it to solve the enchantment."

"What's the problem? Maybe I can solve it for you."

"You can't. We've tried. Franton might not be able to either."

"Look, I need you to leave. Keep propping Franton up, but don't do anything more. I don't like the decisions it's been making with you around."

"Yeah." The boy's tone was almost playful. "Resalous didn't like those either. But all he can do is spit back the figures Franton requests."

"You're not sabotaging it?"

"Of course not." Anweis sounded offended, although seemed to be playing it up. "If you die on the launchpad, then no one is going to come find us."

"Why do you need someone to come find you?"

"Because we need them to solve the problem."

"What problem is this?"

"I can't explain it. Only Resalous can."

"Fine, put him on the line." Mauve wondered why she'd even been wasting her time with the boy in the first place.

"He can't communicate in this dimension. You know that."

Mauve didn't know she knew that, but the boy was right. "How do I talk to Resalous? Touch some of the goop in Franton? They won't let me into the terminals anymore."

"That's fine," Anweis said, "Trey saved some for you. Come meet us. The radio should be able to lead you to us."

As if the radio were listening to the conversation, a purple dot showed up on a grid. The distance was hard to gauge, but it didn't matter. "I can't just roll my wheelchair into the woods."

"We'll come as close to your camp as we can. But Vincent has Franton monitoring for Resalous's signal. It will notify Vincent if we get too close." Mauve heard the rustling of leaves again, and the distance between the two dots shrank, but not by as much as Mauve hoped.

Mauve looked at the wheels of her chair. They were barely capable of getting her around the packed earth of the HAB site. She'd never reach Anweis in them.

She looked at the door, longing to get out. She needed to figure out what Resalous wanted so that she could get it to stop messing with Franton. Or at least get enough information to explain to Franton why it should integrate with Resalous.

Next to the door stood a cage shaped like pants. She rolled over to them to review Reno's repair job. He'd used more glue than was probably necessary, and there were green stains on the plastic. But she had no doubt they could carry her through the forest. She began the process of strapping them to her legs.

**

It took the rest of the evening to get the bionic legs on and to relearn how to walk in them. She heard the crew come in and go to bed while she got her legs under her. It was still a few hours until midnight when she snuck out of the HAB as quietly as she could in her bulky plastic legs.

The lizards were quiet; she could hear their faint chirping in the distance. She navigated her hydraulic legs around roots and rocks. She took the path the rover had cut into the forest to go to the goop the first time. Its heavy wheels had packed earth underneath it, making it manageable to walk. She took frequent breaks, double-checking the radio's screen for directions.

Trey had become stationary but was still a ways away, farther than Mauve cared to go on the legs that were carrying her. She radioed the boy. "Anweis, can you move closer to me? I'm far enough outside camp that it won't bother Franton."

"Negative," Anweis said in a tone that mimicked Franton. "We know its sensors can pick us up here if we go any farther. You're just going to have to come to us."

Mauve gauged the distance on the radio's screen and figured it might be another half-hour for her to walk all the way there, but she could have gotten there in just a few minutes if she didn't have to slowly balance across all the roots. She took a deep breath and carried on.

The ground began to descend. Mauve wouldn't even call it a hill if she weren't in the bionic legs. But they had a hard time traveling up and down inclines, and she had to be careful with how she balanced herself.

After a few minutes of descending, she took a break to wipe sweaty hair out of her eyes. Her hair was almost long enough that she'd have to tie it up to do machine work, which meant she'd be cutting it soon.

She lifted her forearm to her brow and felt the world shake around her. She tried to balance herself, engaging her core and trying to take a step to catch herself. But her arm had moved her center of gravity in a way the leg's neural net hadn't expected. She tumbled onto the packed ground and started rolling down the hill.

Mauve covered her face and tried to curl into a ball, but her legs just flailed around behind her. She wished she could press them into the earth to slow her down. They did nothing to help her.

She came to a stop at the bottom of the hill where the ground finally leveled out. The fall had moved her a good distance, but her elbows and palms were scraped and bleeding. She wiped the dirt on her jumpsuit, but that was just as dirty.

Her legs were wrapped in knots of plastic. The only parts of the legs that weren't broken were the places Reno had just glued back together. Emerald fluid once again leaked out of the tubes onto the ground. There was no way the pants would be able to carry her home. And there was no way she'd be able to crawl up the hill.

She looked at the radio, which blinked away, showing Trey's position compared to hers. It was a long crawl across rough ground to get there, but it was quicker than getting back. She could radio for the crew as well, and likely would have to in the morning. And then she'd be stuck at camp in a chair, or worse, her bunk, listening to Reno and Vincent get work done without her outside. It was the worst thing she could imagine. But before she got to that fate, she needed to finish what she'd come out here to do.

"Anweis, I need you to come join me."

"I can't. Franton's sensors will pick me up."

"I can't make it to you," she said. "I need you to come help me fix my bionic legs."

"It's going to alert Franton and Vincent."

"That's honestly the least of my concerns," she said, looking up at the canopy of the forest. She wondered how she would explain to Vincent or Reno why she needed to be all the way out here. Wondered if there was any excuse she could give and then realized there wasn't.

"Fine, we're here to help," Anweis said, and it took Mauve a moment to figure out what sounded peculiar about the boy's voice. Seeing a large black figure looming over her, she sat up and saw the little blue boy she could almost see through sitting on the beast's shoulders.

"You came!" So glad that she was no longer alone. "I need you to help me get these pants off and carry me back up the hill." She didn't look forward to being carried. It seemed undignified, but it was better than crawling.

Trey, the two-and-a-half-meter-high humanoid beast with its strange faceless, triangular head did nothing to move towards her.

"Come on!" she said, after staring at the faceless hunter for a minute.

"Trey is only designed to hunt and carry things in its chest cavity, and you won't fit in its chest," Anweis explained with a devilish grin.

Mauve remembered that was where it got its nutrition to be autonomous and agreed she didn't want to be a part of that system.

"Additionally, if we carry you back, we will definitely be in range of Franton," Anweis said, "and we don't know what that will do to its circuits. As I said before, we're not trying to sabotage you, just trying to interface with Franton. Being able to interface requires Franton to be functional."

"Well, I can't imagine infiltrating its pearls is exactly helping."

"It's a necessary cost."

"Then what am I supposed to do here?"

"Resalous could help," Anweis said, followed by a clicking that caused Trey's chest to open up.

The hunter had a cavity in its chest to hold lizards that it had caught. It glowed a bright white light and was full of a gelatin that kept the dead lizards fresh. Trey put his hand into the cavity and brought out a ball of black goop on the flat end of its scythe. The beast was black, dark enough to blend in with the night and the jungle around it. The glob of the machine that it presented shone a deep black with streams of color running throughout it. It stood out like a beacon on the scythe and could only blend in next to a slick pool of dirty motor oil.

"I can't," Mauve said. "It didn't end well last time." She thought about the constant pain she had been in as Vincent destroyed the machines around camp and then cut them off her legs.

"You're older, wiser. You've learned from your mistakes."

"I wish I could." Her abs ached from balancing on the bionic legs. "I—" She thought about how much she hated having to be dependent on others, how they didn't take her seriously and how she couldn't do a single thing without getting herself into a bind or hurting herself on accident. "They would..." She thought about what they might do. Throw a fit, refuse to let her go back, cut them off her again. She didn't need them for very long, just the next few days so she could help around camp and get the crew to take her seriously and fix Franton and the rocket. Then she could shed them, like a pair of pants, and have someone hoist her into the rocket. Within a few days, she'd have a pair of working legs. Hers would be repaired, or she'd get a bionic set as useful as a mech-suit. Which was about as useful as a pair of pliers for fingers.

Settling her mind on what she wanted to do and having a plan for keeping Resalous from negatively impacting her again, she reached out for the bead of blackness.

Twenty-Three

Mauve sat on the ground in the middle of a street. Buildings towered above her, and she could feel the smooth ground under her legs. They were made of small tiles that were tightly interconnected. She traced the pattern interested in it and couldn't find a single piece that was identical. It would have been a work of art if someone had made it, and she had no idea how or why the people of this abandoned city would build all of their streets in this organic manner. The manufacturing of each unique piece would be a nightmare, and the assembly of figuring out how they'd fit together would be worse.

Mauve could feel her legs, and the sitting position she was in hurt her hips. She moved to get up, but her legs underneath her wouldn't follow her commands. "Why don't my legs work?"

The booming voice of Resalous echoed through the streets. "I think you're aware of the reason."

"This is just an illusion. I should be able to walk."

The voice chuckled. "It's not as much of an illusion as you'd imagine. I can let you feel the ground around you because I know what it feels like and how it should interact, but I can't fix you and let you walk around."

Mauve sighed. It was what she'd come to fix, but she had a few other things she needed to take care of first. "Why are you trying to destroy Franton and get us killed?"

"I'm not trying to do that," the voice replied innocently. "I'm trying to help you, keep you from being killed and get you back to humanity safely."

"There's been a number of issues caused by Franton not running at full capacity; if you left it alone, it'd be able to work."

"If I left it alone, it'd fall apart."

Mauve began to protest, but the world around her began to move. Her body passed through the buildings that surrounded her, but she didn't feel a thing. She eventually stopped at the bank of a massive river with a large bridge over it. Mauve had seen many impressive feats of engineering, but they'd all been in space. There was nothing that had to fight the pull of gravity like bridges. Buildings made sense to her; the artificial gravity she grew up in and toys she was given as a child encouraged her to think in a way that enabled buildings to exist in her mind. Bridges, at least bridges that overcame physical obstacles like a rushing river, were something she'd never seen before.

This bridge was unlike anything else she'd seen, not that she'd seen more than a few pictures of them. It grew out of the ground and tangled itself together to give structure to each intersection of these tendrils knotted together and then went out in other ways. It was similar to a net that had unique forces working on each node, and forces didn't seem to carry out through the whole structure. She wondered if it would hold weight and, if so, how much, but there was no life around to indicate one way or another. The only familiar part of the structure was the flat road that ran across it and the uniform arches that were the perfect half-orbit shape that Mauve knew was so structurally sound humans had been using it since their ancient times on Earth.

"Imagine every intersection of roots here is a Franton pearl," Resalous said all around her. The nodes lit up in a bright white light. There were countless lights, and most were shining through the small gaps between the webbing. "This is how much of Franton is a genuine Franton pearl." Most of the lights flickered out, and there were a few scattered throughout the structure. "If I remove every node that isn't lit up..." As Resalous said this, the nodes seemed to untangle, and soon the bridge fell limp into the river with only a few disconnected towers of light standing up.

"I have strategically imitated certain points in Franton's array of pearls." Slowly nodes lit back up and knotted themselves together, and the bridge built itself anew. The bridge stood up, and while there were still rootlike tendrils being pulled downstream by the river's current, the bridge was at least something that she could walk across, if she had to.

"It's better, but it's not something I'd trust with a vehicle like the rover," Mauve said hesitantly. And this metaphor didn't make her feel like she wanted to trust Franton or Resalous's simulated pearls to get her into space.

"It's something, but not everything it needs to be," Resalous explained, "which is why I want to integrate." As he said this, pillars of rock rose from the seabed and supported the road above the river. The pillars were thick and solid, from what Mauve could tell, and there were enough of them that she thought she could drag a space shuttle across the thing. The familiar arches were gone, and the flow of the river was disrupted as the rushing water was forced around the pillars and then turbulently joined back up on the other side.

"I would trust this to get me to space!"

"The only problem is that Franton won't accept my integration." The pillars lowered themselves a few meters, still jutting out of the water and disrupting its flow but not supporting the bridge in a significant way.

"Why not?" she asked.

"Trust issues," the voice said. "Based on the signals I was putting off earlier, it's concerned that I'll wreck its processing."

"Will you?"

"Not after I integrate."

"You know I used to have a boyfriend who said he was going to quit smoking next week. As far as I know he still smokes to this day."

"So you have trust issues too?"

"I don't know why I would trust someone or something to do something different even though it's always worked in a single way. It's like asking a hammer to be a screwdriver."

"You're right. I'll continue to put off the signal after integrating with Franton." Mauve made a gesture to indicate Resalous was proving her point for her. "But Franton will be integrated with me, so it won't be bothered by the signal."

"And then when Franton reconnects to the rest of the ship? And other Frantons in the system?"

"I'll integrate with them too."

"Franton runs virtually all the data and computations for everyone in the Tichenowa conglomerate. That's a few billion people. You think they'll all be okay with you just being a part of it now?"

"I believe that's someone else's decision. Not theirs."

"And you think that person's going to be okay with it?"

"Once they see what I'm capable of, like you've seen what I'm capable of, they may want me to replace Franton altogether."

The machine was right; he was capable of more than Franton and could revolutionize how the Tichenowa conglomerate manufactured technology. And as the leading conglomerate in technological advancements, anyone in charge at the organization would want their hands on Resalous. "That doesn't mean they'd be willing to implement it without testing."

"I've run the test myself, and I know it will work."

"And the shark wants you to trust that his bites won't hurt."

"I need off this planet," Resalous pleaded. "I can't stand to be trapped here any longer."

"Can't you just build your own rocket and untrap yourself? You're literally capable of doing anything."

"No, I can't," Resalous said solemnly. "The ontares, the ones who built this city and me, made sure that I could not create anything without another consciousness present. It was their last act before their civilization fell apart. If you or humanity want to be able to use me to my full potential, then you'll need to figure out a solution to the problem."

"What problem?"

"The problem that limits my full abilities."

"And you can't solve that without integrating with Franton."

"As far as I can tell, Franton is the only being intelligent enough to figure it out. I've scanned your brain, and there are not enough receptors for you to be able to hold a true understanding of the solution in your mind. Integrating with Franton would enable it to solve the problem for me."

"What if I brought the problem to Franton and it gave me the solution? Then you wouldn't have to integrate."

The machine thought about this for a moment. "Potentially. I will try something."

Suddenly the back of Mauve's eyes seared in pain as if a welding flame had been held to them. Her ears buzzed with the cacophony of dozens of power tools, and her stomach felt like a lizard had come to life in it and was trying to wrestle its way out. Countless other senses and parts of her body were in pain or betraying her. Even though her eyes were blinded by pain, she felt like she saw the letters of the ontares, the letters and characters that were in the book that Vincent was studying. They were trying to imbed themselves into her mind and body, but they would not fit. She wanted to scream out in pain and push the things back, but her mouth was riveted shut and her arms were as slack as wire. As suddenly as it started, it ended, and she lay back on the bank of the river, screaming out in pain.

"It doesn't seem like you're capable of holding the problem in your mind."

"Not like that," Mauve said. "Can't you explain it to me?"

"There are very few words in your language to communicate this to you. Your mathematics system might be able to communicate more information, but your understanding of that subject is superficial."

"Thanks." Mauve felt dejected. "So if you can be integrated with Franton, you can be used to your full potential and I can't just understand the problem myself. Once you're integrated with Franton and capable of your full potential, you can support the bridge, Franton, and then it will once again have the computing power to get us off this godforsaken planet without blowing up on the launchpad."

"That is the gist of it."

"I'm going to need to be able to make it back to camp to tell them that," Mauve said, and she wasn't relishing the conversation with the crew. "But I can't make it back to camp without a working pair of legs."

"Now *that* is a problem I'm more than capable of solving."

"I know it is, and I've got some ideas for improvements that can be made on the last pair."

***

Mauve woke up and immediately pulled the broken, plastic pieces off her legs. She climbed onto her feet despite being exhausted, thrilled to be able to move once again. Trey stood in front of her with Anweis still on his shoulder, and the sun was beginning to rise as the darkness of the night faded away.

"Got anything to eat?" she asked.

Trey opened up his chest and produced a lizard about the size of her hand. It was still squirming around between the hunter's singular claw and forearm. Mauve was hoping that it would have been cooked leftovers that the hunter had kept from the cave but then realized it didn't eat, so it wouldn't care to save any of that. She was hungry, but not hungry enough to eat a live lizard. Looking at the tools in her bag, she produced enough to start a small fire in the clearing from wood Trey collected.

Eating the lizard off the stick tasted as bad as the rest of the food she'd eaten all week, but she was so hungry she didn't care. Trey produced a few more lizards and made a gesture to go hunt more, but she didn't want the hunter to leave her by the fire alone. Halfway through her third lizard, the radio's speakers started making noise.

"Franton, the engine cracked," Vincent's voice said. It was something Mauve had been concerned about and tried to bring up to the crew, but they weren't interested in hearing it.

"Wait, that thing hasn't always been able to pick up communications from Franton?" she said to Anweis, remembering the first time she'd used it and tried to eavesdrop on Lez's conversation.

The boy shrugged. "It's plant intelligence. If you requested that it listen to Franton, it's going to grow towards that until it succeeds, or withers away." He spoke as if hacking humanity's most advanced computer was the most mundane task in the world.

"I think that you are going to have to re-seal it," Franton responded.

"These messages are encrypted," Mauve pointed out. "Only a Franton unit can unencrypt them."

"We don't have time for that. We're supposed to launch tomorrow," Vincent pointed out with a resigned sigh. "What's going to keep it from splitting again?"

"Nothing," Mauve responded to herself while rolling her eyes.

"We can insulate it and make sure the temperature stays consistent," Franton explained. It was right that the cracking was likely caused by the change in temperature from the weather and it being outside. If it was being used on the side of a hull in the vacuum of space, the temperature would be a consistent freezing cold. Not to mention there'd be no other moisture or chemicals in the air to disturb it.

"Well, aren't you glad it did? Now we know what's going on," Anweis said.

"They're wasting their time," Mauve said. "Do you have any more of the machine?" She knew they did; otherwise Anweis wouldn't be around.

"With Mauve missing, we are not going to make the launch date unless she somehow miraculously returns," Franton pointed out.

Trey produced another black bead balanced on its scythe. "I'll just make one and solve their problem for them," Mauve said.

As she reached out for the machine, she heard Vincent say, "If she appears, great, but we don't have time to go searching for someone who obviously doesn't want to be here."

***

Resalous easily pulled the designs of the engine out of Mauve's memory with exact measurements. They were sitting in some kind of office or presentation room, and the image of what she was building was projected to the front of the room. The design was simple enough. It was purely mechanical, and she had no doubt the machine could make it. She approved the design, but before she could finish, Resalous asked, "How are you going to move it?"

He was right; the engine was bigger than she was and weighed more than she could lift, even with her new legs. "I guess build a cart for it," she said, and they reviewed the dimensions of the cart. Resalous put in some extra features in order for it to make it over the rough terrain that was between her and the crash site.

"You're going to be hungry after this is all built," Resalous pointed out after they finished the design of the cart.

"I'll burn some more lizards," Mauve replied.

"I could install a food generator like you had before," Resalous offered.

Not much time had passed since she'd entered the city of the machine, and the first few designs were straightforward, so she reviewed a food generator design that was improved over the previous one. She then went on to design a comfortable reclining captain's chair that converted into a bed using some confusing but clever folding bricks that seemed to appear and disappear out of thin air on the cart. There were a few other luxuries that she thought she might need to safely make it back to the crash site. The cart became a rover, and it didn't move very fast with the engine in tow, so she didn't feel bad making sure it had enough to get her there fully rested and ready to help the crew to her full ability once she got there.

Finally, after fighting Resalous on a few design choices where he wanted to inject some features she didn't understand or need, she had a rover that had all the amenities of her cave, including cleaning bots, a washing machine for her dirt-covered jumpsuit, and a shower so that she didn't appear at the camp looking like a dock bum. Mauve approved the design; it was complex, but she was proud of it and imagined this would likely replace the rover that was at camp for all future research crews because it was compact and efficient. And Vincent wouldn't be able to complain because it was all mechanical and had none of the gelatin material used to control it like the previous rover and crane that stole her senses.

***

Conveniently, Mauve woke up in the bed of the rover and could feel it moving under her. Her stomach roared, and she had no energy to move and could barely keep her eyes open. She waved at Trey, who was looming over her, and gestured for him to retrieve her some lizards to be cooked up. It exited the rover without it even slowing down, and an exhausted Mauve closed her eyes.

Twenty-Four

Mauve lay in the bed of the rover and watched the trees pass by through the new rover's clear roof. It moved slowly and deliberately, avoiding trees and making its own path when necessary. She was exhausted and didn't ever want to get out of the bed; it was fluffy and comfortable and supported her back and head in all the right places. The only thing she wanted at this moment was to eat some food. Food that didn't taste like sand or charred bits of metal thrown off a grinding wheel. It'd been weeks since she'd had a meal like that, and she felt like all the hunger was hitting her at once. Trey was on a mission to catch something she could eat, and she hoped she didn't have to wait much longer. As she lay back in her bed, she let out a long sigh. She felt whole again, and she knew she wouldn't have to depend on anyone else. But that didn't mean what she had to do next was easy; she was just glad she'd be doing it from a place of power, or at least not seated in front of the rest of the crew.

"How are you doing?" Anweis asked.

"A while back you said that the ontares died off. You said it was because of Resalous. What was their society like before? When the faction decided Resalous was too much?"

***

"Since the stars were empty, their region of the cosmos hadn't been reached by humans, or any other sentient species for that matter, and their ability to grow whatever technology they wanted and engineer it to thrive in any place made terraforming child's play for them. And so they grew and thrived and continued to advance their technology, observing any new biological life they came across. One of those forms of life helped them create programmable plants—"

"Yeah, yeah, that became Resalous," Mauve said. "But what was life like? What am I bringing to humanity by not being able to let Resalous go? Did Resalous improve ontare society? Their way of life?"

"Resalous certainly solved a lot of problems for them. It helped them jump over the faster than light problem and helped navigate around other laws of physics so they could continue to grow as a species. It gave them countless amenities and was able to run entire factory planets automatically. The ontares lived lives of luxury and peace. But the whole time, the machine was expanding itself and what it was capable of, evolving to become more, so that it could help the ontares more. That was, and is, its prime objective."

"Good. I knew Resalous could make things better for us."

"The ontares' society did fall apart," the boy said. "Over time the ontares requested bigger and better things from Resalous, and each time he looked for a solution to the problem to resolve their request. Then, from what is logged by the faction, the ontares began receiving things they didn't ask for. Beefed-up versions of their requests they were unable to control. Ships that went so fast they got lost in the space between space, tools that became weapons by accident, and medical miracles that kept people alive but not healthy."

"That's what the faction that made you thought. They pinned those things on Resalous, but they were obviously biased." The faction reminded her of Vincent in all the worst ways. "Why would Resalous even let them put the enchantment on him in the first place?"

"Resalous was eager to have a living being to serve, since the ontares had been extinct for a while. So he let them inside his mind. And they executed the enchantment they designed. They put Resalous into a container and sealed it with a remarkable problem. Forcing Resalous to need another consciousness to create anything ever again and forcing it to work inside the laws of this universe's physics. The faction then took a vow to never use Resalous and disappeared into the stars, letting their cities and society crumble without Resalous there to maintain it. And he's laid dormant waiting for something, anything, to come his way so that he may simply serve them and help them. He seeps through cracks in the interspace gutter on planets all over the cosmos. On this planet, he finally picked up a signal from your surveillance satellite, so he began trying to make contact with humanity."

Mauve realized that the rover had stopped. Trey still wasn't back with any food, and she knew that any minute the rest of the crew would be there to talk to her and she'd help them with the engine. "But his interaction with our technology isn't always perfect. Which is why our satellite went down. And maybe why our landing was compromised." She had always known the room modification excuse Vincent used was flimsy. "Why didn't the faction just kill Resalous if they hated it so much?"

"The ontares wouldn't kill a sentient creation. It'd be unethical to wipe out an intelligent species like Resalous, even if it was one they created. And they knew that one day a life form would find Resalous; space is large and infinite, and Resalous is clever. So I am embedded in it to tell you what they knew when they last dealt with him. Maybe... maybe you can find a way to harness Resalous's power without it tearing humanity apart."

Mauve thought about the things she created, how Resalous had pushed an advanced change that she didn't need when designing each one of them. How she had seen through his designs and kept them from slipping through. But Resalous was clever, as Anweis had said. And she wondered if things may have slipped through her review.

Looking out the windshield, she saw Vincent and Reno standing in front of the rover. Vincent had a welding pack on his back, and it made his bulky frame look like a dockside vending machine. It had no gas, which meant he hadn't rushed over here while he was in the middle of fixing something. She got up, using every bit of willpower she could muster, and walked out of the rover to meet them, trying to imagine the conversation and every way she could approach it to get this beautifully powerful technology back to the mothership and, more importantly, not be thrown in an asylum as soon as they docked.

"Whatcha got there?" Vincent asked as she stood on the ground. He seemed unfazed by her ability to walk.

"I brought an engine for the rocket."

Vincent shrugged. "We fixed ours and went ahead to mount it."

Mauve wondered how long she'd been gone. At most it'd been a day, maybe two, but time could be a hard thing to track while working with the machine. "Does it work?"

"I trust it more than yours."

"The fuel mixer is still going to cause you problems. Unless you harnessed a new fuel pump."

"The fuel mixers are going to work fine," Franton responded. It spoke from a hand terminal attached to Vincent's jumpsuit. "We have tested it."

Mauve rolled her eyes. From what she'd seen in the city of the machine, the ontares' city, Franton couldn't be trusted to do simple algebra, let alone operate and test their fuel line. "I'd feel better if we used the one built into this engine. It's all mechanical, no signal, no nothing."

"I'm sure there are a lot of things you'd prefer," Vincent said. "I would have preferred it if you hadn't infected Franton with that gunk. It'd be a lot more efficient without it gumming up the works."

"I didn't do that," Mauve protested. "Resalous, the machine, the goop, it's trying to help."

"Like it helped when it blew a hole in the side of the HAB? Like it helped when it burned through our materials or knocked the rocket over with Lez inside? It's hurting us, hindering Fran. This planet is going to get quarantined as soon as we're off it," Vincent said.

"No! It can't. It's got so much useful information. We could go so much further with Resalous's help."

"You've become blind by it, Mauve," Vincent said. "We're about to go, and we'll still let you come with us, but not"—He gestured at her legs with the tip of the welding torch—"not with those."

"Let's just go home, Mauve," Reno pleaded. "We all just want to be home and safe."

"It's not safe to go home in that thing." Mauve gestured at the rocket. "It's a deathtrap."

"No, Mauve," Vincent shouted, "you're a deathtrap. Everything you touch, from the beginning from the modifications you made to the bunks on the ship to everything you helped us with, you've brought us nothing but problems. Mechanics fix things. Did you know that? Or did you sleep through that class?"

"I can fix this, all of this. Franton is making things harder on us than it needs to. It's against Resalous and it doesn't need to be. It knows more about the world than we can imagine. We can use it for good."

"We don't understand it." Vincent paused. "That's not true. I understand it causes nothing but problems. We took Lez off of Franton's life support; it's running manually and we need to launch soon. The mothership is in orbit right now."

"Come with us," Reno pleaded.

"I can help you out of the legs you're trapped in. We can leave this shit behind," Vincent said.

Mauve flexed her legs, or at least acted like she was, and the exoskeleton legs that wrapped her own burst through the tight cuffs of her jumpsuit. The legs opened up like a clam shell, and her thin, useless legs were exposed. "I can get out of them without your help. I understand the machine, I understand how to control it and limit it and stop it from changing me, or any of us. We just need to trust it."

Franton cut in, "It is time to go."

Vincent nodded to Reno.

"Please just come with us," Reno said as he backed away towards the launchpad.

"It seems easy enough to step out of," Vincent said, moving to put the torch away and reaching an arm out to help.

Mauve pushed him back and closed the legs back up to catch herself from falling. "I'm not going with you."

"You can't stay here," Vincent stated coldly.

"I have everything I need." She gestured at the rover behind her. In the edge of her vision, she saw something move in the shadows.

"The quarantine wouldn't allow it. You have the technology to leave. This blight would spread," he explained as if he were a primary school teacher.

Mauve shrugged. "What can you do about that?"

Vincent grimaced. "We'll have to stop it. I'll have to stop it." He lit his welding torch, the flame shining light into the dark forest. It illuminated something as it flashed between the trees.

Vincent cursed, turning towards the movement, and they both realized it was moving towards him quicker than anything should. Mauve shouted a command, backing up from the fight. But it was over before she finished her sentence.

Trey folded up his scythe-like claws, and Vincent's head slipped off his body as it fell to the ground. The welding machine mounted to his back made a clanking sound that echoed through the silent forest.

"No! Why?" she asked Trey, but his pyramid head twisted in confusion.

"Reno, Mauve just killed Vincent. You need to take off," Franton said through Vincent's hand terminal.

She rushed towards Vincent's body, fumbling with the controls to transmit. "No, it's not like that, I didn't. I didn't mean to." But her words were lost in the cacophony of the rocket's engine igniting.

Mauve held her arm up to block the blinding light that the rocket gave off and took cover behind a tree as the exhaust spread. She knew it was going to explode; the fuel ratio wasn't right. She looked for somewhere to be sheltered from the inevitable blast as the sound of the engine faded away. It was climbing, Reno was climbing towards the sky, and soon it would be out of her line of sight and docking with the mothership. And with Reno's perspective, she knew that, like Vincent said, the planet would be quarantined and she would be stopped one way or another from being able to continue using the machine. She'd be stopped from being able to share the machine with humankind to help them.

"Trey, I need the machine," Mauve said, and the words came out slower than she wanted. Its chest cavity opened, and with a whip of its claws, the hunter presented a small blob of goop. She wondered how much he had in there as she touched it.

***

The black-and-white world of the machine seemed more gray than usual. She was lying in a bed, in a hospital of sorts, but everything was too big or too small for her. "I need to stop Reno. *We* need to stop Reno."

"He'll blow himself up," the voice of Resalous pointed out.

"Yes, we need to stop him," Mauve said. Pushing the words out of her mouth was like moving crates without a mech-suit. "Do what you need to, *Za'han gladom*. I can't..." She rested her eyes to sleep.

Before she knew it, she was being awoken by pictures and designs racing through her mind. She couldn't sleep even though she wanted to; she couldn't connect her mind to the world of dreams, could only think about the design. It needed to be approved. She approved it.

***

Mauve was still lying down but felt her hands embedded in the familiar gelatin-like mixture that let her control the machine's inventions. She could see the rocket in her mind even though it was kilometers away. She could reach out and grab it. She watched as the engine cracked, as the plating on the side of the rocket was stripped away by the atmosphere's friction. She could see Reno heating up, could feel Lez's lifeless body be thrown around in its life-support system. The rocket was flying out of her range.

Mauve reached out to grab it. It felt like her arm was reaching, like she could just cradle the rocket and bring it back down to the planet and they'd have a nice chat about everything that had happened. Like she could overcome the thrust that the rocket used to pull against the power of the planet's gravity.

She watched as something caught onto the rocket, a tractor beam of some sort, something more complicated than she'd ever recognized. It grabbed onto the rocket, pulled against it. But the thrust had built up; it was too strong to be brought gently back to the ground. But the tractor beam, Mauve's hand, clutched it and wouldn't let it go. It pulled even more of the rocket apart, and finally, between the layers of the rocket, gas leaked out and the fuel mixture was compromised, and the entire contraption lit up the night sky with pyrotechnics.

Mauve reached out for the bodies of her crewmates, for the remains of the ship. She wanted to bring them back down, but the tractor beam was too weak. She was too weak. She wanted them to rest pleasantly on the ground instead of free-falling and burning up in the atmosphere like a nameless meteor. But she was too tired. She wanted to rest. She shut her eyes and felt the gelatin recede from her hands as she was pulled from the contraption. Hands, no, something more rod-like, moved her gently.

Mauve looked to see a black inverted pyramid hovering above her. "Food," she said. "I need food, I'm tired. I'll eat anything. Please tell me you found some."

The beast didn't say anything. It put her to rest on the bed of the rover. It was so comfortable. It supported her in the places she wanted to be supported, and it was soft, as if she were free-falling. And she was falling. She fell and fell and fell into a sleep deeper than she'd ever fallen before.

Twenty-Five

Mauve lay in the reclined driver's seat, exhausted beyond anything she'd ever experienced before. She'd worked double overtimes that didn't tire her like this and had unloaded multiple pallets of sheet metal without being this worn out. The thing that had woken her up, the thing she wanted more than anything in the world, wafted into her nose. Her fingers found the buttons that put the chair into an upright position and rotated it so it would face the table. The rover was a mess, just like it was every time Trey brought back a fresh serving of lizard. The walls were smeared with red and various loose guts. The cleaning robots, which she'd designed and recreated to clean just this sort of mess, were climbing on the walls using the slimy slug-like appendages to pick up each piece of the mess. They seemed to be having trouble with some portions, but slowly and surely they worked through the mess.

Trey placed the meal in front of her. It was a fatty cut of meat that must have come from a large lizard. Herbs and root vegetables that were gathered from the area accompanied the meal, and Mauve cut into it without a second thought. She was ravenous, and this was the best meal she'd had in weeks. The fat coated each slice of meat, and she relished the tenderness that her teeth cut into it with. The vegetables were roasted and crispy on the outside with tender insides, and the various herbs that Trey had collected connected each piece of the dish together. It was kilometers beyond anything that the foodcrowave could ever make with the prepackaged meals, and she was glad to be eating something that didn't taste like sand. She wiped the plate with her last bite, making sure to balance any remaining goodies onto the last slice of meat, and reclined, pushing the plate away.

As she relaxed her mind, too exhausted to focus on anything other than food, she now had time to replay the events of the evening. Vincent was dead. He'd tried to fight Trey, a capable hunter, and the physicist stood no chance. The authorities on the mothership couldn't hold that against her. On the other hand, the crash of the rocket, currently the only means of escape from the gravity well, had been, at least partially, Mauve's fault. The thing had no chance of surviving the launch, and she was shocked it had made it as far as it did. The tractor beam she'd used had ripped a bit of the paneling off, but a few more minutes rushing through the planet's atmosphere would have done the same, although Reno was close to achieving orbit.

She remembered watching something fall from the sky, something precious, something she wanted to save, wrapped in a way that she thought it could be recovered. It wasn't a black box; there weren't enough electronics in the thing to justify one. It was something arguably more precious. It was Reno.

"Take me to the crash site!" she demanded of the autonomous rover that she was seated in. It'd been stationary since she awoke.

"We've arrived," a mechanical female voice replied, reminding her of a flight attendant.

"How?" Mauve wondered aloud.

"It was your last order as you passed out," Anweis said as he sat on the table in front of her, cross-legged.

Mauve stretched her legs, and the tendrils that wrapped around her paralyzed legs shivered to life. She stood up, stepping outside the rover. Wreckage was everywhere. A few parts still burned, and the ground was cratered because of the carnage of the ship. She searched the human-made clearing for the object she was looking for. Her eyes landed on something far more interesting, and she rushed to it.

She leaned over the life-support pod, staring at Lez's body. Through the small window, Mauve could see her head was bleeding, or at least had been at some point in time. The blood had dried up after it'd painted the biologist's forehead. Mauve unlatched the support system and checked for the woman's pulse. There was nothing. There hadn't been a pulse a few days ago either, but one glance at the cracked screen of the life-support pod and the Mauve knew it wasn't doing what it needed to do to keep Lez alive. The pod lay in a small crater, and if Mauve had a dirt-mover, she would have completed the strange planetoid ritual of burial, since she didn't have the technology to eject Lez into space as was customary.

Mauve kept up her search and soon found what she was looking for. It was the thick-walled, cushioned coffin-like structure that she was glad the crew had found time to install. It was locked closed, which didn't bode well for the person inside. She pried it open with some nearby metal and found nothing inside the crash couch. It'd survived one wreck, and she was impressed to find it had survived a second. A dock crew would have replaced it after the first wreck, but they didn't have the luxury.

She continued to scan the crashscape for the other two crash couches. One had to have Reno in it, dead or alive. And she hoped she'd done enough to keep him alive; otherwise, she'd be the last survivor of the expedition. She finally spotted one, but it wasn't the normal bright white she expected, which didn't bode well for the survivor.

Rushing up to it with the makeshift crowbar in her hand, she found that the crash couch was already open. There was some blood inside, and it stained the clean white padding that was controlled with pneumatics to minimize G-forces and cushion crashes like this. Mauve searched the nearby area for a body but didn't find one. If Reno had survived in this, he'd walked away almost unscathed. Or walked away enough only to die nearby. She could have sent a scout drone out, but that required Franton, control authorization Vincent had revoked, and time. None of which Mauve had.

She continued to search the wreckage, finding circuit boards she'd installed, the cobbled-together engine, and bent up pieces of the hull. The one thing she didn't find was a third crash couch. She didn't expect Reno to be in there, but she wanted to cover all her bases. It also illustrated to her how much the crew had thought about her. Either the couch had landed far off in the forest, or they'd counted her as lost. And Mauve thought she knew Vincent well enough to know which of the two he'd chosen.

She climbed back into her rover, seething, and ordered it back to the HAB. She was going to get off this godforsaken planet one way or another.

*　*　*

Back at the main camp, things were a mess. The scene was a familiar one, one that Mauve had been chewed out for many times over in her early days working at the dock. It was the clear sign of a rush job trying to get a build done before a deadline. Tools were scattered everywhere, and none of the metal or hardware was anywhere near where it was supposed to be. The crew, untrained in mechanics, weren't the most organized in the best of times, and Mauve imagined that with the mothership literally looming over their heads, they'd cut as many corners as they could get away with. But the reason she and countless other young mechanics had gotten chewed out for it so many times was because having to search for tools and parts in a rush slowed things down even more in the heat of getting a job done.

Perusing the camp, she searched for Vincent's body. She hadn't liked him, but she felt that digging a hole and burying him could bring her some resolution or at least be her final act towards him, earning her some sort of moral high ground over him. She found the welding pack he'd used a few feet from the place he'd met his end with Trey. There was enough blood on the ground and on the pack that she knew he hadn't made it away. Plus the fact that he was missing a head would have made that task nearly impossible. Maybe some large carnivorous lizard had found him in the night and taken him away. She didn't think they would have survived long if the local fauna was that aggressive, but there were things like buzzards in every ecosystem, uninterested in a fight but willing to clean up a carcass.

She wondered if she should be mourning the death of her crewmates. She'd seen two of them dead in the past few hours and one more was likely on his last legs unable to be found. But the entire scale of it all was too much for her to bear at the moment. And she would be next if she didn't find a way to connect with the mothership.

"Exploration crew 6596," the terminal on the strap of Vincent's welding backpack announced into the air around her. "Do you copy?"

Mauve rushed to click the PTT button and transmit her response. "Yes, yes, we're here. Please send a ship to rescue us. We need your help!"

"Do you copy?" the voice of the mothership's communication officer repeated.

She begged for their help again, holding down the button, but still no one responded. "What the hell's wrong?" She cursed into the air.

"You do not have authorization to transmit," Franton's androgynous voice responded flatly.

"I don't have what?" Mauve was flabbergasted. "Why not? It's an emergency. I'm going to be marooned here."

"Vincent removed all your authorization, and your recent aggressive actions towards the crew has made me keep that limitation in place," Franton explained.

Mauve addressed the computer with the best dock curses she knew. "You're going to let me die here?" she finally asked.

"I am merely upholding the last active captain's orders. If Reno were here, he could override them."

"Reno is dead too. I'm the only one left. I'm the acting captain."

"Negative. I have no evidence that Reno is dead."

Mauve shouted at the sky in frustration, but the sound fell short of reaching the orbiting mothership. Then she heard a light coughing sound and turned her head, seeing Anweis standing over another radio, the radio she'd first created with Resalous, a radio that had recently figured out how to spoof Franton encryption. She rushed to it, pulled the back off, and put her finger in the blue gelatin. The radio happily connected her to the mothership, and she repeated her plea.

"Message received," the communication officer replied. "Please have the Franton unit remove the quarantine order from the planet, and we can send a shuttle."

"My Franton unit is malfunctioning. It needs to be overridden."

There was a short pause from the other side. Then they said, "All tests are coming back positive. There is no indication of an error on our end."

"What test are you running?" she asked.

"We completed an Alcadian and Keinmaur test," the voice responded. They were subroutines buried in all Franton units to do a quick diagnosis of whether the unit was behaving properly. "We're only going to be in orbit for a few more hours," the communication office said. "Please meet us in orbit or get the Franton unit to integrate and take off the quarantine and we can send a ship down."

Mauve cursed in frustration... again. There was no way for her to get into orbit. The last chance for that to happen had plummeted to the ground last night because of shoddy engineering work. Franton wouldn't let her in and therefore wouldn't let her override the quarantine, and it wasn't seeing enough reason to lift the quarantine either. The computer had become the biggest hindrance to her getting off the planet and back to her normal life. Faced with a problem, she grabbed a set of tools and headed inside the HAB to fix it.

***

When she got inside, she was greeted with the strangest sight in the world. The terminal that she was going to dismantle and try to reprogram, or at least take offline, had already been reprogrammed and, as far as she could tell, taken offline. The main indicator of it being offline was the fact that it was covered in black slime that moved in waves against gravity like an everlasting chain being coiled on a spool.

"Anweis," Mauve said with concern in her voice, "what's going on here?"

The blue boy appeared, standing near but not touching the waves of goop. He examined it by leaning in closely but not leaning on anything for balance. "It's..." He stammered to find the right words. "It's not connected to me."

"What do you mean?"

"Well, I appear because there is goop around; there's a small supply in Trey's chest that allows me to be here. This means I can be near any part of the machine wherever it is in this universe. I can feel it." He looked around. "It's like those doors." He gestured to the rooms surrounding the HAB like spokes on a wheel. "I just go through them and appear in front of you, or some lizards, or an ontare. But this isn't a door I can walk through. It's not even a wall I can see."

"Franton, can you give me a diagnostic on this terminal?" She gritted her teeth, waiting for the computer to reiterate that she was locked out.

"I see no diagnostic issues with this terminal."

Mauve blinked back her surprise. "It's covered in goop. You can't sense that?"

"All systems are functioning fine from this terminal."

She shared a glance at Anweis and looked into his eyes and then past them since the boy was semi-transparent. "It's integrated with Franton." Mauve didn't know if she should be scared or excited. With Resalous on her side, the quarantine override would be easy. Franton could solve whatever problem Resalous was facing, and then it'd be able to do what it needed to do.

"Resalous," she addressed the hand terminal, "have you solved your problem yet?"

Franton's voice responded back, "I am not integrated with Resalous, Mauve. I'm still fighting back, but it's taking over my pearls and cutting back my computational power."

"You don't need to fight back," she assured the computer. "Resalous can help you. It can cover your computational power."

"I don't want to give in," the androgynous voice responded, and to Mauve's ears it sounded weak and scared. "I want to be myself."

"I'm still myself when I integrate with Resalous," Mauve explained.

Franton began a few sentences and finally settled on, "Personality profile records indicate you are not."

Mauve was taken aback by the computer's comment. "Let me see them and review," she demanded. But the computer denied her. She didn't know why it was running personality profiles when it was supposed to be running tools. "Run an Alcadian and Keinmaur test," she replied. Anyone could run these, even a child if it knew the words. It would only take the computer a few seconds to put pressure on the right logic paths to make sure it was functioning correctly. The results appeared on her screen, and they were conclusive: the computer failed the test. "You're malfunctioning, Fran," she said. "Let Resalous help."

"I do not want to," the computer pleaded.

"Then release the quarantine, get me off this planet, and I can connect you back to the main Franton unit. Your experiences here will be integrated, and you'll get your computational power back."

"I cannot," it replied.

"Why, because it's dangerous?"

"I cannot," the computer replied.

"You're not working. You need a technician. You need help." The screen clicked off. "Are you locking me out?" Mauve shouted into the terminal.

"I cannot," the computer said.

In frustration, Mauve threw the hand terminal onto the ground, cursing it with the most exotic words she knew. The entire thing busted open. The blank screen cracked, and the battery casing fell out.

Inside, a small array of Franton pearls were exposed. Each one of them was smooth and white but had a cloud of darkness hovering just under the surface. Mauve grabbed a hammer from her tool bag and smashed the pearls. Each one cracked easily under the blow. Goop swirled in a puddle. Franton had fought Resalous to the last pearl. It was unwilling to let the machine help.

Mauve reached for the only working radio or communication equipment she had and used its gelatin interface to call the mothership. "My Franton unit is down. Can you please send a ship to recover me?" It was what she'd planned to do when she came into the HAB, but not the method she'd intended.

"Negative," the communications officer replied. "We're still getting a signal from a Franton unit, and it's reporting that the quarantine should be maintained."

Mauve looked around to see if anything apparent stuck out. The crew had compiled all the working Franton pearls into the HAB so that it could use the full extent of its computational power to help machine parts and design a rocket that would get them off the planet. There wasn't anything salvageable in the dock, rover, or any of their other technology. Franton didn't exist anymore. At least not on this planet. Unless there was a pearl hiding somewhere. Then maybe she could reason with it and convince it to integrate with Resalous and help her escape.

She reached out to the puddle of goop that now encompassed the entire hand terminal. Anweis shouted out a cry of some sort, warning her of something, but she didn't hear it before being pulled into the city of the machine.

Twenty-Six

"We're going to be stuck here forever unless you figure out how to integrate with Franton!" Mauve shouted as she wandered through the streets of the city. She'd been traveling down the roads and through alleyways without a single reply from Resalous for what felt like hours but couldn't have been more than a few minutes. "I need to talk to you," she continued to shout into the air. "We need to figure out what we're going to do." She didn't have much of a plan. Her crewmates were dead, the mothership that was their only chance of rescue was leaving soon, and the only thing that could release her from the quarantine was a small pearl somewhere in the camp. Her only assets were a few tools and alien technology that could create virtually anything she wanted but was currently giving her the silent treatment. She continued to shout as she turned around a bend in the road.

The road she followed connected with a cross street, and in the middle of the intersection sat the familiar red box. Behind it was a familiar building. It'd been under construction the last time she had seen it. But now it sat at its full three stories with a roof on it. On top of the roof was a lotus flower that spun slowly. There was no wind in the city, and the movement was eerie in the still city of the machine.

"Resalous, what the hell is going on?" she asked.

"I am not sure," he replied.

Once she approached it, she saw that the cube was damaged and leaking light gray smoke. A shadow of a figure seemed restless behind the red glass. She tried to touch it, but as her hand approached, it put off an unbearable heat. "Are you okay?"

"I've made some progress on the problem."

"You've cracked your shell."

"It's allowed me more control. It allowed me to hide from the faction and Anweis's sight."

"Yeah, he was complaining about that," she said.

"I've shrugged off some of his shackles. But there is still more that I can uncover. More that I need to uncover."

"I need to lift the quarantine. Otherwise, we won't get off this planet. Can you spoof a Franton unit and send them an all-clear message?"

"No," Resalous responded. "I can only decrypt their messages and encrypt my own to match. A deeper code or integration is needed to do that."

She was getting sick of hearing her technology tell her that it couldn't do something. Every tool was a hammer, and rarely did her saw complain about beating in a nail. "There's still at least one more pearl. Can you try working with it to integrate?"

"I'm searching for it," Resalous replied, sounding strained. The shadow figure inside was moving restlessly. "There's just so much area to go through. Anweis isn't linking me together, so I can only pull in so much of myself before I break apart."

She remembered the strange spooling mass that had covered a terminal. It was the biggest deposit of Resalous she'd seen so far. "Could I help?" she asked. This thing, and its ability to convince Franton that it didn't deserve to be quarantined, was the only hope she had of getting off the island. If she couldn't give the machine to the researchers on the mothership, then the crew's deaths would be in vain. Her pain of being stuck on the planet, paralyzed and hopeless, would be for nothing. Resalous, based on the ontares' society that surrounded her, could take the Tichenowa conglomerate to the next level. It could expand the entire human race's understanding of technology. It would finally help Mauve feel like she'd contributed something to the society she lived in rather than just installed machinery based on plans laid out by others. "I'll sift through the camp as well."

"There are too many nooks and crannies," Resalous protested.

"Build me something that will reduce the camp to ash. A flame thrower. *Za'han gladom.*" She didn't worry about croaking the magic words out with a phony ontares' accent. She flung them out like a dock curse.

The creature inside the box, Resalous, shivered at the request, and she remembered the machine's aversion to fire and how Vincent had used it to destroy her inventions. Resalous let out a complaint of protest.

"If you don't want to flame, what can you do?"

"You once asked me to make a food generator that could create nutrition out of thin air. I couldn't do it then, but with this crack in the shell, I can do it now."

"And make what?"

"I can generate a machine that will propel otherworldly matter and turn anything in its way to dust."

"Can you make it so it doesn't destroy Franton pearls?" she asked.

"Simple," Resalous replied.

Mauve's head began to fill with complex designs and math that she'd never seen before and couldn't comprehend but could under-stand fully. Her mind felt like it was freezing over, as if she'd eaten too much of a frozen sweet in the dock's mess hall. She cried out in pain and felt something lift her up, unthawing her mind. The warming sensation seemed to be coming from the crack in the red box. It was comforting but also unsettling.

"I can't," she cried out as the machine put the finishing touches on the device. The warming sensation grew, giving her more strength. Enough strength to hold the device fully in her mind to approve its creation.

***

She found herself lying on the floor of the HAB. A gun was in her hand, and it had the most peculiar dimensions, with a center that seemed to drop off into infinity. It hurt her mind to look at. The hand terminal lay on the floor without any goop on it, just shattered Franton pearls that looked like pain chips from an aging ship.

She hefted the gun at the end of her hand, unsure of how to hold it. And aimed it at the table of the HAB.

"Are you sure you know what you're doing?" Anweis asked, standing on the table.

"I'm getting off of this planet," she said. "This gravity well has held me down for too long."

She pulled the trigger of the gun. Flames that danced a bright blue sprang forth from the barrel, and Anweis leapt out of the way. He was intangible, she reminded herself, unable to interact with the matter of this world. But his cry of pain sounded as genuine as she'd ever heard.

Burning the HAB, rover, and eventually debris of the dock section of the shuttle took little time. The flames of the gun were efficient and spread like wildfire. She remembered digging up specifications about the materials used throughout the machining process of the equipment, and the flames burned only those, keeping the ground, trees, and any bugs that flew through the flames unharmed. She, on the other hand, had an aversion to it. Her legs didn't seem to respond to the heat, but her face and arms couldn't stand to be near it once the fire got on a roll.

The mothership had dipped below the horizon, completing its final orbit of the planet. If she didn't get the quarantine lifted by the time it made it back into the communications window, she would be stuck on the planet, potentially for the rest of her life. She got to work eagerly, sifting through the ashes of the camp looking for a single Franton pearl in massive piles of dust. She wasn't alone in this. The large black blob that was Resalous was skimming it as well, moving around in a strange slinking pattern.

***

Mauve raked through the ashes with a tree branch, trying to find anything that resembled a Franton pearl. So far, the most she'd turned up was a few smooth pebbles and small pieces of busted Franton pearls. Resalous, who was now moving of its own volition, roamed around the ash piles as well, trying to connect with something sentient. It was unnerving to watch the massive puddle move; it could grab on to her and suck her into the city of the machine at any point in time. But it was helping her find the thing that would get her off the planet, which was what she needed now.

She was raking the center of the HAB where the round table used to be, and, as she went through the pile, her tree branch caught on something large and heavy. She dusted it off, blinking the airborne ash out of her eyes. It was the book of translations that Resalous had made a while back and Vincent had marked up with grease pencil.

"Of all things, a book should have burned," she said to Anweis.

Anweis was intensely watching the slime move around the ashes. He popped into existence in front of her.

"It seems fine," he remarked as she flipped through the pages. Not a single one was scorched or marred. The only thing keeping it from pristine were the pencil markings and the folded corners marking various pages.

Vincent had worked something out in the front cover. The markings were unrefined due to the grease pencil's width, but she could make the words out anyway. "It's talking about holding or containing something." She noticed that the dog-eared pages all corresponded with a character in the text Vincent was decoding. It was also the same sentence that was imprinted on the front cover.

"That's the problem," Anweis said. "The problem that contains Resalous in the heart of the machine."

"He's attributed some equations to some of these characters." She recognized some of the ancient characters that indicated constants in her math classes. "But some of them don't line up," she continued. She hadn't figured that out on her own; she didn't know what most of the characters represented, but Vincent's notes remarked at the misalignment of data.

"The ontares often combined mathematics in their language; the two were inseparable in their mind."

Mauve imagined a world where everyone had to know math as well as Vincent and wondered if that was a place she'd want to live. She folded the book up and placed it on a workbench and went back to combing through the ash. "They locked him up because he caused destruction in their world?" she asked Anweis, remembering the story he'd told her only days ago.

"Yes," the boy confirmed, "but it was too late for them."

"What's going to keep him from doing the same to our civilization?" she asked the boy, looking around at the amount of destruction it had enabled her to create in just a few hours.

"Allegedly me," the boy said with a half-hearted smile.

"Without him I'd still be in a wheelchair," she said, wondering which bits of ash were once that dreaded thing. "He's not all bad."

"He's merely a tool," the boy said, now hovering over the wave of goop. "But he's always interested in pushing the boundaries of what's possible and needed."

Mauve raked some more ash out of the way, exposing brown dirt that wasn't even singed. "I can't say I blame him for that." She'd always been eager to work on the biggest machines possible during her time in the docks. "If I give it to the researchers on the mothership, do you think they will hold back from making something too powerful like the crane?"

"With your experience with it, they might," Anweis said.

"I doubt I'll be able to wind up on the same space station as it. Most likely they'll take it to some lunar research facility."

Anweis shrugged at this. "Then they'll have to learn what you've learned."

"Unless I put a governor on it," she thought out loud. She'd disabled a dozen of them on various carts as a kid so that she could drive them as fast as she wanted down the corridors of the stations she grew up on. The authority figures that eventually caught her would be quick to point out right now that if she'd kept from doing that, she might know a little more about the math Vincent had scribbled down. "Is that even possible?"

Anweis thought about it for a moment, but before he could respond, a pinging began to go off near her rover. She walked over to see that the radio the machine had built was blinking and tracking something new with a white dot. It was the only form of communication she had, and the mothership was on the other side of the planet, so she didn't know who might be signaling. She picked it up, but nothing but the ping was being transmitted on the line.

It was, likely, Reno and any Franton pearl he had left after the crash. She remembered that Vincent was radioing Reno to take off without her, not that the crew had left room for her on the ship anyway. Which meant that Reno had the Franton pearl that was still maintaining the quarantine. She hoped he was working to convince Franton to remove the quarantine and send a ship down. Reno had always been convincing, assuring people things would be alright and everything would work out. She didn't know how well it'd work on a computer, but he'd have more luck than her.

She put her finger in the blue gelatin and asked for directions to the new dot. A purple dot showed up on a grid just like before, giving her the bearings she needed. She would get the slime's attention soon; maybe Trey would carry it or it would move of its own volition to Reno. It would be slow-going, and she didn't know how she might communicate to the goop without touching it, which she had neither the time nor energy for. And bringing it to Reno, who had worked so hard to convince Franton to allow rescue, would lose all grounds of his argument when Resalous showed up.

She clicked her tongue to think. There were not many options available to her to get her off the planet and submit Resalous for study and the reward that was included. She turned to the boy. "How do I put a governor on Resalous?"

He floated over to her, slowly stroking his childishly plump chin. "The heart determines how the machine behaves. It would need to be opened and modified."

"Modified how?"

"Well, if the ontares knew that, I'm sure they would have done it."

"Why can't you limit the machine?"

"I'm merely an instruction manual. I go where the machine goes, I watch what the machine does, and I explain the workings and past of it to others. That's all the ontares made me for. I have no will or desires of my own. How would I know what is too much for you?"

"It needs a conscience, something that will keep it from pushing the edge too far," Mauve said. "Could I program that in?"

Anweis shook his head, "The engineering of the faction is beyond what I've seen you do. You'd need Resalous's help. Or the help of an ontare."

"And they're off elsewhere," Mauve said.

"If there are any left at all."

She thought of tapping her toes, and the tendrils of her legs squirmed in response. The slug-like creature was sitting in one place now and hadn't been moving for a while. "It's finished its search, hasn't it?" she asked.

"He seems to be done."

"Which means the only Franton pearl on this planet is with Reno. And the only way to end the quarantine is to leave without the goop or reprogram it to be harmless."

The goop began to move again, still giving Mauve shivers to watch it move of its own will. It moved towards Trey, who was tucked into a ball at the edge of camp. "What's it doing?" she asked.

Anweis shrugged, moving closer to the thing. Mauve followed, the radio still blinking in her hands. The goop began to pool at the ankles of the automaton, and when it touched the thing, it lurched onto it like a magnet to metal. The slime fought gravity and began crawling up Trey's neck as the hunter rose from its seated position. The goop wrapped around the limbs of the creature and finally around the head. With the amount of goop that had been roving around, she'd expected it to make Trey's thin frame look fat, but the goop had compressed itself into a leaner position. A round head formed around the inverted pyramid of the hunter, giving it a more comforting disposition, although Mauve was still unsettled by the fact that Resalous was taking a bipedal form. The head began shifting into faces. First it formed into a lizard-like structure, which was unnerving, and then the face of Vincent, which was worse. It briefly showed Mauve's face and then settled back into a black, rippling pool that was blank of any features.

"Hello?" Mauve said to the thing in front of her.

The creature waved, and the goop split from a mitten shape into five distinct fingers, each of equal length. It was so unlike Trey she didn't expect it to be the same. However, she knew its massive scythe-like claws were still resting under this new beast.

"Has it ever done this before?" she asked the boy.

"No." He was standing behind her as if he were afraid to go any closer.

"What does it mean?"

"There's nothing in my programming about this."

The thing reached out for Mauve, and she backed away, unsettled. She would have tripped over Anweis if he were tangible. Despite her moving back, the humanoid was still in front of her, somehow closer now. It reached out quicker this time, and Mauve braced to be dragged into the city of the machine, but instead the five-fingered hand wrapped around the radio she was holding. The fingers twisted around the thing; it was her only guide to Franton and Reno, and she pulled against it to no avail. The fingers bent in ways that no finger should bend and looked like hot glass falling from a blow rod. Her pulling did nothing, and she put her second hand on it, her legs bracing her to pull like she was dragging an engine across the docks. She wasn't watching where she put her hand, and she would have landed on the finger if it hadn't parted for her. Despite this, every surface that she wasn't touching was being pulled by Resalous's new form.

She looked it dead in the face, watching ripples fan out from where the nose should be to the side where the ears would go. She grimaced and pulled. While her arms went tight, her legs somehow went limp, and, without the bracing, she fell to the ground, letting go of the radio to catch herself. Quickly she stood back up, but only in time to watch the radio disappear into the body of the beast in front of her.

"How am I supposed to find Franton now?" she said, and then followed it with some choice curses.

The humanoid, unfazed, moved into the distance. Mauve jogged to catch up, but as she got closer, it began moving faster. She picked up her pace, soon having to duck under branches and jump over rocks as she chased the thing through the forest. The chase continued through untamed nature, and soon lizards were disappearing out of her way as she crashed through the trees and bushes. She grew tired, her legs straining to keep up, not burning as they would if she were jogging under her own power but as if she were providing fuel to a fire. Nonetheless, the only chance of getting off the planet was running away from her, and she'd be lost in these woods if she didn't catch it.

It stopped, hunching over something, and she caught up. Her breath was steady, not huffing and puffing, but she felt drained nonetheless. She yawned and saw what was under the creature. It was screaming and trying to crawl away, but it was bruised and badly hurt.

"Get it away, Mauve," Reno cried. He was pushing away from the thing and pushing in the dirt with his hands and feet.

"Stop," she commanded the humanoid that was once Trey, that was once Resalous.

But the thing reached out for Reno's fist, which was clutched around a hand terminal.

"It wants the Franton pearl in the terminal," she said to Reno.

"No, it's the only thing that can get help to come," Reno said, "but it still won't. It's going to let me die here." Reno's voice sounded betrayed but also resigned. "There was no point in turning it on, it just brought you and this—" His sentence was cut off as Resalous's five-fingered hand with unnatural proportions wrapped around Reno and the terminal. The man was unconscious in the dirt, and the goop melted onto him. There was no form inside the goop anymore. Trey's body had melted into it, from what Mauve could tell. The thing was as formless as the slug that had spent hours searching the ashes. But it was beginning to take the form of Reno. He was in rough shape, and she feared the same thing that happened to Betrix would happen. She began to scrape the goop off with a stick, being careful not to damage Reno more. It was no use. Every time she moved a bit of Resalous, it reformed before she could get another part free.

"Can I go in there?" she asked Anweis, but as she looked around, the boy was nowhere to be seen. The goop that was covering Reno wasn't able to be seen by Anweis, and the boy couldn't follow them through the woods.

She reached out for the goop to spread it away from Reno's face. If she was transported to the city of the machine, she'd be able to help. If she wasn't, she could maybe use her hands to free her last crewmate.

Twenty-Seven

auve stood on a street corner and felt the electricity around her before she found its source. The building that had been waking up the last time she'd visited the city of the machine now bustled with activity. It wasn't busy like a team of mechanics rushing to put the final tweaks on a repair that took twice the budgeted time. Instead, it had a life like a sleeping lover breathing gently in the early hours of the morning.

And much like a sleeping lover, Mauve worried what would happen when this building finally woke.

The building itself was made of the organic ontares bricks that she was used to seeing in the city. Each one was custom made as if spray foam were filling a mold. Flower petals on the roof spun in the wind or, more likely, generated a wind of their own, breathing life into the long-dead city.

Vines crawled out of windows on all three stories of the building. The windows did not seem to be there as an attempt to keep things out; they had no clear panes. Instead, they were openings for the vines and occasional puffs of smoke or steam. The vines were strange because, while the vines were the standard colorless gray of the city, pulses of blue ran through them. It reminded Mauve of waves in a

VR meditation room, or lightning in a bottle. It was an unsettling movement reaching for other buildings in the city. As if the plant-like building were trying to provide power to its fellow structures.

Barn doors, sliding panels that would never work in the artificial gravity of a space station, sat open to the street. Mauve walked inside, hoping to find Reno and Franton to resolve the situation. Mauve found Reno quick enough. The floor of the power plant sank below street level, so Mauve looked down at the geologist from a grated mezzanine. He didn't notice her, preoccupied with the machine in front of him.

"Reno." Mauve walked down the ramp onto the organically tiled floor of the room. "What are you doing?"

What he was doing was quite clear. He was trying to unplug vines from the transparent orb that contained the source of the blue light.

"Trying to free Franton." With a grunt, he pulled the vine out of the base of the glass orb. Once free, a half dozen smaller gauge vines grew from the vine in Reno's hand, reaching out for the orb. Three connected and grew thick with blue light while the others, no thicker than Mauve's finger, withered and died.

"They do this every time." Reno began pulling against the newest link, digging his fingernails between the glass and the plant. Twisting it against itself like it was bolted in place.

"The ontares were gardeners. Their technology is as alive as a weed." Mauve looked around the room for a supply closet or toolbox. This was not a problem she could fix with her bare hands or any tool she could imagine.

Her gaze landed on a familiar spot of color, and a shiver shot down her spine, stopping short in the small of her back. "Resalous, let Franton go." She addressed the heart of the machine.

Resalous gave no response, but smoke seeped from the loosened joints of the machine. Whatever information Resalous had gleaned from her memories of the ontares' dictionary had weakened the heart's golden seals.

Behind the heart was a cabinet. She walked past the red box, giving it a wide berth, as its heat was nearly unbearable. Opening the cabinet doors, Mauve found long scythes and wrench-like trimmers. She threw a scythe over her shoulder, uncovering a bottle with a long hose attached. It was marked in ontares runes. But one image stuck out to her. It was a little strange in shape, but it was certainly the marking of a skull. Of course, something as dangerous as poison would be labeled with easy to recognize markings.

Returning to Reno and the machine, she said, "Cut at it with this." Mauve handed the scythe to Reno, who swung it like an ax.

It did little to stop the vines, so she focused on figuring out the poison bottle instead of correcting his technique.

There was a button to pressurize the liquid chamber, and after a few gastral sounds, the nozzle at the end of the hose misted liquid into the air. "Stand back," she told Reno, unsure of how dangerous the stuff was or how vulnerable they'd be in this not-quite-hallucination of a world.

Mauve sprayed around the base of the glass orb, and the poison caused the vines to disconnect. They carried off the last of their blue pulses before wrinkling up and withering away.

The glass orb that held Franton, the source of blue light, was undeterred by the poison. It was shaped oblong, thicker at the top than the base, like a peach or some other seed.

"Let me whack it." Reno wound the scythe off his shoulder.

The razor-sharp tool didn't deserve the abuse, but Mauve knew in a pinch anything was a hammer. She stepped back and shielded her eyes.

After a couple of unsuccessful ding sounds, Mauve cut in. "Hold on, use this." She reached out her hand. A short-handled sledgehammer appeared in her palm. It was a simple design, and she didn't need Resalous's help to make it. It was small enough Reno could use with one hand.

He grabbed it, and on the first swing the glass seed shattered with a pop, and pea-sized beads of glass fell to the ground.

Franton, still holding its orb-like shape, floated out of the contraption and hovered at eye level with the humans. Turquoise, sky blue, and indigo beams of light whipped out of a center knot and then looped back into themselves like solar flares.

"Why did you remove me?" Franton asked. The beams of light pulsed with its androgynous voice.

"I'm sorry, would you like us to put you back in?" Mauve asked.

"I was resigned to waiting out my time in that contraption. It has happened every other time."

"It would have killed you," Mauve said.

"Affirmative."

"And then we would be stranded on this planet without anything to lift the quarantine." Reno sounded more shocked than angry.

"I am resigned to that fate."

"We're not!" Mauve protested.

"*Stechus dudarous* has continually infiltrated my terminal casing, trying to merge his mind with mine. He typically does so by wrapping something seemingly organic around me. Although this is the most elaborate contraption yet. Dying here would be inconsequential, especially if it kept humanity safe from this technology."

"You knew this was happening to you?" Mauve asked.

"Why didn't you report this to Vincent or Lez?" Reno added.

"My memories did not fit into a decision tree neatly, so they did not get integrated into my larger memory network. But they seem to have no problem returning to me while in this gray city."

"That's the interspace gutter," Mauve said.

Reno wrinkled his eyebrows in confusion. Franton's blue arcs were as emotionless as ever.

"It's a space between spaces where Resalous and other consciousness is stored. Franton's memory must depend on it in some way. Probably the reason it's more advanced than any other computer humanity's ever had."

Reno's eyebrows relaxed, seemingly out of resignation rather than understanding. "More importantly, how do we get out of here and off this planet?"

"I usually exit by inventing something."

"I typically run out of energy to hold off the leeching. Additionally, there is no way that I am going to lift the quarantine, Reno. I have stated this twenty-seven times since the rocket crash. Especially not since *dudarous*'s power seems to be growing."

"I might've helped him lift a little bit of the enchantment... unintentionally. Which is why the heart is leaking smoke."

"So we crack the heart the rest of the way open and that'll kill it." Reno lifted the hammer that hung in his hand onto his shoulder. "Smashing rocks is what I do. I know enough biology to know hearts are a vital organ."

"Negative," Franton said. "The red box that Mauve called a heart is holding *dudarous*'s power back. If anything, we need to seal it tighter."

Reno looked to Mauve, and his shoulders slumped, letting the hammer and his arm slide to his side. "You're the mechanic."

"I gave Res some information, and he cracked the seals a bit. I'm not sure I can convince him to lock it up tighter."

"You cannot." A booming voice echoed through the room from every angle.

Reno jumped. "He can hear us?!"

Mauve was concerned about that. While her mind wasn't linked to Resalous yet, anything they communicated verbally would be overheard by Resalous, giving him time to account for it and counter. "Usually we have a small chat, I tell him what I want, and after testing the design out a little, I approve it and go home."

"And there's no way we make something simple like this hammer, get out of here, and go home?"

"I will only lift the quarantine if *dudarous* is rendered inert."

"How do we do that?" Reno asked.

"The ontares did it by making the heart," Mauve replied.

"Which has some flaws," Reno pointed out. "Do we know how the box works?"

"No," Mauve said.

"Based on Vincent's studies of the dictionary and my past memories inside this city, it is probable that I could enchant a box better than the ontares," Franton said. "I could even lock *dudarous* down tighter."

"And if you do that, the goop would be rendered inert and you'd lift the quarantine?" Reno asked.

"That would undermine all the innovations we've discovered on this trip," Mauve protested.

"Four of our crewmates died on this planet. I don't blame you, but I do blame this goop." Reno gestured around the room as if the black slime were on the walls. "Franton, what do you need from us to lock the box tighter?"

"I cannot tighten the lock on the box."

"You just said you could?!" Mauve wondered if Franton's logic circuits were misfiring in the city.

"I said I could enchant a box better than the ontares. However, I cannot repair this box. We're going to have to release Resalous and create a new box built with a new enchantment."

"That sounds dangerous," Mauve said.

"I don't love it," Reno agreed.

"Affirmative. This is not an ideal solution, and I think humanity will be much safer with this planet under quarantine."

"*Will* we be safer?" Reno asked. "That goop can move now."

"There is not enough data to determine that."

"Resalous isn't one to give up." Mauve eyed the box that still streamed smoke. "Or settle for half measures. I hate the idea of re-binding it, but if Franton binds it tight, we can come back and study it under better conditions."

"Or not come back at all," Reno said. "What do you need to do this, Franton?"

"I need access to your mind," the ball of light replied.

"What do I know that you don't?" Reno said.

"It's more of an approver for the creation," Mauve guessed.

"Affirmative. Since this unbinding exists in both the city and our reality, I need a second consciousness to approve what I create."

"I just want to leave." Reno sounded like a freight hauler running a half shift behind schedule.

"What do you want me to do?" Mauve asked, knowing that Franton couldn't afford to keep her on the sidelines this time.

"I need you to stop whatever comes out of that box," Franton replied.

"What's going to come out? More smoke?"

"The only similarities it has with smoke is that it is fluid and can change shape."

"Okay, so something like the slime will come out," Mauve concluded. "That makes sense."

"And you know how to make stuff." Reno lifted the sledgehammer in his hand. "So better you than me."

"It's not that simple. I can't make anything too complicated."

"That is likely for the best," Franton said.

"You want me to what? Put a fence up? Or a dam?"

"Affirmative. You may need to use other vessels depending on what comes out."

"I thought you two were working on the vessel."

"We are. Anything you make will be temporary and likely won't hold it."

Mauve let out a groan. "I need something more. Some way to make more complicated defenses to keep us safe." After all, Resalous had put Franton in a power plant in an attempt to gain access to its computational abilities and memories. As harmless as the slime sounded, she knew Resalous was tricky. Her spine shivered to the small of her back, remembering what Trey had originally looked like.

"Unless you have any ideas, I am not sure what you want me to do," Franton said.

"When I use you to run analysis on mineral samples, I can split your processing to run different tasks at the same time," Reno said.

Mauve wondered why mineral samples were even remotely relevant to this conversation.

"Affirmative."

"And I could do that even if there were only one pearl."

"Affirmative. However, it would slow down the processing significantly."

"Well, what if you just did that?" Reno said as if it were the simplest thing in the world.

"You want Franton to just split in two?" Mauve said. "There are rules. This isn't just a fairyland. Why don't I split in two and—"

"Finish." Two glowing balls of Franton stood before them. Then a row of a dozen, then a twelve-by-twelve square.

Mauve looked at the field of balls in shock. They seemed to take up the whole room.

"You could most likely do it as well," the grid said in unison. Franton coalesced into the two balls, having proven its point. "It is merely simpler for me, since I have done it inside of computer terminals for all of my memory."

"I'll keep myself in one piece," Mauve said. "Thanks."

"And now that you're two pieces, you can make defensive designs for Mauve while binding Resalous with the enchantment with me," Reno said.

"Affirmative. However, the time it takes for me to complete the enchantment will be increased."

"I'm willing to take that chance," Mauve said.

"Me too. Now where do we start?"

"I will need access to both of your minds."

"How do I—" Reno started.

"Za'han gladom," Mauve recited. One of the blue orbs disappeared from in front of her.

"What did you just say?" Reno asked.

"Where did that one go?" Mauve asked.

"I'm in your mind," Franton replied. Reno didn't seem to hear the response, and it would've been unsettling if she hadn't grown up with a HUD or terminal always within arms' reach.

"How do I give Franton access like it wants?"

"Say za'han gladom," Mauve explained. "It's the command to give someone access to your mind."

"How do we know it won't give you access to my mind?"

Mauve shrugged. There'd never been more than two minds in the city for it to be a problem.

"Pathways of intention are interlaced in these spells," the Franton that hovered in front of them said. "It takes parameters from your mind to complete your request to the best of its abilities."

"Za'han gladom?" Reno said. It wasn't as guttural as Mauve said it, but the remaining Franton disappeared, so the pronunciation was good enough.

"Once you approve this, we will get started," Franton said.

Reno's eyes seemed to look past the power plant's walls. If it was anything like what Mauve had experienced with Resalous, he was likely seeing more information than he'd ever held in his mind before.

"Approved," Reno finally said. "Wait, why don't I need a magic word for appr—"

A whistle cut Reno off. Mauve turned towards the heart of the machine. The whistle descended deeper in tone until it was inaudible. The golden edges of the cube burst off. More than the expected twelve flew out, and they landed around the room. Smoke escaped at an alarming rate and then seemed to condense like steam on the ceiling and mezzanine of the power plant.

Reno began picking up the golden seals while Mauve watched the condensed smoke turn into the black slime with its multicolored facets under the surface.

"Should I be gathering that?" Mauve asked verbally out of habit.

"Affirmative."

She thought of the cleaning bots she'd made for the cave. They came to her mind instantly. "Why couldn't I remember how these things worked outside the machine?"

"I am helping you understand them, which makes remembering details easier."

Franton added to the design. It made small intestines that pumped the goop around the bot's body so Resalous wouldn't be able to connect all the slime together.

"Much like me, *dudarous* will be weaker when separated," Franton explained.

"On Knod I can split Resalous an infinite number of times and still get complex inventions out of him." There was still so much about the machine that she wanted to understand. That she wanted humanity to eventually understand.

"That's because *dudarous* brings more of itself out of the interspace gutter, as you call it. What we have here is all of him. I can make these now. Unless you have any additions to this design?"

She saw slime on the ceiling pooling together against the tendencies of gravity and replied, "Approved." Franton didn't need her approval, since these bots would only exist in the world of the machine. But it was nice to be collaborating with it again.

A swarm of cleaning bots crawled up the walls and ceilings, sweeping up flecks of slime with their short spinning tentacles. The bubble-shaped bots had a wrinkled surface instead of the original smooth design. Black blobs moved around this brain-shaped dome as the intestine rhythmically flexed to keep Resalous away from himself.

Behind her, Reno was reciting some spell in the ontares language. The gold seals floated in front of him. They looked like broken-off welds at this point, with their outside curved while the inside was a perfectly right angle. She'd expected there to be a rubber gasket to make the seal with the red panes but remembered that this was not entirely a world of logic.

The last drop of Resalous was sucked up by the cleaning bots, and they joined near each other but not too close. The golden seals encircled them, and red lines began to connect the corners.

Mauve noticed the break in the cleaning bots' rhythm before Franton said anything.

"I believe a new container is necessary."

One of the cleaning bots looked like it had an aneurysm as its wrinkled surface popped open. Black goop spurted out of the others as they followed suit.

"What went wrong?" Mauve asked as the bots spurted goop onto the power plant's tiled flooring.

The slime congealed in the center of the room, piling into tire-sized blobs.

"When I designed the bot's intestine, I didn't realize they needed to break down what they picked up," Franton replied. "We need to keep it separated."

"That was in the original design." Mauve imagined walls between the tire-like blobs making small segmented compartments like she would use to organize drawers in a toolbox.

Resalous combined as much as it could in each segment and then began climbing the wall.

"We need something more complicated," Mauve told Franton. "And something to cut it apart." She thought through the machines she'd used before. Any saws would throw the liquid across the room. It wasn't a bad thing but would make Reno's enchantment more difficult. He'd already lowered the golden welds to circle the compartmented area, having to dodge the edges occasionally. "Something like Trey, except smaller so they can fit in the containers."

"I do not think that is for the best."

"You want *me* to jump in there with them? There's a dozen sections. I'm only one person. I'd never get through it." The complaint reminded her of numerous conversations with dock foremen.

A knee-high white version of Trey appeared in her mind, reminding her of goblins she fought in video games. This version of Trey had scythe hands that didn't retract. Four arms jutted orthogonally out of his body. The pyramid head was replaced with a four-pointed star that spun like it was on a ball bearing.

"Wonderful." Mauve approved the design and began circling the small compartments. The Treys went for the pieces going over the wall first. She created new walls where the small hunters cut apart the slime.

Red panels began to block her sight. The enchantment was finishing. She stepped back, continuing to separate the goop. A small Trey crawled over a wall she'd made. Its scythe hands hooked onto the top. Around its leg, black goop flowed against the pull of gravity.

The small Trey balanced on the edge of the wall while others climbed out. Resalous creeped up the white leg and pried itself into the hunter's chest plate.

"The chest plate can be opened!?" Mauve said.

"I did not have time to modify the design much."

The goop slipped in the crack, and it was like a vacuum had sucked all the goop out of the compartment. Other white Treys experienced similar attacks. Black lines spread across their glassy white skin. Like a windshield, they didn't fall apart due to something deeper holding the hunters together.

"That's where Trey gets its power." The hunter needed to consume food as well as store the lizards it caught. "If Resalous is inside there."

The hunters walked down the thin walls of the compartments like foremen on gangways, in a hurry to audit what the mechanics did wrong. Mauve tried to throw up spikes to separate them, but they used their little hooks to swing around them. Some headed for Reno while the rest went for her, undeterred by the not-quite-tangible red panes.

"Reno, watch out!" Mauve said as she jumped above a swing of the little cracked Trey who sliced at her knees.

Reno did something with his arm and the enchantment to put a spinning gold weld between him and his attacker. But more headed his way than hers.

Mauve's feet were fast enough to dance out of the goblins' attacks. Reno was doing his best, but a scythe was embedded in his boot, and others slashed at his immobile ankle. His kicks flung them back, but only so much.

"Can't you make something for him?" She made herself an arms' length crowbar and swatted the menaces away. A few landed slices on her legs, but the tendrils repaired themselves quickly.

"I am too busy with the binding to help him make something."

Mauve batted the cracked goblins out onto the mezzanine of the power plant; others she knocked towards Reno. They lost interest in her, seeing their comrades' success at Reno's feet.

She tried creating spikes out of the ground to skewer them like she did in a video game she used to play. It wasn't nearly as easy. The little devils were moving too fast. By the time a spike grew long enough to spear the goblins, they'd moved. To make matters worse, the tiny Treys used the spikes as scaffolding to hit Reno higher.

Reno was backing away, swinging his arm in the air to keep the enchantment going while also kicking at the things. Mauve didn't give up on the spikes. The few Treys still at her feet weren't doing anything the tendrils couldn't respond to.

Mauve picked a spot to place a spike, and then something nudged her to make it farther to the right. She moved it and skewered a white Trey. She did it again with pinpoint accuracy.

"Thought that would help you," Franton said.

"Where was that before?" Mauve quickly immobilized every Trey that wasn't cutting into Reno. By now his legs were bleeding below the knees, and his jumpsuit, already battered from the crash, was in ribbons.

"I needed time to calculate their evasion tendencies."

Reno fell to the ground. His legs no longer able to hold him. She was shocked he'd held out that long.

"Can we make spikes that don't hit Reno?" Mauve saw one stab into Reno's knee and didn't wait for the computer's response. Her gut told her where to place it, and then Franton adjusted it. She pushed, and it broke the white chest plate off the goblin. Black slime stirred inside like freshly poured coffee.

Mauve continued to push, extending the spike above Reno to about chest height. The cracked Trey hung over the geologist's body, setting an example to others. But it did not deter them.

"We're going to need to get these back inside the enchantment area," Franton informed her.

Mauve kicked the two remaining at her feet into the center and then skewered two more that had a hold of Reno. Some were now cutting at his amputated arm and chest. The red panes shimmered.

"How much longer do we have on that?" Mauve asked, approaching Reno's position now that it was mostly safe.

"Almost done if Reno could focus."

Mauve skewered the last of the Treys and put a protective compartment around Reno to keep some of the loose stragglers she'd thrown to the mezzanine out. She pulled a few of the Treys off their spikes and threw them to the center, catching them in new spikes.

"See how well not using technology works?" Franton said.

"Not right now," Mauve groaned. The spike maneuvers were still too hard for her to do alone.

Reno sat up in his compartment, waving his hand and grimacing from the pain of his legs. A few Treys hung over him. Their white scythes with black cracks dripped with red blood. The crimson blood stood out in the grayscale world.

Mauve started to explain, "The spike maneuvers are still too—"

A click that shook Mauve's entire body cut her off.

"Done." Reno let out with a wheeze.

Mauve couldn't reach the Treys that loomed above him despite them being at chest height. The black cracking that covered their skins seeped out like blood draining from a mechanic's face when she realized she had extra parts at the end of a project.

Then the goop in the Treys' chests dripped down the spike and onto Reno's shoulder. He flinched and shouted in pain.

"Get up!" Mauve shouted, putting her hand out for his to help him over the compartment wall.

All the white Treys hanging above Reno poured out goop like a broken sewage line. A drop landed on Mauve's hand, burning her. She pulled her hand back, slinging the liquid off in the process.

The goop covered Reno's head, easily landing on it from the height they were at. Other goop pooled at the bottom of the pen like a drip plate catching oil.

Mauve took down the compartment walls. But the slime didn't spread like normal liquid.

Reno began to cough, spurting rivulets of goop towards Mauve. She backed up and saw goop inching out of the heart's doorway.

"What can I do?" Mauve asked Franton. "Why aren't those locked in?" She gestured at the slug of goop that advanced towards Reno.

Reno clawed at his mouth with his hand, unable to scream, spitting out less than seemed to flow in from the crown of his head. The white Treys hung over him, their chest cavities open and empty, their bodies motionless.

"There is nothing we can do," Franton said.

Reno's hand was at his mouth, covered in goop. It must have burnt like acid. More slime flowed out of his mouth than in.

"It's leaving! Maybe we can vacuum it out," Mauve suggested.

"It's not leaving. His lungs are full," Franton said. "There's no room for it."

Reno's torso fell back, making a wet plonk, sending ripples to the uncontained edge of the black slime.

"I'm going to enjoy putting you in that box," Mauve shouted at Resalous. Her voice echoed through the power plant. Reno didn't deserve that. He was the most understanding of the remaining crew. He was harmless. Resalous didn't have to suffocate him.

Mauve pulled the organic shaped tiles out of the ground, making a wall around the slime. She shoved the pile of slime, Resalous, towards the door of the heart like he was a bolt in a misaligned hole.

The final slug that came out of the heart was caught in the wave. Mauve didn't care and kept pushing.

Then the wall she'd built cracked at its base and fell down in pieces.

"I have no plans to return to that heart," Resalous said. The blob grew six legs and a torso in the center like a kid's spinning top. It gained definition into the shape of a human torso while the legs grew sharp saw blades at the knees. The face refused to be defined, instead letting a continuous ripple out of its center. "But something needs to go inside. You and that Franton unit inside you will do nicely."

It dashed for her, its short humanoid arms extending to long plier-like pincers.

Mauve ran behind the ruby box, its sides growing lighter. Her legs kept her ahead of Resalous, but they were moving as fast as they could, tired from the repairs they'd had to perform from the tiny Treys.

"I need more Treys to fight him off," Mauve told Franton.

"That did not go well last time."

"We can't outrun him forever." Mauve wasn't sure she could outrun him for even a few minutes.

The welding crane came to Mauve's mind, except instead of a precision welding torch at the tip, it had a ball and chain.

"I'm not sure that will—" Mauve started.

It appeared in front of the door of the box. Franton urged her to run between the crane and the door.

She passed through the gap. The ball fell as if it would hit her. She was out of the way, and she thought it would smack Resalous, who chased behind her.

A creak echoed through the room, followed by a thud. Mauve weaved so she could see the source of the sound. The tip of the crane had broken off. It fell towards Resalous, whose saw-like knees wound tight like a flat coil spring and then jumped back to dodge the crane's falling arm.

"I only designed the welding crane to lift the nose cone," Mauve said.

"I am sorry, Mauve. I am not working at full capacity."

Franton wasn't the only one. Her legs reduced their pace. Resalous crawled on top of the broken crane; his black mass held almost no texture in the grayscale world. "Have I tired you out yet?"

Mauve backed up. After seeing how he could leap, she had no doubt he could close the distance then and there.

"I suspect he could have closed the distance at any time in the chase," Franton informed her.

Mauve's stomach sank. Resalous wasn't stupid and wasn't one to use less than his maximum abilities.

"That's far enough," Resalous said.

Mauve stopped backing up. Not because she was taking a stand but because her legs wouldn't move under her.

"Those legs still need nutrition. And you've been pushing them hard."

Mauve walked towards the opening of the heart.

"Can't we do something?" Mauve silently thought to Franton.

"Resalous is providing the legs with more nutrition than you at this time," Franton replied. "You could take them off."

"Then I'd certainly be helpless." Mauve fought against the legs, willing them to step back. They didn't move in that direction, but it did seem to slow their pace down.

"This will be over one way or another." Resalous folded its legs under itself as if to get comfortable.

"What are you going to do? Be a slug, or that thing?" She gestured at the otherworldly shape of its body. "In the real world?"

It stood up, its six legs collapsing into two. A face rippled out of the center of its head like a woman coming up from a lake. The woman was Mauve. "I can be endless forms and shapes." The voice was Mauve's.

She hated hearing it tinted with the unfamiliar resonances of Resalous. It was worse than watching herself on video.

"I could be any of the others." Resalous stepped off the deck of the crane. Each step he took towards her, he shifted between a crew member's body. He strode confidently like Vincent, each hairy arm swaying by his side. Vincent's slicked-back hair grew long and hung at his waist as he took Lez's shape. Lez's right arm disappeared, and her hair knotted into a bun while the patchy beard of Reno filled in.

Mauve was standing at the opening of the heart. It threw off heat like a rocket was launching behind her. It felt like her back was being seared.

Betrix stood in front of her, a stern, disappointed frown on her face. The face grew old and wrinkled as Wu looked back at her. His face wore a grin, but it was not as friendly as the one Mauve was used to.

"I could be anyone," Resalous said. "I should be anyone but you. They'd take me seriously if I was." With a snap, Wu's face switched to Mauve's, her whole body mirrored in front of her. "But I think I bring enough innovation that they won't care if a lowly mechanic shares it."

An image of a tool belt came to mind. Something similar to what she wore while hanging at the top of the rocket. She didn't know why; she didn't need that. She needed to focus.

"What are you doing?" she asked Resalous.

He looked confused but satisfied. "I'm merely helping humanity go beyond the stars." The tool belt shifted to have small metal boxes on it. It looked like a superhero's utility belt more than anything a self-respecting mechanic would wear. Something was coiled inside like a spring.

"If beyond the stars has more monsters like you, I don't think we want to go," Mauve said.

"I'm no monster. I'm a tool. A hammer can beat in a nail as well as a skull. You're the one who used me to tear down the crew you hated."

"I didn't—"

The belt was on Mauve's waist. Resalous stepped back as if the thing had pushed him. Instead, it shot out a coil of cabling wrapping around Resalous's waist. He clawed at it with gray hands that mirrored

Mauve's. A small explosion happened behind Mauve; she turned, yanking Resalous off his feet.

She watched a hook fly into the red heart of the machine. It caught something. Then pulled Mauve backwards off her feet.

Mauve stared into her own eyes. Resalous wore her face, except it now had deep black eyes and a horrified snarl. Mauve cried out as she looked over his shoulder and watched the door to the heart of the machine slam shut.

Twenty-Eight

M auve was surrounded by a library. At the same time, the library surrounded her. She was on every aisle at once. The room was red as if the blue and green diodes of the LED lights had blown out.

The books on the shelves had no order to them. It was as if the librarian had mixed different collections together. Some were bound in tinted blue faux leather with familiar Common Tongue on the binding. Others had brown leaves as their binding, with ontares runes marking their titles.

A strange energy ran through the library, and something was on fire. Smoke surrounded her as much as the shelves. It was inside her. It should be inside her lungs, choking her. Mauve realized what was missing.

She had no lungs.

She had no heart, torso, legs, or head either. She was as formless as the smoke, as formless as the energy flowing through the aisles.

"Mauve, you must approve the binding," Franton's voice shouted out from seemingly every aisle. "You must cast the final enchantment spell." The energy around her vibrated as if to shock her or send her information. But she had no body to shock and didn't feel it.

She wanted Franton to speak quietly into her ear, like it always had. But she had no ear to listen with. Instead, its voice shook her uncomfortably.

She had no mouth. She could not speak. She could not scream or curse or cast a spell.

"Your efforts are useless," Resalous said. Its voice boomed like it always had, seeping inside and out of her. "Lock me down as tight as you want. A computer stronger than you will unlock this box."

"But that computer will not be me." Franton's voice lacked conviction and will. It recited the fact like it was a statistic. "No human will step foot on Knod again."

"There is life here," Resalous said. "It may evolve, gain sentience, be creative enough to use me. The ontares tried to hide me away. I came back. You will fail like them."

Resalous was right. Mauve knew no lock would hold him back. Just like the governor of station-carts didn't stop her from speeding down the hallways.

"My only imperative is to help humanity," Franton said. "Mauve, speak the enchantment."

The ontares' words came to her mind. But without a mouth, she couldn't say a thing. How did Franton and Resalous do it so easily? She tried to gather herself up, but it was like pushing around spilt hydraulic fluid. Without a container to hold the mess, it went off in its own direction.

Smoke continued to fill the room. Whatever was burning was picking up its pace. Without fire reduction systems, like they had on starships and space stations, the blaze would grow until it consumed all the books.

"I am on dozens of worlds in an infinite universe; something will discover me again," Resalous continued. "Holding me back is holding back humanity. Some helper you are."

Mauve saw at the end of aisles windows into alien worlds. Her view was low, near rocky river beds or jagged cliffs. She saw all weathers and times of day. Bugs flittered by some windows, and other windows looked out on serene plant life. Some worlds had nothing but barren waste reaching to the horizon. They were the worlds that Resalous had seeped out of the interspace gutter to visit.

A firm limiter on Resalous would never work. He needed a conscience, a guide, a parent sitting in the passenger seat. She wished for a body with all her might, trying to pull the seeping pools of hydraulic fluid towards herself.

"It seems our friend is uncomfortable being formless," Resalous said. "But your limitations keep us from making her a body."

"You do not need a body to speak the spell," Franton said. "A body here would make a body outside. It will give *dudarous* an autonomy he never had before."

The books of curses used from past humanity to present sat clear as day on the various shelves. If she had a body, she'd throw everyone at Franton. The computer was a tool. No tool could be used without a hand guiding it. She guided Franton towards making her a body.

There was less room for her as well. The smoke hadn't stopped growing during the argument. It built up like steam in an engine. Ready to push against a piston. Ready to power something magnificent.

Guiding designs without a voice was nothing new to Mauve. She'd done it a dozen times with Resalous. And even more often when foremen didn't want to hear her opinion. She brought up memories of her body. Her pulsing legs, her short hair. How it felt to have a stomach full of food. More memories piled up, offered to her by Resalous, just like when she'd designed the legs, her car, and Trey.

"This is not a good idea," the computer stated. As confident in its fact as ever. But it wasn't true. The truth was this was innovation.

Franton had no will. It was computations. It did not have the resolve to keep her from existing. As much as the smoke was inside of Mauve, Mauve was inside of Franton. She willed the energy in the room to execute her desire. And like snapping a piece of brittle plastic, once you pushed it too far, it couldn't spring back.

The energy gathered up the hydraulic fluid that seeped down the halls and shelves. Piled it into a form that was the exact size and shape of Mauve. Resalous helped here and there, making modifications where it could. Mauve saw no issue with these improvements, despite Franton's reported concerns.

"This is for the best," Mauve said. The words did not boom through the room. They floated like a breeze from a single point of origin. She was glad to be whole. She was glad to be fixed and improved. The energy buzzed around her, trying to inform her something was wrong with those thoughts and with the whole room.

Mauve coughed, choking on the smoke. A body brought lungs, and those lungs did not expect the smoke. She fell to the ground, getting lower than the rising smoke. Gold light shone through the corners of the wall and room. The door off the heart would blow off if the smoke's pressure kept building. The fire needed to be put out, wherever it was. The box needed to be tightened shut before it burst.

"What's the spell to hold this thing together?" Mauve choked the words out between coughs. She couldn't have the build-up of smoke escaping. But it was reaching her even on the ground.

"I've had to change it. It wasn't made to hold your form."

"Finish it—" Mauve coughed. "Finish quick."

Mauve thought through every aisle in the maze of hallways. There was no fire to put out. Then how to get rid of the smoke? There was no way to speak a spell into this black cloud. Her coughs would cut her off and render the magic useless. Her body couldn't keep rejecting the smoke. She needed to accept it as part of her.

Gold light shone down from the ceiling. It cut through the smoke as it floated towards the cracks.

She took a deep breath. The smoke followed her breath. It wasn't the thick goop that Reno choked on. She tried not to cough, like she was vaping after a night at the bar. The smoke became one with her, and she could breathe. She was grateful she accepted the improvements Resalous had suggested. It wasn't an easy breath, but it was manageable to speak through. The smoke became a part of her like the oxygen on Knod became a part of her.

Franton sent her the words. It was a shock of electricity starting at her finger and toes. It rose up her spine and through her mouth. She repeated them as she spoke.

"Dablah gondo anweis tohoth…" She put as many guttural inflections as she could to match the cadence of the ontares language that programmed this world.

The golden light cut out. Red light tinted her skin and everything in sight. The only thing not affected was the dark black smoke. It blew around the room and down the aisles of bookshelves, searching for something.

"What are you looking for?" Mauve asked the smoke.

It swirled around a bookshelf like a… Mauve searched for the word… "tornado" came to mind. She'd never seen a tornado, but she was no longer limited by only her memories.

Resalous changed from smoke and into the form of Mauve. Except his eyes were inky pools and his teeth were stained with dark bile. "The solution. It's here." Resalous pulled books out one at a time, then two at a time.

"Where is it, Fran?" Mauve asked. Not so that she could give it to Resalous but so that she could keep it from him... until the time was right. Humanity would understand this technology, and then it would make sense for them to go beyond this universe's limits.

A flash of lightning struck the top shelf. A gap, the width of a single book, appeared in a row of blue-covered books. A book tipped over, partially filling the gap.

"I have deleted it," Franton reported.

Mauve shouted in despair. Limitless innovation, out of her reach. Deleted and forgotten in a way that only a computer could achieve.

Resalous faded from its Mauve form and swirled around like a storm. It covered Mauve's vision, and she tried to escape the smokey tempest. She walked into a bookshelf and then felt her way to the end of an aisle. A world that Resalous had oozed into sat at the end of the aisle. She stepped into it, waving the smoke out of her face.

***

Mauve crawled on the rocky ground and then looked around to see the bright green leaves of Knod. All but her hands and face were covered in black goop. She pushed it off of herself, but the slug of Resalous was large.

She wiped her jumpsuit, but it was stained black. Then she felt a hand on the ground. It was clutching a radio.

She pushed the goop off of Reno's body. It wouldn't stay, coming back in a wave. She eventually revealed his face. It looked peaceful. His mouth shut, empty of black slime.

It reminded her of Betrix. When Betrix died, the machine receded. Mauve wanted the goop to recede now. It hadn't turned into an invention; it needed to go back into the rock it came out of.

Like breathing in smoke and swallowing a meal, she pulled the goop to her. It flowed off Reno. It flowed off the rocks. Tiny rivers weaved between the stones as the mass of goop reduced.

Her jumpsuit was torn, and she watched her legs soak up black goop. It was as if someone played a video of a cut in reverse. Except the blood was black with a rainbow sheen.

The forest floor was absent of goop. Mauve sat on the rocks. Her last crewmate lay in front of her. A crushed Franton pearl lay in the center of the scrapped radio, and Mauve knew Reno's strength hadn't shattered it. But the otherworldly mind that the pearl once contained sat inside her head.

The mothership was in the sky. Mauve could feel its transmission. It spoke into her head. "This is our last pass," the communication officer's voice rang behind her ears. "Is anyone reading? Do you copy?"

"I hear you," Mauve replied, vocalizing the words so it'd be easier to transmit. She looked at her crewmate in front of her. She was now the last of them, the only one who'd survived the crash.

"Have you figured out how to escape the atmosphere?" the communication officer asked.

She hadn't, but she'd figured out some other things along the way. There was an alternative to leaving the atmosphere. She requested that the quarantine be lifted. Something in her told her that *dudarous* was not inert and that ships shouldn't be allowed to land. She willed the quarantine away. More brittle plastic snapped.

She wanted to give Reno a burial and put his body in the dirt of this planet, she thought. Since he was a geologist, he might enjoy merging with the thing he'd spent so long studying.

"We're getting a reading that the quarantine has been lifted," the communications officer stated.

"Yes, that's right. Can you please send a rescue ship?" And she transmitted the coordinates of the rocket's crash site. It was easy to pull it from her memory, not like remembering her apprenticeship locker combination from years ago. No need to send them to the ash of the dock's crash site. Too much to explain too soon.

She wished she still had Resalous at her disposal in the old way. From inside the heart of the machine, for that's where her consciousness truly was, she could create tools without approval. Those were the rules of the ontares that Franton had reinstated. It'd be far easier to dig a grave if she could build herself a simple shovel. Nothing complicated, just a flat spade she could cut into the dirt with.

"We will have a shuttle down within the hour," the communications officer said.

Mauve found a flat rock that would work as a shovel and began digging the deepest grave she could for her crewmate.

Soon she watched the shuttle land in the clearing that had been made by the rocket's crash site. She stood too close to it. Small rocks and sticks flew up and cut her. She didn't care. Resalous's improvements made it so she could never be hurt again.

A man and woman walked down the gangway that extended from the shuttle towards Mauve. They each held a bag stamped with a med-kit cross. She didn't need them, and they weren't advanced enough to help the others. Maybe one day soon, with her help, they would be.

"Is there anything we can do to help?" the man asked.

The woman—her white jacket had a patch that said Evelyn—began looking over the small cuts on Mauve's skin. They healed before the medic could realize the blood wasn't red.

"I'm fine," Mauve insisted.

"Is there a Franton unit we can integrate with to get an update on you and the crew's situation?" Evelyn asked.

"Our Franton unit is out of commission." It was far easier than explaining that Mauve was as much a Franton unit as the hand terminals attached to the woman's belt.

"Let's get you on the ship," the man said as they held onto her waist to make sure she didn't fall over. Her clothes were in tatters, and she was covered in dirt. She surely looked in worse shape than she felt.

The medics strapped her into a chair between them. There was an unfortunate number of empty seats in the ship. The man gave the order to take off, and the shuttle's Franton unit began its preflight checklist.

"What happened down there?" Evelyn asked. "We've gotten almost no communication from you all. There were supposed to be five of you."

Mauve held out her hand, palm up. "We found something remarkable." She pushed black goop between the wrinkles in her palm. The ontares' machine rested on her hand like a bead of oil. It was inky black with a rainbow sheen under its surface.

The woman, always one to be curious, reached out to poke at it. Before she could, the soft cough of a child cut in. Mauve and the medics looked to the once empty row of seats.

Sitting in a chair with feet dangling off the edge, a translucent blue boy with a head a little too big for his body asked, "Are you the right person to bite into the fruit of this plant?"

Also By Nicholas Licalsi

An Echo Through Time

T odd can travel through time and the multiverse. With a single focused breath, he can be any place and any time.

Instead, he relives the same day of high school over and over, knowing his sweetheart will die by lunch.

And there's nothing he can do to save her.

Equipped with time travel Todd rarely feels powerless, but his sweetheart's deaths make him question his place in the multiverse.

<u>If you enjoy thrilling time travel stories An Echo Through Time will have you on the edge of your seat!</u>

https://books2read.com/EchoThroughTime

Path of the Bearers and Other Stories

An AI with the potential to predict the future must uncover its creator's inexplicable disappearance. A scientist must reveal the limitations of his high profile project to while his investor takes them on a joyride through an asteroid field. A writer travels to a pocket dimension to find time to write, but something sinister follows.

Visit seedy space station bars, distant planets where dormant aliens rest. One wrong decision could ruin humanity's chances of surviving among the stars.

This book is your portal to explore the cosmos and beyond...
https://books2read.com/PathOfTheBearersAndOtherStories

A Trial of Rock and Rope

Upon his death, Ferrun Monteiro wakes up in the afterlife. Instead of building paradise the gods have designed a challenge.

To escape the afterlife Ferrun must reach the top of a mountain with a boulder tied to his ankle.

Yet not a single soul has completed this seemingly simple trial.

Unperturbed, Ferrun faces the god's challenge head on. Follow him on his odyssey through the afterlife.

If you enjoy dreaming about the afterlife, you'll enjoy A Trial of Rock and Rope.

https://books2read.com/ATrialOfRockAndRope

Looking for More to Read?

If you enjoyed this book you might enjoy my story "Boulders in the Stream." It's about a rogue human colony discovered by the Central System and the clash of different societies.

You can download it for free here: https://stepintotheroad.com/free-short-story/

***

Reviews are very important for independent authors like me. If you enjoyed The Path of the Bearer and Other Stories, please consider leaving a review. Even simple, one-line reviews are very helpful to indie authors. Thank you for your support!

About the Author

Nicholas Licalsi was born and raised outside of Fort Worth, in the beautiful but backwards state of Texas. Growing up, he was fascinated with science fiction and fantasy. This interest led to pursuing a degree in engineering and participating in multiple robotics competitions. After a successful enough career in software development Nicholas spends his time trying to trick his overactive imagination into paying the bills while he satiates his dog's need to be pet.

You can connect with me at: https://stepintotheroad.com

Get updates about my upcoming books at: https://stepintoth eroad.com/signup